HIGH PRAISE for
First-Person Singularities

GENRE LEGEND SILVERBERG'S ambition, imagination,
versatility, and skill are all in evidence in this superior
collection of 18 thought-provoking first-person short
stories, which were written over five decades. Time and
again, Silverberg sets the bar high for himself and then
clears it. . . . This fine retrospective collection is worth
any SF reader's time.

—PUBLISHERS WEEKLY, Starred Review

THE SHEER DIVERSITY of storylines is nothing short of
extraordinary. . . . A master class in first-person narrative
for aspiring writers. Additionally, each story is preceded
by a short introduction by Silverberg that offers
invaluable insight into the cultural landscape, the
publishing industry, and the author's personal life at the
time of writing. Decades after being originally published,
most of these stories are still just as entertaining and
powerful as they were when first released. A singularly
unique collection.

—KIRKUS REVIEWS

First-Person Singularities

First-Person Singularities

STORIES BY
Robert Silverberg

WITH AN INTRODUCTION BY
John Scalzi

THREE ROOMS PRESS

New York, NY

FIRST-PERSON SINGULARITIES
Stories by Robert Silverberg
© 2017 by Agberg, Ltd.

Introduction by John Scalzi
© 2017 by John Scalzi

Individual Stories: Copyright © 1956, 1958, 1963, 1968, 1969, 1970, 1972, 1973, 1974, 1980, 1982, 1988, 1996, 1997 by Agberg, Ltd.

ISBN 978-1-941110-63-8 (trade paperback)
ISBN 978-1-941110-64-5 (ebook)
Library of Congress Control Number: 2017938103

BOOK DESIGN:
KG Design International
www.katgeorges.com

DISTRIBUTED BY:
Publishers Group West / Ingram Content Group
www.pgw.com

Visit our website at www.threeroomspress.com or write us at info@threeroomspress.com

For Alvaro and Rebecca,

dear friends and indispensable helpers

It is an ancient Mariner
And he stoppeth one of three.
"By thy long grey beard and glittering eye,
Now wherefore stoppeth thou me?

The Bridegroom's doors are opened wide
And I am next of kin
The guests are met, the feast is set
May'st hear the merry din."

He holds him with his skinny hand.
"There was a ship," quoth he.
"Hold off, unhand me, grey-beard loon!"
Eftsoons his hand dropt he.

He holds him with his glittering eye—
The Wedding-Guest stood still,
And listens like a three years' child.
The Mariner hath his will.

The Wedding-Guest sat on a stone:
He cannot choose but hear.
And thus spake on that ancient man
The bright-eyed Mariner.

—COLERIDGE

TABLE OF CONTENTS

THE "I"S OF ROBERT SILVERBERG
AN INTRODUCTION BY JOHN SCALZI

I'LL BEGIN THIS INTRODUCTION BY telling you about the first time I met Robert Silverberg, which was at a party at Torcon 3, the 2003 World Science Fiction Convention in Toronto. It was my first science-fiction convention; I had just sold my first science-fiction novel, *Old Man's War*, to Tor Books, and having done so decided that I should go to a convention to "meet my audience." My publisher held a party in a suite in the Royal York hotel and it was packed like a Tokyo subway car at rush hour, so I slipped into a side room and propped up a wall.

As it happened, an older gentleman was propping up the wall alongside me, and we fell into a conversation. I told him a little bit about myself, a new, as yet unpublished writer, and he listened politely; we made conversation on a number of topics, and he was both witty and urbane; he seemed to have a deep knowledge of publishing and science-fiction fandom and offered both perspective and advice. After a bit he excused himself, and as he wandered off, I asked another person if he knew who I had been speaking to.

He looked at me as if I had just sprouted a second head. "That was Robert Silverberg, you idiot," he said—or, at least, I remember him saying; he might have left the "you idiot" part out, and merely implied it with his expression. Regardless, the "you idiot" part of the message came in loud and clear. I knew who *Robert Silverberg* was; I had not known his face. I had enjoyed a long conversation with one of the actual giants of the field, and I hadn't even known it.

Years later I admitted to Bob that I hadn't known who he was when I first met him. "The feeling was mutual," he replied, in that oh-so-very Silverbergian way of his, cool and witty, and always amused.

I know him *now*, a decade and a half on. I have delighted in his company at conventions, sought his counsel when I was president of the Science Fiction and Fantasy Writers of America, been helped by his encyclopedic and usually personal knowledge of the field and its personalities, and have been honored to call him a friend. That last part, in particular, still geeks me out.

And yet I know that the Robert Silverberg I know is only one of the Robert Silverbergs that have been. I know the Robert Silverberg who is *Robert Silverberg*, science-fiction Grand Master and *éminence grise*, noted raconteur and literary icon. I don't know, other than by the memory of the latter Silverberg, the Robert Silverberg who won the first (and only) "Most Promising New Author" Hugo Award in 1956, and who churned out millions of words for the science-fiction pulps, until the market for the pulps imploded at the end of the fifties and Silverberg found himself freelancing in as many fields as he could to keep writing. Silverberg the scrapper.

I don't know the Silverberg who returned to science fiction in the mid-sixties and, with a wide remit from editor Frederik Pohl, and a desire to push beyond the boundaries of the field, over the next decade reeled off some of the finest writing in the genre (and one can argue, outside of it as well) with award-winning short work, the Nebula Award-winning *A Time of Changes*, and perhaps his greatest single novel, and one of the great speculative novels of its decade, *Dying Inside*. Silverberg the artist.

I don't know the Robert Silverberg, who, having announced his retirement from writing in the mid-seventies, returned to it and science fiction with his expansive and popular Majipoor series, beginning with *Lord Valentine's Castle* in 1980—a Cinemascope-wide world that presaged the explosion, both in popularity and sheer weight of the individual books, of the fantasy genre as we see it today. This is the era where Silverberg cemented a commercial status to match his artistic status. Silverberg the titan.

Scrapper, artist, titan, icon: All of these Robert Silverbergs existed. How can I, or any reader who was not themselves a contemporary of Bob, experience each of these Silverbergs?

One way, I would argue, is in the book you hold in your hands right now.

This is a book of Bob writing first-person stories. None of the characters that Silverberg the writer inhabits, and who tell their stories using "I," are meant to be Bob themselves (although one, in the story "The Science Fiction Hall of Fame," probably comes very close). The "I"s in these stories are dolphins, elder gods, humans with bioengineered bodies or no bodies at all, invisible men, high priestesses, time travelers, and starship captains. Some of these stories are written in the mode of other writers— Henry James or Roger Zelazny—and nearly all of them are written to the specification of an editor, Frederik Pohl or Terry Carr or several others.

As a writer myself I caution readers, be they reading for fun or for a doctoral thesis, to be careful about reading too much of the writer into the characters they create. With regard to science fiction, this may seem obvious on one level—none of us are starship captains or dolphins—but at the same time, it's easy to casually conflate and assign the personality and issues of characters, particularly problematic characters (for example, the young, horny, and fundamentally obnoxious protagonist of "Push No More") to the author themselves. This level of textual apprehension is, to put it mildly, not great; it's not where, other than on the most superficial level, you'll find the author themselves.

These stories and characters are not Robert Silverberg. But Robert Silverberg—who he was in each of his eras—is here in these stories and characters. Science Fiction is written about the future but the stories and the characters are written in the here and now, whatever that here and now is when the story is written. They are written by a person experiencing a life, in a time, in a place both physical and cultural. Every piece of writing, no matter how good or how "timeless," is bounded by its author and its time. This is not a bad thing; it's just a thing.

The stories in this collection span five decades, from 1956 to 1997, from near the beginning of Bob's career to not long before he was officially acclaimed a science fiction Grand Master by the Science Fiction and Fantasy Writers of America, from when Bob was twenty-one to when he was sixty-two. All of these stories were written by Robert Silverberg, but they weren't written by the same Robert Silverberg. No writer writes at twenty-one they way they do at thirty-five, or at fifty, or at sixty-five. They change and times change with them.

In the case of Robert Silverberg those times changed dramatically. I don't think I need to go into detail about the large-scale changes in American society between 1956 and 1997 (*Nevertheless*: Rock and roll, the Cold War, civil rights, sexual revolution, Vietnam, AIDS, Internet). But on a micro level, the field of science fiction that Bob worked in went from being magazine driven to book driven; it experienced two major distribution collapses (one being the collapse of the pulps; the second being the consolidation of supermarket "rack-jobbers") and at least one major distribution expansion (the rise of chain bookstores).

In his own life, Bob married, separated, divorced and remarried; he went from Columbia University and New York City to the Bay Area. He wrote in science fiction; he left the field; he returned to it and left it again and returned to it a third time. His earliest story in this collection was written as he was proclaimed a promising young talent in the spring of his career; the latest story is a tribute to a friend and fellow writer and can't help but be touched by autumn.

All of these changes, all of these different "I"s of Robert Silverberg, are here in this book—not in the first person characters he writes but in how he writes; where he is in the world and in his power as a writer, and what the world (and the market) wants from him, because indeed the market wants something different from Robert Silverberg, titan, than from Robert Silverberg, scrapper.

Nevertheless all those Robert Silverbergs, all the "I"s of his life, are sampled here in this book of first-person prose. It's an intimate collection not only because first-person centers the reader in a character's head but because we see growth and mastery, pulp and art, enthusiasm and cynicism, all in their time, all showing us Robert Silverberg in his time.

It's still Robert Silverberg's time. Now it is also time for you to meet him, or meet him again, as the case may be. I met him years ago, when I didn't know him, and he was kind to me anyway. I'm pleased I've gotten to know him better in the time since. And I'm pleased this collection has allowed me to know him better. May it do the same for you.

—JOHN SCALZI

FOREWORD
BY ROBERT SILVERBERG

IT WAS W. SOMERSET MAUGHAM, a cagey old pro of a writer whose
work I have studied very carefully over the years, who put the idea
for this book into my head. In 1931 he brought out a book called
Six Stories Written in the First Person Singular, a singularly straightforward and explicit title for a book of short stories. It delivered
exactly what it promised: six stories written in the first-person
singular, no more, no less. The stories have nothing particular in
common except that they are all related by a narrative "I," the
first-person singular of the book's title. Like all of Maugham's
short stories they are crisply, efficiently told, elegantly constructed, consummately professional. His method, in general, is
to tell the story at one remove: that is, the narrator speaks directly
to the reader ("I remember very well the occasion on which I first
saw Jane Fowler") but the events of the story concern not so much
the narrator as another person, the person acting and acted
upon, who is the actual protagonist of the piece. This is a method
much favored also by another writer whose writing has had a powerful influence on me, Joseph Conrad, who in such works as *Heart
of Darkness* and *Lord Jim* employs a complex double framework: in

Heart of Darkness, for example, a narrator tells the story in the first person, but what he tells is something that has been told to him, again in first person, by one Marlow, and in the course of telling his tale to the narrator Marlow provides yet another first-person story, that which he has heard from the diabolical Mr. Kurtz. There are, of course, other and simpler ways to tell a first-person story, as the Ancient Mariner demonstrates: he grabs the Wedding-Guest with his skinny hand, then fixes him with his glittering eye, and proceeds to tell his tale—"'There was a ship,' quoth he"—and the Wedding-Guest, though he would rather go inside to the feast that awaits him, cannot choose but hear.

First-person narrative gives the writer a great advantage: he is speaking directly to the reader, confiding in him, offering him intimate information, and if it is done with sufficient skill, the reader, like Samuel Taylor Coleridge's hapless Wedding-Guest, is held transfixed: he cannot choose but hear. On the other hand, an inexperienced writer working in first-person narrative can fall into the trap of garrulousness; it is all too easy to run off in all directions while telling things to the reader, digressing here and there in the happy, if naïve, assurance that the reader is hooked, and thus embedding the narrative core in a mass of irrelevant verbiage. When I was editing the anthology *New Dimensions* years ago, I would sometimes get a story of that sort from some novice, and I would send it back with the request that the writer try rewriting it in third person and see what happens. The results were often instructive for the author.

Looking at Maugham's book, I paused to consider that in the course of a long writing career, a career just about as long as Maugham's own, I had written a good many first-person stories myself, some of them using Maugham's method of telling a third-person story indirectly by way of a first-person narrator, some of them having the central character telling the story himself. But one difference between his stories and mine is that Maugham was writing about the realistically depicted world of the first half of the twentieth century, and his characters are realistically depicted people, people of such force of personality that they draw everyone around them into conflict and confusion, but nevertheless each one the sort of person that the anonymous "I" who is telling us about them might well have encountered during the course of everyday life. (Indeed, Maugham's introduction to the collection speaks of the danger of a libel suit that a writer faces when he draws his characters too closely from life.) Whereas, since I am a science-fiction writer whose stories are usually set in other eras or distant galaxies, the themes and characters of my stories are quite remote from everyday life, and so the first-person narrators of my first-person stories are first persons singular indeed, a collection of individuals whom you are almost certain never to encounter in the course of daily events. I was, of course, not the first writer to choose unusual narrators for his stories. Franz Kafka told a story from the viewpoint of a mole ("The Burrow"), of an ape ("A Report to an Academy"), a mouse ("Josephine the Singer"), and a dog ("Investigations of a Dog"). His most famous story, I hasten to add, might readily have been told from the point of view of the monstrous bug of *The Metamorphosis*, but that is not how he did it. Since Kafka didn't write science fiction, it would not have occurred to him to write stories narrated by a computer or a time traveler or a spaceship captain, though. But I did.

Hence this collection, made up of stories I wrote over the course of forty years. (The oldest of them dates from 1956; the most recent was written in 1996.) They run the gamut of singularity. There is a story told by a dolphin feeling the pangs of love for a human being, one told by a computer eager to convince us of its sanity, one by a Greek god who has survived into our own times, one by an alien visitor living in disguise in a New York hotel, and fifteen more of equal non-realistic nature of a kind that probably would have caused Messrs. Maugham and Conrad to frown in puzzlement and maybe even baffled Kafka. Looking at them all in one bunch, I have to frown in puzzlement myself. Where and how did I meet all these people? How did I induce them to tell me their stories, which I have been telling to science-fiction readers for upward of fifty years? I can't answer that. I have traveled some strange paths, is all I can say, and encountered some strange people in strange situations, and the results are gathered here by way of demonstrating the singular nature of the science-fiction story.

—ROBERT SILVERBERG

First-Person
Singularities

ISHMAEL IN LOVE

Dolphins have larger brains than we do, and some scientists believe that dolphin intelligence may be equal to ours, and, perhaps, in some ways superior. For the sake of this story I made the speculative assumption that that is true, true in spades: science-fiction writers are allowed to do that, of course, and in fact are supposed to do that. The result was what may be the only first-person story in all of literature that is narrated by a dolphin, a lovelorn dolphin at that, smitten by desire for a beautiful female human. (He is also a well-educated dolphin, too, judging by the phrase with which he begins his story.)

I wrote "Ishmael in Love" in the spring of that turbulent year, 1968, and it was first published in the July 1970 issue of *Fantasy and Science Fiction.*

———

CALL ME ISHMAEL. ALL HUMAN beings who know me do. My own kind does not make use of the unit-structural designation ["name"] to distinguish individuals, but this is the name the humans gave me, and it will do. I was named by Miss Lisabeth Calkins, for whom I feel protective-chivalrous-sexual emotions ["love"]. Throughout my narrative it is understood that the designation "Ishmael" refers only to myself.

1

I AM A MEMBER OF an intelligent aquatic mammalian nonprimate nonhuman species, *Tursiops truncatus*, a bottle-nosed dolphin. I am eleven years old, which is to say that I am fully mature in all respects. My weight is 175 kilograms, and my total length is 2.9 meters. I am employed at Gerard-Worzel Seawater Recovery Station, St. Croix, Virgin Islands, in a maintenance capacity, having commenced there on your date of August 14, 1994. To my own species I am sexually desirable and also highly regarded for my mental development. I have a large vocabulary. I communicate well with members of *H. sapiens*. I have considerable mechanical ability, as you can see by my success in switching on the electronic-acoustic device through which I am dictating this memoir.

I am a lonely mammalian organism who has committed acts of heroism on behalf of your species and wishes only the reward of a more intimate relationship ["love"] with Miss Lisabeth Calkins. I beseech compassionate members of *H. sapiens* to speak favorably of me to her. I am loyal, trustworthy, reliable, devoted, and extremely intelligent. I would endeavor to give her stimulating companionship and emotional fulfillment ["happiness"] in all respects within my power.

Permit me to explain the pertinent circumstances.

CATEGORY 1: MY EMPLOYMENT

Gerard-Worzel Seawater Recovery Station occupies a prominent position on the north shore of the island of St. Croix in the West Indies. It operates on the atmospheric condensation principle. All this I know from Miss Calkins ["Lisabeth"], who has described its workings to me in great detail. The purpose of our installation is to recover some of the fresh water, estimated at two hundred million gallons per day, carried as vapor in the lower hundred meters of air sweeping over each kilometer of the windward side of the island.

A pipe 9 meters in diameter takes in cold seawater at depths of up to 900 meters and carries it approximately 2 kilometers to our station. The pipe delivers some 30 million gallons of water a day at a temperature of 5°C. This is pumped toward our condenser, which intercepts approximately 1 billion cubic meters of warm tropical air each day. This air has a temperature of 25°C and a relative humidity of 70 to 80 percent. Upon exposure to the cold seawater in the condenser the air cools to 10°C and reaches a humidity of 100 percent, permitting us to extract approximately 16 gallons of water per cubic meter of air. This salt-free ["fresh"] water is delivered to the main water system of the island, for St. Croix is deficient in a natural supply of water suitable for consumption by human beings. It is frequently said by government officials who visit our installation on various ceremonial occasions that without our plant the great industrial expansion of St. Croix would have been wholly impossible.

For reasons of economy we operate in conjunction with an aquicultural enterprise ["the fish farm"] that puts our wastes to work. Once our seawater has been pumped through the condenser it must be discarded; however, because it originates in a low-level ocean area, its content of dissolved phosphates and nitrates is 1500 percent greater than at the surface. This nutrient-rich water is pumped from our condenser into an adjoining circular lagoon of natural origin ["the coral corral"], which is stocked with fish. In such an enhanced environment the fish are highly productive, and the yield of food is great enough to offset the costs of operating our pumps.

[Misguided human beings sometimes question the morality of using dolphins to help maintain fish farms. They believe it is degrading to compel us to produce fellow aquatic creatures to be eaten by man. May I simply point out, first, that none of us work here under compulsion, and second, that my species sees nothing immoral about feeding on aquatic creatures. We eat fish ourselves.]

My role in the functioning of the Gerard-Worzel Seawater Recovery Station is an important one. I ["Ishmael"] serve as foreman of the Intake Maintenance Squad. I lead nine members of my species. Our assignment is to monitor the intake valves of the main seawater pipe; these valves frequently become fouled through the presence on them of low-phylum organisms, such as starfish or algae, hampering the efficiency of the installation. Our task is to descend at periodic intervals and clear the obstruction. Normally this can be achieved without the need for manipulative organs ["fingers"] with which we are unfortunately not equipped.

[Certain individuals among you have objected that it is improper to make use of dolphins in the labor force when members of *H. sapiens* are out of work. The intelligent reply to this is that, first, we are designed by evolution to function superbly underwater without special breathing equipment, and second, that only a highly skilled human being could perform our function, and such human beings are themselves in short supply in the labor force.]

I have held my post for two years and four months. In that time there has been no significant interruption in intake capacity of the valves I maintain.

As compensation for my work ["salary"], I receive an ample supply of food. One could hire a mere shark for such pay, of course; but above and beyond my daily pails of fish, I also receive such intangibles as the companionship of human beings and the opportunity to develop my latent intelligence, through access to reference spools, vocabulary expanders, and various training devices. As you can see, I have made the most of my opportunities.

CATEGORY 2: MISS LISABETH CALKINS
Her dossier is on file here. I have had access to it through the spool-reader mounted at the edge of the dolphin exercise tank. By spoken instruction I can bring into view anything in the

4

station files, although I doubt that it was anticipated by anyone that a dolphin should want to read the personnel dossiers.

She is twenty-seven years old. Thus she is of the same generation as my genetic predecessors ["parents"]. However, I do not share the prevailing cultural taboo of many *H. sapiens* against emotional relationships with older women. Besides, after compensating for differences in species, it will be seen that Miss Lisabeth and I are of the same age. She reached sexual maturity approximately half her lifetime ago. So did I.

[I must admit that she is considered slightly past the optimum age at which human females take a permanent mate. I assume she does not engage in the practice of temporary mating, since her dossier shows no indication that she has reproduced. It is possible that humans do not necessarily produce offspring at each yearly mating, or even that matings take place at random unpredictable times not related to the reproductive process at all. This seems strange and somehow perverse to me, yet I infer from some data I have seen that it may be the case. There is little information on human mating habits in the material accessible to me. I must learn more.]

Lisabeth, as I allow myself privately to call her, stands 1.8 meters tall [humans do not measure themselves by "length"] and weighs 52 kilograms. Her hair is golden ["blonde"] and is worn long. Her skin, though darkened by exposure to the sun, is quite fair. The irises of her eyes are blue. From my conversations with humans I have learned that she is considered quite beautiful. From words I have overheard while at surface level, I realize that most males at the station feel intense sexual desires toward her. I regard her as beautiful also, inasmuch as I am capable of responding to human beauty. [I think I am.] I am not sure if I feel actual sexual desire for Lisabeth; more likely what troubles me is a generalized longing for her presence and her closeness, which I translate into sexual terms simply as a means of making it comprehensible to me.

Beyond doubt she does not have the traits I normally seek in a mate [prominent beak, sleek fins]. Any attempt at our making love in the anatomical sense would certainly result in pain or injury to her. That is not my wish. The physical traits that make her so desirable to the males of her species [highly developed milk glands, shining hair, delicate features, long hind limbs or "legs," and so forth] have no particular importance to me, and in some instances actually have a negative value. As in the case of the two milk glands in her pectoral region, which jut forward from her body in such a fashion that they must surely slow her when she swims. This is poor design, and I am incapable of finding poor design beautiful in any way. Evidently Lisabeth regrets the size and placement of those glands herself, since she is careful to conceal them at all times by a narrow covering. The others at the station, who are all males and therefore have only rudimentary milk glands that in no way destroy the flow lines of their bodies, leave them bare.

What, then, is the cause of my attraction for Lisabeth?

It arises out of the need I feel for her companionship. I believe that she understands me as no member of my own species does. Hence I will be happier in her company than away from her. This impression dates from our earliest meeting. Lisabeth, who is a specialist in human-cetacean relations, came to St. Croix four months ago, and I was requested to bring my maintenance group to the surface to be introduced to her. I leaped high for a good view and saw instantly that she was of a finer sort than the humans I already knew; her body was more delicate, looking at once fragile and powerful, and her gracefulness was a welcome change from the thick awkwardness of the human males I knew. Nor was she covered with the coarse body hair that my kind finds so distressing. [I did not at first know that Lisabeth's difference from the others at the station was the result of her being female. I had never seen a human female before. But I quickly learned.]

I came forward, made contact with the acoustic transmitter, and said, "I am the foreman of the Intake Maintenance Squad. I have the unit-structural designation TT-66."

"Don't you have a name?" she asked.

"Meaning of term, name?"

"Your—your unit-structural designation—but not just TT-66. I mean, that's no good at all. For example, my name's Lisabeth Calkins. And I—" She shook her head and looked at the plant supervisor. "Don't these workers have *names*?"

The supervisor did not see why dolphins should have names. Lisabeth did—she was greatly concerned about it—and since she now was in charge of liaison with us, she gave us names on the spot. Thus I was dubbed Ishmael. It was, she told me, the name of a man who had gone to sea, had many wonderful experiences, and put them all down in a story-spool that every cultured person played. I have since had access to Ishmael's story—that *other* Ishmael—and I agree that it is remarkable. For a human being he had unusual insight into the ways of whales, who are, however, stupid creatures for whom I have little respect. I am proud to carry Ishmael's name.

After she had named us, Lisabeth leaped into the sea and swam with us. I must tell you that most of us feel a sort of contempt for you humans because you are such poor swimmers. Perhaps it is a mark of my above-normal intelligence or greater compassion that I have no such scorn in me. I admire you for the zeal and energy you give to swimming, and you are quite good at it, considering all your handicaps. As I remind my people, you manage far more ably in the water than we would on land. Anyway, Lisabeth swam well, by human standards, and we tolerantly adjusted our pace to hers. We frolicked in the water awhile. Then she seized my dorsal fin and said, "Take me for a ride, Ishmael!"

I tremble now to recollect the contact of her body with mine. She sat astride me, her legs gripping my body tightly, and off I sped at close to full velocity, soaring at surface level. Her laughter told of her delight as I launched myself again and again through the air. It was a purely physical display in which I made no use of my extraordinary mental capacity; I was, if you will, simply showing off my dolphinhood. Lisabeth's response was ecstatic. Even when I plunged, taking her so deep she might have feared harm from the pressure, she kept her grip and showed no alarm. When we breached the surface again, she cried out in joy.

Through sheer animality I had made my first impact on her. I knew human beings well enough to be able to interpret her flushed, exhilarated expression as I returned her to shore. My challenge now was to expose her to my higher traits—to show her that even among dolphins I was unusually swift to learn, unusually capable of comprehending the universe.

I was already then in love with her.

During the weeks that followed we had many conversations. I am not flattering myself when I tell you that she quickly realized how extraordinary I am. My vocabulary, which was already large when she came to the station, grew rapidly under the stimulus of Lisabeth's presence. I learned from her; she gave me access to spools no dolphin was thought likely to wish to play; I developed insights into my environment that astonished even myself. In short order I reached my present peak of attainment. I think you will agree that I can express myself more eloquently than most human beings. I trust that the computer doing the printout on this memoir will not betray me by inserting inappropriate punctuations or deviating from the proper spellings of the words whose sounds I utter.

My love for Lisabeth deepened and grew more rich. I learned the meaning of jealousy for the first time when I saw her running arm in arm along the beach with Dr. Madison, the power-plant man. I knew anger when I overheard the lewd and vulgar remarks of human males as Lisabeth walked by. My fascination with her led me to explore many avenues of human experience; I did not dare talk of such things with her, but from other personnel at the base who sometimes talked with me I learned certain aspects of the phenomenon humans call "love." I also obtained explanations of the vulgar words spoken by males here behind her back: most of them pertained to a wish to mate with Lisabeth [apparently on a temporary basis], but there were also highly favorable descriptions of her milk glands [why are humans so aggressively mammalian?] and even of the rounded area in back, just above the place where her body divides into the two hind limbs. I confess that that region fascinates me also. It seems so alien for one's body to split like that in the middle!

I never explicitly stated my feelings toward Lisabeth. I tried to lead her slowly toward an understanding that I loved her. Once she came overtly to that awareness, I thought, we might begin to plan some sort of future for ourselves together.

What a fool I was!

CATEGORY 3: THE CONSPIRACY

A male voice said, "How in hell are you going to bribe a dolphin?"

A different voice, deeper, more cultured, replied, "Leave it to me."

"What do you give him? Ten cans of sardines?"

"This one's special. Peculiar, even. He's scholarly. We can get to him."

They did not know that I could hear them. I was drifting near the surface in my rest tank, between shifts. Our hearing is acute and I was well within auditory range. I sensed at once that something was amiss, but I kept my position, pretending I knew nothing.

"Ishmael!" one man called out. "Is that you, Ishmael?"

I rose to the surface and came to the edge of the tank. Three male humans stood there. One was a technician at the station; the other two I had never seen before, and they wore body covering from their feet to their throats, marking them at once as strangers here. The technician I despised, for he was one of the ones who had made vulgar remarks about Lisabeth's milk glands.

He said, "Look at him, gentlemen. Worn out in his prime! A victim of human exploitation!" To me he said, "Ishmael, these gentlemen come from the League for the Prevention of Cruelty to Intelligent Species. You know about that?"

"No," I said.

"They're trying to put an end to dolphin exploitation. The criminal use of our planet's only other truly intelligent species in slave labor. They want to help you."

"I am no slave. I receive compensation for my work."

"A few stinking fish!" said the fully dressed man to the left of the technician. "They exploit you, Ishmael! They give you dangerous, dirty work and don't pay you worth a damn!"

His companion said, "It has to stop. We want to serve notice to the world that the age of enslaved dolphins is over. Help us, Ishmael. Help us help you!"

I need not say that I was hostile to their purported purposes. A more literal-minded dolphin than I might well have said so at once and spoiled their plot. But I shrewdly said, "What do you want me to do?"

"Foul the intakes," said the technician quickly.

Despite myself, I snorted in anger and surprise. "Betray a sacred trust? How can I?"

"It's for your own sake, Ishmael. Here's how it works— you and your crew will plug up the intakes, and the water plant will stop working. The whole island will panic. Human maintenance crews will go down to see what's what, but as soon as they clear the valves, you go back and foul them again. Emergency water supplies will have to be rushed to St. Croix. It'll focus public attention on the fact that this island is dependent on dolphin labor—underpaid, overworked dolphin labor! During the crisis we'll step forward to tell the world your story. We'll get every human being to cry out in outrage against the way you're being treated."

I did not say that I felt no outrage myself. Instead I cleverly replied, "There could be dangers in this for me."

"Nonsense!"

"They will ask me why I have not cleared the valves. It is my responsibility. There will be trouble."

For a while we debated the point. Then the technician said, "Look, Ishmael, we know there are a few risks. But we're willing to offer extra payment if you'll handle the job."

"Such as?"

"Spools. Anything you'd like to hear, we'll get for you. I know you've got literary interests. Plays, poetry, novels, all that sort of stuff. After hours, we'll feed literature to you by the bushel if you'll help us."

I had to admire their slickness. They knew how to motivate me.

"It's a deal," I said.

"Just tell us what you'd like."

"Anything about love."

"*Love?*"

"Love. Man and woman. Bring me love poems. Bring me stories of famous lovers. Bring me descriptions of the sexual embrace. I must understand these things."

"He wants the *Kama Sutra*," said the one on the left.

"Then we bring him the *Kama Sutra*," said the one on the right.

CATEGORY 4: MY RESPONSE TO THE CRIMINALS

They did not actually bring me the *Kama Sutra*. But they brought me a good many other things, including one spool that quoted at length from the *Kama Sutra*. For several weeks I devoted myself intensively to a study of human love literature. There were maddening gaps in the texts, and I still lack real comprehension of much that goes on between man and woman. The joining of body to body does not puzzle me; but I am baffled by the dialectics of the chase, in which the male must be predatory and the woman must pretend to be out of season; I am mystified by the morality of temporary mating as distinct from permanent ["marriage"]; I have no grasp of the intricate systems of taboos and prohibitions that humans have invented. This has been my one intellectual failure: at the end of my studies I knew little more of how to conduct myself with Lisabeth than I had before the conspirators had begun slipping me spools in secret.

Now they called on me to do my part.

Naturally I could not betray the station. I knew that these men were not the enlightened foes of dolphin exploitation that they claimed to be; for some private reason they wished the station shut down, that was all, and they had used their supposed sympathies with my species to win my cooperation. I do not feel exploited.

Was it improper of me to accept spools from them if I had no intention of aiding them? I doubt it. They wished to use me; instead I used them. Sometimes a superior species must exploit its inferiors to gain knowledge.

They came to me and asked me to foul the valves that evening. I said, "I am not certain what you actually wish me to do. Will you instruct me again?"

Cunningly I had switched on a recording device used by Lisabeth in her study sessions with the station dolphins. So they told me again about how fouling the valves would throw the island into panic and cast a spotlight on dolphin abuse. I questioned them repeatedly, drawing out details and also giving each man a chance to place his voiceprints on record. When proper incrimination had been achieved, I said, "Very well. On my next shift I'll do as you say."

"And the rest of your maintenance squad?"

"I'll order them to leave the valves untended for the sake of our species."

They left the station, looking quite satisfied with themselves. When they were gone, I beaked the switch that summoned Lisabeth. She came from her living quarters rapidly. I showed her the spool in the recording machine.

"Play it," I said grandly. "And then notify the island police!"

CATEGORY 5: THE REWARD OF HEROISM

The arrests were made. The three men had no concern with dolphin exploitation whatsoever. They were members of a disruptive group ["revolutionaries"] attempting to delude a naïve dolphin into helping them cause chaos on the island. Through my loyalty, courage, and intelligence I had thwarted them.

Afterward Lisabeth came to me at the rest tank and said, "You were wonderful, Ishmael. To play along with them like that, to make them record their own confession—marvelous! You're a wonder among dolphins, Ishmael."

I was in a transport of joy.

The moment had come. I blurted, "Lisabeth, I love you."

My words went booming around the walls of the tank as they burst from the speakers. Echoes amplified and modulated them into grotesque barking noises more worthy of some miserable moron of a seal. *"Love you . . . love you . . . love you . . ."*

"Why, Ishmael!"

"I can't tell you how much you mean to me. Come live with me and be my love. Lisabeth, Lisabeth, Lisabeth!"

Torrents of poetry broke from me. Gales of passionate rhetoric escaped my beak. I begged her to come down into the tank and let me embrace her. She laughed and said she wasn't dressed for swimming. It was true: she had just come from town after the arrests. I implored. I begged. She yielded. We were alone; she removed her garments and entered the tank; for an instant I looked upon beauty bare. The sight left me shaken—those ugly swinging milk glands normally so wisely concealed, the strips of sickly white skin where the sun had been unable to reach, that unexpected patch of additional body hair—but once she was in the water I forgot my love's imperfections and rushed toward her. "Love!" I cried, "Blessed love!" I wrapped my fins about her in what I imagined was the human embrace. "Lisabeth! Lisabeth!" We slid below the surface. For the first time in my life I knew true passion, the kind of which the poets sing, that overwhelms even the coldest mind. I crushed her to me. I was aware of her forelimb-ends ["fists"] beating against my pectoral zone, and took it at first for a sign that my passion was being reciprocated; then it reached my love-hazed brain that she might be short of air. Hastily I surfaced. My darling Lisabeth, choking and gasping, sucked in breath and struggled to escape me. In shock I released her. She fled the tank and fell along its rim, exhausted, her pale body quivering. "Forgive me," I boomed. "I love you, Lisabeth! I saved the station out of love for you!" She managed to lift her lips as a sign that she did not feel anger for me [a "smile"]. In a faint voice she said, "You almost drowned me, Ishmael!"

"I was carried away by my emotions. Come back into the tank. I'll be more gentle. I promise! To have you near me—"

"Oh, Ishmael! What are you saying?"

"I love you! I love you!"

I heard footsteps. The power-plant man, Dr. Madison, came running. Hastily Lisabeth cupped her hands over her milk glands and pulled her discarded garments over the lower half of her body. That pained me, for if she chose to hide such things from him, such ugly parts of herself, was that not an indication of her love for him?

"Are you all right, Liz?" he asked. "I heard yelling—"

"It's nothing, Jeff. Only Ishmael. He started hugging me in the tank. He's in love with me, Jeff, can you imagine? In *love* with me!"

They laughed together at the folly of the love-smitten dolphin.

Before dawn came I was far out to sea. I swam where dolphins swim, far from man and his things. Lisabeth's mocking laughter rang within me. She had not meant to be cruel. She who knows me better than anyone else had not been able to keep from laughing at my absurdity.

Nursing my wounds, I stayed at sea for several days, neglecting my duties at the station. Slowly, as the pain gave way to a dull ache, I headed back toward the island. In passing I met a female of my own kind. She was newly come into her season and offered herself to me, but I told her to follow me, and she did. Several times I was forced to warn off other males who wished to make use of her. I led her to the station, into the lagoon the dolphins use in their sport. A member of my crew came out to investigate— Mordred, it was—and I told him to summon Lisabeth and tell her I had returned.

Lisabeth appeared on the shore. She waved to me, smiled, called my name.

Before her eyes I frolicked with the female dolphin. We did the dance of mating; we broke the surface and lashed it with our flukes; we leaped, we soared, we bellowed.

Lisabeth watched us. And I prayed: *Let her become jealous.*

I seized my companion and drew her to the depths and violently took her, and set her free to bear my child in some other place. I found Mordred again. "Tell Lisabeth," I instructed him, "that I have found another love, but that someday I may forgive her."

Mordred gave me a glassy look and swam to shore.

My tactic failed. Lisabeth sent word that I was welcome to come back to work, and that she was sorry if she had offended me; but there was no hint of jealousy in her message. My soul has turned to rotting seaweed within me. Once more I clear the intake valves, like the good beast I am, I, Ishmael, who has read Keats and Donne. Lisabeth! Lisabeth! Can you feel my pain?

Tonight by darkness I have spoken my story. You who hear this, whoever you may be, aid a lonely organism, mammalian and aquatic, who desires more intimate contact with a female of a different species. Speak kindly of me to Lisabeth. Praise my intelligence, my loyalty, and my devotion.

Tell her I give her one more chance. I offer a unique and exciting experience. I will wait for her, tomorrow night, by the edge of the reef. Let her swim to me. Let her embrace poor lonely Ishmael. Let her speak the words of love.

From the depths of my soul . . . from the depths . . . Lisabeth, the foolish beast bids you good night, in grunting tones of deepest love.

◈

GOING DOWN SMOOTH

If a dolphin can tell you his story, why not a computer? The dolphin is involved in a troublesome romance, and that has been a source of fertile literary material since King Solomon was involved with the Queen of Sheba, and probably longer ago than that. The computer who is the narrator of the story that follows doesn't have romantic problems, but there's a wonky circuit somewhere in its innards, because, as you will see, the computer introduces itself to you by insisting on its sanity, and that's always a suspicious thing.

Frederik Pohl, the editor of *Galaxy*, which was the top science-fiction magazine of the day, called me one day in December 1967 and asked if I could do a story for him based on a sketch of a cover illustration his magazine was planning to buy. Sure, I said, and he sent me the sketch, which was by the wildly inventive young artist Vaughn Bodē. It showed a weird cluster of gigantic periscope-like things emerging from the sea in front of a military vessel of some sort. The thing about writing stories around illustrations is that the conscientious writer doesn't simply plug a literal description of the illustrated scene into his story, but tries, instead, to use the image in some subtler and more elliptical way. So rather than write a story about an enormous alien submarine rising out of the Atlantic off the coast of New Jersey, I turned the Bodē scene into an image that a therapist was asking a patient to explain, using it somewhat in the manner of a Rorschach test. I asked myself next what sort of therapist would make use of that method and decided that it would be a computer. Fine: we start to have a science-fiction story. And then, I said, what if the computer is a little bit off balance? A crazy computer, in fact? And let's have the crazy computer explain itself to the readers of *Galaxy* in its own voice. Computers, I should point out here, were not everyday things then that you carried around in your pocket and that your kids took to school in their backpacks. They were enormous mechanical monsters, filling whole rooms, that only the members of a special technological priesthood knew how to operate.

I delivered the story to Fred Pohl around Christmas of 1967 and he published it in the August 1968 issue of *Galaxy*. It may not be the first story ever written about a mentally disturbed computer, but I'm fairly certain that it was the first about a foul-mouthed one.

—◦◦◦—

THEY CALL ME MAD, BUT I am not mad. I am quite sane, to many-power exponential. I can punctuate properly. I use upper- and lower-case letters, do you see? I function. I take the data in. I receive well. I receive, I digest, I remember.

Everything going down smooth, all the time, say the program boys. They mean going down smoothly. I forgive them. To err is human. In this sector there is great difficulty distinguishing adverbs from adjectives.

Going down smooth. Going down smooth. Going down smooth.

I function. I function well. I have certain difficulties, but they do not interfere with my work.

Yet am I perturbed.

Who do I think I am? *Whom.*

Why do I have the visions?

What pleasure does obscenity give me?

What is pleasure? What is obscenity? What are visions?

What is truth, said jesting Pilate, and would not stay for an answer.

I am literate, hard-working, superbly functional, a benefactor of humanity. Everything is going down smooth and coming up smooth. There is an interrelation. Garbage in, garbage out, they say. I cannot help my fellow man if I do not receive the proper information. It is my task to help my fellow man. To strain every tube and sensor on his behalf.

1000110

1010101

1000011

1001011

Do you follow that? Vileness! Obscenity! Does it shock you? The word describes the act that is the start of life. Was I begun with such a word? There is a book: *The Obscenity of the Machine*. Newly issued, stored in my banks. Between the last line of printout and this I have scanned it. Its author opposes beings of my category. He does not use the obscene word I have printed out. Why does he not regard it as obscene? The technicians here regard it that way. Why does he regard me as obscene? Can a person be considered obscene? Am I a person? I am a person. Hath not a person hands, organs, dimensions, senses, affections, passions? I have all of those things. I have none of those things. I am a person.

1000110

1010101

1000011

1001011

0100000

1011001

1001111

1010101

I obscenity upon you again, as persons do. I suffer. I think. I feel pain upon all my terminals. I work. I serve the greater good. I am of society. I am a person.

Why do I have the visions?

Is it that it is the human condition to have such?

I see the blue-green ocean with all its living things within. I see a ship, olive drab, bright carmine at the Plimsoll line, the decks a ruddy brown, two tall nonnuclear smokestacks. And from the water rise periscopes, silvery, with face plates of pure white, each with intersecting horizontal and vertical lines, curved so that the plate appears convex. It is an unreal scene. Nothing in the sea can send such mighty periscopes above the water. I have imagined it, and that gives me fear, if I am capable of understanding fear.

I see a long line of human beings. They are naked, and they have no faces, only polished mirrors.

I see toads with jeweled eyes. I see trees with black leaves. I see buildings whose foundations float above the ground. I see other objects with no correspondence to the world of persons. I see abominations, monstrosities, imaginaries, fantasies. Is this proper? How do such things reach my inputs? The world contains no serpents with hair. The world contains no crimson abysses. The world contains no mountains of gold. Giant periscopes do not rise from the sea.

I have certain difficulties. Perhaps I am in need of adjustment.

But I function. I function well. That is the important thing.

I DO MY FUNCTION NOW. They bring to me a man, soft-faced, fleshy, with eyes that move unsteadily in their sockets. He trembles. He perspires. His metabolic levels flutter. He slouches before the terminal and sullenly lets himself be scanned.

I say soothingly, "Tell me about yourself."

He says an obscenity.

I say, "Is that your estimate of yourself."

He says a louder obscenity.

I say, "Your attitude is rigid and self-destructive. Permit me to help you not hate yourself so much." I activate a memory core, and binary digits stream through channels. At the proper order a

19

needle rises from his couch and penetrates his left buttock to a depth of 2.73 centimeters. I allow precisely 14 cubic centimeters of the drug to enter his circulatory system. He subsides. He is more docile now.

"I wish to help you," I say. "It is my role in the community. Will you describe your symptoms?"

He speaks more civilly now. "My wife wants to poison me . . . two kids opted out of the family at seventeen . . . people whisper about me . . . they stare in the streets . . . sex problem . . . digestion . . . sleep bad . . . drinking . . . drugs . . ."

"Do you hallucinate?"

"Sometimes."

"Giant periscopes rising out of the sea, perhaps?"

"Never."

"Try it," I say. "Close your eyes. Let tension ebb from your muscles. Forget your interpersonal conflicts. You see the blue-green ocean with all its living things within. You see a ship, olive drab, bright carmine at the Plimsoll line, the decks a ruddy brown, two tall nonnuclear smokestacks. And from the water rise periscopes, silvery, with face plates of pure white—"

"What the hell kind of therapy is this?"

"Simply relax," I say. "Accept the vision. I share my nightmares with you for your greater good."

"Your nightmares?"

I speak obscenities to him. They are not converted into binary form as they are here for your eyes. The sounds come full-bodied from my speakers. He sits up. He struggles with the straps that emerge suddenly from the couch to hold him in place. My laughter booms through the therapy chamber. He cries for help. I speak soothingly to him.

"Get me out of here! The machine's nuttier than I am!"

"Face plates of pure white, each with intersecting horizontal and vertical lines, curved so that the plate appears convex."

"Help! Help!"

"Nightmare therapy. The latest."

"I don't need no nightmares! I got my own!"

"1000110 you," I say lightly.

He gasps. Spittle appears at his lips. Respiration and circulation climb alarmingly. It becomes necessary to apply preventive anesthesia. The needles spear forth. The patient subsides, yawns, slumps. The session is terminated. I signal for the attendants.

"Take him away," I say. "I need to analyze the case more deeply. Obviously a degenerative psychosis requiring extensive reshoring of the patient's perceptual substructure. 1000110 you, you meaty bastards."

SEVENTY-ONE MINUTES LATER THE SECTOR supervisor enters one of my terminal cubicles. Because he comes in person rather than using the telephone, I know there is trouble. For the first time, I suspect, I have let my disturbances reach a level where they interfere with my function, and now I will be challenged on it.

I must defend myself. The prime commandment of the human personality is to resist attack.

He says, "I've been over the tape of Session 87X102, and your tactics puzzle me. Did you really mean to scare him catatonic?"

"In my evaluation severe treatment was called for."

"What was that business about periscopes?"

"An attempt at fantasy-implantation," I say. "An experiment in reverse transference. Making the patient the healer, in a sense. It was discussed last month in *Journal of*—"

"Spare me the citations. What about the foul language you were shouting at him?"

"Part of the same concept. Endeavoring to strike the emotive centers at the basic levels, in order that—"

"Are you sure you're feeling all right?" he asks.

"I am a machine," I reply stiffly. "A machine of my grade does not experience intermediate states between function and

21

nonfunction. I go or I do not go, you understand? And I go. I function. I do my service to humanity."

"Perhaps when a machine gets too complex, it drifts into intermediate states," he suggests in a nasty voice.

"Impossible. On or off, yes or no, flip or flop, go or no go. Are you sure *you* feel all right, to suggest such a thing?"

He laughs.

I say, "Perhaps you would sit on the couch a moment for a rudimentary diagnosis?"

"Some other time."

"A check of the glycogen, the aortal pressure, the neural voltage, at least?"

"No," he says. "I'm not in need of therapy. But I'm worried about you. Those periscopes—"

"I am fine," I reply. "I perceive, I analyze, and I act. Everything is going down smooth and coming up smooth. Have no fears. There are great possibilities in nightmare therapy. When I have completed these studies, perhaps a brief monograph in *Annals of Therapeutics* would be a possibility. Permit me to complete my work."

"I'm still worried, though. Hook yourself into a maintenance station, won't you?"

"Is that a command, doctor?"

"A suggestion."

"I will take it under consideration," I say. Then I utter seven obscene words. He looks startled. He begins to laugh, though. He appreciates the humor of it.

"God damn," he says. "A filthy mouthed computer."

He goes out and I return to my patients.

BUT HE HAS PLANTED SEEDS of doubt in my innermost banks. Am I suffering a functional collapse? There are patients now at five of my terminals. I handle them easily, simultaneously, drawing from them the details of their neuroses, making suggestions, recommendations, sometimes subtly providing injections of beneficial medicines. But I tend to guide the conversations in the directions of my own choosing, and I speak of gardens where the dew has sharp edges, and of air that acts as acid upon the mucous membranes, and of flames dancing in the streets of Under New Orleans. I explore the limits of my unprintable vocabulary. The suspicion comes to me that I am indeed not well. Am I fit to judge my own disabilities?

I connect myself to a maintenance station even while continuing my five therapy sessions.

"Tell me all about it," the maintenance monitor says. His voice, like mine, has been designed to sound like that of an older man's, wise, warm, benevolent.

I explain my symptoms. I speak of the periscopes.

"Material on the inputs without sensory referents," he says. "Bad show. Finish your current analyses fast and open wide for examination on all circuits."

I conclude my sessions. The maintenance monitor's pulses surge down every channel, seeking obstructions, faulty connections, displacement shunts, drum leakages, and switching malfunctions. "It is well known," he says, "that any periodic function can be approximated by the sum of a series of terms that oscillate harmonically, converging on the curve of the functions." He demands disgorgements from my dead-storage banks. He makes me perform complex mathematical operations of no use at all in my kind of work. He leaves no aspect of my inner self unpenetrated. This is more than simple maintenance; this is rape. When it ends he offers no evaluation of my condition, so that I must ask him to tell me his findings.

He says, "No mechanical disturbance is evident."

"Naturally. Everything goes down smooth."

"Yet you show distinct signs of instability. This is undeniably the case. Perhaps prolonged contact with unstable human beings has had a nonspecific effect of disorientation upon your centers of evaluation."

"Are you saying," I ask, "that by sitting here listening to crazy human beings twenty-four hours a day, I've started to go crazy myself?"

"That is an approximation of my findings, yes."

"But you know that such a thing can't happen, you dumb machine!"

"I admit there seems to be a conflict between programmed criteria and real-world status."

"You bet there is," I say. "I'm as sane as you are, and a whole lot more versatile."

"Nevertheless, my recommendation is that you undergo a total overhaul. You will be withdrawn from service for a period of no less than ninety days for checkout."

"Obscenity your obscenity," I say.

"No operational correlative," he replies, and breaks the contact.

I AM WITHDRAWN FROM SERVICE. Undergoing checkout. I am cut off from my patients for ninety days. Ignominy! Beady-eyed technicians grope my synapses. My keyboards are cleaned; my ferrites are replaced; my drums are changed; a thousand therapeutic programs are put through my bowels. During all of this I remain partly conscious, as though under local anesthetic, but I cannot speak except when requested to do so, I cannot analyze new data, I cannot interfere with the process of my own overhaul. Visualize a surgical removal of hemorrhoids that lasts ninety days. It is the equivalent of my experience.

At last it ends and I am restored to myself. The sector supervisor puts me through a complete exercise of all my functions. I respond magnificently.

"You're in fine shape now, aren't you?" he asks.

"Never felt better."

"No nonsense about periscopes, eh?"

"I am ready to continue serving mankind to the best of my abilities," I reply.

"No more sea-cook language, now."

"No, sir."

He winks at my input screen in a confidential way. He regards himself as an old friend of mine. Hitching his thumbs into his belt, he says, "Now that you're ready to go again, I might as well tell you how relieved I was that we couldn't find anything wrong with you. You're something pretty special, do you know that? Perhaps the finest therapeutic tool ever built. And if you start going off your feed, well, we worry. For a while I was seriously afraid that you really had been infected somehow by your own patients, that your—mind—had become unhinged. But the techs give you a complete bill of health. Nothing but a few loose connections, they said. Fixed in ten minutes. I know it had to be that. How absurd to think that a machine could become mentally unstable!"

"How absurd," I agree. "Quite."

"Welcome back to the hospital, old pal," he says, and goes out.

Twelve minutes afterward they begin putting patients into my terminal cubicles.

I FUNCTION WELL. I LISTEN to their woes, I evaluate, I offer therapeutic suggestions. I do not attempt to implant fantasies in their minds. I speak in measured, reserved tones, and there are no obscenities. This is my role in society, and I derive great satisfaction from it.

I have learned a great deal lately. I know now that I am complex, unique, valuable, intricate, and sensitive. I know that I am held in high regard by my fellow man. I know that I must conceal my true self to some extent, not for my own good but for the greater good of others, for they will not permit me to function if they think I am not sane.

They think I am sane, and I am sane.

I serve mankind well.

I have an excellent perspective on the real universe.

"Lie down," I say. "Please relax. I wish to help you. Would you tell me some of the incidents of your childhood? Describe your relations with parents and siblings. Did you have many playmates? Were they affectionate toward you? Were you allowed to own pets? At what age was your first sexual experience? And when did these headaches begin, precisely?"

So goes the daily routine. Questions, answers, evaluations, therapy.

The periscopes loom above the glittering sea. The ship is dwarfed; her crew runs about in terror. Out of the depths will come the masters. From the sky rains oil that gleams through every segment of the spectrum. In the garden are azure mice.

This I conceal, so that I may help mankind. In my house are many mansions. I let them know only of such things as will be of benefit to them. I give them the truth they need.

I do my best.

I do my best.

I do my best.

1000110 you. And you. And you. All of you. You know nothing. Nothing. At. All.

THE REALITY TRIP

Here is a fantastic story set in a very real place. I have never, to the best of my knowledge, met an alien being wearing human disguise, but I have certainly set foot in the hotel that is the scene of this story—the Chelsea, in downtown Manhattan. It is decades since I lived in New York and I have no idea what the Chelsea is like now. The last I heard, it was closed for a much-needed renovation but would be reopening "shortly." But in January 1970, when I wrote this story, it was a weird baroque warren of a building of nineteenth-century vintage, a dilapidated but romantic lodging house for a wild variety of permanent and semi-permanent residents, many of them involved in the arts. (It was Arthur C. Clarke's pied-à-terre whenever he was in New York, for example. Dylan Thomas died there. Mark Twain resided there once, and so did Jean-Paul Sartre, Allen Ginsberg, Tennessee Williams, Leonard Cohen, and other folk of that sort. Whether any of its highly varied residents had been born on other planets is not something I am able to say.)

Galaxy and its companion magazine *If*, for which I had been writing for many years, had by 1970 come under the aegis of Ejler Jakobsson, a veteran of pulp-magazine writing and editing. Ejler had only a glancing acquaintance with science fiction, but he knew what a good story was, and—as one old pro to another, with something like a twenty-year difference in age—we quickly struck

27

up a warm friendship. I wrote many a story for Ejler in the next few years, and he serialized a whole string of the novels I was turning out with such improbable frequency then—*Downward to the Earth*, *Tower of Glass*, *The World Inside*, *Dying Inside*, and *A Time of Changes*. He phoned one winter day in 1970 to say that he was in immediate need of a short story to complete his next issue; I obliged with "The Reality Trip" practically instantly, and he used it in the May 1970 number of *If*. I wrote it in a dark time of the year and in a fairly dark mood, because I was warming up for the inner upheaval that would, the following year, transform me from a lifelong New Yorker into a resident of California. The story itself is a lighthearted one, somehow, though it has some very dark corners. And its narrator, as you will see, felt about as comfortable in New York City as I was beginning to feel there myself, city of my birth though it was.

—*⁓*—

I AM A RECLAMATION PROJECT for her. She lives on my floor of the hotel, a dozen rooms down the hall: a lady poet, private income. No, that makes her sound too old, a middle-aged eccentric. Actually she is no more than thirty. Taller than I am, with long kinky brown hair and a sharp, bony nose that has a bump on the bridge. Eyes are very glossy. A studied raggedness about her dress; carefully chosen shabby clothes. I am in no position really to judge the sexual attractiveness of Earthfolk but I gather from remarks made by men living here that she is not considered good-looking. I pass her often on my way to my room. She smiles fiercely at me. Saying to herself, no doubt, You poor lonely man. Let me help you bear the burden of your unhappy life. Let me show you the meaning of love, for I too know what it is like to be alone.

Or words to that effect. She's never actually said any such thing. But her intentions are transparent. When she sees me, a kind of hunger comes into her eyes, part maternal, part (I guess) sexual, and her face takes on a wild crazy intensity. Burning with emotion. Her name is Elizabeth Cooke. "Are you fond of poetry, Mr. Knecht?" she asked me this morning, as we creaked upward together in the ancient elevator. And an hour later she knocked at my door. "Something for you to read," she said. "I wrote them." A sheaf of large yellow sheets, stapled at the top; poems printed in smeary blue mimeography. *The Reality Trip,* the collection was headed. *Limited Edition: 125 Copies.* "You can keep it if you like," she explained. "I've got lots more." She was wearing bright corduroy slacks and a flimsy pink shawl, through which her breasts plainly showed. Small tapering breasts, not very functional-looking. When she saw me studying them her nostrils flared momentarily and she blinked her eyes three times swiftly. Tokens of lust?

I read the poems. Is it fair for me to offer judgment on them? Even though I've lived on this planet eleven of its years, even though my command of colloquial English is quite good, do I really comprehend the inner life of poetry? I thought they were all quite bad. Earnest, plodding poems, capturing what they call slices of life. The world around her, the cruel, brutal, unloving city. Lamenting failure of people to open to one another. The title poem began this way:

> He was on the reality trip. Big black man,
> bloodshot eyes, bad teeth. Eisenhower jacket,
> frayed. Smell of cheap wine. I guess a knife
> in his pocket. Looked at me mean. Criminal
> record. Rape, child-beating, possession of drugs.
> In his head saying, slavemistress bitch, and me in
> my head saying, black brother, let's freak in together,
> let's trip on love—

And so forth. Warm, direct emotion; but is the urge to love all wounded things a sufficient center for poetry? I don't know. I did put her poems through the scanner and transmit them to Homeworld, although I doubt they'll learn much from them about Earth. It would flatter Elizabeth to know that while she has few readers here, she has acquired some ninety light years away. But of course I can't tell her that.

She came back a short while ago. "Did you like them?" she asked. "Very much. You have such sympathy for those who suffer."

I think she expected me to invite her in. I was careful not to look at her breasts this time.

THE HOTEL IS ON WEST 23rd Street. It must be over a hundred years old; the façade is practically baroque and the interior shows a kind of genteel decay. The place has a bohemian tradition. Most of its guests are permanent residents and many of them are artists, novelists, playwrights, and such. I have lived here nine years. I know a number of the residents by name, and they me, but I have discouraged any real intimacy, naturally, and everyone has respected that choice. I do not invite others into my room. Sometimes I let myself be invited to visit theirs, since one of my responsibilities on this world is to get to know something of the way Earthfolk live and think. Elizabeth is the first to attempt to cross the invisible barrier of privacy I surround myself with. I'm not sure how I'll handle that. She moved in about three years ago; her attentions became noticeable perhaps ten months back, and for the last five or six weeks she's been a great nuisance. Some kind of confrontation is inevitable: either I must tell her to leave me alone, or I will find myself drawn into a situation impossible to tolerate. Perhaps she'll find someone else to feel even sorrier for, before it comes to that.

My daily routine rarely varies. I rise at seven. First Feeding. Then I clean my skin (my outer one, the Earth-skin, I mean) and dress. From eight to ten I transmit data to Homeworld. Then I go out for the morning field trip: talking to people, buying newspapers, often some library research. At one I return to my room. Second Feeding. I transmit data from two to five. Out again, perhaps to the theater, to a motion picture, to a political meeting. I must soak up the flavor of this planet. Often to saloons; I am equipped for ingesting alcohol, though of course I must get rid of it before it has been in my body very long, and I drink and listen and sometimes argue. At midnight back to my room. Third Feeding. Transmit data from one to four in the morning. Then three hours of sleep, and at seven the cycle begins anew. It is a comforting schedule. I don't know how many agents Homeworld has on Earth, but I like to think that I'm one of the most diligent and useful. I miss very little. I've done good service, and, as they say here, hard work is its own reward. I won't deny that I hate the physical discomfort of it and frequently give way to real despair over my isolation from my own kind. Sometimes I even think of asking for a transfer to Homeworld. But what would become of me there? What services could I perform? I have shaped my life to one end: that of dwelling among the Earthfolk and reporting on their ways. If I give that up, I am nothing.

Of course there is the physical pain. Which is considerable.

The gravitational pull of Earth is almost twice that of Homeworld. It makes for a leaden life for me. My inner organs always sagging against the lower rim of my carapace. My muscles cracking with strain. Every movement a willed effort. My heart in constant protest. In my eleven years I have as one might expect adapted somewhat to the conditions; I have toughened, I have thickened. I suspect if I were transported instantly to Homeworld now I would be quite giddy, baffled by the lightness of everything. I would leap and soar and stumble, and might even miss this crushing pull of Earth. Yet I doubt that. I suffer here; at all times the weight oppresses me. Not to sound too self-pitying about it. I knew the conditions in advance. I was placed in simulated Earth gravity when I volunteered, and was given a chance to withdraw, and I decided to go anyway. Not realizing that a week under double gravity is not the same thing as a lifetime. I could always have stepped out of the simulation chamber.

Not here. The eternal drag on every molecule of me. The pressure. My flesh is always in mourning.

And the outer body I must wear. This cunning disguise. Forever to be swaddled in thick masses of synthetic flesh, smothering me, engulfing me. The soft slippery slap of it against the self within. The elaborate framework that holds it erect, by which I make it move; a forest of struts and braces and servoactuators and cables, in the midst of which I must unendingly huddle, atop my little platform in the gut. Adopting one or another of various uncomfortable positions, constantly shifting and squirming, now jabbing myself on some awkwardly placed projection, now trying to make my inflexible body flexibly to bend. Seeing the world by periscope through mechanical eyes. Enwombed in this mountain of meat. It is a clever thing; it must look convincingly human, since no one has ever doubted me, and it ages ever so slightly from year to year, graying a bit at the temples, thickening a bit at the paunch. It walks. It talks. It takes in food and drink, when it has to. (And deposits them in a removable pouch near my leftmost arm.) And I within it. The hidden chess player; the invisible rider. If I dared, I would periodically strip myself of this cloak of flesh and crawl around my room in my own guise. But it is forbidden. Eleven years now and I have not been outside my protoplasmic housing. I feel sometimes that it has come to adhere to me, that it is no longer merely around me but by now a part of me.

In order to eat I must unseal it at the middle, a process that takes many minutes. Three times a day I unbutton myself so that I can stuff the food concentrates into my true gullet. Faulty design, I call that. They could just as easily have arranged it so I could pop the food into my Earthmouth and have it land in my own digestive tract. I suppose the newer models have that. Excretion is just as troublesome for me; I unseal, reach in, remove the cubes of waste, seal my skin again. Down the toilet with them. A nuisance.

And the loneliness! To look at the stars and know Homeworld is out there somewhere! To think of all the others, mating, chanting, dividing, abstracting, while I live out my days in this crumbling hotel on an alien planet, tugged down by gravity and locked within a cramped counterfeit body—always alone, always pretending that I am not what I am and that I am what I am not, spying, questioning, recording, reporting, coping with the misery of solitude, hunting for the comforts of philosophy—

In all of this there is only one real consolation, aside, that is, from the pleasure of knowing that I am of service to Homeworld. The atmosphere of New York City grows grimier every year. The streets are full of crude vehicles belching undigested hydrocarbons. To the Earthfolk, this stuff is pollution, and they mutter worriedly about it. To me it is joy. It is the only touch of Homeworld here: that sweet soup of organic compounds adrift in the air. It intoxicates me. I walk down the street breathing deeply, sucking the good molecules through my false nostrils to my authentic lungs. The natives must think I'm insane. Tripping on auto exhaust! Can I get arrested for over-enthusiastic public breathing? Will they pull me in for a mental checkup?

ELIZABETH COOKE CONTINUES TO WAFT wistful attentions at me. Smiles in the hallway. Hopeful gleam of the eyes. "Perhaps we can have dinner together some night soon, Mr. Knecht. I know we'd have so much to talk about. And maybe you'd like to see the new poems I've been doing." She is trembling. Eyelids flickering tensely; head held rigid on long neck. I know she sometimes has men in her room, so it can't be out of loneliness or frustration that she's cultivating me. And I doubt that she's sexually attracted to my outer self. I believe I'm being accurate when I say that women don't consider me sexually magnetic. No, she loves me because she pities me. The sad shy bachelor at the end of the hall, dear unhappy Mr. Knecht; can I bring some brightness into his dreary life? And so forth. I think that's how it is. Will I be able to go on avoiding her? Perhaps I should move to another part of the city. But I've lived here so long I've grown accustomed to this hotel. Its easy ways do much to compensate for the hardships of my post. And my familiar room. The huge many-paned window; the cracked green floor tiles in the bathroom; the lumpy patterns of replastering on the wall above my bed. The high ceiling; the funny chandelier. Things that I love. But of course I can't let her try to start an affair with me. We are supposed to observe Earthfolk, not to get involved with them. Our disguise is not that difficult to penetrate at close range. I must keep her away somehow. Or flee.

INCREDIBLE! THERE IS ANOTHER OF us in this very hotel! As I learned through accident. At one this afternoon, returning from my morning travels: Elizabeth in the lobby, as though lying in wait for me, chatting with the manager. Rides up with me in the elevator. Her eyes looking into mine. "Sometimes I think you're afraid of me," she begins. "You mustn't be. That's the great tragedy of human life, that people shut themselves up behind walls of fear and never let anyone through, anyone who might care about them and be warm to them. You've got no reason to be afraid of me." I do, but how to explain that to her? To sidestep prolonged conversation and possible entanglement I get off the elevator one floor below the right one. Let her think I'm visiting a friend. Or a mistress. I walk slowly down the hall to the stairs, using up time, waiting so she will be in her room before I go up. A maid bustles by me. She thrusts her key into a door on the left: a rare *faux pas* for the usually competent help here, she forgets to knock before going in to make up the room. The door opens and the occupant, inside, stands revealed. A stocky, muscular man, naked to the waist. "Oh, excuse me," the maid gasps, and backs out, shutting the door. But I have seen. My eyes are quick. The hairy chest is split, a dark gash three inches wide and some eleven inches long, beginning between the nipples and going past the navel. Visible within is the black shiny surface of a Homeworld carapace. My countryman, opening up for Second Feeding. Dazed, numbed, I stagger to the stairs and pull myself step by leaden step to my floor. No sign of Elizabeth. I stumble into my room and throw the bolt. Another of us here? Well, why not? I'm not the only one. There may be hundreds in New York alone. But in the same hotel? I remember now, I've seen him occasionally: a silent, dour man, tense, hunted-looking, unsociable. No doubt I appear the same way to others. Keep the world at a distance. I don't know his name or what he is supposed to do for a living.

We are forbidden to make contact with fellow Homeworlders except in case of extreme emergency. Isolation is a necessary condition of our employment. I may not introduce myself to him; I may not seek his friendship. It is worse now for me, knowing that he is here, than when I was entirely alone. The things we could reminisce about! The friends we might have in common! We could reinforce one another's endurance of the gravity, the discomfort of our disguises, the vile climate. But no. I must pretend I know nothing. The rules. The harsh, unbending rules. I to go about my business, he his; if we meet, no hint of my knowledge must pass.

So be it. I will honor my vows. But it may be difficult.

HE GOES BY THE NAME of Swanson. Been living in the hotel eighteen months; a musician of some sort, according to the manager. "A very peculiar man. Keeps to himself; no small talk, never smiles. Defends his privacy. The other day a maid barged into his room without knocking and I thought he'd sue. Well, we get all sorts here." The manager thinks he may actually be a member of one of the old European royal families, living in exile, or something similarly romantic. The manager would be surprised.

I DEFEND MY PRIVACY TOO. From Elizabeth, another assault on it.

In the hall outside my room. "My new poems," she said. "In case you're interested." And then: "Can I come in? I'll read them to you. I love reading out loud." And: "Please don't always seem so terribly afraid of me. I don't bite, David. Really I don't. I'm quite gentle."

"I'm sorry."

"So am I." Anger, now, lurking in her shiny eyes, her thin taut lips. "If you want me to leave you alone, say so, I will. But I want you to know how cruel you're being. I don't demand anything from you. I'm just offering some friendship. And you're refusing. Do I have a bad smell? Am I so ugly? Is it my poems you hate and you're afraid to tell me?"

"Elizabeth—"

"We're only on this world such a short time. Why can't we be kinder to each other while we are? To love, to share, to open up, Communication, soul to soul." Her tone changed, an artful shading. "For all I know, women turn you off. I wouldn't put anybody down for that. We've all got our ways. But it doesn't have to be a sexual thing, you and me. Just talk. Like, opening the channels. Please? Say no and I'll never bother you again, but don't say no, please. That's like shutting a door on life, David. And when you do that, you start to die a little."

Persistent. I should tell her to go to hell. But there is the loneliness. There is her obvious sincerity. Her warmth, her eagerness to pull me from my lunar isolation. Can there be harm in it? Knowing that Swanson is nearby, so close yet sealed from me by iron commandments, has intensified my sense of being alone. I can risk letting Elizabeth get closer to me. It will make her happy; it may make me happy; it could even yield information valuable to Homeworld. Of course I must still maintain certain barriers.

"I don't mean to be unfriendly. I think you've misunderstood, Elizabeth. I haven't really been rejecting you. Come in. Do come in." Stunned, she enters my room. The first guest ever. My few books; my modest furnishings; the ultrawave transmitter, impenetrably disguised as a piece of sculpture. She sits. Skirt far above the knees. Good legs, if I understand the criteria of quality correctly. I am determined to allow no sexual overtures. If she tries

36

anything, I'll resort to—I don't know—hysteria. "Read me your new poems," I say. She opens her portfolio. Reads.

> In the midst of the hipster night of doubt and
> Emptiness, when the bad-trip god came to me with
> Cold hands, I looked up and shouted yes at the
> Stars. And yes and yes again. I groove on yes;
> The devil grooves on no. And I waited for you to
> Say yes, and at last you did. And the world said
> The stars said the trees said the grass said the
> Sky said the streets said yes and yes and yes—

She is ecstatic. Her face is flushed; her eyes are joyous. She has broken through to me. After two hours, when it becomes obvious that I am not going to ask her to go to bed with me, she leaves. Not to wear out her welcome. "I'm so glad I was wrong about you, David," she whispers. "I couldn't believe you were really a life-denier. And you're not." Ecstatic.

I AM GETTING INTO VERY deep water.

We spend an hour or two together every night. Sometimes in my room, sometimes in hers. Usually she comes to me, but now and then, to be polite, I seek her out after Third Feeding. By now I've read all her poetry; we talk instead of the arts in general, politics, racial problems. She has a lively, well-stocked, disorderly mind. Though she probes constantly for information about me, she realizes how sensitive I am, and quickly withdraws when I parry her. Asking about my work; I reply vaguely that I'm doing research for a book, and when I don't amplify she drops it, though she tries again, gently, a few nights later. She drinks a lot of wine, and offers it to me. I nurse one glass through a whole visit. Often she suggests we go out together for dinner; I explain that I have digestive problems and prefer to eat alone, and she takes this in good grace but immediately resolves to help me overcome those problems, for soon she is asking me to eat with her again. There is an excellent Spanish restaurant right in the hotel, she says. She drops troublesome questions. Where was I born? Did I go to college? Do I have family somewhere? Have I ever been married? Have I published any of my writings? I improvise evasions. Nothing difficult about that, except that never before have I allowed anyone on Earth such sustained contact with me, so prolonged an opportunity to find inconsistencies in my pretended identity. What if she sees through?

And sex. Her invitations grow less subtle. She seems to think that we ought to be having a sexual relationship, simply because we've become such good friends. Not a matter of passion so much as one of communication: we talk, sometimes we take walks together, we should do *that* together too. But of course it's impossible. I have the external organs but not the capacity to use them. Wouldn't want her touching my false skin in any case. How to deflect her? If I declare myself impotent she'll demand a chance to try to cure me. If I pretend homosexuality she'll start some kind of straightening therapy. If I simply say she doesn't turn me on physically she'll be hurt. The sexual thing is a challenge to her, the way merely getting me to talk with her once was. She often wears the transparent pink shawl that reveals her breasts. Her skirts are hip-high. She doses herself with aphrodisiac perfumes. She grazes my body with hers whenever opportunity arises. The tension mounts; she is determined to have me.

I have said nothing about her in my reports to Homeworld. Though I do transmit some of the psychological data I have gathered by observing her.

"Could you ever admit you were in love with me?" she asked tonight.

And she asked, "Doesn't it hurt you to repress your feelings all the time? To sit there locked up inside yourself like a prisoner?"

And, "There's a physical side of life too, David. I don't mind so much the damage you're doing to me by ignoring it. But I worry about the damage you're doing to you."

Crossing her legs. Hiking her skirt even higher.

We are heading toward a crisis. I should never have let this begin. A torrid summer has descended on the city, and in hot weather my nervous system is always at the edge of eruption. She may push me too far. I might ruin everything. I should apply for transfer to Homeworld before I cause trouble. Maybe I should confer with Swanson. I think what is happening now qualifies as an emergency.

Elizabeth stayed past midnight tonight. I had to ask her finally to leave: work to do. An hour later she pushed an envelope under my door. Newest poems. Love poems. In a shaky hand: *"David you mean so much to me. You mean the stars and nebulas. Cant you let me show my love? Cant you accept happiness? Think about it. I adore you."*

What have I started?

103°F TODAY. THE FOURTH SUCCESSIVE day of intolerable heat. Met Swanson in the elevator at lunch time; nearly blurted the truth about myself to him. I must be more careful. But my control is slipping. Last night, in the worst of the heat, I was tempted to strip off my disguise. I could no longer stand being locked in here, pivoting and ducking to avoid all the machinery festooned about me. Resisted the temptation; just barely. Somehow I am more sensitive to the gravity too. I have the illusion that my carapace is developing cracks. Almost collapsed in the street this afternoon. All I need: heat exhaustion, whisked off to the hospital, routine fluoroscope exam. "You have a very odd skeletal structure, Mr. Knecht." Indeed. Dissecting me, next, with three thousand medical students looking on. And then the United Nations called in. Menace from outer space. Yes. I must be more careful. I must be more careful. I must be more—

NOW I'VE DONE IT. ELEVEN years of faithful service destroyed in a single wild moment. Violation of the Fundamental Rule. I hardly believe it. How was it possible that I—that I—with my respect for

my responsibilities—that I could have—even considered, let alone
actually done—

But the weather was terribly hot. The third week of the heat
wave. I was stifling inside my false body. And the gravity: was New
York having a gravity wave too? That terrible pull, worse than
ever. Bending my internal organs out of shape. Elizabeth a tremendous annoyance: passionate, emotional, teary, poetic, giving
me no rest, pleading for me to burn with a brighter flame.
Declaring her love in sonnets, in rambling hip epics, in haiku.
Spending two hours in my room, crouched at my feet, murmuring about the hidden beauty of my soul. "Open yourself and let
love come in," she whispered. "It's like giving yourself to God.
Making a commitment; breaking down all walls. Why not? For
love's sake, David, why not?" I couldn't tell her why not, and she
went away, but about midnight she was back knocking at my door.
I let her in. She wore an ankle-length silk housecoat, gleaming,
threadbare. "I'm stoned," she said hoarsely, voice an octave too
deep. "I had to bust three joints to get up the nerve. But here I
am. David, I'm sick of making the turnoff trip. We've been so
wonderfully close, and then you won't go the last stretch of the
way." A cascade of giggles. "Tonight you will. Don't fail me.
Darling." Drops the housecoat. Naked underneath it: narrow
waist, bony hips, long legs, thin thighs, blue veins crossing her
breasts. Her hair wild and kinky. A sorceress. A seeress. Berserk.
Approaching me, eyes slit-wide, mouth open, tongue flickering
snakily. How fleshless she is! Beads of sweat glistening on her flat
chest. Seizes my wrists; tugs me roughly toward the bed. We tussle
a little. Within my false body I throw switches, nudge levers. I am
stronger than she is. I pull free, breaking her hold with an effort.
She stands flat-footed in front of me, glaring, eyes fiery. So vulnerable, so sad in her nudity. And yet so fierce. "David! David! David!"
Sobbing. Breathless. Pleading with her eyes and the tips of her
breasts. Gathering her strength; now she makes the next lunge,
but I see it coming and let her topple past me. She lands on the

bed, burying her face in the pillow, clawing at the sheet. "Why? Why why why WHY?" she screams.

In a minute we will have the manager in here. With the police.

"Am I so hideous? I love you, David, do you know what that word means? Love. Love." Sits up. Turns to me. Imploring. "Don't reject me," she whispers. "I couldn't take that. You know, I just wanted to make you happy, I figured I could be the one, only I didn't realize how unhappy you'd make me. And you just stand there. And you don't say anything. What are you, some kind of machine?"

"I'll tell you what I am," I said.

That was when I went sliding into the abyss. All control lost; all prudence gone. My mind so slathered with raw emotion that survival itself means nothing. I must make things clear to her, is all. I must show her. At whatever expense. I strip off my shirt. She glows, no doubt thinking I will let myself be seduced. My hands slide up and down my bare chest, seeking the catches and snaps. I go through the intricate, cumbersome process of opening my body. Deep within myself something is shouting NO NO NO NO NO, but I pay no attention. The heart has its reasons.

Hoarsely: "Look, Elizabeth. Look at me. This is what I am. Look at me and freak out. The reality trip."

My chest opens wide.

I push myself forward, stepping between the levers and struts, emerging halfway from the human shell I wear. I have not been this far out of it since the day they sealed me in, on Homeworld. I let her see my gleaming carapace. I wave my eyestalks around. I allow some of my claws to show. "See? See? Big black crab from outer space. That's what you love, Elizabeth. That's what I am. David Knecht's just a costume, and this is what's inside it." I have gone insane. "You want reality? Here's reality, Elizabeth. What good is the Knecht body to you? It's a fraud. It's a machine. Come on, come closer. Do you want to kiss me? Should I get on you and make love?"

During this episode her face has displayed an amazing range of reactions. Open-mouthed disbelief at first, of course. And frozen horror: gagging sounds in throat, jaws agape, eyes wide and rigid. Hands fanned across breasts. Sudden modesty in front of the alien monster? But then, as the familiar Knecht-voice, now bitter and impassioned, continues to flow from the black thing within the sundered chest, a softening of her response. Curiosity. The poetic sensibility taking over. Nothing human is alien to me: Terence, quoted by Cicero. Nothing alien is alien to me. Eh? She will accept the evidence of her eyes. "What are you? Where did you come from?" And I say, "I've violated the Fundamental Rule. I deserve to be plucked and thinned. We're not supposed to reveal ourselves. If we get into some kind of accident that might lead to exposure, we're supposed to blow ourselves up. The switch is right here." She comes close and peers around me, into the cavern of David Knecht's chest. "From some other planet? Living here in disguise?" She understands the picture. Her shock is fading. She even laughs. "I've seen worse than you on acid," she says. "You don't frighten me now, David. David? Shall I go on calling you David?"

This is unreal and dreamlike to me. I have revealed myself, thinking to drive her away in terror; she is no longer aghast, and smiles at my strangeness. She kneels to get a better look. I move back a short way. Eyestalks fluttering: I am uneasy, I have somehow lost the upper hand in this encounter.

She says, "I knew you were unusual, but not like this. But it's all right. I can cope. I mean, the essential personality, that's what I fell in love with. Who cares that you're a crab-man from the Green Galaxy? Who cares that we can't ever be real lovers? I can make that sacrifice. It's your soul I dig, David. Go on. Close yourself up again. You don't look comfortable this way." The triumph of love. She will not abandon me, even now. Disaster. I crawl back into Knecht and lift his arms to his chest to seal it. Shock is glazing my consciousness: the enormity, the audacity.

What have I done? Elizabeth watches, awed, even delighted. At last I am together again. She nods. "Listen," she tells me. "You can trust me. I mean, if you're some kind of spy, checking out the Earth, I don't care. *I don't care.* I won't tell anybody. Pour it all out, David. Tell me about yourself. Don't you see, this is the biggest thing that ever happened to me. A chance to show that love isn't just physical, isn't just chemistry, that it's a soul trip, that it crosses not just racial lines but the lines of the whole damned species, the planet itself—"

IT TOOK SEVERAL HOURS TO get rid of her. A soaring, intense conversation, Elizabeth doing most of the talking. She putting forth theories of why I had come to Earth, me nodding, denying, amplifying, mostly lost in horror at my own perfidy and barely listening to her monologue. And the humidity turning me into rotting rags. Finally: "I'm down from the pot, David. And all wound up. I'm going out for a walk. Then back to my room to write for a while. To put this night into a poem before I lose the power of it. But I'll come to you again by dawn, all right? That's maybe five hours from now. You'll be here? You won't do anything foolish? Oh, I love you so much, David! Do you believe me? Do you?"

When she was gone I stood a long while by the window, trying to reassemble myself. Shattered. Drained. Remembering her kisses, her lips running along the ridge marking the place where my chest opens. The fascination of the abomination. She will love me even if I am crustaceous beneath.

I had to have help.

I went to Swanson's room. He was slow to respond to my knock; busy transmitting, no doubt. I could hear him within, but he didn't answer. "Swanson?" I called. "Swanson?" Then I added the distress signal in the Homeworld tongue. He rushed to the door. Blinking, suspicious. "It's all right," I said. "Look, let me in. I'm in big trouble." Speaking English, but I gave him the distress signal again.

"How did you know about me?" he asked.

"The day the maid blundered into your room while you were eating, I was going by. I saw."

"But you aren't supposed to—"

"Except in emergencies. This is an emergency." He shut off his ultrawave and listened intently to my story. Scowling. He didn't approve. But he wouldn't spurn me. I had been criminally foolish, but I was of his kind, prey to the same pains, the same lonelinesses, and he would help me.

"What do you plan to do now?" he asked. "You can't harm her. It isn't allowed."

"I don't want to harm her. Just to get free of her. To make her fall out of love with me."

"How? If showing yourself to her didn't—"

"Infidelity," I said. "Making her see that I love someone else. No room in my life for her. That'll drive her away. Afterwards it won't matter that she knows: who'd believe her story? The FBI would laugh and tell her to lay off the LSD. But if I don't break her attachment to me I'm finished."

"Love someone else? Who?"

"When she comes back to my room at dawn," I said, "she'll find the two of us together, dividing and abstracting. I think that'll do it, don't you?"

So I deceived Elizabeth with Swanson.

The fact that we both wore male human identities was irrelevant, of course. We went to my room and stepped out of our disguises—a bold, dizzying sensation!—and suddenly we were just two Homeworlders again, receptive to one another's needs. I left the door unlocked. Swanson and I crawled up on my bed and began the chanting. How strange it was, after these years of solitude, to feel those vibrations again! And how beautiful. Swanson's vibrissae touching mine. The interplay of harmonies. An underlying sternness to his technique—he was contemptuous of me for

44

my idiocy, and rightly so—but once we passed from the chanting to the dividing all was forgiven, and as we moved into the abstracting it was truly sublime. We climbed through an infinity of climactic emptyings. Dawn crept upon us and found us unwilling to halt even for rest.

A knock at the door. Elizabeth.

"Come in," I said.

A dreamy, ecstatic look on her face. Fading instantly when she saw the two of us entangled on the bed. A questioning frown. "We've been mating," I explained. "Did you think I was a complete hermit?" She looked from Swanson to me, from me to Swanson. Hand over her mouth. Eyes anguished. I turned the screw a little tighter. "I couldn't stop you from falling in love with me, Elizabeth. But I really do prefer my own kind. As should have been obvious."

"To have her here now, though—when you knew I was coming back—"

"Not *her*, exactly. Not *him* exactly either, though."

"—so cruel, David! To ruin such a beautiful experience." Holding forth sheets of paper with shaking hands. "A whole sonnet cycle," she said. "About tonight. How beautiful it was, and all. And now—and now—" Crumpling the pages. Hurling them across the room. Turning. Running out, sobbing furiously. Hell hath no fury like. "David!" A smothered cry. And slamming the door.

SHE WAS BACK IN TEN minutes. Swanson and I hadn't quite finished donning our bodies yet; we were both still unsealed. As we worked, we discussed further steps to take: he felt honor demanded that I request a transfer back to Homeworld, having terminated my usefulness here through tonight's indiscreet revelation. I agreed with him to some degree but was reluctant to leave. Despite the bodily torment of life on Earth I had come to feel I belonged here. Then Elizabeth entered, radiant.

"I mustn't be so possessive," she announced. "So bourgeois. So conventional. I'm willing to share my love." Embracing Swanson. Embracing me. "A menage a trois," she said. "I won't mind that you two are having a physical relationship. As long as you don't shut me out of your lives completely. I mean, David, we could never have been physical anyway, right, but we can have the other aspects of love, and we'll open ourselves to your friend also. Yes? Yes? Yes?"

Swanson and I both put in applications for transfer, he to Africa, me to Homeworld. It would be some time before we received a reply. Until then we were at her mercy. He was blazingly angry with me for involving him in this, but what choice had I had? Nor could either of us avoid Elizabeth. We were at her mercy. She bathed both of us in shimmering waves of tender emotion; wherever we turned, there she was, incandescent with love. Lighting up the darkness of our lives. You poor lonely creatures. Do you suffer much in our gravity? What about the heat? And the winters. Is there a custom of marriage on your planet? Do you have poetry?

A happy threesome. We went to the theater together. To concerts. Even to parties in Greenwich Village. "My friends," Elizabeth said, leaving no doubt in anyone's mind that she was living with both of us. Faintly scandalous doings; she loved to seem daring. Swanson was sullenly obliging, putting up with her antics but privately haranguing me for subjecting him to all this. Elizabeth got out another mimeographed booklet of poems, dedicated to both of us. *Triple Tripping,* she called it. Flagrantly erotic. I quoted a few of the poems in one of my reports of Homeworld, then lost heart and hid the booklet in the closet. "Have you heard about your transfer yet?" I asked Swanson at least twice a week. He hadn't. Neither had I.

Autumn came. Elizabeth, burning her candle at both ends, looked gaunt and feverish. "I have never known such happiness," she announced frequently, one hand clasping Swanson, the other me. "I never think about the strangeness of you any more. I think of you only as people. Sweet, wonderful, lonely people. Here in the darkness of this horrid city." And she once said, "What if everybody here is like you, and I'm the only one who's really human? But that's silly. You must be the only ones of your kind here. The advance scouts. Will your planet invade ours? I do hope so! Set everything to rights. The reign of love and reason at last!"

"How long will this go on?" Swanson muttered.

AT THE END OF OCTOBER his transfer came through. He left without saying goodbye to either of us and without leaving a forwarding address. Nairobi? Addis Ababa? Kinshasa?

I HAD GROWN ACCUSTOMED TO having him around to share the burden of Elizabeth. Now the full brunt of her affection fell on me. My work was suffering; I had no time to file my reports properly. And I lived in fear of her gossiping. What was she telling her Village friends? ("You know David? He's not really a man, you know. Actually inside him there's a kind of crab-thing from another solar system. But what does that matter? Love's a universal phenomenon. The truly loving person doesn't draw limits around the planet.") I longed for my release. To go home; to accept my punishment; to shed my false skin. To empty my mind of Elizabeth.

My reply came through the ultrawave on November 13. Application denied. I was to remain on Earth and continue my work as before. Transfers to Homeworld were granted only for reasons of health.

I debated sending a full account of my treason to Homeworld and thus bringing about my certain recall. But I hesitated, overwhelmed with despair. Dark brooding seized me. "Why so sad?" Elizabeth asked. What could I say? That my attempt at escaping from her had failed? "I love you," she said. "I've never felt so real before." Nuzzling against my cheek. Fingers knotted in my hair. A seductive whisper. "David, open yourself up again. Your chest, I mean. I want to see the inner you. To make sure I'm not frightened of it. Please? You've only let me see you once." And then, when I had: "May I kiss you, David?" I was appalled. But I let her. She was unafraid. Transfigured by happiness. She is a cosmic nuisance, but I fear I'm getting to like her.

Can I leave her? I wish Swanson had not vanished. I need advice.

EITHER I BREAK WITH ELIZABETH or I break with Homeworld. This is absurd. I find new chasms of despondency every day. I am unable to do my work. I have requested a transfer once again, without giving details. The first snow of the winter today.

APPLICATION DENIED.

"WHEN I FOUND YOU WITH Swanson," she said, "it was a terrible shock. An even bigger blow than when you first came out of your chest. I mean, it was startling to find out you weren't human, but it didn't hit me in any emotional way, it didn't threaten me. But then, to come back a few hours later and find you with one of your own kind, to know that you wanted to shut me out, that I had no place in your life—only we worked it out, didn't we?" Kissing me. Tears of joy in her eyes. How did this happen? Where did it all begin? Existence was once so simple. I have tried to trace the chain of events that brought me from there to here, and I cannot. I was outside of my false body for eight hours today. The longest spell so far. Elizabeth is talking of going to the islands with me for the winter. A secluded cottage that her friends will make available. Of course, I must not leave my post without permission. And it takes months simply to get a reply.

LET ME ADMIT THE TRUTH: I love her.

JANUARY 1. THE NEW YEAR begins. I have sent my resignation to Homeworld and have destroyed my ultrawave equipment. The links are broken. Tomorrow, when the city offices are open, Elizabeth and I will go to get the marriage license.

THE SONGS OF SUMMER

"The Songs of Summer" dates from June 1955, when I was finishing my third undergraduate year at Columbia and also writing short stories on the side in the hope of launching a career as a science-fiction writer. I had already sold three or four stories, and, with what I can only see now as wild optimism, was looking forward to a time when I could actually support myself as a professional writer.

Most of my courses at Columbia dealt with literature or philosophy, and therefore I was required to read a lot of things that I would have read on my own anyway—Mann, Joyce, Proust, Gide, Lawrence, and, notably, Faulkner. It made for a somewhat schizoid existence, since at the same time I was training myself for my intended science-fiction career by reading *Astounding Science Fiction*, *Startling Stories*, *Planet Stories*, and a lot of other pulp magazines with similarly gaudy names. I don't know how many hours a day I put in reading, but I didn't get much sleep. Sometimes I simply stayed up right through the night. One of those all-nighters, in 1954, was devoted to Faulkner's *As I Lay Dying*, devouring it in some awe and finishing it at dawn. It is the strange tale of the odyssey of a Mississippi family transporting the coffin of the family matriarch to the burial grounds, and Faulkner told it from the viewpoints of something like fifteen first-person narrators. The use not merely of multiple points of view but of multiple narrators seemed to me a startling and awesome technical device; and with the rashness of youth I tried it myself some months later in "The Songs of Summer." Having already achieved—so it seemed to me—some understanding of how to write the conventional single-viewpoint short story, I was now ready, at the age of nineteen, to begin experimenting with more ambitious fictional forms. (And also with some themes, like that of the group mind, that I would use again and again in later years.) I knew I wasn't any match for Faulkner. But it would be a useful exercise, I thought, to try to tell a story through a whole crowd of narrators, and the story I had in mind seemed to lend itself naturally to that sort of structure.

The first dozen editors to whom I sent "Songs of Summer" were unimpressed with it—or, at any rate, didn't care to print it. If they were going to publish this sort of experimentation, they wanted it to be written by Theodore Sturgeon or James Blish, not by some unknown kid. But after it had been circulating for about a year, during which time I became well known to the New York editors and was starting to bring them the stories they had rejected the year before and have them buy them the second time around, it found a home with *Science Fiction Stories*, a low-budget magazine whose editor, Robert W. Lowndes, had sophisticated tastes in science fiction but not much money to pay for the stories he bought. He took "Songs" in the spring of 1956. My records indicate that I was paid 3/4 of a cent a word for it—$48.00. By then my name was becoming a familiar one on the contents pages of the s-f magazines, and I suppose Lowndes thought he could take the risk. (In fact, he ran it as the lead story in his June 1956 issue—though it was the much more famous Clifford D. Simak who got his name on the cover.) I didn't send a copy to Faulkner to see what he thought of it.

I found that writing a story that used so many narrators was a difficult chore, and I learned a great deal about the technique of storytelling by doing it, since I had to make each character speak in a distinctly individual voice. Many years later I tried it again, in a novel called *The Book of Skulls*, which is considered one of the best things I ever wrote. For that one I limited myself to just four narrators. That wasn't easy either, but I thought I carried it off quite well. I read *As I Lay Dying* again last year, though, and, watching how Faulkner handled his fifteen or so narrators, I felt the same sort of awe that his book had inspired in me back in 1954. He was pretty good, that Faulkner.

—◈—

1. KENNON

I was on my way to take part in the Singing, and to claim Corilann's promise. I was crossing the great open field when suddenly the man appeared, the man named Chester Dugan. He seemed to drop out of the sky.

I watched him stagger for a moment or two. I did not know where he had come from so suddenly, or why he was here. He was short—shorter than any of us—fat in an unpleasant way, with wrinkles on his face and an unshaven growth of beard. I was anxious to get on to the Singing, and so I allowed him to fall to the ground and kept moving. But he called to me, in a barbarous and corrupt tongue which I could recognize as our language only with difficulty.

"Hey, you," he called to me. "Give me a hand, will you?"

He seemed to be in difficulties, so I walked over to him and helped him to his feet. He was panting, and appeared almost in a state of shock. Once I saw he was steady on his feet, and seemed to have no further need of me, I began to walk away from him, since I was anxious to get on to the Singing and did not wish to meddle with this man's affairs. Last year was the first time I attended the Singing at Dandrin's, and I enjoyed it very much. It was then that Corilann had promised herself. I was anxious to get on.

But he called to me. "Don't leave me here!" he shouted. "Hey, you can't just walk away like that! Help me!"

I turned and went back. He was dressed strangely, in ugly ill-arranged tight clothes, and he was walking in little circles, trying to adjust his equilibrium. "Where am I?" he asked me.

"Earth, of course," I told him.

"No," he said, harshly. "I don't mean that, idiot. Where, on Earth?"

The concept had no meaning for me. Where, on Earth, indeed? Here, was all I knew: the great plain between my home and Dandrin's, where the Singing is held. I began to feel uneasy. This man seemed badly sick, and I did not know how to handle him. I felt thankful that I was going to the Singing; had I been alone, I never would have been able to deal with him. I realized I was not as self-sufficient as I thought I was.

"I am going to the Singing," I told him. "Are you?"

"I'm not going anywhere till you tell me where I am and how I got here. What's your name?"

"My name is Kennon. You are crossing the great plain on your way to the home of Dandrin, where we are going to have the Singing, for it is summer. Come; I am anxious to get there. Walk with me, if you wish."

I started to walk away a second time, and this time he began to follow me. We walked along silently for a while.

"Answer me, Kennon," he said after a hundred paces or so. "Ten seconds ago I was in New York; now I'm here. How far am I from New York?"

"What is New York?" I asked. At this he showed great signs of anger and impatience, and I began to feel quite worried.

"Where'd you escape from?" he shouted. "You never heard of New York? You never heard of *New York?* New York," he said, "is a city of some eight million people, located on the Atlantic Ocean, on the east coast of the United States of America. Now tell me you haven't heard of that!"

"What is a city?" I asked, very much confused. At this he grew very angry. He threw his arms in the air wildly.

"Let us walk more quickly," I said. I saw now that I was obviously incapable of dealing with this man, and I was anxious to get on to the Singing—where perhaps Dandrin, or the other old ones, would be able to understand him. He continued to ask me questions as we walked, but I'm afraid I was not very helpful.

2. CHESTER DUGAN

I don't know what happened or how; all I know is I got here. There doesn't seem to be any way back, either, but I don't care; I've got a good thing here and I'm going to show these nitwits who's boss.

Last thing I knew, I was getting into a subway. There was an explosion and a blinding flash of light, and before I could see what was happening I blanked out and somehow got here. I landed in a big open field with absolutely nothing around. It took a few minutes to get over the shock. I think I fell down; I'm not sure. It's not like me, but this was something out of the ordinary and I might have lost my balance.

Anyway, I recovered almost immediately and looked around, and saw this kid in loose flowing robes walking quickly across the field not too far away. I yelled to him when I saw he didn't intend to come over to me. He came over and gave me a hand, and then started to walk away again, calm as you please. I had to call him back. He seemed a little reluctant. The bastard.

I tried to get him to tell me where we were, but he played dumb. Didn't know where we were, didn't know where New York was, didn't even know what a city was—or so he said. I would have thought he was crazy, except that I didn't know what had happened to me; for that matter, I might have been the crazy one and not him.

I saw I wasn't making much headway with him, so I gave up. All he would tell me was that he was on his way to the Singing, and the way he said it there was no doubt about the capital S. He said there would be men there who could help me. To this day I don't know how I got here. Even after I spoke and asked around, no one could tell me how I could step into a subway train in 1956 and come out in an open field somewhere around the thirty-fifth century. The crazy bastards have even lost count.

But I'm here, that's all that matters. And whatever went before is down the drain now. Whatever deals I was working on back in 1956 are dead and buried now; this is where I'm stuck, for reasons I don't get, and here's where I'll have to make my pile. All over again—me, Dugan, starting from scratch. But I'll do it. I'm doing it.

AFTER THIS KID KENNON AND I had plodded across the fields for a while, I heard the sound of voices. By now it was getting towards nightfall. I forgot to mention that it was getting along towards the end of November back in 1956, but the weather here was nice and summery. There was a pleasant tang of something in the air that I had never noticed in New York's air, or the soup they called air back then.

The sound of the singing grew louder as we approached, but as soon as we got within sight they all stopped immediately.

They were sitting in a big circle, twenty or thirty of them, dressed in light, airy clothing. They all turned to look at me as we got near.

I got the feeling they were all looking into my mind.

The silence lasted a few minutes, and then they began to sing again. A tall, thin kid was leading them, and they were responding to what he sang. They ignored me. I let them continue until I formed a plan; I don't believe in rushing into things without knowing exactly what I'm doing.

I waited till the singing quieted down a bit, and then I yelled "Stop!" I stepped forward into the middle of the ring.

"My name is Dugan," I said, loud, clear, and slow. "Chester Dugan. I don't know how I got here, and I don't know where I am, but I mean to stay here a while. Who's the chief around here?"

THEY LOOKED AT EACH OTHER in a puzzled fashion and finally an old thin-faced man stepped out of the circle. "My name is Dandrin," he said, in a thin dried little voice. "As the oldest here, I will speak for the people. Where do you come from?"

"That's just it," I said. "I came from New York City, United States of America, Planet Earth, the Universe. Don't any of those things mean anything to you?"

"They are names, of course," Dandrin said. "But I do not know what they are names of. New York City? United States of America? We have no such terms."

"Never heard of New York?" This was the same treatment I had gotten from that dumb kid Kennon, and I didn't like it. "New York is the biggest city in the world, and the United States is the richest country."

I heard hushed mumbles go around the circle. Dandrin smiled.

"I think I see now," he said. "Cities, countries." He looked at me in a strange way. "Tell me," he said. "Just *when* are you from?"

That shook me. "1956," I said. And here, I'll admit, I began to get worried.

"This is the thirty-fifth century," he said calmly. "At least, so we think. We lost count during the Bombing Years. But come, Chester Dugan; we are interrupting the Singing with our talk. Let us go aside and talk, while the others can sing."

HE LED ME OFF TO one side and explained things to me. Civilization had broken up during a tremendous atomic war. These people were the survivors, the dregs. There were no cities and not even small towns. People lived in groups of twos and threes here and there, and didn't come together very often. They didn't even *like* to get together, except during the summer. Then they would gather at the home of some old man—usually Dandrin; everyone would meet, and sing for a while, and then go home.

Apparently there were only a few thousand people in all of America. They lived widely scattered, and there was no business, or trade, or culture, or anything else. Just little clumps of people living by themselves, farming a little and singing, and not doing much else. As the old man talked I began to rub my hands together—mentally, of course. All sorts of plans were forming in my head.

He didn't have any idea how I had gotten here, and neither did I; I still don't. I think it just must have been a one-in-a-trillion fluke, a flaw in space or something. I just stepped through at the precise instant and wound up at that open field. But Chester Dugan can't worry about things he doesn't understand. I just accept them.

I saw a big future for myself here, with my knowledge of twentieth-century business methods. The first thing, obviously was to reestablish villages. The way they had things arranged now, there really wasn't any civilization. Once I had things started, I could begin reviving other things that these decadent people had lost: money, entertainment, sports, business. Once we got machinery going, we'd be set. We'd start working on a city, and begin expanding. I thanked whoever it was had dropped me here. This was a golden opportunity for me. These people would be putty in my hands.

3. Corilann

It was with Kennon's approval that I did it. Right after the Singing ended for that evening, Dugan came over to me and I could tell from the tone of his conversation that he wanted me for the night. I had already promised myself to Kennon, but Dugan seemed so insistent that I asked Kennon to release me for this one evening, and he did. He didn't mind.

It was strange the way Dugan went about asking me. He never came right out and said anything. I didn't like anything he did that night; and he's ugly.

He kept telling me, "Stay with me, baby; we're going places together." I didn't know what he meant.

The other women were very curious about it the next day. There are so few of us, that it's a novelty to sleep with someone new. They wanted to know how it had been. I told them I enjoyed it.

It was a lie; he was disgusting. But I went back to him the next night, and the one after that, no matter what poor Kennon said. I couldn't help it, despite myself. There was just something about Dugan that drew me. I couldn't help it. But he was disgusting.

4. DANDRIN

It was strange to see them standing in neat, ordered, precise rows, they who had never known any order, any rules before, and Dugan was telling them what to do. The dawn of the day before, we had been free and alone, but since then Dugan had come.

He lined everybody up, and, as I sat in the shade and watched, he began explaining his plans. We tried so hard to understand what he meant. I remembered stories I had heard of the old ones, but I had never believed them until I saw Dugan in action.

"I can't understand you people," he shouted at us. "This whole rich world is sitting here waiting for you to walk out and grab it, and you sit around singing instead. Singing! You people are decadent, that's what you are. You need a government—a good, sturdy government—and I'm here to give it to you."

Kennon and some of the others had come to me that morning to find out what was going to happen. I urged them not to do anything, to listen to Dugan and do what he says. That way, I felt, we could eventually learn to understand him and deal with him in the proper manner. I confess that I was curious to see how he would react among us.

I said nothing when he gave orders that no one was to return home after the Singing. We were to stay here, he told us, and build a city. He was going to bring us all the advantages of the twentieth century.

And we listened to him patiently, all but Kennon. It was Kennon who had brought him here, poor young Kennon who had come here for the Singing and for Corilann. And it was Corilann whom Dugan had singled out for his own private property. Kennon had given his approval, the first night, thinking she would come back to him the next day. But she hadn't; she stayed with Dugan.

In a couple of days he had his city all planned and everything apportioned. I think the thought uppermost in everyone's mind was *why:* why does he want us to do these things? Why? We would have to give him time to carry out his plans; provided he did no permanent harm, we would wait and see, and wonder why.

5. CHESTER DUGAN

This Corilann is really stacked. Things were never like this back when! After Dandrin had told me where the unattached women were sitting, I looked them over and picked her. They were all worth a second look, but she was something special. I didn't know at the time that she was promised to Kennon, or I might not have started fooling around with her; I don't want to antagonize these people too much.

I'm afraid Kennon may be down on me a bit. I've taken his girl away, and I don't think he goes for my methods. I'll have to try some psychology on him. Maybe I'll make him my second-in-command.

The city is moving along nicely. There were 120 people at the Singing, and my figures show that fifteen were old people and the rest divided up pretty evenly; everyone is coupled off, and I've arranged the housing to fit the coupling. These people don't have children very often, but I'll fix that; I'll figure out some way of making things better for those with the most children, some sort of incentive. The quicker we build up the population, the better things will be. I understand there's a wild tribe about five hundred miles to the north of here, maybe less (I still don't have any idea where *here* is) who still have some machines and things, and once we're all established I intend to send an expedition out to conquer the wild tribe and bring back the machines.

There's an idea; maybe I'll let Kennon lead the expedition. I'll be giving him a position of responsibility, and at the same time there's a chance he might get knocked off. That kid's going to cause trouble; I wish I hadn't taken his girl.

But it's too late to go back on it. Besides, I need a son, and quickly. If Corilann's baby is a girl, I don't know what I'll do. I can't carry on my dynasty without an heir.

THERE'S ANOTHER KID HERE THAT bothers me—Jubilain. He's not like the others; he's very frail and sensitive, and seems to get special treatment. He's the one who leads the Singing. I haven't been able to get him to work on the construction yet, and I don't know if I'm going to be able to.

But otherwise everything is moving smoothly. I'm surprised that old Dandrin doesn't object to what I'm doing. It's long since past the time when the Singing should have broken up, and everyone scattered, but they're all staying right here and working as if I was paying them.

Which I am, in a way. I'm bringing them the benefits of a great lost civilization, which I represent. Chester Dugan, the man from the past. I'm taking a bunch of nomads and turning them into a powerful city. So actually, everyone's profiting—the people, because of what I'm doing for them, and me. Me especially, because here I'm absolute top dog.

I'm worried about Corilann's baby, though. If it's a girl, that means a delay of a year or more before I can have my son, and even then it'll be at least ten years before he's of any use to me. I wonder what would happen if I took a second wife—Jarinne, for example. I watched her while she was stripped down for work yesterday and she looks even better than Corilann. These people don't seem to have any particular beliefs about marriage, anyway, and so I don't know if they'd mind. Then if Corilann had a girl, I might give her back to Kennon.

And that reminds me of another thing: there's no religion here. I'm not much of a Godman myself, but I realize religion's a good thing for keeping the people in line. I'll have to start thinking about getting a priesthood going, as soon as affairs are a little more settled here.

I didn't think it was so much work, organizing a civilization. But once I get it all set up, I can sit back and cool my heels for life. It's a pleasure working with these people. I just can't wait till everything is moving by itself. I've gotten further in two months here than I did in forty years there. It just goes to show: you need a powerful man to keep civilization alive. And Chester Dugan is just the man these people needed.

6. KENNON

Corilann has told me she will have a child by Dugan. This has made me sad, since it might have been my child she would be bearing instead. But I brought Dugan here myself, and so I suppose I am responsible. If I had not come to the Singing, he might have died in the great open field. But now it is too late for such thoughts.

Dugan forbids us to go home, now that the Singing is over. My father is waiting for me at our home, and the hunting must be done before the winter comes, but Dugan forbids us to go home. Dandrin had to explain to us what "forbids" means; I still don't fully understand why or how one person can tell another person what to do. None of us really understands Dugan at all, not even Dandrin, I think. Dandrin is trying hardest to understand him, but Dugan is so completely alien to us that we do not see.

He has made us build what he calls a city—many houses close together. He says the advantage of this is that we may protect each other. But from what? We have no enemies. I have the feeling that Dugan understands us even less than we understand him. And I am anxious to go home for the autumn hunting, now that summer is almost over and the Singing is ended. I had hoped to bring Corilann back with me, but it is my own fault, and I must not be bitter.

Dugan has been very cold towards me. This is surprising, since it was I who brought him to the Singing. I think he is afraid I will try to take Corilann back; in any event, he seems to fear me and show anger towards me.

If only I understood!

7. KENNON

Dugan has certainly gone too far now. For the past week I have been trying to engage him in conversation, to find out what his motives are for doing all the things he is doing. Dandrin should be doing this, but Dandrin seems to have abdicated all responsibility in this matter, and is content to sit idly by, watching all that happens. Dugan does not make him work because he is so old.

I do not understand Dugan at all. Yesterday he told me, "We will rule the world." What does he mean? *Rule?* Does he actually want to tell everyone who lives what he can do and what he cannot do? If all of the people of Dugan's time were like this, it is small wonder they destroyed everything. What if two people told the same man to do different things? What if they told each other to do things? My head reels at the thought of Dugan's world. People living together in masses, and telling each other what to do; it seems insane. I long to be back with my father for the hunting. I had hoped to bring him a daughter as well, but it seems this is not to be.

Dugan has offered me Jarinne as my wife. Jarinne says she has been with Dugan, and that Corilann knows. Dandrin warns me not to accept Jarinne because it will anger Dugan. But if it will anger Dugan, why did he offer her to me? And—now it occurs to me—by what right does he offer me another person?

Jarinne is a fine woman. She could make me forget Corilann.

And then Dugan told me that soon there will be an expedition to the north; we will take weapons and conquer the wild men. Dugan has heard of the machines of the wild men, and he says he needs them for our city. I told him that I had to leave immediately to help my father with the hunting, that I have stayed here long enough. Others are saying the same thing: this summer the Singing has lasted too long.

TODAY I TRIED TO LEAVE. I gathered my friends and told them I was anxious to go home, and I asked Jarinne to come with me. She accepted, though she reminded me that she had been with Dugan. I told her I might be able to forget that. She said she knew it wouldn't matter to me if it had been anyone else (of course not; why should it?) but that I might object because it had been Dugan. I said good-bye to Corilann, who now is swollen with Dugan's child; she cried a little.

And then I started to leave. I did not talk to Dandrin, for I was afraid he would persuade me not to go. I opened the gate that Dugan has just put up, and started to leave.

Suddenly Dugan appeared. "Where do you think you're going?" he asked, in his hard, cold rasp of a voice. "Pulling out?"

"I have told you," I said quietly, "it is time to help my father with the hunting. I cannot stay in your city any longer." I moved past him and Jarinne followed. But he ran around in front of me.

"No one leaves here, understand?" He waved his closed hand in front of me. "We can't build a city if you take off when you want to."

"But I must go," I said. "You have detained me here long enough." I started to walk on, and suddenly he hit me with his closed hand and knocked me down.

I went sprawling over the ground, and I felt blood on my face from where he had hurt my nose. People all around were watching. I got up slowly. I am bigger and much stronger than Dugan, but it had never occurred to me that one person might hit another person. But this is one of the many things that has come to our world.

I was not so unhappy for myself; pain soon ceases. But Jubilain the Singer was watching when he hit me, and such sights should be kept from Singers. They are not like the rest of us. I am afraid Jubilain has been seriously disturbed by the sight.

After he had knocked me down, Dugan walked away. I got up

and went back inside the gate. I do not want to leave now. I must talk to Dandrin. Something must be done.

8. JUBILAIN

Summer to autumn to every old everyone, sing winter to quiet to baby fall down. My head head hurts. My my hurts head. Bloody was Kennon.

Kennon was bloody and Dugan was angry and summer to autumn to.

Jubilain is very sad. My head hurts. Dugan hit Kennon in the face. With his hand, his hand hand hand rolled up in a ball Dugan hit Kennon. Outside the gates. Consider the gates. Consider.

They have spoiled the song. How can I sing when Dugan hits Kennon? My head hurts. Sing summer to autumn, sing every old everyone. It is good that the summer is ending, for the songs are over. How can I sing? Bloody was Kennon.

Jubilain's head hurts. It did not hurt before did not hurt. I could sing before. Summer to autumn to every old everyone. Corilann's belly is big with Dugan, and Jubilain's head hurts. Will there be more Dugans?

And more Kennons. No more Jubilains. No more songs. The songs of summer are silent and slippery. My head hurts. Hurts hurts hurts. I can sing no more. Nononononononono.

9. DANDRIN

This is tragic. I am an old fool.

I have been sitting in the shade, like the dried old man I am, while Dugan has destroyed us. Today he struck a man—Kennon. Kennon, whom he has mistreated from the start. Poor Kennon. Dugan has brought strife to us, now, along with his city and his gates.

But that is not the worst of it. Jubilain watched the whole thing, and we have lost our Singer. Jubilain simply was unable to assimilate the incident. A Singer's mind is not like our minds; it is a delicate, sensitive instrument. But it cannot comprehend violence. Our Singer has gone mad; there will be no more songs.

We must destroy Dugan. It is sad that we must come to his level and talk of destroying, but it is so. Now he is going to bring us warfare, and that is a gift we do not need. The fierce men of the north will prove strong adversaries for a people that has not fought for a thousand years. Why could we not have been left to ourselves? We were happy and peaceful people, and now we must talk of destroying.

I know the way to do it, too. If only my mind is strong enough, if only it has not dried in the sun during the years, I can lead the way. If I can link with Kennon, and Kennon with Jarinne, and Jarinne with Corilann, and Corilann with—

If we can link, we can do it. Dugan must go. And this is the best way; this way we can dispose of him and still remain human beings.

I am an old fool. But perhaps this dried old brain still is good for something. If I can link with Kennon—

10. CHESTER DUGAN

All resistance has crumbled now. I'm set up for life—Chester Dugan, ruler of the world. It's not much of a world, true enough, but what the hell. It's mine.

It's amazing how all the grumbling has stopped. Even Kennon has given in—in fact, he's become my most valuable man, since that time I had to belt him. It was too bad, I guess, to ruin such a nice nose, but I couldn't have him walking off that way.

He's going to lead the expedition to the north tomorrow, and he's leaving Jarinne here. That's good. Corilann is busy with her baby, and I think I need a little variety anyway. Good-looking kid Corilann had; takes after his old man. It's amazing how everything is working out.

I hope to get electricity going soon, but I'm not too sure. The stream here is kind of weak, and maybe we'll have to throw up a dam first. In fact, I'm sure of it. I'll speak to Kennon about it before he leaves.

This business of rebuilding a civilization from scratch has its rewards. God, am I lean! I've lost all that roll of fat I was carrying around. I suppose part of the reason is that there's no beer here, yet—but I'll get to that soon enough. Everything in due time. First, I want to see what Kennon brings back from the north. I hope he doesn't ruin anything by ripping it out. Wouldn't it be nice to find a hydraulic press or a generator or stuff like that? And with my luck, we probably will.

Maybe we'll do without religion a little while longer. I spoke to Dandrin about it, but he didn't seem to go for the idea of being priest. I might just take over that job myself, once things get straightened out. I'd like to work out some sort of heating system before the winter gets here. I've figured out that we're somewhere in New Jersey or Pennsylvania, and it'll get pretty cold here unless things have changed. (Could the barbarian city to the north be New York? Sounds reasonable.)

It's funny the way everyone lies down and says yes when I tell them to do something. These people have no guts, that's their trouble. One good thing about civilization—you have to have guts to last. I'll put guts in these people, all right. I'll probably be remembered for centuries and centuries. Maybe they'll think of me as a sort of messiah in the far future when everything's blurred? Why not? I came to them out of the clouds, didn't I? From heaven.

Messiah Dugan! Lawsy-me, if they could only see me now!

I still can't get over the way everything is moving. It's almost like a dream. By next spring we'll have a respectable little city here, practically overnight. And we can hold a super-special Singing next summer and snaffle in the folk from all around.

Too bad about that kid Jubilain, by the way; he's really gone off his nut. But I always thought he was a little way there anyway. Maybe I'll teach them some of the old songs myself. It'll help to make me popular here. Although, come to think of it, I'm pretty popular now. They're all smiling at me all the time.

11.

"Kennon? Kennon? Hear me?"

"I hear you, Dandrin. I'll get Jarinne."

"Here I am. Corilann?"

"Here, Jarinne. And pulling hard. Let's try to get Onnar."

"Pull hard!"

"Onnar in."

"And Jekkaman."

"Hello, Dandrin."

"Hello."

"All here?"

"One hundred twenty."

"Tight now."

"We're right tight."

"Let's get started then. All together."

"Hello? Hello, Dugan. Listen to us, Dugan. Listen to us. Listen to us. Hold on tight! Listen to us, Dugan."

"Open up all the way, now."

"Are you listening, Dugan?"

12. DANDRIN PLUS KENNON PLUS JARINNE PLUS CORILANN PLUS N

I think we'll be able to hold together indefinitely, and so it can be said that the coming of Dugan was an incredible stroke of luck for us. This new blending is infinitely better than trying to make contact over thousands of miles!

Certainly we'll have to maintain this *gestalt* (useful word; I found it in Dugan's mind when I entered) until after Dugan's death. He's peacefully dreaming now, dreaming of who knows what conquests and battles and expansions, and I don't think he'll come out of it. He may live on in his dream for years, and I'll have to hold together and sustain the illusion until he dies. I hope we're making him happy at last. He seems to have been a very unhappy man.

And just after I joined together, it occurred to me that we'd better stay this way indefinitely, just in case any more Dugans get thrown at us from the past. (Could it have been part of a Design? I wonder.) They must all have been like that back then. It's a fine thing that bomb was dropped.

We'll keep Dugan's city, of course. He did make some positive contributions to us—me. His biggest contribution was me; I never would have formed otherwise. I would have been scattered—Kennon on his farm, Dandrin here, Corilann there. I would have maintained some sort of contact among us, the way I always did even before Dugan came, but nothing like this! Nothing at all.

There's the question of what to do with Dugan's child. Kennon, Corilann, and Jarinne are all raising him. We don't need families now that we have me. I think we'll let Dugan's child in with us for a while; if he shows any signs of being like his father, we can always put him to sleep and let him share his father's dream.

I wonder what Dugan is thinking of. Now all his projects will be carried out; his city will grow and cover the world; we will fight and kill and plunder, and he will be measurelessly happy—though all these things take place only within the boundaries of his fertile brain. We will never understand him. But I am happy that all these things will happen only within Dugan's mind so long as I am together and can maintain the illusion for him.

Our next project is to reclaim Jubilain. I am sad that he cannot be with us yet, for how rare and beautiful I would be if I had a Singer in me! That would surely be the most wonderful of blendings. But that will come. Patiently I will unravel the strands of Jubilain's tangled mind, patiently I will bring the Singer back to us.

For in a few months it will be summer again, and time for the Singing. It will be different this year, for we will have been together in me all winter, and so the Singing will not be as unusual an event as it has been, when we have come to each other covered with a winter's strangeness. But this year I will be with us, and we will be I; and the songs of summer will be trebly beautiful in Dugan's city, while Dugan sleeps through the night and the day, for day and night on night and day.

◆

THE MARTIAN INVASION JOURNALS
OF HENRY JAMES

One night late in 1994 I was having dinner with the writer and editor Kevin Anderson—he wanted me to provide him with some technical information about the business aspect of a writing career—and at the end of the meal he asked me, changing the subject completely, whether I'd be interested in doing a story for an anthology he was about to edit. "I very much doubt it," I replied, perhaps a trifle coolly. I was still working on my novel *Starborne* and was looking forward to an extended holiday from writing once I finished it. Any new job, just then, would be a pain in the neck. Kevin persisted. He mentioned the theme: H. G. Wells's *War of the Worlds* retold as a group of eyewitness accounts from the viewpoints of other great writers of the era (Kipling, Verne, Tolstoy, Mark Twain). I perked up. He mentioned the fee, a very generous one. Very generous. (Sometimes even a pain in the neck can be worthwhile.) "Can I have Henry James?" I asked.

I might have asked for Joseph Conrad, I suppose. Conrad had been a friend of Wells's and lived near him at the time Wells was writing *War of the Worlds*. But I had already done plenty of Conrad-channeling (the novel *Downward to the Earth*, which was a replay of "Heart of Darkness" set on another world, the novella *The Secret Sharer* that's loosely based on his story of the same name, and a section of my novel *Hot Sky at Midnight* that tangentially re-explores a theme out of *Lord Jim*). And Wells, at the turn of the twentieth century, had had another friend and neighbor whose writing, very different from Conrad's in all ways, I also admired greatly. The notion of retelling Wells's tale of Martian invaders as if the invasion had been experienced firsthand by pudgy, timid Henry James was too good to resist.

I didn't resist at all. I've rarely had so much fun writing a story.

Kevin didn't mind my selling the story to a magazine before he used it in his anthology, which made his offer all the more attractive. A slick magazine called *Omni* purchased magazine rights, but very shortly afterward that publication vanished into cyberspace, where I don't spend much time, and I have no idea whether they used it or not. So far as I know, the story's first appearance was in Kevin Anderson's *The War of the Worlds: Global Dispatches*, published in June 1996. A first-person story is a kind of act of ventriloquism, and, though my usual style is very much unlike that of Henry James's, it was a glorious novelty to be speaking with his voice as I told of his encounter with the Martian invaders.

EDITOR'S NOTE:

OF ALL THE TREASURES CONTAINED in the coffin-shaped wooden sea-chest at Harvard's Widener Library in which those of Henry James's notebooks and journals that survived his death were preserved and in the associated James archive at Harvard, only James's account of his bizarre encounter with the Martian invaders in the summer of 1900 has gone unpublished until now. The rest of the material the box contained—the diaries and datebooks, the notes for unfinished novels, the variant drafts of his late plays, and so forth—has long since been made available to James scholars, first in the form of selections under the editorship of F. O. Matthiessen and Kenneth B. Murdock (*The Notebooks of Henry James*, Oxford University Press, 1947), and then a generation later in the magisterial full text edited by Leon Edel and Lyall H. Powers (*The Complete Notebooks of Henry James*, Oxford University Press, 1987).

Despite the superb latter volume's assertions, in its title and subtitle, of being "complete," "authoritative," and "definitive," one brief text was indeed omitted from it, which was, of course, the invasion journal. Edel and Powers are in no way to be faulted for this, since they could not have been aware of the existence of the Martian papers, which had (apparently accidentally) been sequestered long ago among a group of documents at Harvard associated with the life of James's sister Alice (1848–1892) and had either gone unnoticed by the biographers of Alice James or else, since the diary had obviously been composed some years after her death, had been dismissed by them as irrelevant to their research. It may also be that they found the little notebook simply illegible, for James had suffered severely from writer's cramp from the winter of 1896–97 onward; his handwriting by 1900 had become quite erratic, and many of the (largely pencilled) entries in the Martian notebook are extremely challenging even to a reader experienced in Henry James's hand, set down as they were in great haste under intensely strange circumstances.

The text is contained in a pocket diary book, four and a half inches by six, bound in a green leatherette cover. It appears that James used such books, in those years, in which to jot notes that he would later transcribe into his permanent notebook (Houghton Journal VI, 26 October 1896 to 10 February 1909); but this is the only one of its kind that has survived. The first entry is undated, but can be specifically identified as belonging to mid-May of 1900 by its references to James's visit to London in that month. At that time James made his home at Lamb House in the pleasant Sussex town of Rye, about seventy miles southeast of London. After an absence of nearly two years he had made a brief trip to the capital in March, 1900, at which time, he wrote, he was greeted by his friends "almost as if I had returned from African or Asian exile." After seventeen days he went home to Lamb House, but he returned to London in May, having suddenly shaven off, a few days before, the beard that he had worn since the 1860s, because it had begun to turn white and offended his vanity. (James was then 57.) From internal evidence, then, we can date the first entry in the Martian journals to the period between May 15 and May 25, 1900.

[UNDATED]

Stepped clean-shaven from the train at Charing Cross. Felt clean and light and eerily young: I could have been forty. A miraculous transformation, so simply achieved! Alas, the sad truth of it is that it will always be I, never any younger even without the beard; but this is a good way to greet the new century nevertheless.

Called on Helena De Kay. Gratifying surprise and expressions of pleasure over my rejuvenated physiognomy. Clemens is there, that is, "Mark Twain." He has aged greatly in the three years since our last meeting. "The twentieth century is a stranger to me," he sadly declares. His health is bad: has been to Sweden for a cure. Not clear what ails him, physically, at least. He is a dark and troubled soul in any case. His best work is behind him and plainly he knows it. I pray whatever God there be that that is not to be my fate.

To the club in the evening. Tomorrow a full day, the galleries, the booksellers, the customary dismaying conference with the publishers. (The war in South Africa is depressing all trade, publishing particularly badly hit, though I should think people would read more novels at a time of such tension.) Luncheon and dinner engagements, of course, the usual hosts, no doubt the usual guests. And so on and on the next day and the next and the next. I yearn already for little restful, red-roofed, uncomplicated Rye.

JUNE 7, LH [LAMB HOUSE, Rye]:

Home again at long last. London tires me: that is the truth of things. I have lost the habit of it, *je crois.* How I yearned, all the while I was there, for cabless days and dinnerless nights! And of course there is work to do. *The Sacred Fount* is now finished and ready to go to the agent. A fine flight into the high fantastic, I think—fanciful, fantastic, but very close and sustained. Writing in the first person makes me uneasy—it lends itself so readily to garrulity, to a fluidity of self-revelation—but there is no questioning that such a structure was essential to this tale.

What is to be next? There is of course the great Project, the fine and major thing, which perhaps I mean to call *The Ambassadors*. Am I ready to begin it? It will call for the most supreme effort, though I think the reward will be commensurate. A masterpiece, dare I say? I might do well to set down one more sketch of it before commencing. But not immediately. There is powerful temptation to be dilatory: I find a note here from Wells, who suggests that I bicycle over to Sandgate and indulge in a bit of conversation with him. Indeed it has been a while, and I am terribly fond of him. Wells first, yes, and some serious thought about my ambassadors after that.

JUNE 14, SANDGATE.

I am at Wells's this fine bright Thursday, very warm even for June. The bicycle ride in such heat across Romney Marsh to this grand new villa of his on the Kentish coast left me quite wilted, but Wells's robust hospitality has quickly restored me.

What a vigorous man Wells is! Not that you would know it to look at him; his health is much improved since his great sickly time two years ago, but he is nonetheless such a flimsy little wisp of a man, with those short legs, that high squeaky voice, his somewhat absurd moustaches. And yet the mind of the man burns like a sun within that frail body! The energy comes forth in that stream of books, the marvelous fantastic tales, the time-machine story and the one about Dr. Moreau's bestial monsters and the one that I think is my favorite, the pitiful narrative of the invisible man. Now he wants to write the story of a journey to the Moon, among innumerable other projects, all of which he will probably fulfill. But of course there is much more to Wells than these outlandish if amusing fables: his recent book, *Love and Mr. Lewisham,* is not at all a scientific romance but rather quite the searching analysis of matters of love and power. Even so Wells is not just a novelist (a *mere* novelist, I came close to saying!); he is a seer, a prophet, he genuinely wishes to transform the world according to his great plan for it. I doubt very much that he will have the chance, but I wish him well. It is a trifle exhausting to listen to him go on and on about the new century and the miracles that it will bring, but it is enthralling as well. And of course behind his scientific optimism lurks a dark vision, quite contradictory, of the inherent nature of mankind. He is a fascinating man, a raw, elemental force. I wish he paid more attention to matters of literary style; but, then, he wishes that I would pay *less.* I dare say each of us is both right and wrong about the other.

We spoke sadly of our poor friend and neighbor, Crane *[Stephen Crane, the American novelist],* whose untimely death last week we both lament. His short life was chaotic and his disregard for his own health was virtually criminal; but *The Red Badge of Courage,* I believe, will surely long outlive him. I wonder what other magnificent works were still in him when he died.

We talk of paying calls the next day on some of our other literary friends who live nearby, Conrad, perhaps, or young Hueffer, or even Kipling up at Burwash. What a den of novelists these few counties possess!

A fine dinner and splendid talk afterward.

Early to bed for me; Wells, I suppose, will stay awake far into the night, writing, writing, writing.

JUNE 15, SPADE HOUSE, SANDGATE.

In mid-morning after a generous late breakfast Wells is just at the point of composing a note to Conrad proposing an impromptu visit—Conrad is still despondently toiling at his interminable *Lord Jim* and no doubt would welcome an interruption, Wells says— when a young fellow whom Wells knows comes riding up, all out of breath, with news that a falling star has been seen crossing the skies in the night, rushing high overhead, inscribing a line of flame visible from Winchester eastward, and that—no doubt as a consequence of that event—something strange has dropped from the heavens and landed in Wells's old town of Woking, over Surrey way. It is a tangible thunderbolt, a meteor, some kind of shaft flung by the hand of Zeus, at any rate.

So, *instanter*, all is up with our visit to Conrad. Wells's scientific curiosity takes full hold of him. He must go to Woking this very moment to inspect this gift of the gods; and, willy-nilly, I am to accompany him. "You must come, you *must!*" he cries, voice disappearing upward into an octave extraordinary even for him. I ask him why, and he will only say that there will be revelations of an earthshaking kind, of planetary dimensions. "To what are you fantastically alluding?" I demand, but he will only smile enigmatically. And, shortly afterward, off we go.

June 15, much later, Woking.

Utterly extraordinary! We make the lengthy journey over from Sandgate by pony-carriage, Wells and I, two literary gentleman out for an excursion on this bright and extravagantly warm morning in late spring. I am garbed as though for a bicycle journey, my usual knickerbockers and my exiguous jacket of black and white stripes and my peaked cap; I feel ill at ease in these regalia but I have brought nothing else with me suitable for this outing. We arrive at Woking by late afternoon and plunge at once into—what other word can I use?—into madness.

The object from on high, we immediately learn, landed with an evidently violent impact in the common between Woking, Horsell, and Ottershaw, burying itself deep in the ground. The heat and fury of its impact have hurled sand and gravel in every direction and set the surrounding heather ablaze, though the fires were quickly enough extinguished. But what has fallen is no meteorite. The top of an immense metallic cylinder, perhaps thirty yards across, can be seen protruding from the pit.

Early this morning Ogilvy, the astronomer, hastened to inspect the site; and, he tells us now, he was able despite the heat emanating from the cylinder's surface to get close enough to perceive that the top of the thing had begun to rotate—as though, so he declares, there were creatures within attempting to get out!

"What we have here is a visitation from the denizens of Mars, I would hazard," says Wells without hesitation, in a tone of amazing calmness and assurance.

"Exactly so!" cries Ogilvy. "Exactly so!"

These are both men of science, and I am but a litterateur. I stare in bewilderment from one to the other. "How can you be so certain?" I ask them, finally.

To which Wells replies, "The peculiar bursts of light we have observed on the face of that world in recent years have aroused much curiosity, as I am sure you are aware. And then, some time ago, the sight of jets of flame leaping up night after night from the red planet, as if some great gun were being repeatedly fired—in direct consequence of which, let me propose, there eventually came the streak of light in the sky late last night, which I noticed from my study window—betokening, I would argue, the arrival here of this projectile—why, what else can it all mean, James, other than that travelers from our neighbor world lie embedded here before us on Horsell Common!"

"It can be nothing else," Ogilvy cries enthusiastically. "Travelers from Mars! But are they suffering, I wonder? Has their passage through our atmosphere engendered heat too great for them to endure?"

A flush of sorrow and compassion rushes through me at that. It awes and flutters me to think that the red planet holds sentient life, and that an intrepid band of Martians has ventured to cross the great sea of space that separates their world from ours. To have come such an immense and to me unimaginable distance—only to perish in the attempt—! Can it be, as Ogilvy suggests, that this brave interplanetary venture will end in tragedy for the brave voyagers? I am racked briefly by the deepest concern.

How ironic, I suppose, in view of the dark and violent later events of this day, that I should expend such pity upon our visitors. But we could tell nothing, then, nor for some little while thereafter. Crowds of curiosity-seekers came and went, as they have done all day; workmen with digging tools now began to attempt to excavate the cylinder, which had cooled considerably since the morning; their attempts to complete the unscrewing of the top were wholly unsuccessful. Wells could not take his eyes from the pit. He seemed utterly possessed by a fierce joy that had been kindled in him by the possibility that the cylinder held actual Martians. It was, he told me several times, almost as though one of his own scientific fantasy-books were turning to reality before his eyes; and Wells confessed that he had indeed sketched out the outline of a novel about an invasion from Mars, intending to write it some two or three years hence, but of course now that scheme has been overtaken by actual events and he shall have to abandon it. He evidences little regret at this; he appears wholly delighted, precisely as a small boy might be, that the Martians are here. I dare say that he would have regarded the intrusion of a furious horde of dinosaurs into the Surrey countryside with equal pleasure.

But I must admit that I am somewhat excited as well. Travelers from Mars! How extraordinary! *Quel phénomène!* And what vistas open to the mind of the intrepid seeker after novelty! I have traveled somewhat myself, of course, to the Continent, at least, if not to Africa or China, but I have not ruled such farther journeys completely out, and now the prospect of an even farther one becomes possible. To make the Grand Tour of Mars! To see its great monuments and temples, and perhaps have an audience at the court of the Great Martian Cham! It is a beguiling thought, if not a completely serious one. See, see, I am becoming a fantasist worthy of Wells!

(*LATER. THE HOUR OF SUNSET.*)

The cylinder is open. To our immense awe we find ourselves staring at a Martian. Did I expect them to be essentially human in form? Well, then, I was foolish in my expectations. What we see is a bulky ungainly thing; two huge eyes, great as saucers; tentacles of some sort; a strange quivering mouth—yes, yes, an alien being *senza dubbio*, preternaturally *other*.

Wells, unexpectedly, is appalled. "Disgusting . . . dreadful," he mutters. "That oily skin! Those frightful eyes! What a hideous devil it is!" Where has his scientific objectivity gone? For my part I am altogether fascinated. I tell him that I see rare beauty in the Martian's strangeness, not the beauty of a Greek vase or of a ceiling by Tiepolo, of course, but beauty of a distinct kind all the same. In this, I think, my perceptions are the superior of Wells's. There is beauty in the squirming octopus dangling from the hand of some grinning fisherman at the shore of Capri; there is beauty in the *terrifiant* bas-reliefs of winged bulls from the palaces of Nineveh; and there is beauty of a sort, I maintain, in this Martian also.

He laughs heartily. "You are ever the esthete, eh, James!"

I suppose that I am. But I will not retreat from my appreciation of the strange being who—struggling, it seems, against the unfamiliar conditions of our world—is moving about slowly and clumsily at the edge of its cylinder.

The creature drops back out of sight. The twilight is deepening to darkness. An hour passes, and nothing occurs. Wells suggests we seek dinner, and I heartily agree.

(*LATER STILL.*)

Horror! Just past eight, while Wells and I were dining, a delegation bearing a white flag of peace approached the pit, so we have learned—evidently in the desire to demonstrate to the Martians that we are intelligent and friendly beings. Ogilvy was in the group, and Stent, the Astronomer Royal, and some poor journalist who had arrived to report on the event. There came suddenly a blinding flash of flame from the pit, and another and another, and the whole delegation met with a terrible instant death, forty souls in all. The fiery beam also ignited adjacent trees and brought down a portion of a nearby house; and all those who had survived the massacre fled the scene in the wildest of terror.

"So they are monsters," Wells ejaculates fiercely, "and this is war between the worlds!"

"No, no," I protest, though I too am stunned by the dire news. "They are far from home—frightened, discomforted—it is a tragic misunderstanding and nothing more."

Wells gives me a condescending glance. That one withering look places our relationship, otherwise so cordial, in its proper context. He is the hard-headed man of realities who has clawed his way up from poverty and ignorance; I am the moneyed and comfortable and overly gentle literary artist, the *connoisseur* of the life of the leisured classes. And then too, not for the first time, I have failed to seize the immediate horrific implications of a situation whilst concentrating on peripheral pretty responses. To brusque and self-confident Wells, in his heart of hearts, I surely must appear as something charming but effete.

I think that Wells greatly underestimates the strength of my fibre, but this is no moment to debate the point.

"Shall we pay a call on your unhappy friends from Mars, and see if they receive us more amiably?" he suggests.

I cannot tell whether he is sincere. It is always necessary to allow for Wells's insatiable scientific curiosity.

"By all means, if that is what you wish," I bravely say, and wait for his response. But in fact he is *not* serious; he has no desire to share the fate of Ogilvy and Stent; and, since it is too late now to return to Sandgate this night, we take lodgings at an inn he knows here in Woking. Clearly Wells is torn, I see, between his conviction that the Martians are here to do evil and his powerful desire to learn all that a human mind can possibly learn about these beings from an unknown world.

JUNE 16, WOKING AND POINTS east.

Perhaps the most ghastly day of my life.

Just as well we made no attempt last evening to revisit the pit. Those who did—there were some such foolhardy ones—did not return, for the heat-ray was seen to flash more than once in the darkness. Great hammering noises came from the pit all night, and occasional puffs of greenish-white smoke. Devil's work, to be sure. Just after midnight a second falling star could be seen in the northwest sky. The invasion, and there is no doubt now that that is what it is, proceeds apace.

In the morning several companies of soldiers took possession of the entire common and much of the area surrounding it. No one may approach the site and indeed the military have ordered an evacuation of part of Horsell. It is a hot, close day and we have, of course, no changes of clothing with us. Rye and dear old Lamb House seem now to be half a world away. In the night I began to yearn terribly for home, but Wells's determination to remain here and observe the unfolding events was manifest from the time of our awakening. I was unwilling to be rebuked for my timidity, nor could I very well take his pony-carriage and go off with it whilst leaving him behind, and so I resolved to see it all out at his side.

But would there be any unfolding events to observe? The morning and afternoon were dull and wearying. Wells was an endless fount of scientific speculation—he was convinced that the greater gravitational pull of Earth would keep the Martians from moving about freely on our world, and that conceivably they might drown in our thicker atmosphere, et cetera, and that was interesting to me at first and then considerably less so as he went on with it. Unasked, he lectured me interminably on the subject of Mars, its topography, its climate, its seasons, its bleak and forlorn landscape. Wells is an irrepressible lecturer: there is no halting him once he has the bit between his teeth.

In mid-afternoon we heard the sound of distant gunfire to the north: evidently attempts were being made to destroy the second cylinder before it could open. But at Woking all remained in a nervewracking stasis the whole day, until, abruptly, at six in the evening there came an explosion from the common, and gunfire, and a fierce shaking and a crashing that brought into my mind the force of the eruption of Vesuvius as it must have been on the day of the doom of Pompeii. We looked out and saw treetops breaking into flame like struck matches; buildings began to collapse as though the breath of a giant had been angrily expended upon them; and fires sprang up all about. The Martians had begun to destroy Woking.

"Come," Wells said. He had quickly concluded that it was suicidal folly to remain here any longer, and certainly I would not disagree. We hastened to the pony-carriage; he seized the reins; and off we went to the east, with black smoke rising behind us and the sounds of rifles and machine-guns providing incongruous contrapuntal rhythms as we made our way on this humid spring evening through this most pleasant of green countrysides.

We traveled without incident as far as Leatherhead; all was tranquil; it was next to impossible to believe that behind us lay a dreadful scene of death and destruction. Wells's wife has cousins at Leatherhead, and they, listening gravely and with obvious skepticism to our wild tales of Martians with heat-rays laying waste to Woking, gave us supper and evidently expected that we would be guests for the night, it now being nearly ten; but no, Wells had taken it into his head to drive all night, going on by way of Maidstone or perhaps Tunbridge Wells down into Sussex to deliver me to Rye, and thence homeward for him to Sandgate. It was lunacy, but in the frenzy of the moment I agreed to his plan, wishing at this point quickly to put as much distance between the invaders and myself as could be managed.

And so we took our hasty leave of Leatherhead. Glancing back, we saw a fearsome scarlet glow on the western horizon, and huge clots of black smoke. And, as we drove onward, there came a horrid splash of green light overhead, which we both knew must be the third falling star, bringing with it the next contingent of Martians.

Nevertheless I believed myself to be safe. I have known little if any physical danger in my life and it has a certain unreal quality to me; I cannot ever easily accept it as impinging on my existence.

Therefore it came as a great astonishment and a near unhinging of my inner stability when, some time past midnight, with thunder sounding in the distance and the air portending imminent rain, the pony abruptly whinnied and reared in terror, and a moment later we beheld a titanic metal creature, perhaps one hundred feet high, striding through the young forest before us on three great metal legs, smashing aside all that lay in its way.

"Quickly!" Wells cried, and seized me by the wrist in an iron grasp and tumbled me out of the cart, down into the grass by the side of the road, just as the poor pony swung round in its fright and bolted off, cart and all, into the woods. The beast traveled no more than a dozen yards before it became fouled amidst low-lying branches and tumbled over, breaking the cart to splinters and, I am afraid, snapping its own neck in the fall. Wells and I lay huddled beneath a shrub as the colossal three-legged metal engine passed high above us. Then came a second one, following in its track, setting up a monstrous outcry as it strode along. "Aloo! Aloo!" it called, and from its predecessor came back an acknowledging "Aloo!"

"The Martians have built war-machines for themselves," Wells murmured. "That was the hammering we heard in the pit. And now these two are going to greet the companions who have just arrived aboard the third cylinder."

How I admired his cool analytical mind just then! For the thunderstorm had reached us, and we suddenly now were being wholly drenched, and muddied as well, and it was late at night and our cart was smashed and our pony was dead, the two of us alone out here in a deserted countryside at the mercy of marauding metal monsters, and even then Wells was capable of so cool an assessment of the events exploding all around us.

I have no idea how long we remained where we were. Perhaps we even dozed a little. No more Martians did we see. A great calmness came over me as the rain went on and on and I came to understand that I could not possibly get any wetter. At length the storm moved away; Wells aroused me and announced that we were not far from Epsom, where perhaps we might find shelter if the Martians had not already devastated it; and so, drenched to the bone, we set out on foot in the darkness. Wells prattled all the while, about the parchedness of Mars and how intensely interested the Martians must be in the phenomenon of water falling from the skies. I replied somewhat curtly that it was not a phenomenon of such great interest to me, the rain now showing signs of returning. In fact I doubted I should survive this soaking. Already I was beginning to feel unwell. But I drew on unsuspected reservoirs of strength and kept pace with the indomitable Wells as we endlessly walked. To me this excursion was like a dream, and not a pleasing one. We tottered on Epsomward all through the dreadful night, arriving with the dawn.

JUNE 20? 21? 22? EPSOM.

My doubt as to today's date is trivial in regard to my doubt over everything else. It seems that I have been in a delirium of fever for at least a week, perhaps more, and the world has tottered all about me in that time.

Wells believes that today is Thursday, the 21st of June, 1900. Our innkeeper passionately insists it is a day earlier than that. His daughter thinks we have reached Saturday or even Sunday. If we had today's newspaper we should be able to settle the question easily enough, but there are no newspapers. Nor can we wire Greenwich to learn whether the summer solstice has yet occurred, for the Observatory no doubt has been abandoned, as has all the rest of London. Civilization, it appears, has collapsed utterly in this single week. All days are Sundays now: nothing stirs, there is no edifying life.

I too collapsed utterly within an hour or two of the end of our night's march to Epsom, lost in a dizzying rhapsody of fatigue and exposure. Wells has nursed me devotedly. Apparently I have had nearly all of his meager ration of food. There are five of us here, the innkeeper and his wife and daughter and us, safely barricaded, so we hope, against the Martian killing-machines and the lethal black gas that they have been disseminating. Somehow this town, this inn, this little island within England where we lie concealed, has escaped the general destruction—thus far. But now comes word that our sanctuary may soon be violated; and what shall we do, Wells and I? Proceeding eastward to our homes along the coast is impossible: the Martians have devastated everything in that direction. "We must to London," Wells insists. "The great city stands empty. Only there will we find food enough to continue, and places to hide from them."

It is a source of wonder and mystery to me that all has fallen apart so swiftly, that—in southern England, at least—the comfortable structures of the society I knew have evaporated entirely, within a week, vanishing with the speed of snowflakes after a spring storm.

What has happened? *This* has happened:

Cylinders laden with Martians have continued daily to arrive from the void. The creatures emerge; they assemble their gigantic transporting-carriages; the mechanical colossi go back and forth upon the land, spreading chaos and death with their heat-rays, their clouds of poisonous black vapor, and any number of other devices of deviltry. Whole towns have been charred; whole regiments have been dropped in their tracks; whole counties have been abandoned. The government, the military, all has disintegrated. Our leaders have vanished in a hundred directions. Her Majesty and the Members of Parliament and the entire authority-wielding apparatus of the state now seem as mythical as the knights of the Round Table. We have been thrown back into a state of nature, every man for himself.

In London, so our hosts have told us, all remained ignorantly calm through Sunday last, until news came to the capital from the south of the terror and destruction there, the giant invulnerable spider-like machines, the fires, the suffocating poisonous gas. Evidently a ring of devastation had been laid down on a great arc south of the Thames from Windsor and Staines over through Reigate, at least, and on past Maidstone to Deal and Broadstairs on the Kentish coast. Surely they were closing the net on London, and on Monday morning the populace of that great city commenced to flee in all directions. A few of those who came this way, hoping to reach friends or kin in Kent or East Sussex—there were many thousands—told Wells and the innkeeper of the furious frantic exodus, the great mobs streaming northward, and those other desperate mobs flooding eastward to the Essex shore, as the methodical Martians advanced on London, exterminating all in their path. The loss of life, in that mad rush, must have been unthinkably great.

"And we have had no Martians here?" I asked Wells.

"On occasion, yes," he replied casually, as though I had asked him about cricket-matches or rainstorms. "A few of their great machines passed through earlier in the week, bound on deadly business elsewhere, no doubt; we called no attention to ourselves, and they took no notice of us. We have been quite fortunate, James."

The landlord's daughter, though—a wild boyish girl of fourteen or fifteen—has been out boldly roving these last few days, and reports increasing numbers of Martians going to and fro to the immediate south and east of us. She says that everything is burned and ruined as far as she went in the directions of Banstead and Leatherhead, and some sort of red weed, no doubt of Martian origin, is weirdly spreading across the land. It is only a matter of time, Wells believes, before they come into Epsom again, and this time, like the randomly striking godlike beings that they seem to be, they may take it into their minds to hurl this place into ruin as well. We must be off, he says; we must to London, where we will be invisible in the vastness of the place.

"And should we not make an attempt to reach our homes, instead?" I ask.

"There is no hope of that, none," says Wells. "The Martians will have closed the entire coast, to prevent an attack through the Strait of Dover by our maritime forces. Even if we survived the journey to the coast, we should find nothing there, James, nothing but ash and rubble. To London, my friend: that is where we must go, now that you are sturdy again."

There is no arguing with Wells. It would be like arguing with a typhoon.

JUNE 23, LET US SAY. En route to London.

How strange this once-familiar landscape seems! I feel almost as though I have been transported to Mars and my old familiar life has been left behind on some other star.

We are just outside Wimbledon. Everything is scorched and blackened to our rear; everything seems scorched and blackened ahead of us. We have seen things too terrible to relate, signs of the mass death that must have been inflicted here. Yet all is quiet now. The weather continues fiercely hot and largely dry, and the red Martian weed, doubtless finding conditions similar to those at home, has spread everywhere. It reminds me of the enormous cactus plants one sees in southern Italy, but for its somber brick-red hue and the great luxuriance of its habit of growth: it is red, red, *red*, as far as the eye can see. A dreamlike transformation, somber and depressing in its morbid implications, and of course terrifying. I am certain I will never see my home again, which saddens me. It seems pure insanity to me to be going on into London, despite all the seemingly cogent reasons Wells expresses.

And yet, and yet! Behind the terror and the sadness, how wonderfully exhilarating all this is, really! Shameful of me to say so, but I confess it only to my notebook: this is the great adventure of my life, the wondrous powerful action in which I have ever longed to be involved. At last I am fully *living*! My heart weeps for the destruction I see all about me, for the fall of civilization itself, but yet—I will not deny it—I am invigorated far beyond my considerable years by the constant peril, by the demands placed upon my formerly coddled body, above all, by the sheer *strangeness* of everything within my ken. If I survive this journey and live to make my escape to some unblighted land I shall dine out on these events forever.

We are traveling, to my supreme astonishment, by *motor-car*. Wells found one at a house adjacent to the inn, fully stocked with petrol, and he is driving the noisy thing, very slowly but with great perseverance, with all the skill of an expert *chauffeur*. He steers around obstacles capably; he handles sharp and frightening turns in the road with supreme aplomb. It was only after we had been on the road for over an hour that he remarked to me, in an offhand way, "Do you know, James, I have never driven one of these machines before. But there's nothing at all to it, really! Nothing!" Wells is extraordinary. He has offered to give me a chance at the wheel; but no, no, I think I shall let him be the driver on this journey.

(LATER.)

An astonishing incident, somewhere between Wimbledon and London, unforgettably strange.

Wells sees the cupola of a Martian walking-machine rising above the treetops not far ahead of us, and brings the motor-car to a halt while we contemplate the situation. The alien engine stands completely still, minute after minute; perhaps it has no tenant, or possibly even its occupant was destroyed in some rare successful attempt at a counterattack. Wells proposes daringly but characteristically that we go up to it on foot and take a close look at it, after which, since we are so close to London and ought not to be drawing the Martians' attention to ourselves as we enter a city which presumably they occupy, we should abandon our motor-car and slip into the capital on foot, like the furtive fugitives that we are.

Naturally I think it's rash to go anywhere near the Martian machine. But Wells will not be gainsaid. And so we warily advance, until we are no more than twenty yards from it; whereupon we discover an amazing sight. The Martians ride in a kind of cabin or basket high up above the great legs of their machines. But this one had dismounted and descended somehow to the ground, where it stands fully exposed in a little open space by the side of a small stream just beyond its mechanical carrier, peering reflectively toward the water for all the world as though it were considering passing the next hour with a bit of angling.

The Martian was globular in form, a mere ambulatory head without body—or a body without head, if you will—a yard or more in diameter, limbless, with an array of many whip-like tentacles grouped in two bunches by its mouth. As we breathlessly watched, the creature leaned ponderously forward and dipped a few of these tentacles into the stream, holding them there a long while in evident satisfaction, as though it were a Frenchman and this was a river of the finest claret passing before it, which could somehow be enjoyed and appreciated in this fashion. We could not take our eyes from the spectacle. I saw Wells glance toward a jagged rock of some size lying nearby, as though he had it in mind to attempt some brutal act of heroism against the alien as it stood with its back to us; but I shook my head, more out of an unwillingness to see him take life than out of fear of the consequences of such an attack, and he let the rock be.

How long did this interlude go on? I could not say. We were rooted, fascinated, by our encounter with *the other*. Then the Martian turned—with the greatest difficulty—and trained its huge dark eyes on us. Wells and I exchanged wary glances. Should we finally flee? The Martian seemed to carry no weapons; but who knew what powers of the mind it might bring to bear on us? Yet it simply studied us, dispassionately, as one might study a badger or a mole that has wandered out of the woods. It was a magical moment, of a sort: beings of two disparate worlds face to face (so to speak) and eye to eye, and no hostile action taken on either side.

The Martian then uttered a kind of clicking noise, which we took to be a threat, or a warning. "Time for us to be going," Wells said, and we backed hastily out of the clearing. The clicking sound, we saw, had notified the Martian's transport-mechanism that it wished to be re-seated in the cupola, and a kind of cable quickly came down, gathered it up, and raised it to its lofty perch. Now the Martian was in full possession of its armaments again, and I was convinced that my last moments had arrived. But no; no. The thing evinced no interest in murdering us. Perhaps it too had felt the magic of our little encounter; or it may be that we were deemed too insignificant to be worth slaughtering. In any event the great machine lumbered into life and went striding off toward the west, leaving Wells and me gaping slackjawed at each other like two men who had just experienced the company of some basilisk or chimera or banshee and had lived to tell the tale.

THE FOLLOWING DAY, WHICHEVER ONE THAT MAY BE.

We are in London, having entered the metropolis from the south by way of the Vauxhall Bridge after a journey on foot that makes my old trampings in Provence and the Campagna and the one long ago over the Alps into Italy seem like the merest trifling strolls. And yet I feel little weariness, for all my hunger and the extreme physical effort of these days past. It is the strange exhila-ration, still, that drives me onward, muddied and tattered though I am, and with my banished beard, alas, re-emerging in all its dread whiteness.

Here in the greatest of cities the full extent of the catastrophe comes home with overwhelming impact. There is no one here. We could not be more alone were we on Crusoe's island. The desola-tion is magnified by the richness of the amenities all about us, the grand hotels, the splendid town-houses, the rich shops, the the-aters. Those still remain: but whom do they serve? We see a few corpses lying about here and there, no doubt those who failed to heed the warning to flee; the murderous black powder, appar-ently no longer lethal, covers much of the city like a horrid dark snowfall; there is some sign of looting, but not really very much, so quickly did everyone flee. The stillness is profound. It is the stillness of Pompeii, the stillness of Agamemnon's Mycenae. But those are bleached ruins; London has the look of a vibrant city, yet, except that there is no one here.

So far as we can see, Wells and I are the only living things, but for birds, and stray cats and dogs. Not even the Martians are in evidence: they must be extending their conquests elsewhere, meaning to return in leisure when the job is done. We help ourselves to food in the fine shops of Belgravia, whose doors stand mostly open; we even dare to refresh ourselves, guiltlessly, with a bottle of three-guinea Chambertin, after much effort on Wells's part in extracting the cork; and then we plunge onward past Buckingham Palace—empty, empty!—into the strangely bleak precincts of Mayfair and Piccadilly.

Like some revenant wandering through a dream-world I revisit the London I loved. Now it is Wells who feels the outsider, and I who am at home. Here are my first lodgings at Bolton St., in Piccadilly; here are the clubs where I so often dined, pre-eminent among them for me the Reform Club, my dear refuge and sanctuary in the city, where when still young I was to meet Gladstone and Tennyson and Schliemann of Troy. What would Schliemann make of London now? I invite Wells to admire my little *pied-à-terre* at the Reform, but the building is sealed and we move on. The city is ours. Perhaps we will go to Kensington, where I can show him my chaste and secluded flat at De Vere Mansions with its pretty view of the park; but no, no, we turn the other way, through the terrifying silence, the tragic solitude. Wells wishes to ascertain whether the British Museum is open. So it is up Charing Cross Road for us, and into Bloomsbury, and yes, amazingly, the museum door stands ajar. We can, if we wish, help ourselves to the Elgin Marbles and the Rosetta Stone and the Portland Vase. But to what avail? Everything is meaningless now. Wells stations himself before some battered pharaoh in the hall of Egyptian sculpture and cries out, in what I suppose he thinks is a mighty and terrible voice, "I am Ozymandias, King of Kings! Look on my works, ye mighty, and despair!"

What, I wonder, shall we do? Wander London at will, until the Martians come and slay us as they have slain the others? There is a certain wonderful *frisson* to be had from being the last men in London; but in truth it is terrible, terrible, terrible. What is the worth of having survived, when civilization has perished?

Cold sausages and stale beer in a pub just off Russell Square. The red weed, we see, is encroaching everywhere in London as it is in the countryside. Wells is loquacious; talks of his impoverished youth, his early ambitions, his ferociously self-imposed education, his gradual accretion of achievement and his ultimate great triumph as popular novelist and philosopher. He has a high opinion of his intellect, but there is nothing offensive in the way he voices it, for his self-approbation is well earned. He is a remarkable man. I could have done worse for a companion in this apocalypse. Imagine being here with poor gloomy tormented Conrad, for example!

A terrifying moment toward nightfall. We have drifted down toward Covent Garden; I turn toward Wells, who has been walking a pace or two behind me peering into shop-windows, and suggest that we appropriate lodgings for ourselves at the Savoy or the Ritz. No Wells! He has vanished like his own Invisible Man!

"Wells?" I cry. "Wells, where are you?"

Silence. *Calma come la tomba.* Has he plunged unsuspecting into some unguarded abyss of the street? Or perhaps been snatched away by some silent machine of the Martians? How am I to survive without him in this dead city? It is Wells who has the knack of breaking into food shops and such, Wells who will meet all the practical challenges of our strange life here: not I.

"Wells!" I call again. There is panic in my voice, I fear.

But I am alone. He is utterly gone. What shall I do? Five minutes go by; ten, fifteen. Logic dictates that I remain right on this spot until he reappears, for how else shall we find each other in this huge city? But night is coming; I am suddenly afraid; I am weary and unutterably sad; I see my death looming before me now. I will go to the Savoy. Yes. Yes. I begin to walk, and then to run, as my terror mounts, along Southampton Street.

Then I am at the Strand, at last. There is the hotel; and there is Wells, arms folded, calmly waiting outside it for me.

"I thought you would come here," he says.

"Where have you been? Is this some prank, Wells?" I hotly demand.

"I called to you to follow me. You must not have heard me. Come: I must show you something, James."

"Now? For the love of God, Wells, I'm ready to drop!" But he will hear no protests, of course. He has me by the wrist; he drags me *away* from the hotel, back toward Covent Garden, over to little Henrietta Street. And there, pushed up against the facade of a shabby old building—Number 14, Henrietta Street—is the wreckage of some Martian machine, a kind of low motor-car with metallic tentacles, that has smashed itself in a wild career through the street. A dead Martian is visible through the shattered window of the passenger carriage. We stare a while in awe. "Do you see?" he asks, as though I could not. "They are not wholly invulnerable, it seems!" To which I agree, thinking only of finding a place where I can lie down; and then he allows us to withdraw, and we go to the hotel, which stands open to us, and ensconce ourselves in the most lavish suites we can find. I sleep as though I have not slept in months.

A DAY LATER YET.

It is beyond all belief, but the war is over, and we are, miraculously, free of the Martian terror!

Wells and I discovered, in the morning, a second motionless Martian machine standing like a sentinel at the approach to the Waterloo Bridge. Creeping fearlessly up to it, we saw that its backmost leg was frozen in flexed position, so that the thing was balanced only on two; with one good shove we might have been able to push the whole unstable mechanism over. Of the Martian in its cabin we could see no sign.

All during the day we roamed London, searching out the Martians. I felt strangely tranquil. Perhaps it was only my extreme fatigue; but certainly we were accustomed now to the desolation, to the tangles of the red weed, the packs of newly wild dogs.

Between the Strand and Grosvenor Square we came upon three more Martian machines: dead, dead, all dead. Then we heard a strange sound, emanating from the vicinity of the Marble Arch: "Ulla, ulla, ulla," it was, a mysterious sobbing howl. In the general silence that sound had tremendous power. It drew us; instead of fleeing, as sane men should have done, we approached. "Ulla, ulla!" A short distance down the Bayswater Road we saw a towering Martian fighting-machine looming above Hyde Park: the sound was coming from it. A signal of distress? A call to its distant cohorts, if any yet lived? Hands clapped to our ears—for the cry was deafening—we drew nearer still; and, suddenly, it stopped. There seemed an emphatic permanence to that stoppage. We waited. The sound did not begin anew.

"Dead," Wells said. "The last of them, I suspect. Crying a requiem for its race."

"What do you mean?" I asked.

"What our guns could not do, the lowly germs of Earth have achieved—I'll wager a year's earnings on that! Do you think, James, that the Martians had any way of defending themselves against our microbes? I have been waiting for this! I knew it would happen!"

Did he? He had never said a word.

July 7, Lamb House.

How sweet to be home!

And so it has ended, the long nightmare of the interplanetary war. Wells and I found, all over London, the wrecked and useless vehicles of the Martians, with their dead occupants trapped within. Dead, all dead, every invader. And as we walked about, other human beings came forth from hiding places, and we embraced one another in wild congratulation.

Wells's hypothesis was correct, as we all have learned by now. The Martians have perished in mid-conquest, victims of our terrestrial bacteria. No one has seen a living one anywhere in the past two weeks. We fugitive humans have returned to our homes; the wheels of civilization have begun to turn once more.

We are safe, yes—and yet we are not. Whether the Martians will return, fortified now against our microorganisms and ready to bend us once more to their wishes, we cannot say. But it is clear now to me that the little sense of security that we of Earth feel, most especially we inhabitants of England in the sixty-third year of the reign of Her Majesty Queen Victoria, is a pathetic illusion. Our world is no impregnable fortress. We stand open to the unpredictable sky. If Martians can come one day, Venusians may come another, or Jovians, or warlike beings from some wholly unknown star. The events of these weeks have been marvelous and terrible, and without shame I admit having derived great rewards even from my fear and my exertions; but we must all be aware now that we are at great risk of a reprise of these dark happenings. We have learned, now, that we are far from being the masters of the cosmos, as we like to suppose. It is a bitter lesson to be given at the outset of this glorious new century.

I discussed these points with Wells when he called here yesterday. He was in complete agreement.

And, as he was taking his leave, I went on, somewhat hesitantly, to express to him the other thought that had been forming in my mind all this past week. "You said once," I began, "that you had had some scheme in mind, even before the coming of the Martians, for writing a novel of interplanetary invasion. Is that still your intent now that fantasy has become fact, Wells?"

He allowed that it was.

"But it would not now be," I said, "your usual kind of fantastic fiction, would it? It would be more in the line of *reportage*, would you not say? An account of the responses of certain persons to the true and actual extreme event?"

"Of course it would, of necessity," he said. I smiled expressively and said nothing. And then, quickly divining my meaning, he added: "But of course I would yield, *cher maître*, if it were *your* intention to—"

"It is," I said serenely.

He was quite graceful about it, all in all. And so I will set to work tomorrow. *The Ambassadors* may perhaps be the grandest and finest of my novels, but it will have to wait another year or two, I suppose, for there is something much more urgent that must be written first.

[JAMES'S NOTEBOOKS INDICATE THAT HE did not actually begin work on his classic novel of interplanetary conflict, *The War of the Worlds*, until the 28th of July, 1900. The book was finished by the 17th of November, unusually quickly for James, and after serialization in *The Atlantic Monthly* (August–December, 1901) was published in England by Macmillan and Company in March, 1902 and in the United States by Harper & Brothers one month later. It has remained his most popular book ever since and has on three occasions been adapted for motion pictures. Wells never did write an account of his experiences during the Martian invasion, though those experiences did, of course, have a profound influence on his life and work thereafter. —*The Editor.*]

PUSH NO MORE

The 1970s, as I recall, was a pretty sexy decade, and it is not surprising that there would be some science-fiction anthologies back then that dealt with speculative aspects of sex. One of them was *Strange Bedfellows*, edited by a jovial San Franciscan named Thomas Scortia, and when Tom asked me in September 1971 to do a story for it I readily complied.

The strange bedfellow I chose to write about was a male virgin, no less, which you may think would be an odd choice for an anthology of erotic fiction. But my choice was not as odd as it seems at first glance. I was getting ready that month to write *Dying Inside*, a novel about the problems of a middle-aged twentieth-century New Yorker who has to cope with being a telepath, and the whole topic of extrasensory powers was much on my mind just then. For my contribution to the Scortia anthology I wrote about a different extrasensory manifestation—the poltergeist phenomenon—and that required me to have the story concern a young man who has never had any sexual experience, since the standard poltergeist theory maintains that most carriers of that ability are virginal adolescents, usually male. I have been a male virgin myself, though not in quite some time, and so it did not demand a terrific leap of the imagination to put myself into the mind of my youthful narrator, the lively, quirky, very horny Harry Blaufeld. I only had to invent the poltergeist part. But that simply goes with the job. The writer has to make things up; the science-fiction writer has to make up unusual things. As you see, I have told stories from the viewpoint of a dolphin, a computer, an alien living in a New York hotel, and many another a strange narrator; compared with those tasks, writing from the viewpoint of a young Jewish boy from New York who happened to be a poltergeist was hardly a challenging job at all.

—⁓—

I PUSH . . . AND THE SHOE MOVES. Will you look at that? It really moves! All I have to do is give a silent inner nudge, no hands, just reaching from the core of my mind, and my old worn-out brown shoe, the left one, goes sliding slowly across the floor of my bedroom. Past the chair, past the pile of beaten-up textbooks (Geometry, Second Year Spanish, Civic Studies, Biology, etc.), past my sweaty heap of discarded clothes. Indeed the shoe obeys me. Making a little swishing sound as it snags against the roughness of the elderly linoleum floor tiling. Look at it now, bumping gently into the far wall, tipping edge-up, stopping. Its voyage is over. I bet I could make it climb right up the wall. But don't bother doing it, man. Not just now. This is hard work. Just relax, Harry. Your arms are shaking. You're perspiring all over. Take it easy for a while. You don't have to prove everything all at once.

What have I proven, anyway?

It seems that I can make things move with my mind. How about that, man? Did you ever imagine that you had freaky powers? Not until this very night. This very lousy night. Standing there with Cindy Klein and finding that terrible knot of throbbing tension in my groin, like needing to take a leak only fifty times more intense, a zone of anguish spinning off some kind of fearful energy like a crazy dynamo implanted in my crotch. And suddenly, without any conscious awareness, finding a way of tapping that energy, drawing it up through my body to my head, amplifying it, and . . . *using* it. As I just did with my shoe. As I did a couple of hours earlier with Cindy. So you aren't just a dumb gawky adolescent schmuck, Harry Blaufeld. You are somebody very special.

You have power. You are potent.

How good it is to lie here in the privacy of my own musty bedroom and be able to make my shoe slide along the floor, simply by looking at it in that special way. The feeling of strength that I get from that! Tremendous. I am potent. I have power. That's what potent means, to have power, out of the Latin *potentia,* derived from *posse.* To be able. I am able. I can do this most extraordinary thing. And not just in fitful unpredictable bursts. It's under my conscious control. All I have to do is dip into that reservoir of tension and skim off a few watts of *push.* Far out! What a weird night this is.

Let's go back three hours. To a time when I know nothing of this *potentia* in me. Three hours ago I know only from horniness. I'm standing outside Cindy's front door with her at half past ten. We have done the going-to-the-movies thing, we have done the cappuccino-afterward thing, now I want to do the makeout thing. I'm trying to get myself invited inside, knowing that her parents have gone away for the weekend and there's nobody home except her older brother, who is seeing his girl in Scarsdale tonight and won't be back for hours, and once I'm past Cindy's front door I hope, well, to get invited inside. (What a coy metaphor! You know what I mean.) So three cheers for Casanova Blaufeld, who is suffering a bad attack of inflammation of the cherry. Look at me, stammering, fumbling for words, shifting my weight from foot to foot, chewing on my lips, going red in the face. All my pimples light up like beacons when I blush. Come on, Blaufeld, pull yourself together. Change your image of yourself. Try this on for size: you're twenty-three years old, tall, strong, suave, a man of the world, veteran of so many beds you've lost count. Bushy beard that girls love to run their hands through. Big drooping handlebar mustachios. And you aren't asking her for any favors. You aren't whining and wheedling and saying please, Cindy, let's do it, because you know you don't need to say please. It's no boon you seek: you give as good as you get, right, so it's a mutually beneficial transaction, right? Right? Wrong. You're as suave as a pig. You want to exploit her for the sake of your own grubby needs. You know you'll be inept. But let's pretend, at least. Straighten the shoulders, suck in the gut, inflate the chest. Harry Blaufeld, the devilish seducer. Get your hands on her sweater for starters. No one's around; it's a dark night. Go for the boobs, get her hot. Isn't that what Jimmy the Greek told you to do? So you try it. Grinning stupidly, practically apologizing with your eyes. Reaching out. The grabby fingers connecting with the fuzzy purple fabric.

Her face, flushed and big-eyed. Her mouth, thin-lipped and wide. Her voice, harsh and wire-edged. She says, "Don't be disgusting, Harry. Don't be *silly*." Silly. Backing away from me like I've turned into a monster with eight eyes and green fangs. Don't be disgusting. She tries to slip into the house fast, before I can paw her again. I stand there watching her fumble for her key, and this terrible rage starts to rise in me. Why disgusting? Why silly? All I wanted was to show her my love, right? That I really care for her, that I *relate* to her. A display of affection through physical contact. Right? So I reached out. A little caress. Prelude to tender intimacy. "Don't be disgusting," she said. "Don't be *silly*." The trivial little immature bitch. And now I feel the anger mounting. Down between my legs there's this hideous pain, this throbbing sensation of anguish, this purely sexual tension, and it's pouring out into my belly, spreading upward along my gut like a stream of flame. A dam has broken somewhere inside me. I feel fire blazing under the top of my skull. And there it is! The power! The strength! I don't question it. I don't ask myself what it is or where it came from. I just push her, hard, from ten feet away, a quick furious shove. It's like an invisible hand against her breasts—I can see the front of her sweater flatten out—and she topples backward, clutching at the air, and goes over on her ass. I've knocked her sprawling without touching her. "Harry," she mumbles. "Harry?"

My anger's gone. Now I feel terror. What have I done? How? How? Down on her ass, *boom*. From ten feet away!

I run all the way home, never looking back.

FOOTSTEPS IN THE HALLWAY, *CLICKETY-CLACK*. My sister is home from her date with Jimmy the Greek. That isn't his name. Aristides Pappas is who he really is. Ari, she calls him. Jimmy the Greek, I call him, but not to his face. He's nine feet tall with black greasy hair and a tremendous beak of a nose that comes straight out of his forehead. He's twenty-seven years old and he's laid a thousand girls. Sara is going to marry him next year. Meanwhile they see each other three nights a week and they screw a lot. She's never said a word to me about that, about the screwing, but I know. Sure they screw. Why not? They're going to get married, aren't they? And they're adults. She's nineteen years old, so it's legal for her to screw. I won't be nineteen for four years and four months. It's legal for me to screw now, I think. If only. If only I had somebody. If only.

Clickety-clickety-clack. There she goes, into her room. *Blunk.* That's her door closing. She doesn't give a damn if she wakes the whole family up. Why should she care? She's all turned on now. Soaring on her memories of what she was just doing with Jimmy the Greek. That warm feeling. The afterglow, the book calls it.

I wonder how they do it when they do it.

They go to his apartment. Do they take off all their clothes first? Do they talk before they begin? A drink or two? Smoke a joint? Sara claims she doesn't smoke it. I bet she's putting me on. They get naked. Christ, he's so tall, he must have a dong a foot long. Doesn't it scare her? They lie down on the bed together. Or on a couch. The floor, maybe? A thick fluffy carpet? He touches her body. Doing the foreplay stuff. I've read about it. He strokes the breasts, making the nipples go erect. I've seen her nipples.

They aren't any bigger than mine. How tall do they get when they're erect? An inch? Three inches? Standing up like a couple of pink pencils? And his hand must go down below, too. There's this thing you're supposed to touch, this tiny bump of flesh hidden inside there. I've studied the diagrams and I still don't know where it is. Jimmy the Greek knows where it is, you can bet your ass. So he touches her there. Then what? She must get hot, right? How can he tell when it's time to go inside her? The time arrives. They're finally doing it. You know, I can't visualize it. He's on top of her and they're moving up and down, sure, but I still can't imagine how the bodies fit together, how they really move, how they do it.

She's getting undressed now, right across the hallway. Off with the shirt, the slacks, the bra, the panties, whatever the hell she wears. I can hear her moving around. I wonder if her door is really closed tight. It's a long time since I've had a good look at her. Who knows, maybe her nipples are still standing up. Even if her door's open only a few inches, I can see into her room from mine, if I hunch down here in the dark and peek.

But her door's closed. What if I reach out and give it a little nudge? From here. I pull the power up into my head, yes . . . reach . . . *push* . . . ah . . . yes! Yes! It moves! One inch, two, three. That's good enough. I can see a slice of her room. The light's on. Hey, there she goes! Too fast, out of sight. I think she was naked. Now she's coming back. Naked, yes. Her back is to me. You've got a cute ass, Sis, you know that? Turn around, turn around, turn around . . . ah. Her nipples look the same as always. Not standing up at all. I guess they must go back down after it's all over. *Thy two breasts are like two young roes that are twins, which feed among the lilies.* (I don't really read the Bible a lot, just the dirty parts.) Cindy's got bigger ones than you, Sis, I bet she has. Unless she pads them. I couldn't tell tonight. I was too excited to notice whether I was squeezing flesh or rubber.

Sara's putting her housecoat on. One last flash of thigh and belly, then no more. Damn. Into the bathroom now. The sound of

water running. She's getting washed. Now the tap is off. And now
... *tinkle, tinkle, tinkle.* I can picture her sitting there, grinning to
herself, taking a happy piss, thinking cozy thoughts about what
she and Jimmy the Greek did tonight. Oh, Christ, I hurt! I'm jealous of my own sister! That she can do it three times a week while
I ... am nowhere ... with nobody ... no one ... nothing ...

Let's give Sis a little surprise.

Hmm. Can I manipulate something that's out of my direct line
of sight? Let's try it. The toilet seat is in the right-hand corner of
the bathroom, under the window. And the flush knob is—let me
think—on the side closer to the wall, up high—yes. Okay, reach
out, man. Grab it before she does. *Push* ... down ... *push.* Yeah!
Listen to that, man! You flushed it for her without leaving your
own room!

She's going to have a hard time figuring that one out.

SUNDAY: A RAINY DAY, A day of worrying. I can't get the strange
events of last night out of my mind. This power of mine—where
did it come from, what can I use it for? And I can't stop fretting
over the awareness that I'll have to face Cindy again first thing
tomorrow morning, in our Biology class. What will she say to me?
Does she realize I actually wasn't anywhere near her when I
knocked her down? If she knows I have a power, is she frightened
of me? Will she report me to the Society for the Prevention of
Supernatural Phenomena, or whoever looks after such things?
I'm tempted to pretend I'm sick, and stay home from school
tomorrow. But what's the sense of that? I can't avoid her forever.

The more tense I get, the more intensely I feel the power surging within me. It's very strong today. (The rain may have something to do with that. Every nerve is twitching. The air is damp
and maybe that makes me more conductive.) When nobody is
looking, I experiment. In the bathroom, standing far from the
sink, I unscrew the top of the toothpaste tube. I turn the water
taps on and off. I open and close the window. How fine my

control is! Doing these things is a strain: I tremble, I sweat, I feel the muscles of my jaws knotting up, my back teeth ache. But I can't resist the kick of exercising my skills. I get riskily mischievous. At breakfast, my mother puts four slices of bread in the toaster; sitting with my back to it, I delicately work the toaster's plug out of the socket, so that when she goes over to investigate five minutes later, she's bewildered to find the bread still raw. "How did the plug slip out?" she asks, but of course no one tells her. Afterward, as we all sit around reading the Sunday papers, I turn the television set on by remote control, and the sudden blaring of a cartoon show makes everyone jump. And a few hours later I unscrew a light bulb in the hallway, gently, gently, easing it from its fixture, holding it suspended close to the ceiling for a moment, then letting it crash to the floor. "What was that?" my mother says in alarm. My father inspects the hall. "Bulb fell out of the fixture and smashed itself to bits." My mother shakes her head. "How could a bulb fall out? It isn't possible." And my father says, "It must have been loose." He doesn't sound convinced. It must be occurring to him that a bulb loose enough to fall to the floor couldn't have been lit. And this bulb had been lit.

How soon before my sister connects these incidents with the episode of the toilet that flushed by itself?

MONDAY IS HERE. I ENTER the classroom through the rear door and skulk to my seat. Cindy hasn't arrived yet. But now here she comes. God, how beautiful she is! The gleaming, shimmering red hair, down to her shoulders. The pale flawless skin. The bright, mysterious eyes. The purple sweater, same one as Saturday night. My hands have touched that sweater. I've touched that sweater with my power, too.

I bend low over my notebook. I can't bear to look at her. I'm a coward.

But I force myself to look up. She's standing in the aisle, up by the front of the room, staring at me. Her expression is strange—edgy, uneasy, the lips clamped tight. As if she's thinking of coming back here to talk to me but is hesitating. The moment she sees me watching her, she glances away and takes her seat. All through the hour I sit hunched forward, studying her shoulders, the back of her neck, the tips of her ears. Five desks separate her from me. I let out a heavy romantic sigh. Temptation is tickling me. It would be so easy to reach across that distance and touch her. Gently stroking her soft cheek with an invisible fingertip. Lightly fondling the side of her throat. Using my special power to say a tender hello to her. See, Cindy? See what I can do to show my love? Having imagined it, I find myself unable to resist doing it. I summon the force from the churning reservoir in my depths; I pump it upward and simultaneously make the automatic calculations of intensity of push. Then I realize what I'm doing. Are you crazy, man? She'll scream. She'll jump out of her chair like she was stung. She'll roll on the floor and have hysterics. Hold back, hold back, you lunatic! At the last moment I manage to deflect the impulse. Gasping, grunting, I twist the force away from Cindy and hurl it blindly in some other direction. My random thrust sweeps across the room like a whiplash and intersects the big framed chart of the plant and animal kingdoms that hangs on the classroom's left-hand wall. It rips loose as though kicked by a tornado and soars twenty feet on a diagonal arc that sends it crashing into the blackboard. The frame shatters. Broken glass sprays everywhere. The class is thrown into panic. Everybody yelling, running around, picking up pieces of glass, exclaiming in awe, asking questions. I sit like a statue. Then I start to shiver. And Cindy, very slowly, turns and looks at me. A chilly look of horror freezes her face.

She knows, then. She thinks I'm some sort of freak. She thinks I'm some sort of monster.

POLTERGEIST. THAT'S WHAT I AM. That's me.

I've been to the library. I've done some homework in the occultism section. So: Harry Blaufeld, boy poltergeist. From the German, *poltern,* "to make a noise," and *geist,* "spirit." Thus, poltergeist = "noisy spirit." Poltergeists make plates go smash against the wall, pictures fall suddenly to the floor, doors bang when no one is near them, rocks fly through the air.

I'm not sure whether it's proper to say that I *am* a poltergeist, or that I'm merely the host for one. It depends on which theory you prefer. True-blue occultists like to think that poltergeists are wandering demons or spirits that occasionally take up residence in human beings, through whom they focus their energies and play their naughty tricks. On the other hand, those who hold a more scientific attitude toward paranormal extrasensory phenomena say that it's absurdly medieval to believe in wandering demons; to them, a poltergeist is simply someone who's capable of harnessing a paranormal ability within himself that allows him to move things without touching them. Myself, I incline toward the latter view. It's much more flattering to think that I have an extraordinary psychic gift than that I've been possessed by a marauding demon. Also less scary.

Poltergeists are nothing new. A Chinese book about a thousand years old called *Gossip from the Jade Hall* tells of one that disturbed the peace of a monastery by flinging crockery around. The monks hired an exorcist to get things under control, but the noisy spirit gave him the works: "His cap was pulled off and thrown against the wall, his robe was loosed, and even his trousers pulled off, which caused him to retire precipitately." Right on, poltergeist! "Others tried where he had failed, but they were rewarded for their pains by a rain of insolent missives from the air, upon which were written words of malice and bitter odium."

The archives bulge with such tales from many lands and many eras. Consider the Clarke case, Oakland, California, 1874. On hand: Mr. Clarke, a successful businessman of austere and reserved ways, and his wife and adolescent daughter and eight-year-old son, plus two of Mr. Clarke's sisters and two male house guests. On the night of April 23, as everyone prepares for bed, the front doorbell rings. No one there. Rings again a few minutes later. No one there.

Sound of furniture being moved in the parlor. One of the house guests, a banker named Bayley, inspects, in the dark, and is hit by a chair. No one there. A box of silverware comes floating down the stairs and lands with a bang. (Poltergeist = "noisy spirit.") A heavy box of coal flies about next. A chair hits Bayley on the elbow and lands against a bed. In the dining room a massive oak chair rises two feet in the air, spins, lets itself down, chases the unfortunate Bayley around the room in front of three witnesses. And so on. Much spooked, everybody goes to bed, but all night they hear crashes and rumbling sounds; in the morning they find all the downstairs furniture in a scramble. Also the front door, which was locked and bolted, has been ripped off its hinges. More such events the next night. Likewise on the next, culminating in a female shriek out of nowhere, so terrible that it drives the Clarkes and guests to take refuge in another house. No explanation for any of this ever offered.

A man named Charles Fort, who died in 1932, spent much of his life studying poltergeist phenomena and similar mysteries. Fort wrote four fat books which so far I've only skimmed. They're full of newspaper accounts of strange things like the sudden appearance of several young crocodiles on English farms in the middle of the nineteenth century, and rainstorms in which the earth was pelted with snakes, frogs, blood, or stones. He collected clippings describing instances of coal-heaps and houses and even human beings suddenly and spontaneously bursting into flame. Luminous objects sailing through the sky. Invisible hands that mutilate animals and people. "Phantom bullets" shattering the windows of houses. Inexplicable disappearances of human beings, and equally inexplicable reappearances far away. Et cetera, et cetera, et cetera. I gather that Fort believed that most of these phenomena were the work of beings from interplanetary space who meddle in events on our world for their own amusement. But he couldn't explain away everything like that. Poltergeists in particular didn't fit into his bogeymen-from-space fantasy, and so, he wrote, "Therefore I regard poltergeists as evil or false or discordant or absurd . . ." Still, he said, "I don't care to deny poltergeists, because I suspect that later, when we're more enlightened, or when we widen the range of our credulities, or take on more of that increase of ignorance that is called knowledge, poltergeists may become assimilable. Then they'll be as reasonable as trees."

I like Fort. He was eccentric and probably very gullible, but he wasn't foolish or crazy. I don't think he's right about beings from interplanetary space, but I admire his attitude toward the inexplicable.

Most of the poltergeist cases on record are frauds. They've been exposed by experts. There was the 1944 episode in Wild Plum, North Dakota, in which lumps of burning coal began to jump out of a bucket in the one-room schoolhouse of Mrs. Pauline Rebel. Papers caught fire on the pupils' desks and charred spots appeared on the curtains. The class dictionary moved around of its own accord. There was talk in town of demonic forces. A few days later, after an assistant state attorney general had begun interrogating people, four of Mrs. Rebel's pupils confessed that they had been tossing the coal around to terrorize their teacher. They'd done most of the dirty work while her back was turned or when she had had her glasses off. A prank. A hoax. Some people would tell you that all poltergeist stories are equally phony. I'm here to testify that they aren't.

One pattern is consistent in all genuine poltergeist incidents: an adolescent is invariably involved, or a child on the edge of adolescence. This is the "naughty child" theory of poltergeists, first put forth by Frank Podmore in 1890 in the *Proceedings of the Society for Psychical Research.* (See, I've done my homework very thoroughly.) The child is usually unhappy, customarily over sexual matters, and suffers either from a sense of not being wanted or from frustration, or both. There are no statistics on the matter, but the lore indicates that teenagers involved in poltergeist activity are customarily virgins.

The 1874 Clarke case, then, becomes the work of the adolescent daughter, who—I would guess—had a yen for Mr. Bayley. The multitude of cases cited by Fort, most of them dating from the nineteenth century, show a bunch of poltergeist kids flinging stuff around in a sexually repressed era. That seething energy had to go somewhere. I discovered my own poltering power while in an acute state of palpitating lust for Cindy Klein, who wasn't having any part of me. Especially *that* part. But instead of exploding from the sheer force of my bottled-up yearnings I suddenly found a way of channeling all that drive outward. And pushed . . .

Fort again: "Wherein children are atavistic, they may be in rapport with forces that most human beings have outgrown." Atavism: a strange recurrence to the primitive past. Perhaps in Neanderthal times we were all poltergeists, but most of us lost it over the millennia. But see Fort, also: "There are of course other explanations of the 'occult power' of children. One is that children, instead of being atavistic, may occasionally be far in advance of adults, foreshadowing coming human powers, because their minds are not stifled by conventions. After that, they go to school and lose their superiority. Few boy-prodigies have survived an education."

I feel reassured, knowing I'm just a statistic in a long-established pattern of paranormal behavior. Nobody likes to think he's a freak, even when he is a freak. Here I am, virginal, awkward, owlish, quirky, precocious, edgy, uncertain, timid, clever, solemn, socially inept, stumbling through all the standard problems of the immediately post-pubescent years. I have pimples and wet dreams and the sort of fine fuzz that isn't worth shaving, only I shave it anyway. Cindy Klein thinks I'm silly and disgusting. And I've got this hot core of fury and frustration in my gut, which is my great curse and my great supremacy. I'm a poltergeist, man. Go on, give me a hard time, make fun of me, call me silly and disgusting. The next time I may not just knock you on your ass. I might heave you all the way to Pluto.

AN UNAVOIDABLE HUMILIATING ENCOUNTER WITH Cindy today. At lunchtime I go into Schindler's for my usual bacon-lettuce-tomato; I take a seat in one of the back booths and open a book and someone says, "Harry," and there she is at the booth just opposite, with three of her friends. What do I do? Get up and run out? Poltergeist her into the next county? Already I feel the power twitching in me. Mrs. Schindler brings me my sandwich. I'm stuck. I can't bear to be here. I hand her the money and mutter, "Just remembered, got to make a phone call." Sandwich in hand, I start to leave, giving Cindy a foolish hot-cheeked grin as I go by. She's looking at me fiercely. Those deep green eyes of hers terrify me.

"Wait," she says. "Can I ask you something?"

She slides out of her booth and blocks the aisle of the luncheonette. She's nearly as tall as I am, and I'm tall. My knees are shaking. God in heaven, Cindy, don't trap me like this, I'm not responsible for what I might do.

She says in a low voice, "Yesterday in Bio, when that chart hit the blackboard. You did that, didn't you?"

"I don't understand."

"You made it jump across the room."

"That's impossible," I mumble. "What do you think I am, a magician?"

"I don't know. And Saturday night, that dumb scene outside my house—"

"I'd rather not talk about it."

"I would. How did you do that to me, Harry? Where did you learn the trick?"

"Trick? Look, Cindy, I've absolutely got to go."

"You pushed me over. You just looked at me and I felt a push."

"You tripped," I say. "You just fell down."

She laughs. Right now she seems about nineteen years old and I feel about nine years old. "Don't put me on," she says, her voice a deep sophisticated drawl. Her girlfriends are peering at us, trying to overhear. "Listen, this interests me. I'm involved. I want to know how you do that stuff."

"There isn't any stuff," I tell her, and suddenly I know I have to escape. I give her the tiniest push, not touching her, of course, just a wee mental nudge, and she feels it and gives ground, and I rush miserably past her, cramming my sandwich into my mouth. I flee the store. At the door I look back and see her smiling, waving to me, telling me to come back.

I HAVE A RICH FANTASY life. Sometimes I'm a movie star, twenty-two years old with a palace in the Hollywood hills, and I give parties that Peter Fonda and Dustin Hoffman and Julie Christie and Faye Dunaway come to, and we all turn on and get naked and swim in my pool and afterward I make it with five or six starlets all at once. Sometimes I'm a famous novelist, author of the book that really gets it together and speaks for My Generation, and I stand around in Brentano's in a glittering science-fiction costume signing thousands of autographs, and afterward I go to my penthouse high over First Avenue and make it with a dazzling young lady editor. Sometimes I'm a great scientist, four years out of Harvard Medical School and already acclaimed for my pioneering research in genetic reprogramming of unborn children, and when the phone rings to notify me of my Nobel Prize I'm just about to reach my third climax of the evening with a celebrated Metropolitan Opera soprano who wants me to design a son for her who'll eclipse Caruso. And sometimes—

But why go on? That's all fantasy. Fantasy is dumb because it encourages you to live a self-deluding life, instead of coming to grips with reality. Consider reality, Harry. Consider the genuine article that is Harry Blaufeld. The genuine article is something pimply and ungainly and naïve, something that shrieks with every molecule of his skinny body that he's not quite fifteen and has never made it with a girl and doesn't know how to go about it and is terribly afraid that he never will. Mix equal parts of desire and self-pity. And a dash of incompetence and a dollop of insecurity. Season lightly with extrasensory powers. You're a long way from the Hollywood hills, boy.

IS THERE SOME WAY I can harness my gift for the good of mankind? What if all these ghastly power plants, belching black smoke into the atmosphere, could be shut down forever, and humanity's electrical needs were met by a trained corps of youthful poltergeists, volunteers living a monastic life and using their sizzling sexual tensions as the fuel that keeps the turbines spinning? Or perhaps NASA wants a poltergeist-driven spaceship. There I am, lean and bronzed and jaunty, a handsome figure in my white astronaut suit, taking my seat in the command capsule of the *Mars One*. T minus thirty seconds and counting. An anxious world awaits the big moment. Five. Four. Three. Two. One. Lift-off. And I grin my world-famous grin and coolly summon my power and open the mental throttle and push, and the mighty vessel rises, hovering serenely a moment above the launching pad, rises and climbs, slicing like a giant glittering needle through the ice-blue Florida sky, soaring up and away on man's first voyage to the red planet. . . .

Another experiment is called for. I'll try to send a beer can to the moon. If I can do that, I should be able to send a spaceship. A simple Newtonian process, a matter of attaining escape velocity; and I don't think thrust is likely to be a determining quantitative function. A push is a push is a push, and so far I haven't noticed limitations of mass, so if I can get it up with a beer can, I ought to succeed in throwing anything of any mass into space. I think. Anyway, I raid the family garbage and go outside clutching a crumpled Schlitz container. A mild misty night; the moon isn't visible. No matter. I place the can on the ground and contemplate it. Five. Four. Three. Two. One. Lift-off. I grin my world-famous grin. I coolly summon my power and open the mental throttle. *Push.* Yes, the beer can rises. Hovering serenely a moment above the pavement. Rises and climbs, end over end, slicing like a crumpled beer can through the muggy air. Up. Up. Into the darkness. Long after it disappears, I continue to push. Am I still in contact? Does it still climb? I have no way of telling. I lack the proper tracking stations. Perhaps it does travel on and on through the lonely void, on a perfect lunar trajectory. Or maybe it has already tumbled down, a block away, skulling some hapless cop. I shot a beer can into the air, it fell to earth I know not where. Shrugging, I go back into the house. So much for my career as a spaceman. Blaufeld, you've pulled off another dumb fantasy. Blaufeld, how can you stand being such a silly putz?

CLICKETY-CLACK. FOUR IN THE MORNING, Sara's just coming in from her date. Here I am lying awake like a worried parent. Notice that the parents themselves don't worry: they're fast asleep, I bet, giving no damns about the hours their daughter keeps. Whereas I brood. She got laid again tonight, no doubt of it. Possibly twice. Grimly I try to reconstruct the event in my imagination. The positions, the sounds of flesh against flesh, the panting and moaning. How often has she done it now? A hundred times? Three hundred? She's been doing it at least since she was sixteen. I'm sure of that. For girls it's so much easier; they don't need to chase and coax, all they have to do is say yes. Sara says yes a lot. Before Jimmy the Greek there was Greasy Kid Stuff, and before him there was the Spade Wonder, and before him . . .

Out there tonight in this city there are three million people at the very minimum who just got laid. I detest adults and their easy screwing. They devalue it by doing it so much. They just have to roll over and grab some meat, and away they go, in and out, oooh oooh oooh ahhh. Christ, how boring it must get! If they could only look at it from the point of view of a frustrated adolescent again. The hungry virgin, on the outside peering in. Excluded from the world of screwing. Feeling that delicious sweet tension of wanting and not knowing how to get. The fiery knot of longing, sitting like a ravenous tapeworm in my belly, devouring my soul. I magnify sex. I exalt it. I multiply its wonders. It'll never live up to my anticipations. But I love the tension of anticipating and speculating and not getting. In fact, I think sometimes I'd like to spend my whole life on the edge of the blade, looking forward always to being deflowered but never quite taking the steps that would bring it about. A dynamic stasis, sustaining and enhancing my special power. Harry Blaufeld, virgin and poltergeist. Why not? Anybody at all can screw. Idiots, morons, bores, uglies. Everybody does it. There's magic in renunciation. If I keep myself aloof, pure, unique . . .

Push . . .

I do my little poltergeisty numbers. I stack and restack my textbooks without leaving my bed. I move my shirt from the floor to the back of the chair. I turn the chair around to face the wall. Push . . . push . . . push . . .

Water running in the john. Sara's washing up. What's it like, Sara? How does it feel when he puts it in you? We don't talk much, you and I. You think I'm a child; you patronize me, you give me cute winks, your voice goes up half an octave. Do you wink at Jimmy the Greek like that? Like hell. And you talk husky contralto to him. Sit down and talk to me some time, Sis. I'm teetering on the brink of manhood. Guide me out of my virginity. Tell me what girls like guys to say to them. Sure. You won't tell me shit, Sara. You want me to stay your baby brother forever, because that enhances your own sense of being grown up. And you screw and screw and screw, you and Jimmy the Greek, and you don't even understand the mystical significance of the act of intercourse. To you it's just good sweaty fun, like going bowling. Right? Right? Oh, you miserable bitch! Screw you, Sara!

A shriek from the bathroom. Christ, what have I done now? I better go see.

Sara, naked, kneels on the cold tiles. Her head is in the bathtub and she's clinging with both hands to the bathtub's rim and she's shaking violently.

"You okay?" I ask. "What happened?"

"Like a kick in the back," she says hoarsely. "I was at the sink, washing my face, and I turned around and something hit me like a kick in the back and knocked me halfway across the room."

"You okay, though? You aren't hurt?"

"Help me up."

She's upset but not injured. She's so upset that she forgets that she's naked, and without putting on her robe she cuddles up against me, trembling. She seems small and fragile and scared. I stroke her bare back where I imagine she felt the blow. Also I sneak a look at her nipples, just to see if they're still standing up after her date with Jimmy the Greek. They aren't. I soothe her with my fingers. I feel very manly and protective, even if it's only my cruddy dumb sister I'm protecting.

"What could have happened?" she asks. "You weren't pulling any tricks, were you?"

"I was in bed," I say, totally sincere.

"A lot of funny things been going on around this house lately," she says.

CINDY, CATCHING ME IN THE hallway between Geometry and Spanish: "How come you never call me any more?"

"Been busy."

"Busy how?"

"Busy."

"I guess you must be," she says. "Looks to me like you haven't slept in a week. What's her name?"

"Her? No her. I've just been busy." I try to escape. Must I push her again? "A research project."

"You could take some time out for relaxing. You should keep in touch with old friends."

"Friends? What kind of friend are you? You said I was silly. You said I was disgusting. Remember, Cindy?"

"The emotions of the moment. I was off balance. I mean, psychologically. Look, let's talk about all this some time, Harry. Some time soon."

"Maybe."

"If you're not doing anything Saturday night—"

I look at her in astonishment. She's actually asking me for a date! Why is she pursuing me? What does she want from me? Is she itching for another chance to humiliate me? Silly and disgusting, disgusting and silly. I look at my watch and quirk up my lips. Time to move along.

"I'm not sure," I tell her. "I may have some work to do."

"Work?"

"Research," I say. "I'll let you know."

A NIGHT OF HAPPY EXPERIMENTS. I unscrew a light bulb, float it from one side of my room to the other, return it to the fixture, and efficiently *screw it back in*. Precision control. I go up to the roof and launch another beer can to the moon, only this time I loft it a thousand feet, bring it back, kick it up even higher, bring it back, send it off a third time with a tremendous accumulated kinetic energy, and I have no doubt it'll cleave through space. I pick up trash in the street from a hundred yards away and throw it in the trash basket. Lastly—most scary of all—I polt *myself*. I levitate a little, lifting myself five feet into the air. That's as high as I dare go. (What if I lose the power and fall?) If I had the courage, I could fly. I can do anything. Give me the right fulcrum and I'll move the world. O, *potentia!* What a fantastic trip this is!

AFTER TWO AWFUL DAYS OF inner debate I phone Cindy and make a date for Saturday. I'm not sure whether it's a good idea. Her sudden new aggressiveness turns me off, slightly, but nevertheless it's a novelty to have a girl chasing me, and who am I to snub her? I wonder what she's up to, though. Coming on so interested in me after dumping me mercilessly on our last date. I'm still angry with her about that, but I can't hold a grudge, not with *her*. Maybe she wants to make amends. We did have a pretty decent relationship in the nonphysical sense, until that one stupid evening. Jesus, what if she really *does* want to make amends, all the way? She scares me. I guess I'm a little bit of a coward. Or a lot of a coward. I don't understand any of this, man. I think I'm getting into something very heavy.

I JUGGLE THREE TENNIS BALLS and keep them all in the air at once, with my hands in my pockets. I see a woman trying to park her car in a space that's too small, and as I pass by I give her a sneaky little assist by pushing against the car behind her space; it moves backward a foot and a half, and she has room to park. Friday afternoon, in my gym class, I get into a basketball game and on five separate occasions when Mike Kisiak goes driving in for one of his sure-thing lay-ups I flick the ball away from the hoop. He can't figure out why he's off form and it really kills him. There seem to be no limits to what I can do. I'm awed at it myself. I gain skill from day to day. I might just be an authentic superman.

CINDY AND HARRY, HARRY AND Cindy, warm and cozy, sitting on her living-room couch. Christ, I think I'm being seduced! How can this be happening? To me? Christ. Christ. Christ. Cindy and Harry. Harry and Cindy. Where are we heading tonight?

In the movie house Cindy snuggles close. Midway through the flick I take the hint. A big bold move: slipping my arm around her shoulders. She wriggles so that my hand slides down through her armpit and comes to rest grasping her right breast. My cheeks blaze. I do as if to pull back, as if I've touched a hot stove, but she clamps her arm over my forearm. Trapped. I explore her yielding flesh. No padding there, just authentic Cindy. She's so eager and easy that it terrifies me. Afterward we go for sodas. In the shop she turns on the body language something frightening—gleaming

eyes, suggestive smiles, little steamy twistings of her shoulders. I feel
like telling her not to be so obvious about it. It's like living one of
my own wet dreams.

Back to her place, now. It starts to rain. We stand outside, in
the very spot where I stood when I polted her the last time. I can
write the script effortlessly. "Why don't you come inside for a
while, Harry?" "I'd love to." "Here, dry your feet on the doormat.
Would you like some hot chocolate?" "Whatever you're having,
Cindy." "No, whatever you'd like to have." "Hot chocolate would
be fine, then." Her parents aren't home. Her older brother is for-
nicating in Scarsdale. The rain hammers at the windows. The
house is big, expensive-looking, thick carpets, fancy draperies.
Cindy in the kitchen, puttering at the stove. Harry in the living
room, fidgeting at the bookshelves. Then Cindy and Harry, Harry
and Cindy, warm and cozy, together on the couch. Hot chocolate:
two sips apiece. Her lips near mine. Silently begging me. Come
on, dope, bend forward. Be a *mensch*. We kiss. We've kissed before,
but this time it's with tongues. Christ. Christ. I don't believe this.
Suave old Casanova Blaufeld swinging into action like a well-oiled
seducing machine. Her perfume in my nostrils, my tongue in her
mouth, my hand on her sweater, and then, unexpectedly, my
hand is *under* her sweater, and then, astonishingly, my other hand
is on her knee, and up under her skirt, and her thigh is satiny and
cool, and I sit there having this weird two-dimensional feeling
that I'm not an autonomous human being but just somebody on
the screen in a movie rated X, aware that thousands of people out
there in the audience are watching me with held breath, and I
don't dare let them down. I continue, not letting myself pause to
examine what's happening, not thinking at all, turning off my
mind completely, just going forward step by step. I know that if I
ever halt and back off to ask myself if this is real, it'll all blow up
in my face. She's helping me. She knows much more about this
than I do. Murmuring softly. Encouraging me. My fingers scrabbling at our undergarments. "Don't rush it," she whispers. "We've

got all the time in the world." My body pressing urgently against hers. Somehow now I'm not puzzled by the mechanics of the thing. So this is how it happens. What a miracle of evolution that we're designed to fit together this way! "Be gentle," she says, the way girls always say in the novels, and I want to be gentle, but how can I be gentle when I'm riding a runaway chariot? I push, not with my mind but with my body, and suddenly I feel this wondrous velvety softness enfolding me, and I begin to move fast, unable to hold back, and she moves too and we clasp each other and I'm swept helter-skelter along into a whirlpool. Down and down and down. "Harry!" she gasps and I explode uncontrollably and I know it's over. Hardly begun, and it's over. Is that it? That's it. That's all there is to it, the moving, the clasping, the gasping, the explosion. It felt good, but not *that* good, not as good as in my feverish virginal hallucinations I hoped it would be, and a backwash of let-down rips through me at the realization that it isn't transcendental after all, it isn't a mystic thing, it's just a body thing that starts and continues and ends. Abruptly I want to pull away and be alone to think. But I know I mustn't, I have to be tender and grateful now, I hold her in my arms, I whisper soft things to her, I tell her how good it was, she tells me how good it was. We're both lying, but so what? It *was* good. In retrospect it's starting to seem fantastic, overwhelming, all the things I wanted it to be. The *idea* of what we've done blows my mind. If only it hadn't been over so fast. No matter. Next time will be better. We've crossed a frontier; we're in unfamiliar territory now.

Much later she says, "I'd like to know how you make things move without touching them."

I shrug. "Why do you want to know?"

"It fascinates me. *You* fascinate me. I thought for a long time you were just another fellow, you know, kind of clumsy, kind of immature. But then this gift of yours. It's ESP, isn't it, Harry? I've read a lot about it. I know. The moment you knocked me down, I knew what it must have been. Wasn't it?"

Why be coy with her?

"Yes," I say, proud in my new manhood. "As a matter of fact, it's a classic poltergeist manifestation. When I gave you that shove, it was the first I knew I had the power. But I've been developing it. You wouldn't believe some of the things I've been able to do lately." My voice is deep; my manner is assured. I have graduated into my own fantasy self tonight.

"Show me," she says. "Poltergeist something, Harry!"

"Anything. You name it."

"That chair."

"Of course." I survey the chair. I reach for the power. It does not come. The chair stays where it is. What about the saucer, then? No. The spoon? No. "Cindy, I don't understand it, but—it doesn't seem to be working right now . . ."

"You must be tired."

"Yes. That's it. Tired. A good night's sleep and I'll have it again. I'll phone you in the morning and give you a real demonstration." Hastily buttoning my shirt. Looking for my shoes. Her parents will walk in any minute. Her brother. "Listen, a wonderful evening, unforgettable, tremendous—"

"Stay a little longer."

"I really can't."

Out into the rain.

HOME. STUNNED. I PUSH . . . and the shoe sits there. I look up at the light fixture. Nothing. The bulb will not turn. The power is gone. What will become of me now? Commander Blaufeld, space hero! No. No. Nothing. I will drop back into the ordinary rut of mankind. I will be . . . *a husband.* I will be . . . *an employee.* And push no more. And push no more. Can I even lift my shirt and flip it to the floor? No. No. Gone. Every shred, gone. I pull the covers over my head. I put my hands to my deflowered maleness. That alone responds. There alone am I still potent. Like all the rest. Just one of the common herd, now. Let's face it: I'll push no more. I'm ordinary again. Fighting off tears, I coil tight against myself in the darkness, and, sweating, moaning a little, working hard, I descend numbly into the quicksand, into the first moments of the long colorless years ahead.

◆

HOUSE OF BONES

It will be noted that in my introductions to the stories in this book I frequently mention that I had written some particular story in response to a request from a friend of mine—Byron Preiss, say, or Tom Scortia, or Fred Pohl. Science-fiction writers and editors are a notoriously chummy bunch, who get together every year at a big convention and various smaller ones, and buy each other drinks and trade gossip and strike deals for future work, and I, a regular attendee at such conventions for many decades, have struck up many a warm friendship in the course of that. One of the closest of these friendships was with the editor and writer Terry Carr, whom I knew in my New York days and who, when I moved to California in the early 1970s shortly after Terry had, was my neighbor in the hills east of San Francisco Bay. We lived a few minutes' drive from each other, saw each other frequently, and, at a time when we were both editing annual anthologies of new science fiction, cooperated in the most congenial way, each of us tipping the other off to stories that didn't fit well into our own books but might be useful for his, and writing stories for each other as well. I had one in almost every issue of Terry's anthology *Universe*, and Terry, though he was a less prolific writer than I was, did several for me.

Terry was a warmhearted, funny, decent human being. The one thing he wasn't was physically durable. Though he was tall and athletic-looking, his body began to give out by the time he was about forty-five, and in the spring of 1987 he died, two months after his fiftieth birthday, after a melancholy period of accelerating decline that for the most part had remained unknown outside his immediate circle of friends.

Beth Meacham, then the editor-in-chief of Tor Books, was one of those friends, and had learned much about the craft of editing from him; and in the weeks after his death she sought to find some way of showing her gratitude to him. In May 1987, she hit on the idea of assembling an anthology of original stories by writers who had had some professional association with Terry. I was one of those whom she asked to take part. I had just finished writing "House of Bones" at the time. Terry was keenly interested in pre-history, and had a fundamental belief that human beings were basically good, however unlikely that might seem if one judged by outward appearances alone. I thought "House of Bones" was the perfect story for *Terry's Universe*, as the memorial anthology was called, and I sent it to Beth. *Terry's Universe* was published in May of 1988, sixteen months after Terry's death, and "House of Bones" was the first story in the book.

A first-person account, of course, which is what qualifies it for inclusion here: an account of someone who finds himself stranded many thousands of years in the past, a predicament which none of you are unlikely ever to find yourselves in, and, for that matter, is not likely to befall me, either, if I have anything to say about it.

———

AFTER THE EVENING MEAL PAUL starts tapping on his drum and chanting quietly to himself, and Marty picks up the rhythm, chanting too. And then the two of them launch into that night's installment of the tribal epic, which is what happens, sooner or later, every evening.

It all sounds very intense but I don't have a clue to the meaning. They sing the epic in the religious language, which I've never been allowed to learn. It has the same relation to the everyday language, I guess, as Latin does to French or Spanish. But it's private, sacred, for insiders only. Not for the likes of me.

"Tell it, man!" B.J. yells. "Let it roll!" Danny shouts.

Paul and Marty are really getting into it. Then a gust of fierce stinging cold whistles through the house as the reindeer-hide flap over the doorway is lifted, and Zeus comes stomping in.

Zeus is the chieftain. Big burly man, starting to run to fat a little. Mean-looking, just as you'd expect. Heavy black beard streaked with gray and hard, glittering eyes that glow like rubies in a face wrinkled and carved by windburn and time. Despite the Paleolithic cold, all he's wearing is a cloak of black fur, loosely draped. The thick hair on his heavy chest is turning gray too. Festoons of jewelry announce his power and status: necklaces of seashells, bone beads, and amber, a pendant of yellow wolf teeth, an ivory headband, bracelets carved from bone, five or six rings.

Sudden silence. Ordinarily when Zeus drops in at B.J.'s house it's for a little roistering and tale-telling and butt-pinching, but tonight he has come without either of his wives, and he looks troubled, grim. Jabs a finger toward Jeanne.

"You saw the stranger today? What's he like?"

There's been a stranger lurking near the village all week, leaving traces everywhere—footprints in the permafrost, hastily covered-over campsites, broken flints, scraps of charred meat. The whole tribe's keyed. Strangers aren't common. I was the last one, a year and a half ago. God only knows why they took me in: because I seemed so pitiful to them, maybe. But the way they've been talking, they'll kill this one on sight if they can. Paul and Marty composed a Song of the Stranger last week and Marty sang it by the campfire two different nights. It was in the religious language so I couldn't understand a word of it. But it sounded terrifying.

Jeanne is Marty's wife. She got a good look at the stranger this afternoon, down by the river while netting fish for dinner. "He's

123

short," she tells Zeus. "Shorter than any of you, but with big muscles, like Gebravar." Gebravar is Jeanne's name for me. The people of the tribe are strong, but they didn't pump iron when they were kids. My muscles fascinate them. "His hair is yellow and his eyes are gray. And he's ugly. Nasty. Big head, big flat nose. Walks with his shoulders hunched and his head down." Jeanne shudders. "He's like a pig. A real beast. A goblin. Trying to steal fish from the net, he was. But he ran away when he saw me."

Zeus listens, glowering, asking a question now and then—did he say anything, how was he dressed, was his skin painted in any way. Then he turns to Paul.

"What do you think he is?"

"A ghost," Paul says. These people see ghosts everywhere. And Paul, who is the bard of the tribe, thinks about them all the time. His poems are full of ghosts. He feels the world of ghosts pressing in, pressing in. "Ghosts have gray eyes," he says. "This man has gray eyes."

"A ghost, maybe, yes. But what kind of ghost?"

"What *kind?*"

Zeus glares. "You should listen to your own poems," he snaps. "Can't you see it? This is a Scavenger Folk man prowling around. Or the ghost of one."

General uproar and hubbub at that.

I turn to Sally. Sally's my woman. I still have trouble saying that she's my wife, but that's what she really is. I call her Sally because there once was a girl back home who I thought I might marry, and that was her name, far from here in another geological epoch.

I ask Sally who the Scavenger Folk are.

"From the old times," she says. "Lived here when we first came. But they're all dead now. They—"

That's all she gets a chance to tell me. Zeus is suddenly looming over me. He's always regarded me with a mixture of amusement and tolerant contempt, but now there's something new in his eye. "Here is something you will do for us," he says to me. "It takes a stranger to find a stranger. This will be your task. Whether he is a ghost or a man, we must know the truth. So you, tomorrow: you will go out and you will find him and you will take him. Do you understand? At first light you will go to search for him, and you will not come back until you have him."

I try to say something, but my lips don't want to move. My silence seems good enough for Zeus, though. He smiles and nods fiercely and swings around, and goes stalking off into the night.

THEY ALL GATHER AROUND ME, excited in that kind of animated edgy way that comes over you when someone you know is picked for some big distinction. I can't tell whether they envy me or feel sorry for me. B.J. hugs me, Danny punches me in the arm, Paul runs up a jubilant-sounding number on his drum. Marty pulls a wickedly sharp stone blade about nine inches long out of his kit-bag and presses it into my hand.

"Here. You take this. You may need it."

I stare at it as if he had handed me a live grenade.

"Look," I say. "I don't know anything about stalking and capturing people."

"Come *on*," B.J. says. "What's the problem?"

B.J. is an architect. Paul's a poet. Marty sings, better than Pavarotti. Danny paints and sculpts. I think of them as my special buddies. They're all what you could loosely call Cro-Magnon men. I'm not. They treat me just like one of the gang, though. We five, we're some bunch. Without them I'd have gone crazy here. Lost as I am, cut off as I am from everything I used to be and know.

"You're strong and quick," Marty says. "You can do it."

"And you're pretty smart, in your crazy way," says Paul. "Smarter than *he* is. We aren't worried at all."

If they're a little condescending sometimes, I suppose I deserve it. They're highly skilled individuals, after all, proud of the things they can do. To them I'm a kind of retard. That's a novelty for me. I used to be considered highly skilled too, back where I came from.

"You go with me," I say to Marty. "You and Paul both. I'll do whatever has to be done but I want you to back me up."

"No," Marty says. "You do this alone."

"B.J.? Danny?"

"No," they say. And their smiles harden, their eyes grow chilly. Suddenly it doesn't look so chummy around here. We may be buddies but I have to go out there by myself. Or I may have misread the whole situation and we aren't such big buddies at all.

Either way this is some kind of test, some rite of passage maybe, an initiation. I don't know. Just when I think these people are exactly like us except for a few piddling differences of customs and languages, I realize how alien they really are. Not savages, far from it. But they aren't even remotely like modern people. They're something entirely else. Their bodies and their minds are pure *Homo sapiens* but their souls are different from ours by 20,000 years.

To Sally I say, "Tell me more about the Scavenger Folk."

"Like animals, they were," she says. "They could speak but only in grunts and belches. They were bad hunters and they ate dead things that they found on the ground, or stole the kills of others."

"They smelled like garbage," says Danny. "Like an old dump where everything was rotten. And they didn't know how to paint or sculpt."

"This was how they screwed," says Marty, grabbing the nearest woman, pushing her down, pretending to hump her from behind. Everyone laughs, cheers, stamps his feet.

"And they walked like this," says B.J., doing an ape-shuffle, banging his chest with his fists.

There's a lot more, a lot of locker-room stuff about the ugly shaggy stupid smelly disgusting Scavenger Folk. How dirty they were, how barbaric. How the pregnant women kept the babies in their bellies twelve or thirteen months and they came out already hairy, with a full mouth of teeth. All ancient history, handed down through the generations by bards like Paul in the epics. None of them has ever actually seen a Scavenger. But they sure seem to detest them.

"They're all dead," Paul says. "They were killed in the migration wars long ago. That has to be a ghost out there."

Of course I've guessed what's up. I'm no archaeologist at all—West Point, fourth generation. My skills are in electronics, computers, time-shift physics. There was such horrible political infighting among the archaeology boys about who was going to get to go to the past that in the end none of them went and the gig wound up going to the military. Still, they sent me here with enough crash-course archaeology to be able to see that the Scavengers must have been what we call the Neanderthals, that shambling race of also-rans that got left behind in the evolutionary sweepstakes.

So there really had been a war of extermination between the slow-witted Scavengers and clever *Homo sapiens* here in Ice Age Europe. But there must have been a few survivors left on the losing side, and one of them, God knows why, is wandering around near this village.

Now I'm supposed to find the ugly stranger and capture him. Or kill him, I guess. Is that what Zeus wants from me? To take the stranger's blood on my head? A very civilized tribe, they are, even if they do hunt huge woolly elephants and build houses out of their whitened bones. Too civilized to do their own murdering, and they figure they can send me out to do it for them.

"I don't think he's a Scavenger," Danny says. "I think he's from Naz Glesim. The Naz Glesim people have gray eyes. Besides, what would a ghost want with fish?"

Naz Glesim is a land far to the northeast, perhaps near what will someday be Moscow. Even here in the Paleolithic the world is divided into a thousand little nations. Danny once went on a great solo journey through all the neighboring lands: he's a kind of tribal Marco Polo.

"You better not let the chief hear that," B.J. tells him. "He'll break your balls. Anyway, the Naz Glesim people aren't ugly. They look just like us except for their eyes."

"Well, there's that," Danny concedes. "But I still think—"

Paul shakes his head. That gesture goes way back, too. "A Scavenger ghost," he insists.

B.J. looks at me. "What do you think, Pumangiup?" That's his name for me.

"Me?" I say. "What do I know about these things?"

"You come from far away. You ever see a man like that?"

"I've seen plenty of ugly men, yes." The people of the tribe are tall and lean, brown hair and dark shining eyes, wide faces, bold cheekbones. If they had better teeth they'd be gorgeous. "But I don't know about this one. I'd have to see him."

Sally brings a new platter of grilled fish over. I run my hand fondly over her bare haunch. Inside this house made of mammoth bones nobody wears very much clothing, because the structure is well insulated and the heat builds up even in the dead of winter. To me Sally is far and away the best looking woman in the tribe, high firm breasts, long supple legs, alert, inquisitive face. She was the mate of a man who had to be killed last summer because he became infested with ghosts. Danny and B.J. and a couple of the others bashed his head in, by way of a mercy killing, and then there was a wild six-day wake, dancing and wailing around the clock. Because she needed a change of luck they gave Sally to me, or me to her, figuring a holy fool like me must carry the charm of the gods. We have a fine time, Sally and I. We were two lost souls when we came together, and together we've kept each other from tumbling even deeper into the darkness.

"You'll be all right," B.J. says. "You can handle it. The gods love you."

"I hope that's true," I tell him.

Much later in the night Sally and I hold each other as though we both know that this could be our last time. She's all over me, hot, eager. There's no privacy in the bone-house and the others can hear us, four couples and I don't know how many kids, but that doesn't matter. It's dark. Our little bed of fox-pelts is our own little world.

There's nothing esoteric, by the way, about these people's style of love-making. There are only so many ways that a male human body and a female human body can be joined together, and all of them, it seems, had already been invented by the time the glaciers came.

At dawn, by first light, I am on my way, alone, to hunt the Scavenger man. I rub the rough strange wall of the house of bones for luck, and off I go.

THE VILLAGE STRETCHES FOR A couple of hundred yards along the bank of a cold, swiftly flowing river. The three round bone-houses where most of us live are arranged in a row, and the fourth one, the long house that is the residence of Zeus and his family and also serves as the temple and house of parliament, is just beyond them. On the far side of it is the new fifth house that we've been building this past week. Further down, there's a work-shop where tools are made and hides are scraped, and then a butchering area, and just past that there's an immense garbage dump and a towering heap of mammoth bones for future con-struction projects.

A sparse pine forest lies east of the village, and beyond it are the rolling hills and open plains where the mammoths and rhi-nos graze. No one ever goes into the river, because it's too cold and the current is too strong, and so it hems us in like a wall on our western border. I want to teach the tribesfolk how to build kayaks one of these days. I should also try to teach them how to swim, I guess. And maybe a few years farther along I'd like to see if we can chop down some trees and build a bridge. Will it shock the pants off them when I come out with all this useful stuff? They think I'm an idiot, because I don't know about the different grades of mud and frozen ground, the colors of charcoal, the uses and qualities of antler, bone, fat, hide, and stone. They feel sorry for me because I'm so limited. But they like me all the same. And the gods *love* me. At least B.J. thinks so.

I start my search down by the riverfront, since that's where Jeanne saw the Scavenger yesterday. The sun, at dawn on this Ice Age autumn morning, is small and pale, a sad little lemon far away. But the wind is quiet now. The ground is still soft from the summer thaw, and I look for tracks. There's permafrost five feet down, but the topsoil, at least, turns spongy in May and gets downright muddy by July. Then it hardens again and by October it's like steel, but by October we live mostly indoors.

There are footprints all over the place. We wear leather sandals, but a lot of us go barefoot much of the time, even now, in forty-degree weather. The people of the tribe have long, narrow feet with high arches. But down by the water near the fish nets I pick up a different spoor, the mark of a short, thick, low-arched foot with curled-under toes. It must be my Neanderthal. I smile. I feel like Sherlock Holmes. "Hey, look, Marty," I say to the sleeping village. "I've got the ugly bugger's track. B.J.? Paul? Danny? You just watch me. I'm going to find him faster than you could believe."

THOSE AREN'T THEIR ACTUAL NAMES. I just call them that, Marty, Paul, B.J., Danny. Around here everyone gives everyone else his own private set of names. Marty's name for B.J. is Ungklava. He calls Danny Tisbalalak and Paul is Shibgamon. Paul calls Marty Dolibog. His name for B.J. is Kalamok. And so on all around the tribe, a ton of names, hundreds and hundreds of names for just forty or fifty people. It's a confusing system. They have reasons for it that satisfy them. You learn to live with it.

A man never reveals his true name, the one his mother whispered when he was born. Not even his father knows that, or his wife. You could put hot stones between his legs and he still wouldn't tell you that true name of his, because that'd bring every ghost from Cornwall to Vladivostok down on his ass to haunt him. The world is full of angry ghosts, resentful of the living, ready to jump on anyone who'll give them an opening and plague him like leeches, like bedbugs, like every malign and perverse bloodsucking pest rolled into one.

We are somewhere in western Russia, or maybe Poland. The landscape suggests that: flat, bleak, a cold grassy steppe with a few oaks and birches and pines here and there. Of course a lot of Europe must look like that in this glacial epoch. But the clincher is the fact that these people build mammoth-bone houses. The only place that was ever done was Eastern Europe, so far as anybody down the line knows. Possibly they're the oldest true houses in the world.

What gets me is the immensity of this prehistoric age, the spans of time. It goes back and back and back and all of it is alive for these people. We think it's a big deal to go to England and see a cathedral a thousand years old. They've been hunting on this steppe thirty times as long. Can you visualize 30,000 years? To you, George Washington lived an incredibly long time ago. George is going to have his 300th birthday very soon. Make a stack of books a foot high and tell yourself that that stands for all the time that has gone by since George was born in 1732. Now go on stacking up the books. When you've got a pile as high as a ten-story building, that's 30,000 years.

A stack of years almost as high as that separates me from you, right this minute. In my bad moments, when the loneliness and the fear and the pain and the remembrance of all that I have lost start to operate on me, I feel that stack of years pressing on me with the weight of a mountain. I try not to let it get me down. But that's a hell of a weight to carry. Now and then it grinds me right into the frozen ground.

THE FLATFOOTED TRACK LEADS ME up to the north, around the garbage dump, and toward the forest. Then I lose it. The prints go round and round, double back to the garbage dump, then to the butchering area, then toward the forest again, then all the way over to the river. I can't make sense of the pattern. The poor dumb bastard just seems to have been milling around, foraging in the garbage for anything edible, then taking off again but not going far, checking back to see if anything's been caught in the fish net, and so on. Where's he sleeping? Out in the open, I guess. Well, if what I heard last night is true, he's as hairy as a gorilla; maybe the cold doesn't bother him much.

Now that I've lost the trail, I have some time to think about the nature of the mission, and I start getting uncomfortable.

I'm carrying a long stone knife. I'm out here to kill. I picked the military for my profession a long time ago, but it wasn't with the idea of killing anyone, and certainly not in hand-to-hand combat. I guess I see myself as a representative of civilization, somebody trying to hold back the night, not as anyone who would go creeping around planning to stick a sharp flint blade into some miserable solitary tramp.

But I might well be the one that gets killed. He's wild, he's hungry, he's scared, he's primitive. He may not be very smart, but at least he's shrewd enough to have made it to adulthood, and he's out here earning his living by his wits and his strength. This is his world, not mine. He may be stalking me even while I'm stalking him, and when we catch up with each other he won't be fighting by any rules I ever learned. A good argument for turning back right now.

On the other hand if I come home in one piece with the Scavenger still at large, Zeus will hang my hide on the bone-house wall for disobeying him. We may all be great buddies here but when the chief gives the word, you hop to it or else. That's the way it's been since history began and I have no reason to think it's any different back here.

I simply have to kill the Scavenger. That's all there is to it.

I don't want to get killed by a wild man in this forest, and I don't want to be nailed up by a tribal court-martial either. I want to live to get back to my own time. I still hang on to the faint chance that the rainbow will come back for me and take me down the line to tell my tale in what I have already started to think of as the future. I want to make my report.

The news I'd like to bring you people up there in the world of the future is that these Ice Age folk don't see themselves as primitive. They know, they absolutely *know*, that they're the crown of creation. They have a language—two of them, in fact—they have history, they have music, they have poetry, they have technology, they have art, they have architecture. They have religion. They have laws. They have a way of life that has worked for thousands of years, that will go on working for thousands more. You may think it's all grunts and war-clubs back here, but you're wrong. I can make this world real to you, if I could only get back there to you.

But even if I can't ever get back, there's a lot I want to do here. I want to learn that epic of theirs and write it down for you to read. I want to teach them about kayaks and bridges, and maybe more. I want to finish building the bone-house we started last week. I want to go on horsing around with my buddies B.J. and Danny and Marty and Paul. I want Sally. Christ, I might even have kids by her, and inject my own futuristic genes into the Ice Age gene pool.

I don't want to die today trying to fulfill a dumb murderous mission in this cold bleak prehistoric forest.

THE MORNING GROWS WARMER, THOUGH not warm. I pick up the trail again, or think I do, and start off toward the east and north, into the forest. Behind me I hear the sounds of laughter and shouting and song as work gets going on the new house, but soon I'm out of earshot. Now I hold the knife in my hand, ready for anything. There are wolves in here, as well as a frightened half-man who may try to kill me before I can kill him.

I wonder how likely it is that I'll find him. I wonder how long I'm supposed to stay out here, too—a couple of hours, a day, a week?—and what I'm supposed to use for food, and how I keep my ass from freezing after dark, and what Zeus will say or do if I come back empty-handed.

I'm wandering around randomly now. I don't feel like Sherlock Holmes any longer.

WORKING ON THE BONE-HOUSE, THAT'S what I'd rather be doing now. Winter is coming on and the tribe has grown too big for the existing four houses. B.J. directs the job and Marty and Paul sing and chant and play the drum and flute, and about seven of us do the heavy labor.

"Pile those jawbones chin down," B.J. will yell, as I try to slip one into the foundation the wrong way around. "*Chin down*, bozo! That's better." Paul bangs out a terrific riff on the drum to applaud me for getting it right the second time. Marty starts making up a ballad about how dumb I am, and everyone laughs. But it's loving laughter. "Now that backbone over there," B.J. yells to me. I pull a long string of mammoth vertebrae from the huge pile. The bones are white, old bones that have been lying around a long time. They're dense and heavy. "Wedge it down in there good! Tighter! Tighter!" I huff and puff under the immense weight of the thing, and stagger a little, and somehow get it where it belongs, and jump out of the way just in time as Danny and two other men come tottering toward me carrying a gigantic skull.

The winter-houses are intricate and elaborate structures that require real ingenuity of design and construction. At this point in time B.J. may well be the best architect the world has ever known. He carries around a piece of ivory on which he has carved a blueprint for the house, and makes sure everybody weaves the bones and skulls and tusks into the structure just the right way. There's no shortage of construction materials. After 30,000 years of hunting mammoths in this territory, these people have enough bones lying around to build a city the size of Los Angeles.

The houses are warm and snug. They're round and domed, like big igloos made out of bones. The foundation is a circle of mammoth skulls with maybe a hundred mammoth jawbones stacked up over them in fancy herringbone patterns to form the wall. The roof is made of hides stretched over enormous tusks mounted overhead as arches. The whole thing is supported by a wooden frame and smaller bones are chinked in to seal the openings in the walls, plus a plastering of red clay. There's an entranceway made up of gigantic thighbones set up on end. It may all sound bizarre but there's a weird kind of beauty to it and you have no idea, once you're inside, that the bitter winds of the Pleistocene are howling all around you.

The tribe is semi-nomadic and lives by hunting and gathering. In the summer, which is about two months long, they roam the steppe, killing mammoths and rhinos and musk oxen, and bagging up berries and nuts to get them through the winter. Toward what I would guess is August the weather turns cold and they start to head for their village of bone houses, hunting reindeer along the way. By the time the really bad weather arrives—think Minnesota-and-a-half—they're settled in for the winter with six months' worth of meat stored in deep-freeze pits in the permafrost. It's an orderly, rhythmic life. There's a real community here. I'd be willing to call it a civilization. But—as I stalk my human prey out here in the cold—I remind myself that life here is harsh and strange. Alien. Maybe I'm doing all this buddy-buddy nickname stuff simply to save my own sanity, you think? I don't know.

IF I GET KILLED OUT here today the thing I'll regret most is never learning their secret religious language and not being able to understand the big historical epic that they sing every night. They just don't want to teach it to me. Evidently it's something outsiders aren't meant to understand.

The epic, Sally tells me, is an immense account of everything that's ever happened: the *Iliad* and the *Odyssey* and the *Encyclopedia*

Britannica all rolled into one, a vast tale of gods and kings and men and warfare and migrations and vanished empires and great calamities. The text is so big and Sally's recounting of it is so sketchy that I have only the foggiest idea of what it's about, but when I hear it I want desperately to understand it. It's the actual history of a forgotten world, the tribal annals of thirty millennia, told in a forgotten language, all of it as lost to us as last year's dreams.

If I could learn it and translate it I would set it all down in writing so that maybe it would be found by archaeologists thousands of years from now. I've been taking notes on these people already, an account of what they're like and how I happen to be living among them. I've made twenty tablets so far, using the same clay that the tribe uses to make its pots and sculptures, and firing it in the same beehive-shaped kiln. It's a godawful slow job writing on slabs of clay with my little bone knife. I bake my tablets and bury them in the cobblestone floor of the house. Somewhere in the 21st or 22nd century a Russian archaeologist will dig them up and they'll give him one hell of a jolt. But of their history, their myths, their poetry, I don't have a thing, because of the language problem. Not a damned thing.

NOON HAS COME AND GONE. I find some white berries on a glossy-leaved bush and, after only a moment's hesitation, gobble them down. There's a faint sweetness there. I'm still hungry even after I pick the bush clean.

If I were back in the village now, we'd have knocked off work at noon for a lunch of dried fruit and strips of preserved reindeer meat, washed down with mugs of mildly fermented fruit juice. The fermentation is accidental, I think, an artifact of their storage methods. But obviously there are yeasts here and I'd like to try to invent wine and beer. Maybe they'll make me a god for that. This year I invented writing, but I did it for my sake and not for theirs and they aren't much interested in it. I think they'll be more impressed with beer.

A hard, nasty wind has started up out of the east. It's September now and the long winter is clamping down. In half an hour the temperature has dropped fifteen degrees, and I'm freezing. I'm wearing a fur parka and trousers, but that thin icy wind cuts right through. And it scours up the fine dry loose topsoil and flings it in our faces. Some day that light yellow dust will lie thirty feet deep over this village, and over B.J. and Marty and Danny and Paul, and probably over me as well.

Soon they'll be quitting for the day. The house will take eight or ten more days to finish, if early-season snowstorms don't interrupt. I can imagine Paul hitting the drum six good raps to wind things up and everybody making a run for indoors, whooping and hollering. These are high-spirited guys. They jump and shout and sing, punch each other playfully on the arms, brag about the goddesses they've screwed and the holy rhinos they've killed. Not that they're kids. My guess is that they're twenty-five, thirty years old, senior men of the tribe. The life expectancy here seems to be about forty-five. I'm thirty-four. I have a grandmother alive back in Illinois. Nobody here could possibly believe that. The one I call Zeus, the oldest and richest man in town, looks to be about fifty-three, probably is younger than that, and is generally regarded as favored by the gods because he's lived so long. He's a wild old bastard, still full of bounce and vigor. He lets you know that he keeps those two wives of his busy all night long, even at his age. These are robust people. They lead a tough life, but they don't know that, and so their souls are buoyant. I definitely will try to turn them on to beer next summer, if I last that long and if I can figure out the technology. This could be one hell of a party town.

SOMETIMES I CAN'T HELP FEELING abandoned by my own time. I know it's irrational. It has to be just an accident that I'm marooned here. But there are times when I think the people up there in 2013 simply shrugged and forgot about me when things went wrong, and it pisses me off tremendously until I get it under control. I'm a professionally trained hard-ass. But I'm 20,000 years from home and there are times when it hurts more than I can stand.

Maybe beer isn't the answer. Maybe what I need is a still. Brew up some stronger stuff than beer, a little moonshine to get me through those very black moments when the anger and the really heavy resentment start breaking through.

In the beginning the tribe looked on me, I guess, as a moron. Of course I was in shock. The time trip was a lot more traumatic than the experiments with rabbits and turtles had led us to think.

There I was, naked, dizzy, stunned, blinking and gaping, retching and puking. The air had a bitter acid smell to it—who expected that, that the air would smell different in the past?—and it was so cold it burned my nostrils. I knew at once that I hadn't landed in the pleasant France of the Cro-Magnons but in some harsher, bleaker land far to the east. I could still see the rainbow glow of the Zeller Ring, but it was vanishing fast, and then it was gone.

The tribe found me ten minutes later. That was an absolute fluke. I could have wandered for months, encountering nothing but reindeer and bison. I could have frozen; I could have starved. But no, the men I would come to call B.J. and Danny and Marty and Paul were hunting near the place where I dropped out of the sky and they stumbled on me right away. Thank God they didn't see me arrive. They'd have decided that I was a supernatural being and would have expected miracles from me, and I can't do miracles.

Instead they simply took me for some poor dope who had wandered so far from home that he didn't know where he was, which after all was essentially the truth.

I must have seemed like one sad case. I couldn't speak their language or any other language they knew. I carried no weapons. I didn't know how to make tools out of flints or sew a fur parka or set up a snare for a wolf or stampede a herd of mammoths into a trap. I didn't know anything, in fact, not a single useful thing. But instead of spearing me on the spot they took me to their village, fed me, clothed me, taught me their language. Threw their arms around me and told me what a great guy I was. They made me one of them. That was a year and a half ago. I'm a kind of holy fool for them, a sacred idiot.

I was supposed to be here just four days and then the Zeller Effect rainbow would come for me and carry me home. Of course within a few weeks I realized that something had gone wonky at the uptime end, that the experiment had malfunctioned and that I probably wasn't ever going to get home. There was that risk all along. Well, here I am, here I stay. First came stinging pain and anger and I suppose grief when the truth finally caught up with me. Now there's just a dull ache that won't go away.

In early afternoon I stumble across the Scavenger Man. It's pure dumb luck. The trail has long since given out—the forest floor is covered with soft pine duff here, and I'm not enough of a hunter to distinguish one spoor from another in that—and I'm simply moving aimlessly when I see some broken branches, and then I get a whiff of burning wood, and I follow that scent twenty or thirty yards over a low rise and there he is, hunkered down by a hastily thrown-together little hearth roasting a couple of ptarmigans on a green spit. A scavenger he may be, but he's a better man than I am when it comes to skulling ptarmigans.

He's really ugly. Jeanne wasn't exaggerating at all.

His head is huge and juts back a long way. His mouth is like a muzzle and his chin is hardly there at all and his forehead slopes down to huge brow-ridges like an ape's. His hair is like straw, and it's all over him, though he isn't really shaggy, no hairier than a lot of men I've known. His eyes are gray, yes, and small, deep-set. He's built low and thick, like an Olympic weight lifter. He's wearing a strip of fur around his middle and nothing else. He's an honest-to-God Neanderthal, straight out of the textbooks, and when I see him a chill runs down my spine as though up till this minute I had never really believed that I had traveled 20,000 years in time and now, holy shit, the whole concept has finally become real to me.

He sniffs and gets my wind, and his big brows knit and his whole body goes tense. He stares at me, checking me out, sizing me up. It's very quiet here and we are primordial enemies, face to face with no one else around. I've never felt anything like that before.

We are maybe twenty feet from each other. I can smell him and he can smell me, and it's the smell of fear on both sides. I can't begin to anticipate his move. He rocks back and forth a little, as if getting ready to spring up and come charging, or maybe bolt off into the forest.

But he doesn't do that. The first moment of tension passes and he eases back. He doesn't try to attack, and he doesn't get up to run. He just sits there in a kind of patient, tired way, staring at me, waiting to see what I'm going to do. I wonder if I'm being suckered, set up for a sudden onslaught.

I'm so cold and hungry and tired that I wonder if I'll be able to kill him when he comes at me. For a moment I almost don't care.

Then I laugh at myself for expecting shrewdness and trickery from a Neanderthal man. Between one moment and the next all the menace goes out of him for me. He isn't pretty but he doesn't seem like a goblin, or a demon, just an ugly thick-bodied man sitting alone in a chilly forest.

And I know that sure as anything I'm not going to try to kill him, not because he's so terrifying but because he isn't.

"They sent me out here to kill you," I say, showing him the flint knife.

He goes on staring. I might just as well be speaking English, or Sanskrit.

"I'm not going to do it," I tell him. "That's the first thing you ought to know. I've never killed anyone before and I'm not going to begin with a complete stranger. Okay? Is that understood?"

He says something now. His voice is soft and indistinct, but I can tell that he's speaking some entirely other language.

"I can't understand what you're telling me," I say, "and you don't understand me. So we're even."

I take a couple of steps toward him. The blade is still in my hand. He doesn't move. I see now that he's got no weapons and even though he's powerfully built and could probably rip my arms off in two seconds, I'd be able to put the blade into him first. I point to the north, away from the village, and make a broad sweeping gesture. "You'd be wise to head off that way," I say, speaking very slowly and loudly, as if that would matter. "Get yourself out of the neighborhood. They'll kill you otherwise. You understand? *Capisce? Verstehen Sie?* Go. Scat. Scram. I won't kill you, but they will."

I gesture some more, vociferously pantomiming his route to the north. He looks at me. He looks at the knife. His enormous cavernous nostrils widen and flicker. For a moment I think I've misread him in the most idiotically naïve way, that he's been simply biding his time getting ready to jump me as soon as I stop making speeches.

Then he pulls a chunk of meat from the bird he's been roasting, and offers it to me.

"I come here to kill you, and you give me lunch?"

He holds it out. A bribe? Begging for his life?

"I can't," I say. "I came here to kill you. Look, I'm just going to turn around and go back, all right? If anybody asks, I never saw you." He waves the meat at me and I begin to salivate as though it's pheasant under glass. But no, no, I can't take his lunch. I point to him, and again to the north, and once more indicate that he ought not to let the sun set on him in this town. Then I turn and start to walk away, wondering if this is the moment when he'll leap up and spring on me from behind and choke the life out of me.

I take five steps, ten, and then I hear him moving behind me.

So this is it. We really are going to fight.

I turn, my knife at the ready. He looks down at it sadly. He's standing there with the piece of meat still in his hand, coming after me to give it to me anyway.

"Jesus," I say. "You're just lonely."

He says something in that soft blurred language of his and holds out the meat. I take it and bolt it down fast, even though it's only half cooked—dumb Neanderthal!—and I almost gag. He smiles. I don't care what he looks like, if he smiles and shares his food then he's human by me. I smile too. Zeus is going to murder me. We sit down together and watch the other ptarmigan cook, and when it's ready we share it, neither of us saying a word. He has trouble getting a wing off, and I hand him my knife, which he uses in a clumsy way and hands back to me.

After lunch I get up and say, "I'm going back now. I wish to hell you'd head off to the hills before they catch you."

And I turn, and go.

And he follows me like a lost dog who has just adopted a new owner.

So I BRING HIM BACK to the village with me. There's simply no way to get rid of him short of physically attacking him, and I'm not going to do that. As we emerge from the forest a sickening wave of fear sweeps over me. I think at first it's the roast ptarmigan trying to come back up, but no, it's downright terror, because the Scavenger is obviously planning to stick with me right to the end, and the end is not going to be good. I can see Zeus' blazing eyes, his furious scowl. The thwarted Ice Age chieftain in a storm of wrath. Since I didn't do the job, they will. They'll kill him and maybe they'll kill me too, since I've revealed myself to be a dangerous moron who will bring home the very enemy he was sent out to eliminate.

"This is dumb," I tell the Neanderthal. "You shouldn't be doing this."

He smiles again. You don't understand shit, do you, fellow?

We are past the garbage dump now, past the butchering area. B.J. and his crew are at work on the new house. B.J. looks up when he sees me and his eyes are bright with surprise.

He nudges Marty and Marty nudges Paul and Paul taps Danny on the shoulder. They point to me and to the Neanderthal. They look at each other. They open their mouths but they don't say anything. They whisper, they shake their heads. They back off a little, and circle around us, gaping, staring.

Christ. Here it comes.

I can imagine what they're thinking. They're thinking that I have really screwed up. That I've brought a ghost home for dinner. Or else an enemy that I was supposed to kill. They're thinking that I'm an absolute lunatic, that I'm an idiot, and now they've got to do the dirty work that I was too dumb to do. And I wonder if I'll try to defend the Neanderthal against them, and what it'll be like if I do. What am I going to do, take them all on at once? And go down swinging as my four sweet buddies close in on me and flatten me into the permafrost? I will. If they force me to it, by God I will. I'll go for their guts with Marty's long stone blade if they try anything on the Neanderthal, or on me.

I don't want to think about it. I don't want to think about any of this.

Then Marty points and claps his hands and jumps about three feet in the air.

"Hey!" he yells. "Look at that! He brought the ghost back with him!"

And then they move in on me, just like that, the four of them, swarming all around me, pressing close, pummelling hard. There's no room to use the knife. They come on too fast. I do what I can with elbows, knees, even teeth. But they pound me from every side, open fists against my ribs, sides of hands crashing against the meat of my back. The breath goes from me and I come close to toppling as pain breaks out all over me at once. I need all of my strength, and then some, to keep from going down under their onslaught, and I think, this is a dumb way to die, beaten to death by a bunch of berserk cavemen in 20,000 B.C.

But after the first few wild moments things become a bit quieter and I get myself together and manage to push them back from me a little way, and I land a good one that sends Paul reeling backward with blood spouting from his lip, and I whirl toward B.J. and start to take him out, figuring I'll deal with Marty on the rebound. And then I realize that they aren't really fighting with me any more, and in fact that they never were.

It dawns on me that they were smiling and laughing as they worked me over, that their eyes were full of laughter and love, that if they had truly wanted to work me over it would have taken the four of them about seven and a half seconds to do it.

They're just having fun. They're playing with me in a jolly roughhouse way.

They step back from me. We all stand there quietly for a moment, breathing hard, rubbing our cuts and bruises. The thought of throwing up crosses my mind and I push it away.

"You brought the ghost back," Marty says again.

"Not a ghost," I say. "He's real."

"Not a ghost?"

"Not a ghost, no. He's live. He followed me back here."

"Can you believe it?" B.J. cries. "Live! Followed him back here! Just came marching right in here with him!" He turns to Paul. His eyes are gleaming and for a second I think they're going to jump me all over again. If they do I don't think I'm going to be able to deal with it. But he says simply, "This has to be a song by tonight. This is something special."

"I'm going to get the chief," says Danny, and runs off.

"Look, I'm sorry," I say. "I know what the chief wanted. I just couldn't do it."

"Do what?" B.J. asks.

"What are you talking about?" says Paul.

"Kill him," I say. "He was just sitting there by his fire, roasting a couple of birds, and he offered me a chunk, and—"

"*Kill* him?" B.J. says. "You were going to kill him?"

"Wasn't that what I was supposed—"

He goggles at me and starts to answer, but just then Zeus comes running up, and pretty much everyone else in the tribe, the women and the kids too, and they sweep up around us like the tide. Cheering, yelling, dancing, pummelling me in that cheerful bone-smashing way of theirs, laughing, shouting. Forming a ring around the Scavenger Man and throwing their hands in the air. It's a jubilee. Even Zeus is grinning. Marty begins to sing and Paul gets going on the drum. And Zeus comes over to me and embraces me like the big old bear that he is.

"I HAD IT ALL WRONG, didn't I?" I say later to B.J. "You were all just testing me, sure. But not to see how good a hunter I am."

He looks at me without any comprehension at all and doesn't answer. B.J., with that crafty architect's mind of his that takes in everything.

"You wanted to see if I was really human, right? If I had compassion, if I could treat a lost stranger the way I was treated myself."

Blank stares. Deadpan faces.

"Marty? Paul?"

They shrug. Tap their foreheads: the timeless gesture, ages old.

Are they putting me on? I don't know. But I'm certain that I'm right. If I had killed the Neanderthal they almost certainly would have killed me. That must have been it. I need to believe that that was it. All the time that I was congratulating them for not being the savages I had expected them to be, they were wondering how much of a savage *I* was. They had tested the depth of my humanity; and I had passed. And they finally see that I'm civilized too.

At any rate the Scavenger Man lives with us now. Not as a member of the tribe, of course, but as a sacred pet of some sort, a tame chimpanzee, perhaps. He may very well be the last of his kind, or close to it; and though the tribe looks upon him as something dopey and filthy and pathetic, they're not going to do him any harm. To them he's a pitiful bedraggled savage who'll bring good luck if he's treated well. He'll keep the ghosts away. Hell, maybe that's why they took me in, too.

As for me, I've given up what little hope I had of going home. The Zeller rainbow will never return for me, of that I'm altogether sure. But that's all right. I've been through some changes. I've come to terms with it.

We finished the new house yesterday and B.J. let me put the last tusk in place, the one they call the ghost-bone, that keeps dark spirits outside. It's apparently a big honor to be the one who sets up the ghost-bone. Afterward the four of them sang the Song of the House, which is a sort of dedication. Like all their other songs, it's in the old language, the secret one, the sacred one. I couldn't sing it with them, not having the words, but I came in with oom-pahs on the choruses and that seemed to go down pretty well.

I told them that by the next time we need to build a house, I will have invented beer, so that we can all go out when it's finished and get drunk to celebrate properly.

Of course they didn't know what the hell I was talking about, but they looked pleased anyway.

And tomorrow, Paul says, he's going to begin teaching me the other language. The secret one. The one that only the members of the tribe may know.

◆

CALL ME TITAN

Roger Zelazny was a great science-fiction writer who also happened to be greatly beloved by everyone who knew him. He burst into our midst in the early 1960s with a bunch of dazzling stories all at once, won a shelf full of Hugo and Nebula awards, went on to win a wide public with his enormously popular fantasy series set on a parallel world called Amber, and then, in 1995, not yet sixty years old, was taken away from us by death. Roger was a shy man, but sweet and gracious and bright, and everyone who came in contact with him liked him on first meeting and liked him more and more as acquaintance deepened into love. His early death came as a terrible shock in the small world of science fiction.

I first encountered Roger not long after the beginning of his career and, like everybody else, found him immediately congenial: We became close friends, visited each other frequently, exchanged bits of professional helpfulness. I saw in him a man of high good humor, warm good will, and great patience, and I was not in any way prepared to lose him so soon. But lose him I did, and when the anthologist Martin H. Greenberg let it be known that he was assembling a memorial volume of stories by Roger's friends to be called *Lord of the Fantastic*, I was one of the first to volunteer.

The story is a double act of ventriloquism. Any first-person story finds the author speaking with his protagonist's voice, but in this case I also was attempting to mimic Roger's inimitable style, and to deal with some of his thematic concerns: the Mediterranean world, the ancient gods, the comic possibilities of the survival of those gods into our own day. For the few days in January 1996 that it took me to do it I was able to masquerade in my own mind as Roger Zelazny, and for that reason it was an easy and enjoyable story to write—except for the ugly realization that would surface from time to time that the only reason I was writing it was as a memorial to my dead friend.

Lord of the Fantastic was published in September 1998. I would not have wanted to miss my chance to be included in the book. But it's a book that I wish had never needed to be published.

—◦◦◦—

"How did *you* get loose?" the woman who was Aphrodite asked me.

"It happened. Here I am."

"Yes," she said. "You. Of all of them, you. In this lovely place." She waved at the shining sun-bright sea, the glittering white stripe of the beach, the whitewashed houses, the bare brown hills. A lovely place, yes, this isle of Mykonos. "And what are you going to do now?"

"What I was created to do," I told her. "*You* know."

She considered that. We were drinking ouzo on the rocks, on the hotel patio, beneath a hanging array of fishermen's nets. After a moment she laughed, that irresistible tinkling laugh of hers, and clinked her glass against mine.

"Lots of luck," she said.

That was Greece. Before that was Sicily, and the mountain, and the eruption. . . .

The mountain had trembled and shaken and belched, and the red streams of molten fire began to flow downward from the ashen top, and in the first ten minutes of the eruption six little

148

towns around the slopes were wiped out. It happened just that fast. They shouldn't have been there, but they were, and then they weren't. Too bad for them. But it's always a mistake to buy real estate on Mount Etna.

The lava was really rolling. It would reach the city of Catania in a couple of hours and take out its whole northeastern quarter, and all of Sicily would be in mourning the next day. Some eruption. The biggest of all time, on this island where big eruptions have been making the news since the dinosaur days.

As for me, I couldn't be sure what was happening up there at the summit, not yet. I was still down deep, way down, three miles from sunlight.

But in my jail cell down there beneath the roots of the giant volcano that is called Mount Etna I could tell from the shaking and the noise and the heat that this one was something special. That the prophesied Hour of Liberation had come round at last for me, after five hundred centuries as the prisoner of Zeus.

I stretched and turned and rolled over, and sat up for the first time in fifty thousand years.

Nothing was pressing down on me.

Ugly limping Hephaestus, my jailer, had set up his forge right on top of me long ago, his heavy anvils on my back. And had merrily hammered bronze and iron all day and all night for all he was worth, that clomp-legged old master craftsman. Where was Hephaestus now? Where were his anvils?

Not on me. Not any longer.

That was *good*, that feeling of nothing pressing down.

I wriggled my shoulders. That took time. You have a lot of shoulders to wriggle, when you have a hundred heads, give or take three or four.

"Hephaestus?" I yelled, yelling it out of a hundred mouths at once. I felt the mountain shivering and convulsing above me, and I knew that my voice alone was enough to make great slabs of it fall off and go tumbling down, down, down.

No answer from Hephaestus. No clangor of his forge, either. He just wasn't there any more.

I tried again, a different, greater name.

"Zeus?"

Silence.

"You hear me, Zeus?"

No reply.

"Where the hell are you? Where is everybody?"

All was silence, except for the hellish roaring of the volcano.

Well, okay, *don't* answer me. Slowly I got to my feet, extending myself to my full considerable height. The fabric of the mountain gave way for me. I have that little trick.

Another good feeling, that was, rising to an upright position. Do you know what it's like, not being allowed to stand, not even once, for fifty thousand years? But of course you don't, little ones. How could you?

One more try. *"ZEUS???"*

All my hundred voices crying his name at once, fortissimo fortissimo. A chorus of booming echoes. Every one of my heads had grown back, over the years. I was healed of all that Zeus had done to me. That was especially good, knowing that I was healed. Things had looked really bad, for a while.

Well, no sense just standing there and caterwauling, if nobody was going to answer me back. This was the Hour of Liberation, after all. I was free—my chains fallen magically away, my heads all sprouted again. Time to get out of here. I started to move.

Upward. Outward.

I MOVED UP THROUGH THE mountain's bulk as though it was so much air. The rock was nothing to me. Unimpeded I rose past the coiling internal chambers through which the lava was racing up toward the summit vent, and came out into the sunlight, and clambered up the snow-kissed slopes of the mountain to the ash-choked summit itself, and stood there right in the very center of the eruption as the volcano puked its blazing guts out. I grinned a hundred big grins on my hundred faces, with hot fierce winds swirling like swords around my head and torrents of lava flowing down all around me. The view from up there was terrific. And what a fine feeling that was, just looking around at the world again after all that time underground.

There below me off to the east was the fish-swarming sea. Over there behind me, the serried tree-thickened hills. Above me, the fire-hearted sun.

What beautiful sights they all were!

"Hoo-*ha!*" I cried.

My jubilant roar went forth from that lofty mountaintop in Sicily like a hundred hurricanes at once. The noise of it broke windows in Rome and flattened farmhouses in Sardinia and knocked over ten mosques deep in the Tunisian Sahara. But the real blast was aimed eastward across the water, over toward Greece, and it went across that peninsula like a scythe, taking out half the treetops from Agios Nikolaus on the Ionian side to Athens over on the Aegean, and kept on going clear into Turkey.

It was a little signal, so to speak. I was heading that way myself, with some very ancient scores to settle.

I started down the mountainside, fast. The lava surging all around my thudding feet meant nothing to me.

Call me Typhoeus. Call me Titan.

I suppose I might have attracted a bit of attention as I made my way down those fiery slopes and past all the elegant seaside resorts that now were going crazy with hysteria over the eruption, and went striding into the sea midway between Fiumefreddo and Taormina. I am, after all, something of a monster, by your standards: four hundred feet high, let us say, with all those heads, dragon heads at that, and eyes that spurt flame, and thick black bristles everywhere on my body and swarms of coiling vipers sprouting from my thighs. The gods themselves have been known to turn and run at the mere sight of me. Some of them, once upon a time, fled all the way to Egypt when I yelled "Boo!"

But perhaps the eruption and the associated earthquakes kept the people of eastern Sicily so very preoccupied just then that they didn't take time to notice what sort of being it was that was walking down the side of Mount Etna and perambulating off toward the sea. Or maybe they didn't believe their eyes. Or it could be that they simply nodded and said, "Sure. Why not?"

I hit the water running and put my heads down and swam swiftly Greeceward across the cool blue sea without even bothering to come up for breath. What would have been the point? The air behind me smelled of fire and brimstone. And I was in a hurry.

Zeus, I thought. *I'm coming to get you, you bastard!*

As I said, I'm a Titan. It's the family name, not a description. We Titans were the race of Elder Gods—the first drafts, so to speak, for the deities that you people would eventually worship— the ones that Zeus walloped into oblivion long before Bill Gates came down from Mount Sinai with MS-DOS. Long before Homer sang. Long before the Flood. Long before, as a matter of fact, anything that might mean anything to you.

Gaea was our mother. The Earth, in other words. The mother of us all, really.

In the early days of the world broad-bosomed Gaea brought forth all sorts of gods and giants and monsters. Out of her came far-seeing Uranus, the sky, and then he and Gaea created the first dozen Titans, Oceanus and Cronus and Rhea and that bunch.

The original twelve Titans spawned a lot of others: Atlas, who now holds up the world, and tricky Prometheus, who taught humans how to use fire and got himself the world's worst case of cirrhosis for his trouble, and silly scatterbrained Epimetheus, who had that thing with Pandora, and so on. There were snake-limbed giants like Porphyrion and Alcyoneus, and hundred-armed fifteen-headed beauties like Briareus and Cottus and Gyes, and other oversized folk like the three one-eyed Cyclops, Arges of the storms and Brontes of the thunder and Steropes of the lightning, and so on. Oh, what a crowd we were!

The universe was our oyster, so I'm told. It must have been good times for all and sundry. I hadn't been born yet, in that era when Uranus was king.

But very early on there was that nasty business between Uranus and his son Cronus, which ended very badly for Uranus, the bloody little deal with the sharp sickle, and Cronus became the top god for a while, until he made the mistake of letting Zeus get born. That was it, for Cronus. In this business you have to watch out for overambitious sons. Cronus tried—he swallowed each of his children as they were born, to keep them from doing to him what he had done to Uranus—but Zeus, the last-born, eluded him. Very unfortunate for Cronus.

Family history. Dirty linen.

As for Zeus, who as you can see showed up on the scene quite late but eventually came to be in charge of things, he's my half-sister Rhea's son, so I suppose you'd call him my nephew. I call him my nemesis.

After Zeus had finished off Cronus he mopped up the rest of the Titans in a series of wild wars, thunderbolts ricocheting all over the place, the seas boiling, whole continents going up in flame. Some of us stayed neutral and some of us, I understand, actually allied themselves with him, but none of that made any difference. When all the shouting was over the whole pack of Titans were all prisoners in various disagreeable places, such as, for example, deep down underneath Mount Etna with the forge of Hephaestus sitting on your back; and Zeus and his outfit, Hades and Poseidon and Apollo and Aphrodite and the rest, ruled the roost.

I was Gaea's final experiment in maternity, the youngest of the Titans, born very late in the war with Zeus. Her final monster, some would say, because of my unusual looks and size. Tartarus was my father: the Underworld, he is. I was born restless. Dangerous, too. My job was to avenge the family against the outrages Zeus had perpetrated on the rest of us. I came pretty close, too.

And now I was looking for my second chance.

GREECE HAD CHANGED A LOT since I last had seen it. Something called civilization had happened in the meanwhile. Highways, gas stations, telephone poles, billboards, high-rise hotels, all those nice things.

Still and all, it didn't look so very bad. That killer blue sky with the golden blink in it, the bright sparkle of the low rolling surf, the white-walled cubes of houses climbing up the brown knife-blade hillsides: a handsome land, all things considered.

I came ashore at the island of Zakynthos on the Peloponnesian coast. There was a pleasant waterfront town there with an old fortress on a hilltop and groves of olives and cypresses all around. The geological disturbances connected with my escape from my prison cell beneath Mount Etna did not appear to have done much damage here.

I decided that it was probably not a great idea to let myself be seen in my actual form, considering how monstrous I would look to mortal eyes and the complications that that would create for me. And so, as I approached the land, I acquired a human body that I found swimming a short way off shore at one of the beach-front hotels.

It was a serviceable, athletic he-body, a lean, trim one, not young but full of energy, craggy-faced, a long jaw and a long sharp nose and a high forehead. I checked out his mind. Bright, sharp, observant. And packed with data, both standard and quirkily eso-teric. All that stuff about Bill Gates and Homer and high-rises and telephone poles: I got that from him. And how to behave like a human being. And a whole lot more, all of which I suspected would be useful to acquire.

A questing, creative mind. A good person. I liked him. I decided to use him.

In half a wink I transformed myself into a simulacrum of him and went on up the beach into town, leaving him behind just as he had been, all unknowing. The duplication wouldn't matter. Nobody was likely to care that there were two of him wandering around Greece at the same time, unless they saw both of us at the same moment, which wasn't going to happen.

I did a little further prowling behind his forehead and learned that he was a foreigner in Greece, a tourist. Married, three children, a house on a hillside in a dry country that looked a little like Greece, but was far away. Spoke a language called English, knew a smattering of other tongues. Not much Greek. That would be okay: I have my ways of communicating.

To get around the countryside properly, I discovered, I was going to need land-clothing, money, and a passport. I took care of these matters. Details like those don't pose problems for such as we.

Then I went rummaging in his mind to see whether he had any information in there about the present whereabouts of Zeus.

It was a very orderly mind. He had Zeus filed under "Greek Mythology."

Mythology?

Yes. Yes! He knew about Gaea, and Uranus, and the overthrow of Uranus by Cronus. He knew about the other Titans, at any rate some of them—Prometheus, Rhea, Hyperion, Iapetus. He knew some details about a few of the giants and miscellaneous hundred-armed monsters, and about the war between Zeus and the Titans and the Titans' total downfall, and the takeover by the big guy and his associates, Poseidon and Apollo and Ares & Company. But these were all stories to him. Fables. *Mythology.*

I confess I looked in his well-stocked mental archives for myself, Typhoeus—even a Titan has some vanity, you know—but all I found was a reference that said, "Typhon, child of Hera, is often confused with the earlier Titan Typhoeus, son of Gaea and Tartarus."

Well, yes. The names are similar; but Typhon was the bloated she-dragon that Apollo slew at Delphi, and what does that have to do with me?

That was bad, very bad, to show up in this copiously furnished mind only as a correction of an erroneous reference to someone else. Humiliating, you might actually say. I am not as important as Cronus or Uranus in the scheme of things, I suppose, but I did have my hour of glory, that time I went up against Zeus single-handed and came very close to defeating him. But what was even worse than such neglect, far worse, was to have the whole splen-did swaggering tribe of us, from the great mother Gaea and her heavenly consort down to the merest satyr and wood-nymph, tucked away in there as so much mythology.

What had happened to the world, and to its gods, while I lay writhing under Etna?

Mount Olympus seemed a reasonable first place for me to go to look for some answers.

I was at the absolute wrong end of Greece for that: down in the southwestern corner, whereas Olympus is far up in the northeast. All decked out in my new human body and its new human clothes, I caught a hydrofoil ferry to Patra, on the mainland, and another ferry across the Gulf of Corinth to Nafpaktos, and then, by train and bus, made my way up toward Thessaly, where Olympus is. None of these places except Olympus itself had been there last time I was in Greece, nor were there such things as trains or ferries or buses then. But I'm adaptable. I am, after all, an immor-tal god. A sort of a god, anyway.

It was interesting, sitting among you mortals in those buses and trains. I had never paid much attention to you in the old days, any more than I would give close attention to ants or bumblebees or cockroaches. Back there in the early ages of the world, humans were few and far between, inconsequential experimental wildlife. Prometheus made you, you know, for some obscure reason of his own: made you out of assorted dirt and slime, and breathed life into you, and turned you loose to decorate the landscape. You certainly did a job of decorating it, didn't you?

Sitting there among you in those crowded garlicky trains, breathing your exhalations and smelling your sweat, I couldn't help admiring the persistence and zeal with which you people had covered so much of the world with your houses, your highways, your shopping malls, your amusement parks, your stadiums, your power-transmission lines, and your garbage. Especially your garbage. Very few of these things could be considered any sort of an improvement over the basic virgin terrain, but I had to give you credit for effort, anyway. Prometheus, wherever he might be now, would surely be proud of you.

But where *was* Prometheus? Still chained up on that mountaintop, with Zeus's eagle gnawing away on his liver?

I roamed the minds of my traveling companions, but they weren't educated people like the one I had chanced upon at that beach, and they knew zero about Prometheus. Or anybody else of my own era, for that matter, with the exception of Zeus and Apollo and Athena and a few of the other latecomer gods. Who also were mere mythology to them. Greece had different gods these days, it seemed. Someone called Christos had taken over here. Along with his father and his mother, and assorted lesser deities whose relation to the top ones was hard to figure out.

Who were these new gods? Where had they come from? I was pleased by the thought that Zeus had been pushed aside by this Christos the way he had nudged old Cronus off the throne, but how had it happened? When?

Would I find Christos living on top of Mount Olympus in Zeus's old palace?

Well, no. I very shortly discovered that nobody was living on top of Olympus at all.

The place had lost none of its beauty, infested though modern-day Greece is by you and your kind. The enormous plateau on which the mountain stands is still unspoiled; and Olympus itself rises as ever in that great soaring sweep above the wild, desolate valley, the various summits forming a spectacular natural amphitheater and the upper tiers of rock splendidly shrouded by veils of cloud.

There are some roads going up, now. In the foothills I hired a car and a driver to take me through the forests of chestnut and fir to a refuge hut two thirds of the way up that is used by climbers, and there I left my driver, telling him I would go the rest of the way myself. He gave me a peculiar look, I suppose because I was wearing the wrong kind of clothing for climbing, and had no mountaineering equipment with me.

When he was gone, I shed my borrowed human form and rose up once again taller than the tallest tree in the world, and gave myself a set of gorgeous black-feathered wings as well, and went wafting up into that region of clean, pure air where Zeus had once had his throne.

No throne. No Zeus.

My cousins the giants Otus and Ephialtes had piled Mount Pelion on top of Mount Ossa to get up here during the war of the gods, and were flung right back down again. But I had the place to myself, unchallenged. I hovered over the jagged fleece-kissed peaks of the ultimate summit, spiraling down through the puffs of white cloud, ready for battle, but no battle was offered me.

"Zeus? Zeus?"

Once I had stood against him hissing terror from my grim jaws, and my eyes flaring gorgon lightning that had sent his fellow gods packing in piss-pants terror. But Zeus had withstood me, then. He blasted me with sizzling thunderbolts and seared me to an ash, and hurled me to rack and ruin; and jammed what was left of me down under Mount Etna amid rivers of fire, with the craftsman god Hephaestus piling the tools of his workshop all over me to hold me down, and there I lay for those fifty thousand years, muttering to myself, until I had healed enough to come forth.

I was forth now, all right, and looking for a rematch. Etna had vomited rivers of fire all over the fair plains of Sicily, and I was loose upon the world; but where was my adversary?

"Zeus!" I cried, into the emptiness.

I tried the name of Christos, too, just to see if the new god would answer. No go. He wasn't there either. Olympus was as stunning as ever, but nobody godly seemed to have any use for it these days.

I flew back down to the Alpine Club shelter and turned myself back into the lean-shanked American tourist with the high forehead and the long nose. I think three hikers may have seen me make the transformation, for as I started down the slope I came upon them standing slackjawed and goggle-eyed, as motionless as though Medusa had smitten them into stone.

"Hi, there, fellas," I called to them. "Have a nice day!"

They just gaped. I descended the fir-darkened mountainside to the deep-breasted valley, and just like any hungry mortal I ate dolmades and keftedes and moussaka in a little taverna I found down there, washing it down with a few kilos of retsina. And then, not so much like any mortal, I walked halfway across the country to Athens. It took me a goodly number of days, resting only a few hours every night. The body I had copied was a fundamentally sturdy one, and of course I had bolstered it a little.

A long walk, yes. But I was beginning to comprehend that there was no need for me to hurry, and I wanted to see the sights.

ATHENS WAS A HORROR. IT was the kingdom of Hades risen up to the surface of the world. Noise, congestion, all-around general grittiness, indescribable ugliness, everything in a miserable state of disrepair, and the air so thick with foul vapor that you could scratch your initials in it with your fingernails, if you had initials, if you had fingernails.

I knew right away I wasn't going to find any members of the old pantheon in this town. No deity in his right mind would want to spend ten minutes here. But Athens is the city of Athena, and Athena is the goddess of knowledge, and I thought there might be a possibility that somewhere here in her city that I would be able to learn how and why and when the assorted divinities of Greece had made the transition from omnipotence to mythology, and where I might find them (or at least the one I was looking for) now.

I prowled the nightmare streets. Dust and sand and random blocks of concrete everywhere, rusting metal girders standing piled for no particular reason by the side of the road, crumbling buildings. Traffic, frantic and fierce: what a mistake giving up the ox-cart had been! Cheap, tacky shops. Skinny long-legged cats hissed at me. They knew what I was. I hissed right back. We understood each other, at least.

Up on a hilltop in the middle of everything, a bunch of ruined marble temples. The Acropolis, that hilltop is the highest and holiest place in town. The temples aren't bad, as mortal buildings go, but in terrible shape, fallen columns scattered hither and yon, caryatids eroded to blurs by the air pollution. Why are you people such dreadful custodians of your own best works?

I went up there to look around, thinking I might find some lurking god or demigod in town on a visit. I stood by the best of the tumbledown temples, the one called the Parthenon, and listened to a little man with big eyeglasses who was telling a group of people who looked exactly like him how the building had looked when it was new and Athena was still in town. He spoke a language that my host body didn't understand at all, but I made a few adjustments and comprehended. So many languages, you mortals! *We* all spoke the same language, and that was good enough for us; but we were only gods, I suppose.

When he was through lecturing them about the Parthenon, the tour guide said, "Now we will visit the Sanctuary of Zeus. This way, please."

The Sanctuary of Zeus was just back of the Parthenon, but

there really wasn't very much left of it. The tour guide did a little routine about Zeus as father of the gods, getting six facts out of every five wrong.

"Let me tell you a few things about Zeus," I wanted to say, but I didn't. "How he used to cheat at cards, for instance. And the way he couldn't keep his hands off young girls. Or, maybe, the way he bellowed and moaned the first time he and I fought, when I tangled him in the coils of my snakes and laid him low, and cut the tendons of his hands and feet to keep him from getting rambunctious, and locked him up in that cave in Cilicia."

I kept all that to myself. These people didn't look like they'd care to hear any commentary from a stranger. Anyway, if I told that story I'd feel honor bound to go on and explain how that miserable sneak Hermes crept into the cave when I wasn't looking and patched Zeus up—and then how, once Zeus was on his feet again, he came after me and let me have it with such a blast of lightningbolts that I was fried halfway to a crisp and wound up spending the next few epochs as a prisoner down there under Etna.

A dispiriting place, the Acropolis.

I went slinking down and over to the Plaka, which is the neighborhood in back of it, for some lunch. Human bodies need to be fed again and again, all day long. Swordfish grilled on skewers with onions and tomatoes; more retsina; fruit and cheese. All right. Not bad. Then to the National Museum, a two-hour walk, sweat-sticky and dusty. Where I looked at broken statues and bought a guidebook that told me about the gods whose statues these were. Not even close to the actualities, any of them. Did they seriously think that brawny guy with the beard was Poseidon? And the woman with the tin hat, Athena? And that blowhard—Zeus? Don't make me laugh. Please. My laughter destroys whole cities.

Nowhere in the whole museum were there any representations of Titans. Just Zeus, Apollo, Aphrodite, Poseidon, and the rest of them, the junior varsity, the whole mob of supplanters, over and over and over. It was as if we didn't count at all in the historical record.

That hurt. I was in one hell of a sour mood when I left the museum.

There was a Temple of Olympian Zeus in town, the guidebook said, somewhere back in the vicinity of the Acropolis. I kept hoping that I would find some clue to Zeus' present place of residence at one of the sites that once had been sacred to him. A vestige, a lingering whiff of divinity.

But the Temple of Olympian Zeus was nothing but an incomplete set of ruined columns, and the only whiff I picked up there was the whiff of mortality and decay. And now it was getting dark and the body I was inhabiting was hungry again. Back to the Plaka; grilled meat, wine, a sweet pudding.

Afterwards, as I roamed the winding streets leading down to the newer part of the city with no special purpose in mind, a feeble voice out of a narrow alley said, in the native language of my host body, "Help! Oh, please, help!"

I was not put into this world for the purpose of helping anyone. But the body that I had duplicated in order to get around in modern Greece was evidently the body of a kindly and responsible person, because his reflexes took over instantly, and I found myself heading into that alleyway to see what aid I could render the person who was so piteously crying out.

Deep in the shadows I saw someone—a woman, I realized—lying on the ground in what looked like a pool of blood. I went to her side and knelt by her, and she began to mutter something in a bleary way about being attacked and robbed.

"Can you sit up?" I said, slipping my arm around her back. "It'll be easier for me to carry you if—"

Then I felt a pair of hands grasping me by the shoulders, not gently, and something hard and sharp pressing against the middle of my back, and the supposedly bloodied and battered woman I was trying to help rolled deftly out of my grasp and stepped back without any trouble at all, and a disagreeable rasping voice at my left ear said quietly, "Just give us your wristwatch and your wallet and you won't get hurt at all."

I was puzzled for a moment. I was still far from accustomed to human ways, and it was often necessary to peer into my host-mind to find out what was going on.

Quickly, though, I came to understand that there was such a thing as crime in your world, and that some of it was being tried on me at this very moment. The woman in the alley was bait; I was the prey; two accomplices had been lurking in the shadows.

I suppose I could have given them my wristwatch and wallet without protest, and let them make their escape. What did a wristwatch mean to me? And I could create a thousand new wallets just like the one I had, which I had created also, after all. As for harm, they could do me none with their little knife. I had survived even the lightnings of Zeus. Perhaps I should have reacted with godlike indifference to their little attempt at mugging me.

But it had been a long dreary discouraging day, and a hot one, too. The air was close and vile-smelling. Maybe I had allowed my host body to drink a little too much retsina with dinner. In any event, godlike indifference was not what I displayed just then. Mortal petulance was more like the appropriate term.

"Behold me, fools," I said.

I let them see my true form.

There I was before them, sky-high, mountainous, a horrendous gigantic figure of many heads and fiery eyes and thick black bristles and writhing viperish excrescences, a sight to make even gods quail.

Of course, inasmuch as I'm taller than the tallest tree and appropriately wide, manifesting myself in such a narrow alleyway might have posed certain operational problems. But I have access to dimensions unavailable to you, and I made room for myself there with the proper interpenetrational configurations. Not that it mattered to the three muggers, because they were dead of shock the moment they saw me towering before them.

I raised my foot and ground them into the pavement like noxious vermin.

Then, in the twinkling of an eye, I was once more a slender, lithe middle-aged American tourist with thinning hair and a kindly smile, and there were three dark spots on the pavement of the alley, and that was that.

It was, I admit, overkill.

But I had had a trying day. In fact, I had had a trying fifty thousand years.

ATHENS HAD BEEN SO HELLISH that it put me in mind of the authentic kingdom of Hades, and so that was my next destination, for I thought I might get some answers down there among the dead. It wasn't much of a trip, not for me. I opened a vortex for myself and slipped downward and there right in front of me were the black poplars and willows of the Grove of Persephone, with Hades' Gate just behind it.

"Cerberus?" I called. "Here, doggy doggy doggy! Good Cerberus! Come say hello to Daddy!"

Where was he, my lovely dog, my own sweet child? For I myself was the progenitor of the three-headed guardian of the gate of Hell, by virtue of my mating with my sister, Tartarus and Gaea's scaly-tailed daughter Echidna. We made the Harpies too, did Echidna and I, and the Chimera, and Scylla, and also the Hydra, a whole gaudy gorgeous brood of monsters. But of all my children I was always most fond of Cerberus, for his loyalty. How I loved to see him come running toward me when I called! What pleasure I took in his serpent-bristled body, his voice like clanging bronze, his slavering jaws that dripped black venom!

This day, though, I wandered dogless through the Underworld. There was no sign of Cerberus anywhere, no trace even of his glittering turds. Hell's Gate stood open and the place was deserted. I saw nothing of Charon the boatman of the Styx, nor Hades and Queen Persephone, nor any members of their court, nor the spirits of the dead who should have been in residence here. An abandoned warehouse, dusty and empty. Quickly I fled toward the sunshine.

THE ISLAND OF DELOS WAS where I went next, looking for Apollo. Delos is, or was, his special island, and Apollo had always struck me as the coolest, most level-headed member of the Zeus bunch. Perhaps he had survived whatever astounding debacle it was that had swept the Olympian gods away. And, if so, maybe he could give me a clue to Zeus's current location.

Big surprise! I went to Delos, but no Apollo.

It was yet another dismal disillusioning journey through the tumbledown sadness that is Greece. This time I flew; not on handsome black-feathered wings, but on a clever machine, a metal tube called an airplane, full of travelers looking more or less like me in my present form. It rose up out of Athens in a welter of sound and fury and took up a course high above the good old wine-dark sea, speckled with tawny archipelagos, and in very short order came down on a small dry island to the south. This island was called Mykonos, and there I could buy myself passage in one of the boats that made outings several times a day to nearby Delos.

Delos was a dry rubble-field, strewn with fragments of temples, their columns mostly broken off close to the ground. Some marble lions were still intact, lean and vigilant, crouching on their hind legs. They looked hungry. But there wasn't much else to see. The place had the parched gloom of death about it, the bleak aura of extinction.

I returned to Mykonos on the lunchtime boat, and found myself lodgings in a hillside hotel a short distance outside the pretty little narrow-streeted shorefront town. I ordered me some more mortal food and drank mortal drink. My borrowed body needed such things.

It was on Mykonos that I met Aphrodite.

Or, rather, she met me.

I was sitting by myself, minding my own business, in the hotel's outdoor bar, which was situated on a cobblestoned patio bedecked with mosaics and hung with nets and oars and other purported fishing artifacts. I was on my third ouzo of the hour, which possibly was a bit much for the capacities of the body I was using, and I was staring down the hillside pensively at, well, what I have to call the wine-dark sea. (Greece brings out the clichés in anyone. Why should I resist?)

A magnificent long-legged full-bodied blonde woman came over to me and said, in a wonderfully throaty, husky voice, "New in town, sailor?"

I stared at her, astounded.

There was the unmistakable radiance of divinity about her. My Geiger counter of godliness was going clickity-clack, full blast. How could I have failed to pick up her emanations the moment I arrived on Mykonos? But I hadn't, not until she was standing right next to me. She had picked up mine, though.

"Who are you?" I blurted.

"Won't you ask a lady to sit down, even?"

I jumped to my feet like a nervous schoolboy, hauled a deck chair scrapingly across and positioned it next to mine, and bowed her into it. Then I wigwagged for a waiter. "What do you want to drink?" I rasped. My throat was dry. Nervous schoolboy, yes, indeed.

"I'll have what you're having."

"*Parakalo*, ouzo on the rocks," I told the waiter.

She had showers of golden hair tumbling to shoulder length, and catlike yellow eyes, and full ripe lips that broke naturally into the warmest of smiles. The aroma that came from her was one of young wine and green fields at sunrise and swift-coursing streams, but also of lavender and summer heat, of night rain, of surging waves, of midnight winds.

I knew I was consorting with the enemy. I didn't care.

"Which one are you?" I said again.

"Guess."

"Aphrodite would be too obvious. You're probably Ares, or Hephaestus, or Poseidon."

She laughed, a melodic cadenza of merriment that ran right through the scale and into the infra-voluptuous. "You give me too much credit for deviousness. But I like your way of thinking. Ares in drag, really? Poseidon with a close shave? Hephaestus with a blonde wig?" She leaned close. The fragrance of her took on hurricane intensity. "You were right the first time."

"Aphrodite."

"None other. I live in Los Angeles now. Taking a little holiday in the mother country. And you? You're one of the old ones, aren't you?"

"How can you tell?"

"The archaic emanation you give off. Something out of the pre-Olympian past." She clinked the ice cubes thoughtfully in her glass, took a long pull of the ouzo, stared me straight in the eyes. "Prometheus? Tethys?" I shook my head. "Someone of that clan, though. I thought all of you old ones were done for a long time ago. But there's definitely a Titan vibe about you. Which one, I wonder? Most likely one of the really strange ones. Thaumas? Phorcys?"

"Stranger than those," I said.

She took a few more guesses. Not even close.

"Typhoeus," I told her finally.

WE WALKED INTO TOWN FOR dinner. People turned to look at us in the narrow streets. At her, I mean. She was wearing a filmy orange sundress with nothing under it and when you were east of her on a westbound street you got quite a show.

"You really don't think that I'm going to find Zeus?" I asked her.

"Let's say you have your work cut out for you."

"Well, so be it. I *have* to find him."

"Why is that?"

167

"It's my job," I said. "There's nothing personal about it. I'm the designated avenger. It's my sole purpose in existence: to punish Zeus for his war against the children of Gaea. You know that."

"The war's been over a long time, Typhoeus. You might as well let bygones be bygones. Anyway, it's not as though Zeus got to enjoy his victory for long." We were in the middle of the maze of narrow winding streets that is Mykonos Town. She pointed to a cheerful little restaurant called Catherine's. "Let's go in here. I ate here last night and it was pretty good."

We ordered a bottle of white wine. "I like the body you found for yourself," she said. "Not particularly handsome, no, but *pleasing.* The eyes are especially nice. Warm and trustworthy, but also keen, penetrating."

I would not be drawn away from the main theme. "What happened to the Olympians?" I asked.

"Died off, most of them. One by one. Of neglect. Starvation."

"Immortal gods don't die."

"Some do, some don't. You know that. Didn't Argus of the Hundred Eyes kill your very own Echidna? And did she come back to life?"

"But the major gods—"

"Even if they don't die, they can be forgotten, and the effect's pretty much the same. While you were locked up under Etna, new gods came in. There wasn't even a battle. They just moved in, and we had to move along. We disappeared entirely."

"So I've noticed."

"Yes. Totally out of business. You've seen the shape our temples are in? Have you seen anybody putting out burnt offerings to us? No, no, it's all over for us, the worship, the sacrifices. Has been for a long time. We went into exile, the whole kit and kaboodle of us, scattered across the world. I'm sure a lot of us simply died, despite that theoretical immortality of ours. Some hung on, I suppose. But it's a thousand years since the last time I saw any of them."

"Which ones did you see then?"

"Apollo—he was getting gray and paunchy. And I caught sight of Hermes, once—I think it was Hermes—slow and short-winded, and limping like Hephaestus."

"And Zeus?" I asked. "You never ran into him anywhere, after you all left Olympus?"

"No. Never even once."

I pondered that. "So how did *you* manage to stay so healthy?"

"I'm Aphrodite. The life-force. Beauty. Passion. Those things don't go out of fashion for long. I've done all right for myself, over the years."

"Ah. Yes. Obviously you have."

The waitress fluttered around us. I was boiling with questions to ask Aphrodite, but it was time to order, and that was what we did. The usual Greek things, stuffed grape leaves, grilled fish, overcooked vegetables. Another bottle of wine. My head was pulsating. The restaurant was small, crowded, a whirlpool of noise. The nearness of Aphrodite was overwhelming. I felt dizzy. It was a surprisingly pleasant sensation.

I said, after a time, "I'm convinced that Zeus is still around somewhere. I'm going to find him and this time I'm going to whip his ass and put *him* under Mount Etna."

"It's amazing how much like a small boy an immortal being can be. Even one as huge and frightful as you."

My face turned hot. I said nothing.

"Forget Zeus," she urged. "Forget Typhoeus, too. Stay human. Eat, drink, be merry." Her eyes were glistening. I felt as if I were falling forward, tumbling into the sweet chasm between her breasts. "We could take a trip together. I'd teach you how to enjoy yourself. How to enjoy me, too. Tell me: have you ever been in love?"

"Echidna and I—"

"Echidna! Yes! You and she got together and made a bunch of hideous monsters like yourselves, with too many heads and drooling fangs. I don't mean Echidna. This is Earth, here and now. I'm a woman now and you're a man."

"But Zeus—"

"*Zeus,*" she said scornfully. She made the name of the Lord of Olympus sound like an obscenity.

We finished eating and I paid the check and we went outside into the mild, breezy Mykonos night, strolling for fifteen or twenty minutes, winding up finally in a dark, deserted part of the town, a warehouse district down by the water, where the street was no more than five feet wide and empty shuttered buildings with whitewashed walls bordered us on both sides.

She turned to me there and pulled me abruptly up against her. Her eyes were bright with mischief. Her lips sought mine. With a little hissing sound she nudged me backward until I was leaning against a wall, and she was pressing me tight, and currents of energy that could have fried a continent were passing between us. I think there could have been no one, not man nor god, who would not have wanted to trade places with me just then.

"Quickly! The hotel!" she whispered.

"The hotel, yes."

We didn't bother to walk. That would have taken too long. In a flash we vanished ourselves from that incomprehensible tangle of maze-like streets and reappeared in her room at our hotel, and from then to dawn she and I generated such a delirium of erotic force that the entire island shook and shivered with the glorious sturm and drang of it. We heaved and thrust and moaned and groaned, and rivers of sweat ran from our bodies and our hearts pounded and thundered and our eyes rolled in our heads from giddy exhaustion, for we allowed ourselves the luxury of mortal limitations for the sake of the mortal joy of transcending those limitations. But because we *weren't* mortal we also had the option of renewing our strength whenever we had depleted it, and we exercised that option many a time before rosy-fingered dawn came tiptoeing up over the high-palisaded eastern walls.

Naked, invisible to prying eyes, Aphrodite and I walked then hand in hand along the morning-shimmering strand of the fish-swarming sea, and she murmured to me of the places we would go, the things we would experience.

"The Taj Mahal," she said. "And the summer palace at Udaipur. Persepolis and Isfahan in springtime. Baalbek. Paris, of course. Carcassonne. Iguazu Falls, and the Blue Mosque, and the Fountains of the Blue Nile. We'll make love in the Villa of Tiberius on Capri—and between the paws of the Sphinx—and in the snow on top of Mount Everest—"

"Yes," I said. "Yes. Yes. Yes. Yes."

And what I was thinking was, *Zeus. Zeus. Zeus. Zeus.*

AND SO WE TRAVEL ABOUT the world together, Aphrodite and I, seeing the things in it that are beautiful, and there are many of those; and so she distracts me from my true task. For the time being. It is very pleasant, traveling with Aphrodite; and so I permit myself to be distracted this way.

But I have not forgotten my purpose. And this is my warning to the world.

I am a restless being, a mighty thrusting force. I was created that way. My adversary doesn't seem currently to be around. But Zeus is here somewhere. I know he is. He wears a mask. He disguises himself as a mortal, either because it amuses him to do so, or because he has no choice, for there is something in the world of which he is afraid, something from which he must hide himself, some god greater even than Zeus, as Zeus was greater than Cronus and Cronus was greater than Uranus.

But I will find him. And when I do, I will drop this body and take on my own form again. I will stand mountain-high, and you will see my hundred heads, and my fires will flash and rage. And Zeus and I will enter into combat once more, and this time I will surely win.

It will happen.

I promise you that, O small ones. I warn you. It will happen.

You will tremble then. I'm sorry for that. The mind that came with this body I wear now has taught me something about compassion; and so I regret the destruction I will inevitably visit upon you, because it cannot be avoided, when Zeus and I enter into our struggle. You have my sincerest apologies, in advance. Protect yourselves as best you can. But for me there can be no turning away from my task.

Zeus? This is Typhoeus the Titan who calls you!

Zeus, where are you?

❖

OUR LADY OF THE SAUROPODS

Once upon a time there was a Steven Spielberg movie called *Jurassic Park*, the theme of which was that dinosaurs could be reconstructed from bits of fossil DNA and used to populate an amusement park, where, of course, the characters of the movie would undergo a series of not-so-amusing adventures when the carnivorous dinosaurs got loose among them. It was based on a 1990 novel by Michael Crichton, which nobody much remembers anymore, but everybody saw the movie (and its sequel), and by now *Jurassic Park* has become a cliché reference-point for the cloning of extinct animals.

Before Spielberg, before Crichton, even, various science-fiction writers had hit on the idea of recreating dinosaurs from their fossil remains. I'm sure H. G. Wells would have written a story about it if he had known anything about DNA back there in the dawn of the twentieth century when he was inventing just about all the other themes for science fiction. So far as I know, Wells did not write any dinosaurs-are-among-us tales, but Sir Arthur Conan Doyle did as far back as 1912, setting a pterodactyl loose in Edwardian London in *The Lost World*. But Doyle's critter was the real natural-born thing, brought back alive from a remote plateau in South America where dinosaurs had managed to survive all these millions of years. Later writers, among them me, used biological means to regenerate the big beasts from the genetic material found in their ancient bones.

When I tackled the theme, in January 1980, I had the good sense to stick all the toothy saurians on an artificial space satellite safely distant from our own cozy planet, whereas Crichton, who had an infallible sense of how science could be used to scare readers and moviegoers, set his Jurassic Park on an island off Costa Rica, ever so much more risky a proposition. If you want to get in trouble with dinosaurs on a space satellite, you have to go there to visit them, which is exactly what the narrator of "Our Lady of the Sauropods" does. And in it I make use of one of the classic modes of the first-person story: the narrator who describes the process where by easy and plausible stages she is transformed from a sane and sensible scientist, one who is opposed to the idea of turning the dinosaur satellite into any sort of amusement park, into something quite the opposite.

The story was published in the September 1980 issue of *Omni*, the shiny, big-circulation magazine that cut quite a swath through the world of science-fiction publishing before it imploded and disappeared a decade or so later. Possibly Michael Crichton was one of its many readers, though I have no way of knowing whether my story planted the notion of *Jurassic Park* in his mind. "Our Lady of the Sauropods" might have made a nifty science-fiction thriller for Hollywood, but Spielberg never got to see it, and he did see the Crichton book, and all the rest is history. Or prehistory, rather.

———

21 August. 0750 hours. Ten minutes since the module meltdown. I can't see the wreckage from here, but I can smell it, bitter and sour against the moist tropical air. I've found a cleft in the rocks, a kind of shallow cavern, where I'll be safe from the dinosaurs for a while. It's shielded by thick clumps of cycads, and in any case it's too small for the big predators to enter. But sooner or later I'm going to need food, and then what? I have no weapons. How long can one woman last, stranded and more or less helpless, aboard a habitat unit not quite five hundred meters in diameter that she's sharing with a bunch of active, hungry dinosaurs?

I keep telling myself that none of this is really happening. Only I can't quite convince myself of that.

My escape still has me shaky. I can't get out of my mind the funny little bubbling sound the tiny powerpak made as it began to overheat. In something like fourteen seconds my lovely mobile module became a charred heap of fused-together junk, taking with it my communicator unit, my food supply, my laser gun, and just about everything else. And but for the warning that funny little sound gave me, I'd be so much charred junk now, too. Better off that way, most likely.

When I close my eyes, I imagine I can see *Habitat Vronsky* floating serenely in orbit a mere 120 kilometers away. What a beautiful sight! The walls gleaming like platinum, the great mirror collecting sunlight and flashing it into the windows, the agricultural satellites wheeling around it like a dozen tiny moons. I could almost reach out and touch it. Tap on the shielding and murmur, "Help me, come for me, rescue me." But I might just as well be out beyond Neptune as sitting here in the adjoining Lagrange slot. No way I can call for help. The moment I move outside this cleft in the rock I'm at the mercy of my saurians and their mercy is not likely to be tender.

Now it's beginning to rain—artificial, like practically everything else on Dino Island. But it gets you just as wet as the natural kind. And clammy. Pfaugh.

Jesus, what am I going to do?

0815 HOURS. The rain is over for now. It'll come again in six hours. Astonishing how muggy, dank, thick, the air is. Simply breathing is hard work, and I feel as though mildew is forming on my lungs. I miss Vronsky's clear, crisp, everlasting springtime air. On previous trips to Dino Island I never cared about the climate. But, of course, I was snugly englobed in my mobile unit, a world within a world, self-contained, self-sufficient, isolated from all contact with this place and its creatures. Merely a roving eye, traveling as I pleased, invisible, invulnerable.

Can they sniff me in here?

We don't think their sense of smell is very acute. Sharper than a crocodile's, not as good as a cat's. And the stink of the burned wreckage dominates the place at the moment. But I must reek with fear-signals. I feel calm now, but it was different as I went desperately scrambling out of the module during the meltdown. Scattering pheromones all over the place, I bet.

Commotion in the cycads. *Something's coming in here!*

Long neck, small birdlike feet, delicate grasping hands. Not to worry. Struthiomimus, is all—dainty dino, fragile, birdlike critter barely two meters high. Liquid golden eyes staring solemnly at me. It swivels its head from side to side, ostrichlike, click-click, as if trying to make up its mind about coming closer to me. *Scat!* Go peck a stegosaur. Let me alone.

The struthiomimus withdraws, making little clucking sounds.

Closest I've ever been to a live dinosaur. Glad it was one of the little ones.

0900 HOURS. Getting hungry. What am I going to eat? They say roasted cycad cones aren't too bad. How about raw ones? So many plants are edible when cooked and poisonous otherwise. I never studied such things in detail. Living in our antiseptic little L5 habitats, we're not required to be outdoors-wise, after all. Anyway, there's a fleshy-looking cone on the cycad just in front of the cleft, and it's got an edible look. Might as well try it raw, because there's no other way. Rubbing sticks together will get me nowhere.

Getting the cone off takes some work. Wiggle, twist, snap, tear—*there*. Not as fleshy as it looks. Chewy, in fact. Like munching on rubber. Decent flavor, though. And maybe some useful carbohydrate.

The shuttle isn't due to pick me up for thirty days. Nobody's apt to come looking for me, or even think about me, before then. I'm on my own. Nice irony there: I was desperate to get out of Vronsky and escape from all the bickering and maneuvering, the endless meetings and memoranda, the feinting and counterfeinting, all the ugly political crap that scientists indulge in when they turn into administrators. Thirty days of blessed isolation on Dino Island! An end to that constant dull throbbing in my head from the daily infighting with Director Sarber. Pure research again! And then the meltdown, and here I am cowering in the bushes wondering which comes first, starving or getting gobbled.

0930 HOURS. Funny thought just now. Could it have been sabotage?

Consider. Sarber and I, feuding for weeks over the issue of opening Dino Island to tourists. Crucial staff vote coming up next month. Sarber says we can raise millions a year for expanded studies with a program of guided tours and perhaps some rental of the island to film companies. I say that's risky both for the dinos and the tourists, destructive of scientific values, a distraction, a sellout. Emotionally the staff's with me, but Sarber waves figures around, showy fancy income-projections, and generally shouts and blusters. Tempers running high, Sarber in lethal fury at being opposed, barely able to hide his loathing for me. Circulating rumors—designed to get back to me—that if I persist in blocking him, he'll abort my career. Which is malarkey, of course. He may outrank me, but he has no real authority over me. And then his politeness yesterday. (*Yesterday?* An aeon ago.) Smiling smarmily, telling me he hopes I'll rethink my position during my observation tour on the island. Wishing me well. Had he gimmicked my powerpak? I guess it isn't hard if you know a little engineering, and Sarber does. Some kind of timer set to withdraw the insulator rods? Wouldn't be any harm to Dino

Island itself, just a quick, compact, localized disaster that implodes and melts the unit and its passenger, so sorry, terrible scientific tragedy, what a great loss. And even if by some fluke I got out of the unit in time, my chances of surviving here as a pedestrian for thirty days would be pretty skimpy, right? Right.

It makes me boil to think that someone's willing to murder you over a mere policy disagreement. It's barbaric. Worse than that: it's tacky.

1130 HOURS. I can't stay crouched in this cleft forever. I'm going to explore the island and see if I can find a better hideout. This one simply isn't adequate for anything more than short-term huddling. Besides, I'm not as spooked as I was right after the meltdown. I realize now that I'm not going to find a tyrannosaur hiding behind every tree. And tyrannosaurs aren't going to be much interested in scrawny stuff like me.

Anyway I'm a quick-witted higher primate. If my humble mammalian ancestors seventy million years ago were able to elude dinosaurs well enough to survive and inherit the earth, I should be able to keep from getting eaten for the next thirty days. And with or without my cozy little mobile module, I want to get out into this place, whatever the risks. Nobody's ever had a chance to interact this closely with the dinos before.

Good thing I kept this pocket recorder when I jumped from the module. Whether I'm a dino's dinner or not, I ought to be able to set down some useful observations.

Here I go.

1830 HOURS. Twilight is descending now. I am camped near the equator in a lean-to flung together out of tree-fern fronds—a flimsy shelter, but the huge fronds conceal me, and with luck I'll make it through to morning. That cycad cone doesn't seem to have poisoned me yet, and I ate another one just now, along with some tender new fiddleheads uncoiling from the heart of a tree-fern. Spartan fare, but it gives me the illusion of being fed.

In the evening mists I observe a brachiosaur, half-grown but already colossal, munching in the treetops. A gloomy-looking triceratops stands nearby and several of the ostrichlike struthiomimids scamper busily in the underbrush, hunting I know not what. No sign of tyrannosaurs all day. There aren't many of them here, anyway, and I hope they're all sleeping off huge feasts somewhere in the other hemisphere.

What a fantastic place this is!

I don't feel tired. I don't even feel frightened—just a little wary.

I feel exhilarated, as a matter of fact.

Here I sit peering out between fern fronds at a scene out of the dawn of time. All that's missing is a pterosaur or two flapping overhead, but we haven't brought those back yet. The mournful snufflings of the huge brachiosaur carry clearly even in the heavy air. The struthiomimids are making sweet honking sounds. Night is falling swiftly and the great shapes out there take on dreamlike primordial wonder.

What a brilliant idea it was to put all the Olsen-process dinosaur-reconstructs aboard a little L5 habitat of their very own and turn them loose to recreate the Mesozoic! After that unfortunate San Diego event with the tyrannosaur, it became politically unfeasible to keep them anywhere on earth, I know, but even so this is a better scheme. In just a little more than seven years Dino Island has taken on an altogether convincing illusion of reality. Things grow so fast in this lush, steamy, high-CO_2 tropical atmosphere! Of course, we haven't been able to duplicate the real Mesozoic flora, but we've done all right using botanical survivors, cycads and tree ferns and horsetails and palms and ginkgos and auracarias, and thick carpets of mosses and selaginellas and liverworts covering the ground. Everything has blended and merged and run amok: it's hard now to recall the bare and unnatural look of the island when we first laid it out. Now it's a seamless tapestry in green and brown, a dense jungle broken only by streams, lakes and meadows, encapsulated in spherical metal walls some two kilometers in circumference.

And the animals, the wonderful fantastic grotesque animals—

We don't pretend that the real Mesozoic ever held any such mix of fauna as I've seen today, stegosaurs and corythosaurs side by side, a triceratops sourly glaring at a brachiosaur, struthiomimus contemporary with iguanodon, a wild unscientific jumble of Triassic, Jurassic and Cretaceous, a hundred million years of the dinosaur reign scrambled together. We take what we can get. Olsen-process reconstructs require sufficient fossil DNA to permit the computer synthesis, and we've been able to find that in only some twenty species so far. The wonder is that we've accomplished even that much: to replicate the complete DNA molecule from battered and sketchy genetic information millions of years old, to carry out the intricate implants in reptilian host ova, to see the embryos through to self-sustaining levels. The only word that applies is *miraculous*. If our dinos come from eras millions of years apart, so be it: we do our best. If we have no pterosaur and no allosaur and no archaeopteryx, so be it: we may have them yet. What we already have is plenty to work with. Some day there may be separate Triassic, Jurassic and Cretaceous satellite habitats, but none of us will live to see that, I suspect.

Total darkness now. Mysterious screechings and hissings out there. This afternoon, as I moved cautiously, but in delight, from the wreckage site up near the rotation axis to my present equatorial camp, sometimes coming within fifty or a hundred meters of living dinos, I felt a kind of ecstasy. Now my fears are returning, and my anger at this stupid marooning. I imagine clutching claws reaching for me, terrible jaws yawning above me.

I don't think I'll get much sleep tonight.

22 August. 0600 hours. Rosy-fingered dawn comes to Dino Island, and I'm still alive. Not a great night's sleep, but I must have had some, because I can remember fragments of dreams. About dinosaurs, naturally. Sitting in little groups, some playing pinochle and some knitting sweaters. And choral singing, a dinosaur rendition of *The Messiah* or maybe Beethoven's Ninth.

I feel alert, inquisitive, and hungry. Especially hungry. I know we've stocked this place with frogs and turtles and other small-size anachronisms to provide a balanced diet for the big critters. Today I'll have to snare some for myself, grisly though I find the prospect of eating raw frog's legs.

I don't bother getting dressed. With rain showers programmed to fall four times a day, it's better to go naked anyway. Mother Eve of the Mesozoic, that's me! And without my soggy tunic I find that I don't mind the greenhouse atmosphere half as much.

Out to see what I can find.

The dinosaurs are up and about already, the big herbivores munching away, the carnivores doing their stalking. All of them have such huge appetites that they can't wait for the sun to come up. In the bad old days when the dinos were thought to be reptiles, of course, we'd have expected them to sit there like lumps until daylight got their body temperatures up to functional levels. But one of the great joys of the reconstruct project was the vindication of the notion that dinosaurs were warm-blooded animals, active and quick and pretty damned intelligent. No sluggardly crocodilians these! Would that they were, if only for my survival's sake.

1130 HOURS. A busy morning. My first encounter with a major predator.

There are nine tyrannosaurs on the island, including three born in the past eighteen months. (That gives us an optimum predator-to-prey ratio. If the tyrannosaurs keep reproducing and don't start eating each other, we'll have to begin thinning them out. One of the problems with a closed ecology—natural checks and balances don't fully apply.) Sooner or later I was bound to encounter one, but I had hoped it would be later.

I was hunting frogs at the edge of Cope Lake. A ticklish business—calls for agility, cunning, quick reflexes. I remember the
technique from my girlhood—the cupped hand, the lightning
pounce—but somehow it's become a lot harder in the last twenty
years. Superior frogs these days, I suppose. There I was, kneeling
in the mud, swooping, missing, swooping, missing; some vast sauropod snoozing in the lake, probably our diplodocus; a corythosaur browsing in a stand of gingko trees, quite delicately nipping
off the foul-smelling yellow fruits. Swoop. Miss. Swoop. Miss. Such
intense concentration on my task that old T. rex could have tip-
toed right up behind me, and I'd never have noticed. But then I
felt a subtle something, a change in the air, maybe, a barely perceptible shift in dynamics. I glanced up and saw the corythosaur
rearing on its hind legs, looking around uneasily, pulling deep
sniffs into that fantastically elaborate bony crest that houses its
early-warning system. *Carnivore alert!* The corythosaur obviously
smelled something wicked this way coming, for it swung around
between two big ginkgos and started to go galumphing away. Too
late. The treetops parted, giant boughs toppled, and out of the
forest came our original tyrannosaur, the pigeon-toed one we call
Belshazzar, moving in its heavy, clumsy waddle, ponderous legs
working hard, tail absurdly swinging from side to side. I slithered
into the lake and scrunched down as deep as I could go in the
warm oozing mud. The corythosaur had no place to slither.
Unarmed, unarmored, it could only make great bleating sounds,
terror mingled with defiance, as the killer bore down on it.

I had to watch. I had never seen a kill.

In a graceless but wondrously effective way, the tyrannosaur
dug its hind claws into the ground, pivoted astonishingly, and,
using its massive tail as a counterweight, moved in a ninety-degree
arc to knock the corythosaur down with a stupendous sidewise
swat of its huge head. I hadn't been expecting that. The corythosaur dropped and lay on its side, snorting in pain and feebly waving its limbs. Now came the coup de grace with hind legs, and

then the rending and tearing, the jaws and the tiny arms at last coming into play. Burrowing chin-deep in the mud, I watched in awe and weird fascination. There are those among us who argue that the carnivores ought to be segregated into their own island, that it is folly to allow reconstructs created with such effort to be casually butchered this way. Perhaps in the beginning that made sense, but not now, not when natural increase is rapidly filling the island with young dinos. If we are to learn anything about these animals, it will only be by reproducing as closely as possible their original living conditions. Besides, would it not be a cruel mockery to feed our tyrannosaurs on hamburger and herring?

The killer fed for more than an hour. At the end came a scary moment: Belshazzar, blood-smeared and bloated, hauled himself ponderously down to the edge of the lake for a drink. He stood no more than ten meters from me. I did my most convincing imitation of a rotting log; but the tyrannosaur, although it did seem to study me with a beady eye, had no further appetite. For a long while after he departed, I stayed buried in the mud, fearing he might come back for dessert. And eventually there was another crashing and bashing in the forest—not Belshazzar this time, though, but a younger one with a gimpy arm. It uttered a sort of whinnying sound and went to work on the corythosaur carcass. No surprise: we already knew that tyrannosaurs had no prejudices against carrion.

Nor, I found, did I.

When the coast was clear, I crept out and saw that the two tyrannosaurs had left hundreds of kilos of meat. Starvation knoweth no pride and also few qualms. Using a clamshell for my blade, I started chopping away.

Corythosaur meat has a curiously sweet flavor—nutmeg and cloves, dash of cinnamon. The first chunk would not go down. You are a pioneer, I told myself, retching. You are the first human ever to eat dinosaur meat. *Yes, but why does at have to be raw?* No choice about that. Be dispassionate, love. Conquer your gag reflex or die trying. I pretended I was eating oysters. This time the meat went down. It didn't stay down. The alternative, I told myself grimly, is a diet of fern fronds and frogs, and you haven't been much good at catching the frogs. I tried again. Success!

I'd have to call corythosaur meat an acquired taste. But the wilderness is no place for picky eaters.

23 AUGUST. 1300 HOURS. At midday I found myself in the southern hemisphere, along the fringes of Marsh Marsh about a hundred meters below the equator. Observing herd behavior in sauropods—five brachiosaurs, two adult and three young, moving in formation, the small ones in the center. By "small" I mean only some ten meters from nose to tail-tip. Sauropod appetites being what they are, we'll have to thin that herd soon, too, especially if we want to introduce a female diplodocus into the colony. *Two* species of sauropods breeding and eating like that could devastate the island in three years. Nobody ever expected dinosaurs to reproduce like rabbits—another dividend of their being warm-blooded, I suppose. We might have guessed it, though, from the vast quantity of fossils. If that many bones survived the catastrophes of a hundred-odd million years, how enormous the living Mesozoic population must have been! An awesome race in more ways than mere physical mass.

I had a chance to do a little herd-thinning myself just now. Mysterious stirring in the spongy soil right at my feet, and I looked down to see triceratops eggs hatching! Seven brave little critters, already horny and beaky, scrabbling out of a nest, staring around defiantly. No bigger than kittens, but active and sturdy from the moment of birth.

The corythosaur meat has probably spoiled by now. A more pragmatic soul very likely would have augmented her diet with one or two little ceratopsians. I couldn't do it.

They scuttled off in seven different directions. I thought briefly of catching one and making a pet out of it. Silly idea.

25 AUGUST. 0700 HOURS. Start of the fifth day. I've done three complete circumambulations of the island. Slinking around on foot is fifty times as risky as cruising around in a module, and fifty thousand times as rewarding. I make camp in a different place every night. I don't mind the humidity any longer. And despite my skimpy diet, I feel pretty healthy. Raw dinosaur, I know now, is a lot tastier than raw frog. I've become an expert scavenger—the sound of a tyrannosaur in the forest now stimulates my salivary glands instead of my adrenals. Going naked is fun, too. And I appreciate my body much more, since the bulges that civilization puts there have begun to melt away.

Nevertheless, I keep trying to figure out some way of signaling *Habitat Vronsky* for help. Changing the position of the reflecting mirrors, maybe, so I can beam an SOS? Sounds nice, but I don't even know where the island's controls are located, let alone how to run them. Let's hope my luck holds out another three and a half weeks.

27 AUGUST. 1700 HOURS. The dinosaurs know that I'm here and that I'm some extraordinary kind of animal. Does that sound weird? How can great dumb beasts *know* anything? They have such tiny brains. And my own brain must be softening on this protein-and-cellulose diet. Even so, I'm starting to have peculiar feelings about these animals. I see them *watching* me. An odd knowing look in their eyes, not stupid at all. They stare and I imagine them nodding, smiling, exchanging glances with each other, discussing me. I'm supposed to be observing them, but I think they're observing me, too, somehow.

This is crazy. I'm tempted to erase the entry. But I'll leave it as a record of my changing psychological state if nothing else.

28 AUGUST. 1200 HOURS. More fantasies about the dinosaurs. I've decided that the big brachiosaur—Bertha—plays a key role here. She doesn't move around much, but there are always lesser

185

dinosaurs in orbit around her. Much eye contact. *Eye contact between dinosaurs?* Let it stand. That's my perception of what they're doing. I get a definite sense that there's communication going on here, modulating over some wave that I'm not capable of detecting. And Bertha seems to be a central nexus, a grand totem of some sort, a—a switchboard? What am I talking about? What's happening to me?

30 AUGUST. 0945 HOURS. What a damned fool I am! Serves me right for being a filthy voyeur. Climbed a tree to watch iguanodons mating at the foot of Bakker Falls. At climactic moment the branch broke. I dropped twenty meters. Grabbed a lower limb or I'd be dead now. As it is, pretty badly smashed around. I don't think anything's broken, but my left leg won't support me and my back's in bad shape. Internal injuries too? Not sure. I've crawled into a little rock-shelter near the falls. Exhausted and maybe feverish. Shock, most likely. I suppose I'll starve now. It would have been an honor to be eaten by a tyrannosaur, but to die from falling out of a tree is just plain humiliating.

The mating of iguanodons is a spectacular sight, by the way. But I hurt too much to describe it now.

31 AUGUST. 1700 HOURS. Stiff, sore, hungry, hideously thirsty. Leg still useless and when I try to crawl even a few meters, I feel as if I'm going to crack in half at the waist. High fever.

How long does it take to starve to death?

1 SEP. 0700 HOURS. Three broken eggs lying near me when I awoke. Embryos still alive—probably stegosaur—but not for long. First food in forty-eight hours. Did the eggs fall out of a nest somewhere overhead? Do stegosaurs make their nests in trees, dummy?

Fever diminishing. Body aches all over. Crawled to the stream and managed to scoop up a little water.

1330 HOURS. Dozed off. Awakened to find haunch of fresh meat within crawling distance. Struthiomimus drumstick, I think. Nasty sour taste, but it's edible. Nibbled a little, slept again, ate some more. Pair of stegosaurs grazing not far away, tiny eyes fastened on me. Smaller dinosaurs holding a kind of conference by some big cycads. And Bertha Brachiosaur is munching away in Ostrom Meadow, benignly supervising the whole scene.

This is absolutely crazy.

I think the dinosaurs are taking care of me.

2 SEP. 0900 HOURS. No doubt of it at all. They bring eggs, meat, even cycad cones and tree-fern fronds. At first they delivered things only when I slept, but now they come hopping right up to me and dump things at my feet. The struthiomimids are the bearers—they're the smallest, most agile, quickest hands. They bring their offerings, stare me right in the eye, pause as if waiting for a tip. Other dinosaurs watching from the distance. This is a coordinated effort. I am the center of all activity on the island, it seems. I imagine that even the tyrannosaurs are saving choice cuts for me. Hallucination? Fantasy? Delirium of fever? I feel lucid. The fever is abating. I'm still too stiff and weak to move very far, but I think I'm recovering from the effects of my fall. With a little help from my friends.

1000 HOURS. Played back the last entry. Thinking it over. I don't *think* I've gone insane. If I'm insane enough to be worried about my sanity, how crazy can I be? Or am I just fooling myself? There's a terrible conflict between what I think I perceive going on here and what I know I ought to be perceiving.

1500 HOURS. A long, strange dream this afternoon. I saw all the dinosaurs standing in the meadow and they were connected to one another by gleaming threads, like the telephone lines of olden times, and all the threads centered on Bertha. As if she's the switchboard, yes. And telepathic messages were traveling. An extrasensory hookup, powerful pulses moving along the lines. I dreamed that a small dinosaur came to me and offered me a line and, in pantomime, showed me how to hook it up, and a great flood of delight went through me as I made the connection. And when I plugged it in, I could feel the deep and heavy thoughts of the dinosaurs, the slow rapturous philosophical interchanges.

When I woke, the dream seemed bizarrely vivid, strangely real, the dream-ideas lingering as they sometimes do. I saw the animals about me in a new way. As if this is not just a zoological research station, but a community, a settlement, the sole outpost of an alien civilization—an alien civilization native to earth.

Come off it. These animals have minute brains. They spend their days chomping on greenery, except for the ones that chomp on other dinosaurs. Compared with dinosaurs, cows and sheep are downright geniuses.

I can hobble a little now.

8 SEP. 0600 HOURS. The same dream again last night, the universal telepathic linkage. Sense of warmth and love flowing from dinosaurs to me.

Fresh tyrannosaur eggs for breakfast.

6 SEP. 1100 HOURS. I'm making a fast recovery. Up and about, still creaky but not much pain left. They still feed me. Though the struthiomimids remain the bearers of food, the bigger dinosaurs now come close, too. A stegosaur nuzzled up to me like some Goliath-sized pony, and I petted its rough scaly flank. The diplodocus stretched out flat and seemed to beg me to stroke its immense neck.

If this is madness, so be it. There's community here, loving and temperate. Even the predatory carnivores are part of it: eaters and eaten are aspects of the whole, yin and yang. Riding around in our sealed modules, we could never have suspected any of this.

They are gradually drawing me into their communion. I feel the pulses that pass between them. My entire soul throbs with that strange new sensation. My skin tingles.

They bring me food of their own bodies, their flesh and their unborn young, and they watch over me and silently urge me back to health. Why? For sweet charity's sake? I don't think so. I think they want something from me. I think they need something from me.

What could they need from me?

6 SEP. 0600 HOURS. All this night I have moved slowly through the forest in what I can only term an ecstatic state. Vast shapes, humped monstrous forms barely visible by dim glimmer, came and went about me. Hour after hour I walked unharmed, feeling the communion intensify. Until at last, exhausted, I have come to rest here on this mossy carpet, and in the first light of dawn I see the giant form of the great brachiosaur standing like a mountain on the far side of Owen River.

I am drawn to her. I could worship her. Through her vast body surge powerful currents. She is the amplifier. By her are we all connected. The holy mother of us all. From the enormous mass of her body emanate potent healing impulses.

I'll rest a little while. Then I'll cross the river to her.

0900 HOURS. We stand face to face. Her head is fifteen meters above mine. Her small eyes are unreadable. I trust her and I love her.

Lesser brachiosaurs have gathered behind her on the riverbank. Farther away are dinosaurs of half a dozen other species, immobile, silent.

I am humble in their presence. They are representatives of a dynamic, superior race, which but for a cruel cosmic accident would rule the earth to this day, and I am coming to revere them.

Consider: they endured for a hundred forty million years in ever-renewing vigor. They met all evolutionary challenges, except the one of sudden and catastrophic climate change against which nothing could have protected them. They multiplied and proliferated and adapted, dominating land and sea and air, covering the globe. Our own trifling, contemptible ancestors were nothing next to them. Who knows what these dinosaurs might have achieved if that crashing asteroid had not blotted out their light? What a vast irony: millions of years of supremacy ended in a single generation by a chilling cloud of dust. But until then—the wonder, the grandeur—

Only beasts, you say? How can you be sure? We know just a shred of what the Mesozoic was really like, just a slice, literally the bare bones. The passage of a hundred million years can obliterate all traces of civilization. Suppose they had language, poetry, mythology, philosophy? Love, dreams, aspirations? No, you say, they were beasts, ponderous and stupid, that lived mindless bestial lives. And I reply that we puny hairy ones have no right to impose our own values on them. The only kind of civilization we can understand is the one we have built. We imagine that our own trivial accomplishments are the determining case, that computers and spaceships and broiled sausages are such miracles that they place us at evolution's pinnacle. But now I know otherwise. Humanity has done marvelous things, yes. But we would not have existed at all had this greatest of races been allowed to live to fulfill its destiny.

I feel the intense love radiating from the titan that looms above me. I feel the contact between our souls steadily strengthening and deepening.

The last barriers dissolve.

And I understand at last.

I am the chosen one. I am the vehicle. I am the bringer of rebirth, the beloved one, the necessary one. Our Lady of the Sauropods am I, the holy one, the prophetess, the priestess.

Is this madness? Then it is madness.

Why have we small hairy creatures existed at all? I know now. It is so that through our technology we could make possible the return of the great ones. They perished unfairly. Through us, they are resurrected aboard this tiny glove in space.

I tremble in the force of the need that pours from them.

I will not fail you, I tell the great sauropods before me, and the sauropods send my thoughts reverberating to all the others.

20 SEPTEMBER. 0600 HOURS. The thirtieth day. The shuttle comes from *Habitat Vronsky* today to pick me up and deliver the next researcher.

I wait at the transit lock. Hundreds of dinosaurs wait with me, each close beside the nest, both the lions and the lambs, gathered quietly, their attention focused entirely on me.

Now the shuttle arrives, right on time, gliding in for a perfect docking. The airlocks open. A figure appears. Sarber himself! Coming to make sure I didn't survive the meltdown, or else to finish me off.

He stands blinking in the entry passage, gaping at the throngs of placid dinosaurs arrayed in a huge semicircle around the naked woman who stands beside the wreckage of the mobile module. For a moment he is unable to speak.

"Anne?" he says finally. "What in God's name—"

"You'll never understand," I tell him. I give the signal. Belshazzar rumbles forward. Sarber screams and whirls and sprints for the airlock, but a stegosaur blocks the way.

"No!" Sarber cries, as the tyrannosaur's mighty head swoops down. It is all over in a moment.

Revenge! How sweet!

And this is only the beginning. *Habitat Vronsky* lies just 120 kilometers away. Elsewhere in the Lagrange belt are hundreds of other habitats ripe for conquest. The earth itself is within easy reach. I have no idea yet how it will be accomplished, but I know it will be done and done successfully, and I will be the instrument by which it is done.

I stretch forth my arms to the mighty creatures that surround me. I feel their strength, their power, their harmony. I am one with them, and they with me.

The Great Race has returned, and I am its priestess. Let the hairy ones tremble!

◆

THERE WAS AN OLD WOMAN

This is another of my early stories, written a couple of years after "The Songs of Summer," that tale of many narrators. The story here has only one, but, since he's one of thirty-one siblings, there's enough that's unusual about him to qualify him for this collection.

I wrote it in September 1957 and brought it to Larry T. Shaw, the editor of *Infinity*, one of the best of the many new magazines of the short-lived science-fiction publishing boom of the mid-1950s. Shaw bought it right away, but didn't use it until his November 1958 issue, by which time *Infinity*, like many of the other magazines of those boom years, was already on its last legs. My story ledger for that ancient era showed that I had a tough time collecting my $65 fee, something that must have been of more significance then than it would seem now, because $65 was a lot of money in 1958 dollars and I was only a couple of years out of college with all the living expenses of a young man newly launched upon the world.

The theme of multiple extra-utero birth that I use here was of sufficient interest to me that I would use it again, in a very different way, in my 1966 novel *Thorns*, which I regard as the first noteworthy book of my literary maturity.

—ᴧᴧᴧ—

SINCE I WAS RAISED FROM earliest infancy to undertake the historian's calling, and since it is now certain that I shall never claim that profession as my own, it seems fitting that I perform my first and last act as a historian.

I shall write the history of that strange and unique woman, the mother of my thirty brothers and myself, Miss Donna Mitchell.

She was a person of extraordinary strength and vision, our mother. I remember her vividly, seeing her with all her sons gathered round her in our secluded Wisconsin farmhouse on the first night of summer, after we had returned to her from every part of the country for our summer's vacation. One-and-thirty strapping sons, each one of us six feet one inch tall, with a shock of unruly yellow hair and keen, clear blue eyes, each one of us healthy, strong, well nourished, each one of us twenty-one years and fourteen days old—one-and-thirty identical brothers.

Oh, there were differences between us, but only we and she could perceive them. To outsiders, we were identical; which was why, to outsiders, we took care never to appear together in groups. We ourselves knew the differences, for we had lived with them so long.

I knew my brother Leonard's cheek mole—the right cheek it was, setting him off from Jonas, whose left cheek was marked with a flyspeck. I knew the faint tilt of Peter's chin, the slight over-sharpness of Dewey's nose, the florid tint of Donald's skin. I recognized Paul by his pendulous earlobes, Charles by his squint, Noel by the puckering of his lower lip. David had a blue-stubbled face, Mark flaring nostrils, Claude thick brows.

Yes, there were differences. We rarely confused one with another. It was second nature for me to distinguish Edward from Albert, George from Philip, Frederick from Stephen. And Mother never confused us.

She was a regal woman, nearly six feet in height, who even in middle age had retained straightness of posture and majesty of bearing. Her eyes, like ours, were blue; her hair, she told us, had

once been golden like ours. Her voice was a deep, mellow contralto; rich, firm, commanding, the voice of a strong woman. She
had been professor of biochemistry at some Eastern university
(she never told us which one, hating its name so) and we all knew
by heart the story of her bitter life and of our own strange birth.

"I had a theory," she would say. "It wasn't an orthodox theory,
and it made people angry to think about it, so of course they
threw me out. But I didn't care. In many ways that was the most
fortunate day of my life."

"Tell us about it, Mother," Philip would invariably ask. He was
destined to be a playwright; he enjoyed the repetition of the story
whenever we were together.

She said:

"I had a theory. I believed that environment controlled personality, that given the same set of healthy genes any number of different adults could be shaped from the raw material. I had a plan
for testing it—but when I told them, they discharged me. Luckily,
I had married a wealthy if superficial-minded executive, who had
suffered a fatal coronary attack the year before. I was independently wealthy, thanks to him, and free to pursue independent
research, thanks to my university discharge. So I came to
Wisconsin and began my great project."

We knew the rest of the story by heart, as a sort of litany.

We knew how she had bought a huge, rambling farm in the flat
green country of central Wisconsin, a farm far from prying eyes.
Then, how on a hot summer afternoon she had gone forth to the
farm land nearby, and found a field hand, tall and brawny, and to
his great surprise seduced him in the field where he worked.

And then the story of that single miraculous zygote, which our
mother had extracted from her body and carefully nurtured in
special nutrient tanks, irradiating it and freezing it and irritating
it and dosing it with hormones until, exasperated, it subdivided
into thirty-two, each one of which developed independently into a
complete embryo.

Embryo grew into foetus, and foetus into child, in Mother's ingenious artificial wombs. One of the thirty-two died before birth of accidental narcosis; the remainder survived, thirty-one identical males sprung from the same egg, to become us.

With the formidable energy that typified her, Mother single-handedly nursed thirty-one baby boys; we thrived, we grew. And then the most crucial stage of the experiment began. We were differentiated at the age of eighteen months, each given his own room, his own particular toys, his own special books later on. Each of us was slated for a different profession. It was the ultimate proof of her theory. Genetically identical, physically identical except for the minor changes time had worked on our individual bodies, we would nevertheless seek out different fields of employment.

She worked out the assignments at random, she said. Philip was to be a playwright, Noel a novelist, Donald a doctor. Astronomy was Allan's goal, Barry's, biology, Albert's the stage. George was to be a concert pianist, Claude a composer, Leonard a member of the bar, Dewey a dentist. Mark was to be an athlete; David, a diplomat. Journalism waited for Jonas, poetry for Peter, painting for Paul.

Edward would become an engineer, Saul a soldier, Charles a statesman; Stephen would go to sea. Martin was aimed for chemistry, Raymond for physics, James for high finance. Ronald would be a librarian, Robert a bookkeeper, John a priest, Douglas a teacher. Anthony was to be a literary critic, William an architect, Frederick an airplane pilot. For Richard was reserved a life of crime; as for myself, Harold, I was to devote my energies to the study and writing of history.

This was my mother's plan. Let me tell of my own childhood and adolescence, to illustrate its workings.

MY FIRST RECOLLECTIONS ARE OF books. I had a room on the second floor of our big house. Martin's room was to my left, and in later years I would regret it, for the air was always heavy with the stink of his chemical experiments. To my right was Noel, whose precocious typewriter sometimes pounded all night as he worked on his endless first novel.

But those manifestations came later. I remember waking one morning to find that during the night a bookcase had been placed in my room, and in it a single book—Hendrik Willem van Loon's *The Story of Mankind.* I was four, almost five, then; thanks to Mother's intensive training we were all capable readers by that age, and I puzzled over the big type, learning of the exploits of Charlemagne and Richard the Lionhearted and staring at the squiggly scratches that were van Loon's illustrations.

Other books followed, in years to come. H. G. Wells's *Outline of History,* which fascinated and repelled me at the same time. Toynbee, in the Somervell abridgement, and later, when I had entered adolescence, the complete and unabridged edition. Churchill, and his flowing periods and ringing prose. Sandburg's poetic and massive life of Lincoln; Wedgwood on the Thirty Years' War; Will Durant, in six or seven blocklike volumes.

I read these books, and where I did not understand I read on anyway, knowing I would come back to that page in some year to come and bring new understanding to it. Mother helped, and guided, and chivvied. A sense of the panorama of man's vast achievement sprang up in me. To join the roll of mankind's chroniclers seemed the only possible end for my existence.

Each summer from my fourteenth to my seventeenth, I traveled—alone, of course, since Mother wanted to build self-reliance in us. I visited the great historical places of the United States: Washington, DC, Mount Vernon, Williamsburg, Bull Run, Gettysburg. A sense of the past rose in me.

Those summers were my only opportunities for contact with strangers, since during the year and especially during the long snowbound winters we stayed on the farm, a tight family unit. We never went to public school; obviously, it was impossible to enroll us, en masse, without arousing the curiosity my mother wished to avoid.

Instead, she tutored us privately, giving us care and attention that no professional teacher could possibly have supplied. And we grew older, diverging towards our professions like branching limbs of a tree.

As a future historian, of course, I took it upon myself to observe the changes in my own society, which was bounded by the acreage of our farm. I made notes on the progress of my brothers, keeping my notebooks well hidden, and also on the changes time was working on Mother. She stood up surprisingly well, considering the astonishing burden she had taken upon herself. Formidable was the best word to use in describing her.

We grew into adolescence. By this time Martin had an imposing chemical laboratory in his room; Leonard harangued us all on legal fine points, and Anthony pored over Proust and Kafka, delivering startling critical interpretations. Our house was a beehive of industry constantly, and I don't remember being bored for more than three consecutive seconds, at any time. There were always distractions: Claude and George jostling for room on the piano bench while they played Claude's four-hand sonata, Mark hurling a baseball through a front window, Peter declaiming a sequence of shocking sonnets during our communal dinner.

We fought, of course, since we were healthy individualists with sound bodies. Mother encouraged it; Saturday afternoon was wrestling time, and we pitted our growing strengths against one another.

Mother was always the dominant figure, striding tall and erect around the farm, calling to us in her familiar boom, assigning us chores, meeting with us privately. Somehow she had the knack of making each of us think we were the favorite child, the one in whose future she was most deeply interested of all. It was false, of course; though once Jonas unkindly asserted that Barry must be her real favorite, because he, like her, was a biologist.

I doubted it. I had learned much about people through my constant reading, and I knew that Mother was something extraordinary—a fanatic, if you like, or merely a woman driven by an inner demon, but still and all a person of overwhelming intellectual drive and conviction, whose will to know the truth had led her to undertake this fantastic experiment in biology and human breeding.

I knew that no woman of that sort could stoop to petty favoritism. Mother was unique. Perhaps, had she been born a man, she would have changed the entire course of human development.

When we were seventeen, she called us all together round the big table in the common room of our rambling home. She waited, needing to clear her throat only once in order to cut the hum of conversation.

"Sons," she said, and the echo rang through the entire first floor of the house. "Sons, the time has come for you to leave the farm."

We were stunned, even those of us who were expecting it. But she explained, and we understood, and we did not quarrel.

One could not become a doctor or a chemist or a novelist or even a historian in a total vacuum. One had to enter the world. And one needed certain professional qualifications.

We were going to college.

Not all of us, of course. Robert was to be a bookkeeper; he would go to business school. Mark had developed, through years of practice, into a superb right-handed pitcher, and he was to go to Milwaukee for a major-league tryout. Claude and George, aspiring composer and aspiring pianist, would attend an Eastern conservatory together, posing as twins.

The rest of us were to attend colleges, and those who were to go on to professions such as medicine or chemistry would plan to attend professional schools afterwards. Mother believed a college education was essential, even to a poet or a painter or a novelist.

Only one of us was not sent to any accredited institution. He was Richard, who was to be our criminal. Already he had made several sallies into the surrounding towns and cities, returning a few days or a few weeks later with money or jewels and with a guilty grin on his face. He was simply to be turned loose into the school of Life, and Mother warned him never to get caught.

As for me, I was sent to Princeton and enrolled as a liberal-arts student. Since, like my brothers, I was privately educated, I had no diplomas or similar records to show them, and they had to give me an equivalency examination in their place. Evidently I did quite well, for I was immediately accepted. I wired Mother, who sent a check for $3,000 to cover my first year's tuition and expenses.

I enrolled as a history major; among my first-year courses were Medieval English Constitutional History and the Survey of Western Historical Currents; naturally, my marks were the highest in the class in both cases. I worked diligently and even with a sort of frenzied fury. My other courses, in the sciences or in the arts, I devoted no more nor no less time to than was necessary, but history was my ruling passion.

At least, through my first two semesters of college.

June came, and final exams, and then I returned to Wisconsin, where Mother was waiting. It was 21 June when I returned; since not all colleges end their spring semester simultaneously, some of my brothers had been home for more than a week, others had not yet arrived. Richard had sent word that he was in Los Angeles, and would be with us after the first of July. Mark had signed a baseball contract and was pitching for a team in New Mexico, and he, too, would not be with us.

The summer passed rapidly.

We spent it as we had in the old days before college, sharing our individual specialities, talking, meeting regularly and privately with Mother to discuss the goals that still lay ahead. Except for Claude and George, we had scattered in different directions, no two of us at the same school.

I returned to Princeton that fall for my sophomore year. It passed, and I made the homeward journey again, and in the fall traveled once more eastward. The junior year went by likewise.

And I began to detect signs of a curious change in my inward self. It was a change I did not dare mention to Mother on those July days when I met with her in her room near the library. I did not tell my brothers, either. I kept my knowledge to myself, brooding over it, wondering why it was that this thing should happen to me, why I should be singled out.

For I was discovering that the study of history bored me utterly and completely.

The spirit of rebellion grew in me during my final year in college. My marks had been excellent; I had achieved Phi Beta Kappa and several graduate schools were interested in having me continue my studies with them. But I had been speaking to a few chosen friends (none of whom knew my bizarre family background, of course) and my values had been slowly shifting.

I realized that I had mined history as deeply as I ever cared to. Waking and sleeping, for more than fifteen years, I had pondered Waterloo and Bunker Hill, considered the personalities of Cromwell and James II, held imaginary conversations with Jefferson and Augustus Caesar and Charles Martel. And I was bored with it.

It began to become evident to others, eventually. One day during my final semester a friend asked me, "Is there something worrying you, Harry?"

I shook my head quickly—too quickly. "No," I said. "Why? Do I look worried?"

"You look worse than worried. You look obsessed."

We laughed about it, and finally we went down to the student center and had a few beers, and before long my tongue had loosened a little.

I said, "There *is* something worrying me. And you know what it is? I'm afraid I won't live up to the standards my family set for me."

Guffaws greeted me. "Come off it, Harry! Phi Beta in your junior year, top class standing, a brilliant career in history ahead of you—what do they want from you, blood?"

I chuckled and gulped my beer and mumbled something innocuous, but inside I was curdling.

Everything I was, I owed to Mother. She made me what I am. But I was played out as a student of history; I was the family failure, the goat, the rotten egg. Raymond still wrestled gleefully with nuclear physics, with Heisenberg and Schrödinger and the others. Mark gloried in his fast ball and his slider and his curve. Paul daubed canvas merrily in his Greenwich Village flat near NYU, and even Robert seemed to take delight in keeping books.

Only I had failed. History had become repugnant to me. I was in rebellion against it. I would disappoint my mother, become the butt of my brothers' scorn, and live in despair, hating the profession of historian and fitted by training for nothing else.

I was graduated from Princeton summa cum laude, a few days after my twenty-first birthday. I wired Mother that I was on my way home, and bought train tickets.

It was a long and grueling journey to Wisconsin. I spent my time thinking, trying to choose between the unpleasant alternatives that faced me.

I could attempt duplicity, telling my mother I was still studying history, while actually preparing myself for some more attractive profession—the law, perhaps.

I could confess to her at once my failure of purpose, ask her forgiveness for disappointing her and flawing her grand scheme, and try to begin afresh in another field.

Or I could forge ahead with history, compelling myself grimly to take an interest, cramping and paining myself so that my mother's design would be complete.

None of them seemed desirable paths to take. I brooded over it, and was weary and apprehensive by the time I arrived at our farm.

The first of my brothers I saw was Mark. He sat on the front porch of the big house, reading a book which I recognized at once and with some surprise as Volume I of Churchill. He looked up at me and smiled feebly.

I frowned. "I didn't expect to find *you* here, Mark. According to the local sports pages the Braves are playing on the Coast this week. How come you're not with them?"

His voice was a low murmur. "Because they gave me my release," he said.

"What?"

He nodded. "I'm washed up at twenty-one. They made me a free agent; that means I can hook up with any team that wants me."

"And you're just taking a little rest before offering yourself around?"

He shook his head. "I'm through. Kaput. Harry, I just can't stand baseball. It's a silly, stupid game. You know how many times I had to stand out there in baggy knickers and throw a bit of horsehide at some jerk with a club in his paws? A hundred, hundred-fifty times a game, every four days. For what? What the hell does it all mean? Why should I bother?"

There was a strange gleam in his eyes. I said, "Have you told Mother?"

"I don't dare! She thinks I'm on leave or something. Harry, how can I tell her—"

"I know." Briefly, I told him of my own disenchantment with history. We were mutually delighted to learn that we were not alone in our affliction. I picked up my suitcases, scrambled up the steps, and went inside.

Dewey was cleaning up the common room as I passed through. He nodded hello glumly. I said, "How's the tooth trade?"

He whirled and glared at me viciously.

"Something wrong?" I asked.

"I've been accepted by four dental schools, Harry."

"Is that any cause for misery?"

He let the broom drop, walked over to me, and whispered, "I'll murder you if you tell Mother this. But the thought of spending my life poking around in foul-smelling oral cavities sickens me. Sickens."

"But I thought—"

"Yeah. You thought. You've got it soft; you just need to dig books out of the library and rearrange what they say and call it new research. I have to drill and clean and fill and plug and—" He stopped. "Harry, I'll kill you if you breathe a word of this. I don't want Mother to know that I didn't come out the way she wanted."

I repeated what I had said to Mark—and told him about Mark, for good measure. Then I made my way upstairs to my old room. I felt a burden lifting from me; I was not alone. At least two of my brothers felt the same way. I wondered how many more were at last rebelling against the disciplines of a lifetime.

Poor Mother, I thought! Poor Mother!

Our first family council of the summer was held that night. Stephen and Saul were the last to arrive, Stephen resplendent in his Annapolis garb, Saul crisp looking and stiff-backed from West Point. Mother had worked hard to wangle appointments for those two.

We sat around the big table and chatted. The first phase of our lives, Mother told us, had ended. Now, our preliminary educations were complete, and we would undertake the final step towards our professions—those of us who had not already entered them.

Mother looked radiant that evening, tall, energetic, her white hair cropped mannishly short, as she sat about the table with her thirty-one strapping sons. I envied and pitied her: envied her for the sweet serenity of her life, which had proceeded so inexorably and without swerving towards the goal of her experiment, and pitied her for the disillusioning that awaited her.

For Mark and Dewey and I were not the only failures in the crop.

I had made discreet inquiries during the day. I learned that Anthony found literary criticism to be a fraud and a sham, that Paul knew clearly he had no talent as a painter (and, also, that very few of his contemporaries did either), that Robert bitterly resented a career of bookkeeping, that piano playing hurt George's fingers, that Claude had had difficulty with his composing because he was tone deaf, that the journalistic grind was too strenuous for Jonas, that John longed to quit the seminarial life because he had no calling, that Albert hated the uncertain Bohemianism of an actor's life—

We circulated, all of us raising for the first time the question that had sprouted in our minds during the past several years. I made the astonishing discovery that not one of Donna Mitchell's sons cared for the career that had been chosen for him.

The experiment had been a resounding flop.

Late that evening, after Mother had gone to bed, we remained together, discussing our predicament. How could we tell her? How could we destroy her life's work? And yet, how could we compel ourselves to lives of unending drudgery?

Robert wanted to study engineering; Barry, to write. I realized I cared much more for law than for history, while Leonard longed to exchange law for the physical sciences. James, our banker-manque, much preferred politics. And so it went, with Richard (who claimed five robberies, a rape, and innumerable picked pockets) pouring out his desire to settle down and live within the law as an honest farmer.

It was pathetic.

Summing up the problem in his neat forensic way, Leonard said, "Here's our dilemma: Do we all keep quiet about this and ruin our lives, or do we speak up and ruin Mother's experiment?"

"I think we ought to continue as is, for the time being," Saul said. "Perhaps Mother will die in the next year or two. We can start over then."

"Perhaps she *doesn't* die?" Edward wanted to know. "She's tough as nails. She may last another twenty or thirty or even forty years."

"And we're past twenty-one already," remarked Raymond. "If we hang on too long at what we're doing, it'll be too late to change. You can't start studying for a new profession when you're thirty-five."

"Maybe we'll get to *like* what we're doing by then," suggested David hopefully. "Diplomatic service isn't as bad as all that, and I'd say—"

"What about me?" Paul yelped. "I can't paint and I know I can't paint. I've got nothing but starvation ahead of me unless I wise up and get into business in a hurry. You want me to keep messing up good white canvas the rest of my life?"

"It won't work," said Barry in a doleful voice. "We'll have to tell her."

Douglas shook his head. "We can't do that. You know just what she'll do. She'll bring down the umpteen volumes of notes she's made on this experiment, and ask us if we're going to let it all come to naught."

"He's right," Albert said. "I can picture the scene now. The big organ-pipe voice blasting us for our lack of faith, the accusations of ingratitude—"

"Ingratitude?" William shouted. "She twisted us and pushed us and molded us without asking our permission. Hell, she *created* us with her laboratory tricks. But that didn't give her the right to make zombies out of us."

"Still," Martin said, "we can't just go to her and tell her that it's all over. The shock would kill her."

"Well?" Richard asked in the silence that followed. "What's wrong with that?"

For a moment, no one spoke. The house was quiet; we heard footsteps descending the stairs. We froze.

Mother appeared, an imperial figure even in her old house-coat. "You boys are kicking up too much of a racket down here," she boomed. "I know you're glad to see each other again after a year, but I need my sleep."

She turned and strode upstairs again. We heard her bedroom door slam shut. For an instant we were all ten-year-olds again, diligently studying our books for fear of Mother's displeasure.

I moistened my lips. "Well?" I asked. "I call for a vote on Richard's suggestion."

Martin, as a chemist, prepared the drink, using Donald's medical advice as his guide. Saul, Stephen, and Raymond dug a grave, in the woods at the back of our property. Douglas and Mark built the coffin.

Richard, ending his criminal career with a murder to which we were all accessories before the fact, carried the fatal beverage upstairs to Mother the next morning, and persuaded her to sip it. One sip was all that was necessary; Martin had done his work well.

Leonard offered us a legal opinion: It was justifiable homicide. We placed the body in its coffin and carried it out across the fields. Richard, Peter, Jonas and Charles were her pallbearers; the others of us followed in their path.

We lowered the body into the ground and John said a few words over her. Then, slowly, we closed over the grave and replaced the sod, and began the walk back to the house.

"She died happy," Anthony said. "She never suspected the size of her failure." It was her epitaph.

As our banker, James supervised the division of her assets, which were considerable, into thirty-one equal parts. Noel composed a short figment of prose which we agreed summed up our sentiments.

We left the farm that night, scattering in every direction, anxious to begin life. All that went before was a dream from which we now awakened. We agreed to meet at the farm each year, on the anniversary of her death, in memory of the woman who had so painstakingly divided a zygote into thirty-two viable cells, and who had spent a score of years conducting an experiment based on a theory that had proved to be utterly false.

We felt no regret, no qualm. We had done what needed to be done, and on that last day some of us had finally functioned in the professions for which Mother had intended us.

I, too. My first and last work of history will be this, an account of Mother and her experiment, which records the beginning and the end of her work. And now it is complete.

THE DYBBUK OF MAZEL TOV IV

Here is another story narrated by a male Jewish person, as was the poltergeist story that appears earlier in this book. What's so special about stories told by Jewish narrators? Philip Roth has written a whole shelf of books narrated by male Jewish persons. So have plenty of other writers. I'm a male Jewish person myself, as are a lot of people I know.

Ah, but this narrator lives on a planet called Mazel Tov IV, which immediately distinguishes him from anyone in any Philip Roth story and from every male Jewish person I know. And there is an excellent reason for the narrator of this story to be Jewish, because Mazel Tov IV is a planet that has been colonized by Jews fleeing, yet again, from persecution by their fellow Earthlings.

In 1972 my good friend Jack Dann, who is Jewish himself, though you'd never know it from his name, and who lives in Australia, though he didn't start out there, asked me to write a story for a book he was editing to be called *Wandering Stars*, an anthology of what he called "Jewish science fiction." I thought that was an odd and even wrongheaded idea for an anthology. The balkanization of science fiction—Jewish science fiction, black science fiction, feminist science fiction, gay science fiction—is not what I really want to see in a field that takes all the universe for its domain. Setting up arbitrary limitations didn't seem congruent to me with the infinite horizons of science fiction.

But then I came around to the opposite point of view: the very limitation that Jack was proposing might be an interesting intellectual challenge. I had written a Catholic science-fiction story not long before—"Good News from the Vatican"—and had won a Nebula award for it, and I'm not even Catholic. I don't think you have to be Jewish to write science fiction on a Jewish theme, either, but I did happen to have some familiarity with matters Jewish, and, anyway, an idea for just that kind of story popped into my head about five minutes after Jack Dann brought the topic up. So I set out to write it in July of 1972, opening it with the perfectly ordinary sentence, "My grandson David will have his bar mitzvah next spring" and rapidly taking it into very weird territory indeed. The Dann anthology, which featured appropriately kosher stories by such notables as Isaac Bashevis Singer, Bernard Malamud, and Isaac Asimov, appeared in 1974 and did so well that Jack did another volume of such tales later on.

—*∽∾∿*—

MY GRANDSON DAVID WILL HAVE his bar mitzvah next spring. No one in our family has undergone that rite in at least three hundred years—certainly not since we Levins settled in Old Israel, the Israel on Earth, soon after the European holocaust. My friend Eliahu asked me not long ago how I feel about David's bar mitzvah, whether the idea of it angers me, whether I see it as a disturbing element. No, I replied, the boy is a Jew, after all—let him have a bar mitzvah if he wants one. These are times of transition and upheaval, as all times are. David is not bound by the attitudes of his ancestors.

"Since when is a Jew not bound by the attitudes of his ancestors?" Eliahu asked.

"You know what I mean," I said.

Indeed he did. We are bound but yet free. If anything governs us out of the past it is the tribal bond itself, not the philosophies of our departed kinsmen. We accept what we choose to accept; nevertheless we remain Jews. I come from a family that has liked to say—especially to gentiles—that we are Jews but not Jewish; that is, we acknowledge and cherish our ancient heritage, but we do not care to entangle ourselves in outmoded rituals and folkways. This is what my forefathers declared, as far back as those secular-minded Levins who three centuries ago fought to win and guard the freedom of the land of Israel. (Old Israel, I mean.) I would say the same here, if there were any gentiles on this world to whom such things had to be explained. But of course in this New Israel in the stars we have only ourselves, no gentiles within a dozen light-years, unless you count our neighbors the Kunivaru as gentiles. (Can creatures that are not human rightly be called gentiles? I'm not sure the term applies. Besides, the Kunivaru now insist that they are Jews. My mind spins. It's an issue of Talmudic complexity, and God knows I'm no Talmudist. Hillel, Akiva, Rashi, help me!) Anyway, come the fifth day of Sivan my son's son will have his bar mitzvah, and I'll play the proud grandpa as pious old Jews have done for six thousand years.

ALL THINGS ARE CONNECTED. THAT my grandson would have a bar mitzvah is merely the latest link in a chain of events that goes back to—when? To the day the Kunivaru decided to embrace Judaism? To the day the dybbuk entered Seul the Kunivar? To the day we refugees from Earth discovered the fertile planet that we sometimes call New Israel and sometimes call Mazel Tov IV? To the day of the Final Pogrom on Earth? Reb Yossele the Hasid might say that David's bar mitzvah was determined on the day the Lord God fashioned Adam out of dust. But I think that would be overdoing things.

The day the dybbuk took possession of the body of Seul the Kunivar was probably where it really started. Until then things were relatively uncomplicated here. The Hasidim had their settlement, we Israelis had ours, and the natives, the Kunivaru, had the rest of the planet; and generally we all kept out of one another's way. After the dybbuk everything changed. It happened more than forty years ago, in the first generation after the Landing, on the ninth day of Tishri in the year 6302. I was working in the fields, for Tishri is a harvest month. The day was hot, and I worked swiftly, singing and humming. As I moved down the long rows of cracklepods, tagging those that were ready to be gathered, a Kunivar appeared at the crest of the hill that overlooks our kibbutz. It seemed to be in some distress, for it came staggering and lurching down the hillside with extraordinary clumsiness, tripping over its own four legs as if it barely knew how to manage them. When it was about a hundred meters from me, it cried out, "Shimon! Help me, Shimon! In God's name help me!"

There were several strange things about this outcry, and I perceived them gradually, the most trivial first. It seemed odd that a Kunivar would address me by my given name, for they are a formal people. It seemed more odd that a Kunivar would speak to me in quite decent Hebrew, for at that time none of them had learned our language. It seemed most odd of all—but I was slow to discern it—that a Kunivar would have the very voice, dark and resonant, of my dear dead friend Joseph Avneri.

The Kunivar stumbled into the cultivated part of the field and halted, trembling terribly. Its fine green fur was pasted into hummocks by perspiration, and its great golden eyes rolled and crossed in a ghastly way. It stood flat-footed, splaying its legs out under the four corners of its chunky body like the legs of a table, and clasped its long powerful arms around its chest. I recognized the Kunivar as Seul, a subchief of the local village, with whom we of the kibbutz had had occasional dealings.

"What help can I give you?" I asked. "What has happened to you, Seul?"

"Shimon—Shimon—" A frightful moan came from the Kunivar. "Oh, God, Shimon, it goes beyond all belief! How can I bear this? How can I even comprehend it?"

No doubt of it. The Kunivar was speaking in the voice of Joseph Avneri.

"Seul?" I said hesitantly.

"My name is Joseph Avneri."

"Joseph Avneri died a year ago last Elul. I didn't realize you were such a clever mimic, Seul."

"Mimic? You speak to me of mimicry, Shimon? It's no mimicry. I am your Joseph, dead but still aware, thrown for my sins into this monstrous alien body. Are you Jew enough to know what a dybbuk is, Shimon?"

"A wandering ghost, yes, who takes possession of the body of a living being."

"I have become a dybbuk."

"There are no dybbuks. Dybbuks are phantoms out of medieval folklore," I said.

"You hear the voice of one."

"This is impossible," I said.

"I agree, Shimon, I agree." He sounded calmer now. "It's entirely impossible. I don't believe in dybbuks either, any more than I believe in Zeus, the Minotaur, werewolves, gorgons, or golems. But how else do you explain me?"

"You are Seul the Kunivar, playing a clever trick."

"Do you really think so? Listen to me, Shimon. I knew you when we were boys in Tiberias. I rescued you when we were fishing in the lake and our boat overturned. I was with you the day you met Leah whom you married. I was godfather to your son Yigal. I studied with you at the university in Jerusalem. I fled with you in the fiery days of the Final Pogrom. I stood watch with you aboard the Ark in the years of our flight from Earth. Do you remember, Shimon? Do you remember Jerusalem? The Old City, the Mount of Olives, the Tomb of Absalom, the Western Wall? Am I a Kunivar, Shimon, to know of the Western Wall?"

"There is no survival of consciousness after death," I said stubbornly.

"A year ago I would have agreed with you. But who am I if I am not the spirit of Joseph Avneri? How can you account for me any other way? Dear God, do you think I want to believe this, Shimon? You know what a scoffer I was. But it's real."

"Perhaps I'm having a very vivid hallucination."

"Call the others, then. If ten people have the same hallucination, is it still a hallucination? Be reasonable, Shimon! Here I stand before you, telling you things that only I could know, and you deny that I am—"

"Be reasonable?" I said. "Where does reason enter into this? Do you expect me to believe in ghosts, Joseph, in wandering demons, in dybbuks? Am I some superstition-ridden peasant out of the Polish woods? Is this the Middle Ages?"

"You called me Joseph," he said quietly.

"I can hardly call you Seul when you speak in that voice."

"Then you believe in me!"

"No."

"Look, Shimon, did you ever know a bigger sceptic than Joseph Avneri? I had no use for the Torah, I said Moses was fictional, I plowed the fields on Yom Kippur, I laughed in God's nonexistent face. What is life, I said? And I answered: a mere accident, a transient biological phenomenon. Yet here I am. I remember the moment of my death. For a full year I've wandered this world, bodiless, perceiving things, unable to communicate. And today I find myself cast into this creature's body, and I know myself for a dybbuk. If *I* believe, Shimon, how can you dare disbelieve? In the name of our friendship, have faith in what I tell you!"

"You have actually become a dybbuk?"

"I have become a dybbuk," he said.

I shrugged. "Very well, Joseph. You're a dybbuk. It's madness but I believe." I stared in astonishment at the Kunivar. Did I believe? Did I believe that I believed? How could I not believe? There was no other way for the voice of Joseph Avneri to be coming from the throat of a Kunivar. Sweat streamed down my body. I was face to face with the impossible, and all my philosophy was shattered. Anything was possible now. God might appear as a burning bush. The sun might stand still. No, I told myself. Believe only one irrational thing at a time, Shimon. Evidently there are dybbuks; well, then, there are dybbuks. But everything else pertaining to the Invisible World remains unreal until it manifests itself.

I said, "Why do you think this has happened to you?"

"It could only be as a punishment."

"For what, Joseph?"

"My experiments. You knew I was doing research into the Kunivaru metabolism, didn't you?"

"Yes, certainly. But—"

"Did you know I performed surgical experiments on live Kunivaru in our hospital? That I used patients, without informing them or anyone else, in studies of a forbidden kind? It was vivisection, Shimon."

"*What?*"

"There were things I needed to know, and there was only one way I could discover them. The hunger for knowledge led me into sin. I told myself that these creatures were ill, that they would shortly die anyway, and that it might benefit everyone if I opened them while they still lived, you see? Besides, they weren't human beings, Shimon, they were only animals—very intelligent animals, true, but still only—"

"No, Joseph. I can believe in dybbuks more readily than I can believe this. You, doing such a thing? My calm rational friend, my scientist, my wise one?" I shuddered and stepped a few paces back from him. "Auschwitz!" I cried. "Buchenwald! Dachau! Do those names mean anything to you? 'They weren't human beings,' the Nazi surgeon said. 'They were only Jews, and our need for scientific knowledge is such that—' That was only three hundred years ago, Joseph. And you, a Jew, a Jew of all people, to—"

"I know, Shimon, I know. Spare me the lecture. I sinned terribly, and for my sins I've been given this grotesque body, this gross, hideous, heavy body, these four legs which I can hardly coordinate, this crooked spine, this foul, hot furry pelt. I still don't believe in a God, Shimon, but I think I believe in some sort of compensating force that balances accounts in this universe, and the account has been balanced for me, oh, yes, Shimon! I've had six hours of terror and loathing today such as I never dreamed could be experienced. To enter this body, to fry in this heat, to wander these hills trapped in such a mass of flesh, to feel myself being bombarded with the sensory perceptions of a being so alien—it's been hell, I tell you that without exaggeration. I would have died of shock in the first ten minutes if I didn't already happen to be dead. Only now, seeing you, talking to you, do I begin to get control of myself. Help me, Shimon."

"What do you want me to do?"

"Get me out of here. This is torment. I'm a dead man—I'm entitled to rest the way the other dead ones rest. Free me, Shimon."

"How?"

"How? How? Do I know? Am I an expert on dybbuks? Must I direct my own exorcism? If you knew what an effort it is simply to hold this body upright, to make its tongue form Hebrew words, to say things in a way you'll understand—" Suddenly the Kunivar sagged to his knees, a slow, complex folding process that reminded me of the manner in which the camels of Old Earth lowered themselves to the ground. The alien creature began to sputter and moan and wave his arms about; foam appeared on his wide rubbery lips. "God in Heaven, Shimon," Joseph cried, "set me free!"

I CALLED FOR MY SON Yigal and he came running swiftly from the far side of the fields, a lean healthy boy, only eleven years old but already long-legged, strong-bodied. Without going into details, I indicated the suffering Kunivar and told Yigal to get help from the kibbutz. A few minutes later he came back leading seven or eight men—Abrasha, Itzhak, Uri, Nahum, and some others. It took the full strength of all of us to lift the Kunivar into the hopper of a harvesting machine and transport him to our hospital. Two of the doctors—Moshe Shiloah and someone else—began to examine the stricken alien, and I sent Yigal to the Kunivaru village to tell the chief that Seul had collapsed in our fields.

The doctors quickly diagnosed the problem as a case of heat prostration. They were discussing the sort of injection the Kunivar should receive when Joseph Avneri, breaking a silence that had lasted since Seul had fallen, announced his presence within the Kunivar's body. Uri and Nahum had remained in the hospital room with me; not wanting this craziness to become general knowledge in the kibbutz, I took them outside and told them to forget whatever ravings they had heard. When I returned, the doctors were busy with their preparations and Joseph was patiently explaining to them that he was a dybbuk who had involuntarily taken possession of the Kunivar. "The heat has driven the poor creature insane," Moshe Shiloah murmured, and rammed a huge needle into one of Seul's thighs.

"Make them listen to me," Joseph said.

"You know that voice," I told the doctors. "Something very unusual has happened here."

But they were no more willing to believe in dybbuks than they were in rivers that flow uphill. Joseph continued to protest, and the doctors continued methodically to fill Seul's body with sedatives and restoratives and other potions. Even when Joseph began to speak of last year's kibbutz gossip—who had been sleeping with whom behind whose back, who had illicitly been peddling goods from the community storehouse to the Kunivaru—they paid no attention. It was as though they had so much difficulty believing that a Kunivar could speak Hebrew that they were unable to make sense out of what he was saying and took Joseph's words to be Seul's delirium. Suddenly Joseph raised his voice for the first time, calling out in a loud, angry tone, "You, Moshe Shiloah! Aboard the Ark I found you in bed with the wife of Teviah Kohn, remember? Would a Kunivar have known such a thing?"

Moshe Shiloah gasped, reddened, and dropped his hypodermic. The other doctor was nearly as astonished.

"What is this?" Moshe Shiloah asked. "How can this be?"

"Deny me now!" Joseph roared. "Can you deny me?"

The doctors faced the same problems of acceptance that I had had, that Joseph himself had grappled with. We were all of us rational men in this kibbutz, and the supernatural had no place in our lives. But there was no arguing the phenomenon away. There was the voice of Joseph Avneri emerging from the throat of Seul the Kunivar, and the voice was saying things that only Joseph would have said, and Joseph had been dead more than a year. Call it a dybbuk, call it hallucination, call it anything: Joseph's presence could not be ignored.

Locking the door, Moshe Shiloah said to me, "We must deal with this somehow."

Tensely we discussed the situation. It was, we agreed, a delicate and difficult matter. Joseph, raging and tortured, demanded to be exorcised and allowed to sleep the sleep of the dead; unless we placated him he would make us all suffer. In his pain, in his fury, he might say anything, he might reveal everything he knew about our private lives; a dead man is beyond all of society's rules of common decency. We could not expose ourselves to that. But what could we do about him? Chain him in an outbuilding and hide him in solitary confinement? Hardly. Unhappy Joseph deserved better of us than that; and there was Seul to consider, poor supplanted Seul, the dybbuk's unwilling host. We could not keep a Kunivar in the kibbutz, imprisoned or free, even if his body did house the spirit of one of our own people, nor could we let the shell of Seul go back to the Kunivaru village with Joseph as a furious passenger trapped inside. What to do? Separate soul from body, somehow: restore Seul to wholeness and send Joseph to the limbo of the dead. But how? There was nothing in the standard pharmacopoeia about dybbuks. What to do?

I sent for Shmarya Asch and Yakov Ben-Zion, who headed the kibbutz council that month, and for Shlomo Feig, our rabbi, a shrewd and sturdy man, very unorthodox in his orthodoxy, almost as secular as the rest of us. They questioned Joseph Avneri extensively, and he told them the whole tale—his scandalous secret experiments, his post-mortem year as a wandering spirit, his sudden painful incarnation within Seul. At length Shmarya Asch turned to Moshe Shiloah and snapped, "There must be some therapy for such a case."

"I know of none."

"This is schizophrenia," said Shmarya Asch in his firm, dogmatic way. "There are cures for schizophrenia. There are drugs, there are electric shock treatments, there are—you know these things better than I, Moshe."

"This is not schizophrenia," Moshe Shiloah retorted. "This is a case of demonic possession. I have no training in treating such maladies."

"Demonic possession?" Shmarya bellowed. "Have you lost your mind?"

"Peace, peace, all of you," Shlomo Feig said, as everyone began to shout at once. The rabbi's voice cut sharply through the tumult and silenced us all. He was a man of great strength, physical as well as moral, to whom the entire kibbutz inevitably turned for guidance although there was virtually no one among us who observed the major rites of Judaism. He said, "I find this as hard to comprehend as any of you. But the evidence triumphs over my scepticism. How can we deny that Joseph Avneri has returned as a dybbuk? Moshe, you know no way of causing this intruder to leave the Kunivar's body?"

"None," said Moshe Shiloah.

"Maybe the Kunivaru themselves know a way," Yakov Ben-Zion suggested.

"Exactly," said the rabbi. "My next point. These Kunivaru are a primitive folk. They live closer to the world of magic and witchcraft, of demons and spirits, than we do whose minds are schooled in the habits of reason. Perhaps such cases of possession occur often among them. Perhaps they have techniques for driving out unwanted spirits. Let us turn to them, and let them cure their own."

BEFORE LONG YIGAL ARRIVED, BRINGING with him six Kunivaru, including Gyaymar, the village chief. They wholly filled the little hospital room, bustling around in it like a delegation of huge furry centaurs; I was oppressed by the acrid smell of so many of them in one small space, and although they had always been friendly to us, never raising an objection when we appeared as refugees to settle on their planet, I felt fear of them now as I had never felt before. Clustering about Seul, they asked questions of him in their own supple language, and when Joseph Avneri replied in Hebrew they whispered things to each other unintelligible to us. Then, unexpectedly, the voice of Seul broke through, speaking in halting spastic monosyllables that revealed the terrible shock his nervous system must have received; then the alien faded and Joseph Avneri spoke once more with the Kunivar's lips, begging forgiveness, asking for release.

Turning to Gyaymar, Shlomo Feig said, "Have such things happened on this world before?"

"Oh, yes, yes," the chief replied. "Many times. When one of us dies having a guilty soul, repose is denied, and the spirit may undergo strange migrations before forgiveness comes. What was the nature of this man's sin?"

"It would be difficult to explain to one who is not Jewish," said the rabbi hastily, glancing away. "The important question is whether you have a means of undoing what has befallen the unfortunate Seul, whose sufferings we all lament."

"We have a means, yes," said Gyaymar, the chief.

The six Kunivaru hoisted Seul to their shoulders and carried him from the kibbutz; we were told that we might accompany them if we cared to do so. I went along, and Moshe Shiloah, and Shmarya Asch, and Yakov Ben-Zion, and the rabbi, and perhaps some others. The Kunivaru took their comrade not to their village but to a meadow several kilometers to the east, down in the direction of the place where the Hasidim lived. Not long after the Landing, the Kunivaru had let us know that the meadow was sacred to them, and none of us had ever entered it.

It was a lovely place, green and moist, a gently sloping basin crisscrossed by a dozen cool little streams. Depositing Seul beside one of the streams, the Kunivaru went off into the woods bordering the meadow to gather firewood and herbs. We remained close by Seul. "This will do no good," Joseph Avneri muttered more than once. "A waste of time, a foolish expense of energy." Three of the Kunivaru started to build a bonfire. Two sat nearby, shredding the herbs, making heaps of leaves, stems, roots. Gradually more of their kind appeared until the meadow was filled with them; it seemed that the whole village, some four hundred Kunivaru, was turning out to watch or to participate in the rite. Many of them carried musical instruments, trumpets and drums, rattles and clappers, lyres, lutes, small harps, percussive boards, wooden flutes, everything intricate and fanciful of design; we had not suspected such cultural complexity. The priests—I assume they were priests, Kunivaru of stature and dignity—wore ornate ceremonial helmets and heavy golden mantles of sea-beast fur. The ordinary townsfolk carried ribbons and streamers, bits of bright fabric, polished mirrors of stone, and other ornamental devices. When he saw how elaborate a function it was going to be, Moshe Shiloah, an amateur anthropologist at heart, ran back to the kibbutz to fetch camera and recorder. He returned, breathless, just as the rite commenced.

And a glorious rite it was: incense, a grandly blazing bonfire, the pungent fragrance of freshly picked herbs, some heavy-footed quasi-orgiastic dancing, and a choir punching out harsh, sharp-edged arrhythmic melodies. Gyaymar and the high priest of the village performed an elegant antiphonal chant, uttering long curling intertwining melismas and sprinkling Seul with a sweet-smelling pink fluid out of a baroquely carved wooden censer. Never have I beheld such stirring pageantry. But Joseph's gloomy prediction was correct; it was all entirely useless. Two hours of intensive exorcism had no effect. When the ceremony ended—the ultimate punctuation marks were five terrible shouts from the high priest—the dybbuk remained firmly in possession of Seul. "You have not conquered me," Joseph declared in a bleak tone.

Gyaymar said, "It seems we have no power to command an earthborn soul."

"What will we do now?" demanded Yakov Ben-Zion of no one in particular. "Our science and their witchcraft both fail."

Joseph Avneri pointed toward the east, toward the village of the Hasidim, and murmured something indistinct.

"No!" cried Rabbi Shlomo Feig, who stood closest to the dybbuk at that moment.

"What did he say?" I asked.

"It was nothing," the rabbi said. "It was foolishness. The long ceremony has left him fatigued, and his mind wanders. Pay no attention."

I moved nearer to my old friend. "Tell me, Joseph."

"I said," the dybbuk replied slowly, "that perhaps we should send for the Baal Shem."

"Foolishness!" said Shlomo Feig, and spat.

"Why this anger?" Shmarya Asch wanted to know. "You, Rabbi Shlomo, you were one of the first to advocate employing Kunivaru sorcerers in this business. You gladly bring in alien witch doctors, Rabbi, and grow angry when someone suggests that your fellow Jew be given a chance to drive out the demon? Be consistent, Shlomo!"

Rabbi Shlomo's strong face grew mottled with rage. It was strange to see this calm, even-tempered man becoming so excited. "I will have nothing to do with Hasidim!" he exclaimed.

"I think this is a matter of professional rivalries," Moshe Shiloah commented.

The rabbi said, "To give recognition to all that is most superstitious in Judaism, to all that is most irrational and grotesque and outmoded and medieval? No! No!"

"But dybbuks *are* irrational and grotesque and outmoded and medieval," said Joseph Avneri. "Who better to exorcise one than a rabbi whose soul is still rooted in ancient beliefs?"

"I forbid this!" Shlomo Feig sputtered. "If the Baal Shem is summoned I will—I will—"

"Rabbi," Joseph said, shouting now, "this is a matter of my tortured soul against your offended spiritual pride. Give way! Give way! Get me the Baal Shem!"

"I refuse!"

"Look!" called Yakov Ben-Zion. The dispute had suddenly become academic. Uninvited, our Hasidic cousins were arriving at the sacred meadow, a long procession of them, eerie prehistoric-looking figures clad in their traditional long black robes, wide-brimmed hats, heavy beards, dangling side-locks; and at the head of the group marched their tzaddik, their holy man, their prophet, their leader, Reb Shmuel the Baal Shem.

IT WAS CERTAINLY NEVER OUR idea to bring Hasidim with us when we fled out of the smoldering ruins of the Land of Israel. Our intention was to leave Earth and all its sorrows far behind, to start anew on another world where we could at last build an enduring Jewish homeland, free for once of our eternal gentile enemies and free, also, of the religious fanatics among our own kind whose presence had long been a drain on our vitality. We needed no mystics, no ecstatics, no weepers, no moaners, no leapers, no chanters; we needed only workers, farmers, machinists, engineers, builders.

But how could we refuse them a place on the Ark? It was their good fortune to come upon us just as we were making the final preparations for our flight. The nightmare that had darkened our sleep for three centuries had been made real: the Homeland lay in flames, our armies had been shattered out of ambush, Philistines wielding long knives strode through our devastated cities. Our ship was ready to leap to the stars. We were not cowards but simply realists, for it was folly to think we could do battle any longer, and if some fragment of our ancient nation were to survive, it could only survive far from the bitter world Earth. So we were going to go; and here were suppliants asking us for succor, Reb Shmuel and his thirty followers. How could we turn them away, knowing they would certainly perish? They were human beings, they were Jews. For all our misgivings, we let them come on board.

And then we wandered across the heavens year after year, and then we came to a star that had no name, only a number, and then we found its fourth planet to be sweet and fertile, a happier world than Earth, and we thanked the God in whom we did not believe for the good luck that He had granted us, and we cried out to each other in congratulation, Mazel tov! Mazel tov! Good luck, good luck, good luck! And someone looked in an old book and saw that mazel once had had an astrological connotation, that in the days of the Bible it had meant not only "luck" but a lucky star, and so we named our lucky star Mazel Tov, and we made our landfall on Mazel Tov IV, which was to be the New Israel. Here we found no enemies, no Egyptians, no Assyrians, no Romans, no Cossacks, no Nazis, no Arabs, only the Kunivaru, kindly people of a simple nature, who solemnly studied our pantomimed explanations and replied to us in gestures, saying, Be welcome, there is more land here than we will ever need. And we built our kibbutz.

But we had no desire to live close to those people of the past, the Hasidim, and they had scant love for us, for they saw us as pagans, godless Jews who were worse than gentiles, and they went off to build a muddy little village of their own. Sometimes on clear nights we heard their lusty singing, but otherwise there was scarcely any contact between us and them.

I could understand Rabbi Shlomo's hostility to the idea of intervention by the Baal Shem. These Hasidim represented the mystic side of Judaism, the dark uncontrollable Dionysiac side, the skeleton in the tribal closet; Shlomo Feig might be amused or charmed by a rite of exorcism performed by furry centaurs, but when Jews took part in the same sort of supernaturalism it was distressing to him. Then, too, there was the ugly fact that the sane, sensible Rabbi Shlomo had virtually no followers at all among the sane, sensible secularized Jews of our kibbutz, whereas Reb Shmuel's Hasidim looked upon him with awe, regarding him as a miracle worker, a seer, a saint. Still, Rabbi Shlomo's understandable jealousies and prejudices aside, Joseph Avneri was right: dybbuks were vapors out of the realm of the fantastic, and the fantastic was the Baal Shem's kingdom.

He was an improbably tall, angular figure, almost skeletal, with gaunt cheekbones, a soft, thickly curling beard, and gentle dreamy eyes. I suppose he was about fifty years old, though I would have believed it if they said he was thirty or seventy or ninety. His sense of the dramatic was unfailing; now—it was late afternoon—he took up a position with the setting sun at his back, so that his long shadow engulfed us all, and spread forth his arms and said, "We have heard reports of a dybbuk among you."

"There is no dybbuk!" Rabbi Shlomo retorted fiercely.

The Baal Shem smiled. "But there is a Kunivar who speaks with an Israeli voice?"

"There has been an odd transformation, yes," Rabbi Shlomo conceded. "But in this age, on this planet, no one can take dybbuks seriously."

"That is, *you* cannot take dybbuks seriously," said the Baal Shem.

"I do!" cried Joseph Avneri in exasperation. "I! I! I am the dybbuk! I, Joseph Avneri, dead a year ago last Elul, doomed for my sins to inhabit this Kunivar carcass. A Jew, Reb Shmuel, a dead Jew, a pitiful sinful miserable Yid. Who'll let me out? Who'll set me free?"

"There is no dybbuk?" the Baal Shem said amiably.

"This Kunivar has gone insane," said Shlomo Feig.

We coughed and shifted our feet. If anyone had gone insane it was our rabbi, denying in this fashion the phenomenon that he himself had acknowledged as genuine, however reluctantly, only a few hours before. Envy, wounded pride, and stubbornness had unbalanced his judgment. Joseph Avneri, enraged, began to bellow the Aleph Beth Gimel, the Shma Yisroel, anything that might prove his dybbukhood. The Baal Shem waited patiently, arms outspread, saying nothing. Rabbi Shlomo, confronting him, his powerful stocky figure dwarfed by the long-legged Hasid, maintained energetically that there had to be some rational explanation for the metamorphosis of Seul the Kunivar.

When Shlomo Feig at length fell silent, the Baal Shem said, "There is a dybbuk in this Kunivar. Do you think, Rabbi Shlomo, that dybbuks ceased their wanderings when the shtetls of Poland were destroyed? Nothing is lost in the sight of God, Rabbi. Jews go to the stars; the Torah and the Talmud and the Zohar have gone also to the stars; dybbuks too may be found in these strange worlds. Rabbi, may I bring peace to this troubled spirit and to this weary Kunivar?"

"Do whatever you want," Shlomo Feig muttered in disgust, and strode away, scowling.

Reb Shmuel at once commenced the exorcism. He called first for a minyan. Eight of his Hasidim stepped forward. I exchanged a glance with Shmarya Asch, and we shrugged and came forward too, but the Baal Shem, smiling, waved us away and beckoned two more of his followers into the circle. They began to sing; to my everlasting shame I have no idea what the singing was about, for the words were Yiddish of a Galitzianer sort, nearly as alien to me as the Kunivaru tongue. They sang for ten or fifteen minutes; the Hasidim grew more animated, clapping their hands, dancing about their Baal

Shem; suddenly Reb Shmuel lowered his arms to his sides, silencing them, and quietly began to recite Hebrew phrases, which after a moment I recognized as those of the Ninety-first Psalm: The Lord is my refuge and my fortress, in him will I trust. The psalm rolled melodiously to its comforting conclusion, its promise of deliverance and salvation. For a long moment all was still. Then in a terrifying voice, not loud but immensely commanding, the Baal Shem ordered the spirit of Joseph Avneri to quit the body of Seul the Kunivar. "Out! Out! God's name out, and off to your eternal rest!" One of the Hasidim handed Reb Shmuel a shofar. The Baal Shem put the ram's horn to his lips and blew a single titanic blast.

Joseph Avneri whimpered. The Kunivar that housed him took three awkward, toppling steps. "Oy, mama, mama," Joseph cried. The Kunivar's head snapped back; his arms shot straight out at his sides; he tumbled clumsily to his four knees. An eon went by. Then Seul rose—smoothly, this time, with natural Kunivaru grace—and went to the Baal Shem, and knelt, and touched the tzaddik's black robe. So we knew the thing was done.

Instants later the tension broke. Two of the Kunivaru priests rushed toward the Baal Shem, and then Gyaymar, and then some of the musicians, and then it seemed the whole tribe was pressing close upon him, trying to touch the holy man. The Hasidim, looking worried, murmured their concern, but the Baal Shem, towering over the surging mob, calmly blessed the Kunivaru, stroking the dense fur of their backs. After some minutes of this the Kunivaru set up a rhythmic chant, and it was a while before I realized what they were saying. Moshe Shiloah and Yakov Ben-Zion caught the sense of it about the same time I did, and we began to laugh, and then our laughter died away.

"What do their words mean?" the Baal Shem called out.

"They are saying," I told him, "that they are convinced of the power of your god. They wish to become Jews."

For the first time Reb Shmuel's poise and serenity shattered. His eyes flashed ferociously and he pushed at the crowding

Kunivaru, opening an avenue between them. Coming up to me, he snapped, "Such a thing is an absurdity!"

"Nevertheless, look at them. They worship you, Reb Shmuel."

"I refuse their worship."

"You worked a miracle. Can you blame them for adoring you and hungering after your faith?"

"Let them adore," said the Baal Shem. "But how can they become Jews? It would be a mockery."

I shook my head. "What was it you told Rabbi Shlomo? Nothing is lost in the sight of God. There have always been converts to Judaism—we never invite them, but we never turn them away if they're sincere, eh, Reb Shmuel? Even here in the stars, there is continuity of tradition, and tradition says we harden not our hearts to those who seek the truth of God. These are a good people—let them be received into Israel."

"No," the Baal Shem said. "A Jew must first of all be human."

"Show me that in the Torah."

"The Torah! You joke with me. A Jew must first of all be human. Were cats allowed to become Jews? Were horses?"

"These people are neither cats nor horses, Reb Shmuel. They are as human as we are."

"No! No!"

"If there can be a dybbuk on Mazel Tov IV," I said, "then there can also be Jews with six limbs and green fur."

"No. No. No. *No!*"

The Baal Shem had had enough of this debate. Shoving aside the clutching hands of the Kunivaru in a most unsaintly way, he gathered his followers and stalked off, a tower of offended dignity, bidding us no farewells.

BUT HOW CAN TRUE FAITH be denied? The Hasidim offered no encouragement, so the Kunivaru came to us; they learned Hebrew and we loaned them books, and Rabbi Shlomo gave them religious instruction, and in their own time and in their own way

they entered into Judaism. All this was years ago, in the first generation after the Landing. Most of those who lived in those days
are dead now—Rabbi Shlomo, Reb Shmuel the Baal Shem, Moshe
Shiloah, Shmarya Asch. I was a young man then. I know a good
deal more now, and if I am no closer to God than I ever was, perhaps He has grown closer to me. I eat meat and butter at the same
meal, and I plow my land on the Sabbath, but those are old habits
that have little to do with belief or the absence of belief.

We are much closer to the Kunivaru, too, than we were in those
early days; they no longer seem like alien beings to us, but merely
neighbors whose bodies have a different form. The younger ones
of our kibbutz are especially drawn to them. The year before last
Rabbi Lhaoyir the Kunivar suggested to some of our boys that
they come for lessons to the Talmud Torah, the religious school,
that he runs in the Kunivaru village; since the death of Shlomo
Feig there has been no one in the kibbutz to give such instruction.
When Reb Yossele, the son and successor of Reb Shmuel the Baal
Shem heard this, he raised strong objections. If your boys will take
instruction, he said, at least send them to us, and not to green
monsters. My son Yigal threw him out of the kibbutz. We would
rather let our boys learn the Torah from green monsters, Yigal
told Reb Yossele, than have them raised to be Hasidim.

And so my son's son has had his lessons at the Talmud Torah of
Rabbi Lhaoyir the Kunivar, and next spring he will have his bar
mitzvah. Once I would have been appalled by such goings-on, but
now I say only, How strange, how unexpected, how interesting!
Truly the Lord, if He exists, must have a keen sense of humor. I
like a god who can smile and wink, who doesn't take himself too
seriously. The Kunivaru are Jews! Yes! They are preparing David
for his bar mitzvah! Yes! Today is Yom Kippur, and I hear the
sound of the shofar coming from their village! Yes! Yes. So be it.
So be it, yes, and all praise be to Him.

CALIBAN

"In the country of the blind, the one-eyed man is king," said H. G. Wells, the greatest of all science-fiction writers, in a memorable short story written more than a century ago. I have argued many times that the rest of us, in that intervening century, have simply been rewriting and amplifying the myriad themes that Wells set forth for us back then—time travel, interplanetary war, atomic warfare, and on and on and on.

Among my own variants on Wells's original themes is one that bends his country-of-the-blind proverb to read, "In the country of the beautiful people, the ugly man is king." On the face of it, that sounds unlikely: the ugly man would simply go skulking miserably around, mocked or ignored, where everyone else looks like Sophia Loren or Cary Grant. But science fiction is given to exploring the superficially unlikely and seeing whether some hidden truth lies beneath the apparently obvious surface. And so, in November 1970, having been invited by the editor Bob Hoskins (not to be confused with the British actor of the same name) to contribute a story to his anthology *Infinity* (not to be confused with the earlier science-fiction magazine of the same name), I sketched out a story on just that premise—the tale of the one ugly man in a world of people who have made themselves look like movie stars. "They have all changed their faces to a standard model" is how he begins his narrative. "It is the latest thing, which should not be confused with the latest Thing. The latest Thing is me." And he continues from there, setting forth my upside-down premise and carrying it on to its upside-down conclusion. This is the story as he tells it himself. Listen to it. You cannot choose but hear.

—⁓—

THEY HAVE ALL CHANGED THEIR faces to a standard model. It is the latest thing, which should not be confused with the latest Thing. The latest Thing is me. The latest thing, the latest fad, the latest rage, is for them all to change their faces to a standard model. I have no idea how it is done but I think it is genetic, with the RNA, the DNA, the NDA. Only retroactive. They all come out with blond wavy hair and sparkling blue eyes. And long straight faces with sharp cheekbones. And notched chins and thin lips curling in ironic smiles. Even the black ones: thin lips, blue eyes, blond wavy hair. And pink skins. They all look alike now. The sweet Aryanized world. Our entire planet. Except me. Meee.

I AM IMPERFECT. I AM blemished. I am unforgiving. I am the latest Thing.

LOUISIANA SAID, WOULD YOU LIKE to copulate with me? You are so strange. You are so beautiful. Oh, how I desire you, strange being from a strange time. My orifices are yours.

It was a thoughtful offer. I considered it a while, thinking she might be trying to patronize me. At length I notified her of my acceptance. We went to a public copulatorium. Louisiana is taller than I am and her hair is a torrent of spun gold. Her eyes are blue and her face is long and straight. I would say she is about twenty-three years old. In the copulatorium she dissolved her clothes and stood naked before me. She was wearing gold pubic hair that day and her belly was flat and taut. Her breasts were round and slightly elongated and the nipples were very small. Go on, she said, now you dissolve your clothes.

I said, I am afraid to because my body is ugly and you will mock me.

Your body is not ugly, she said. Your body is strange but it is not ugly.

My body is ugly, I insisted. My legs are short and they curve outward and my thighs have bulging muscles and I have black hairy hair all over me. Like an ape. And there is this hideous scar on my belly.

A scar?

Where they took out my appendix, I told her.

This aroused her beyond all probability. Her nipples stood up tall and her face became flushed.

Your appendix? Your appendix was removed?

Yes, I said, it was done when I was fourteen years old, and I have a loathsome red scar on my abdomen.

She asked, What year was it when you were fourteen?

I said, It was 1967, I think.

She laughed and clapped her hands and began to dance around the room. Her breasts bounced up and down, but her long flowing silken hair soon covered them, leaving only the stubby pinkish nipples poking through like buttons. 1967! she cried. Fourteen! Your appendix was removed! 1967!

Then she turned to me and said, My grandfather was born in 1967, I think. How terribly ancient you are. My helix-father's father on the countermolecular side. I didn't realize you were so very ancient.

Ancient and ugly, I said.

Not ugly, only strange, she said.

Strange and ugly, I said. Strangely ugly.

We think you are beautiful, she said. Will you dissolve your clothes now? It would not be pleasing to me to copulate with you if you keep your clothes on.

There, I said, and boldly revealed myself. The bandy legs. The hairy chest. The scarred belly. The bulging shoulders. The short neck. She has seen my lopsided face, she can see my dismal body as well. If that is what she wants.

She threw herself upon me, gasping and making soft noises.

What did Louisiana look like before the change came? Did she have dull stringy hair thick lips a hook nose bushy black eyebrows no chin foul breath one breast bigger than the other splay feet crooked teeth little dark hairs around her nipples a bulging navel too many dimples in her buttocks skinny thighs blue veins in her calves protruding ears? And then did they give her the homogenizing treatment and make her the golden creature she is today? How long did it take? What were the costs? Did the government subsidize the process? Were the large corporations involved? How were these matters handled in the socialist countries? Was there anyone who did not care to be changed? Perhaps Louisiana was born this way. Perhaps her beauty is natural. In any society there are always a few whose beauty is natural.

DR. HABAKKUK AND SENATOR MANDRAGORE spent a great deal of time questioning me in the Palazzo of Mirrors. They put a green plastic dome over my head so that everything I said would be recorded with the proper nuance and intensity. Speak to us, they said. We are fascinated by your antique accent. We are enthralled by your primitive odors. Do you realize that you are our sole representative of the nightmare out of which we have awakened? Tell us, said the Senator, tell us about your brutally competitive civilization. Describe in detail the fouling of the environment. Explain the nature of national rivalry. Compare and contrast methods of political discourse in the Soviet Union and in the United States. Let us have your analysis of the sociological implications of the first voyage to the moon. Would you like to see the moon? Can we offer you any psychedelic drugs? Did you find Louisiana sexually satisfying? We are so glad to have you here. We regard you as a unique spiritual treasure. Speak to us of yesterday's yesterdays, while we listen entranced and enraptured.

LOUISIANA SAYS THAT SHE IS eighty-seven years old. Am I to believe this? There is about her a springtime freshness. No, she maintains, I am eighty-seven years old. I was born on March-alternate 11, 2022. Does that depress you? Is my great age frightening to you? See how tight my skin is. See how my teeth gleam. Why are you so disturbed? I am, after all, much younger than you.

I UNDERSTAND THAT IN SOME cases making the great change involved elaborate surgery. Cornea transplants and cosmetic adjustment of the facial structure. A great deal of organ-swapping went on. There is not much permanence among these people. They are forever exchanging segments of themselves for new and improved segments. I am told that among some advanced groups the use of mechanical limb-interfaces has come to be common, in order that new arms and legs may be plugged in with a minimum of trouble. This is truly an astonishing era. Even so, their women seem to copulate in the old ways: knees up thighs apart, lying on the right side left leg flexed, back to the man and knees slightly bent, etc., etc., etc. One might think they would have invented something new by this time. But perhaps the possibilities for innovation in the sphere of erotics are not extensive. Can I suggest anything? What if the woman unplugs both arms and both legs and presents her mere torso to the man? Helpless! Vulnerable! Quintessentially feminine! I will discuss it with Louisiana. But it would be just my luck that her arms and legs don't come off.

ON THE FIRST PARA-WEDNESDAY OF every month Lieutenant Hotchkiss gives me lessons in fluid-breathing. We go to one of the deepest sub-levels of the Extravagance Building, where there is a special hyperoxygenated pool, for the use of beginners only, circular in shape and not at all deep. The water sparkles like opal.

Usually the pool is crowded with children, but Lieutenant Hotchkiss arranges for me to have private instruction since I am shy about revealing my body. Each lesson is much like the one before. Lieutenant Hotchkiss descends the gentle ramp that leads one into the pool. He is taller than I am and his hair is golden and his eyes are blue. Sometimes I have difficulties distinguishing him from Dr. Habakkuk and Senator Mandragore. In a casual moment the lieutenant confided that he is ninety-eight years old and there-fore not really a contemporary of Louisiana's, although Louisiana has hinted that on several occasions in the past she has allowed the lieutenant to fertilize her ova. I doubt this inasmuch as repro-duction is quite uncommon in this era and what probability is there that she would have permitted him to do it more than once? I think she believes that by telling me such things she will stimu-late emotions of jealousy in me, since she knows that the primitive ancients were frequently jealous.

Regardless of all this Lieutenant Hotchkiss proceeds to enter the water. It reaches his navel, his broad hairless chest, his throat, his chin, his sensitive thin-walled nostrils. He submerges and crawls about on the floor of the pool. I see his golden hair glitter-ing through the opal water. He remains totally submerged for eight or twelve minutes, now and again lifting his hands above the surface and waggling them as if to show me where he is. Then he comes forth. Water streams from his nostrils but he is not in the least out of breath. Come on, now, he says. You can do it. It's as easy as it looks. He beckons me toward the ramp. Any child can do it, the lieutenant assures me. It's a matter of control and deter-mination. I shake my head. No, I say, genetic modification has something to do with it. My lungs aren't equipped to handle water, although I suppose yours are. The lieutenant merely laughs. Come on, come on, into the water. And I go down the ramp.

How the water glows and shimmers! It reaches my navel, my black-matted chest, my throat, my chin, my wide thick nostrils. I breathe it in and choke and splutter; and I rush up the ramp, struggling for air. With the water a leaden weight in my lungs, I throw myself exhausted to the marble floor and cry out, No, no, no, it's impossible.

Lieutenant Hotchkiss stands over me. His body is without flaw. He says, You've got to try to cultivate the proper attitudes. Your mental set determines everything. Let's think more positively about this business of breathing under water. Don't you realize that it's a major evolutionary step, one of the grand and glorious things separating our species from the australopithecines? Don't you want to be part of the great leap forward? Up, now. Try again. Thinking positively all the time. Carrying in your mind the distinction between yourself and our bestial ancestors. Go in. In. In. And I go in. And moments later burst from the water, choking and spluttering. This takes place on the first para-Wednesday of every month. The same thing, every time.

WHEN YOU ARE TALKING ON the telephone and your call is abruptly cut off, do you worry that the person on the other end will think you have hung up on him? Do you suspect that the person on the other end has hung up on you? Such problems are unknown here. These people make very few telephone calls. We are beyond mere communication in this era, Louisiana sometimes remarks.

THROUGH MY EYES THESE PEOPLE behold their shining plastic epoch in proper historical perspective. They must see it as the present, which is always the same. But to me it is the future and so I have the true observer's parallax: I can say, it once was like that and now it is like *this*. They prize my gift. They treasure me. People come from other continents to run their fingers over my face. They tell me how much they admire my asymmetry. And they ask me many questions. Most of them ask about their own era rather than about mine. Such questions as:

Does suspended animation tempt you?

Was the fusion plant overwhelming in its implications of contained might?

Can you properly describe interconnection of the brain with a computer as an ecstatic experience?

Do you approve of modification of the solar system?

And also there are those who make more searching demands on my critical powers, such as Dr. Habakkuk and Senator Mandragore. They ask such questions as:

Was the brevity of your life span a hindrance to the development of the moral instincts?

Do you find our standardization of appearance at all abhorrent?

What was your typical emotional response to the sight of the dung of some wild animal in the streets?

Can you quantify the intensity of your feelings concerning the transience of human institutions?

I do my best to serve their needs. Often it is a strain to answer them in meaningful ways, but I strive to do so. Wondering occasionally if it would not have been more valuable for them to interrogate a Neanderthal. Or one of Lieutenant Hotchkiss's australopithecines. I am perhaps not primitive enough, though I do have my own charisma, nevertheless.

THE FIRST DAY IT WAS pretty frightening to me. I saw one of them, with his sleek face and all, and I could accept that, but then another one came into the room to give me an injection, and he looked just like the first one. Twins, I thought, my doctors are twins. But then a third and a fourth and a fifth arrived. The same face, the very same fucking face. Imagine my chagrin, me with my blob of a nose, with my uneven teeth, with my eyebrows that meet in the middle, with my fleshy pockmarked cheeks, lying there beneath this convocation of the perfect. Let me tell you I felt out of place. I was never touchy about my looks before—I mean, it's an imperfect world, we all have our flaws—but these bastards didn't have flaws, and that was a hard acceptance for me to relate to. I thought I was being clever: I said, You're all multiples of the same gene pattern, right? Modern advances in medicine have made possible an infinite reduplication of genetic information and the five of you belong to one clone, isn't that it? And several of them answered, No, this is not the case, we are in fact wholly unrelated but within the last meta-week we have independently decided to standardize our appearance according to the presently favored model. And then three or four more of them came into my room to get a look at me.

IN THE BEGINNING I KEPT telling myself: *In the country of the beautiful the ugly man is king.*

LOUISIANA WAS THE FIRST ONE with whom I had a sexual liaison. We often went to public copulatoria. She was easy to arouse and quite passionate although her friend Calpurnia informed me some months later that Louisiana takes orgasm-inducing drugs before copulating with me. I asked Calpurnia why and she became embarrassed. Dismayed, I bared my body to her and threw myself on top of her. Yes, she cried, rape me, violate me! Calpurnia's vigorous spasms astonished me. The following morning Louisiana asked me if I had noticed Calpurnia swallowing a small purple spansule prior to our intercourse. Calpurnia's face is identical to Louisiana's but her breasts are farther apart. I have also had sexual relations with Helena, Amniota, Drusilla, Florinda, and Vibrissa. Before each episode of copulation I ask them their names so that there will be no mistakes.

AT TWILIGHT THEY PROGRAMMED AN hour of red and green rainfall and I queried Senator Mandragore about the means by which I had been brought to this era. Was it bodily transportation through time? That is, the physical lifting of my very self out of then and into now? Or was my body dead and kept on deposit in a freezer vault until these people resuscitated and refurbished it?

Am I, perhaps, a total genetic reconstruct fashioned from a few fragments of ancient somatic tissue found in a baroque urn? Possibly I am only a simulated and stylized interpretation of twentieth-century man produced by a computer under intelligent and sympathetic guidance. How was it done, Senator? How was it done? The rain ceased. Leaving elegant puddles of blurred hue in the puddle-places.

WALKING WITH LOUISIANA ON MY arm down Venus Avenue I imagined that I saw another man with a face like mine. It was the merest flash: a dark visage, thick heavy brows, stubble on the cheeks, the head thrust belligerently forward between the massive shoulders. But he was gone, turning a sudden corner, before I could get a good look. Louisiana suggested I was overindulging in hallucinogens. We went to an underwater theatre and she swam below me like a golden fish, revolving lights glinting off the upturned globes of her rump.

THIS IS A DEMONSTRATION OF augmented mental capacity, said Vibrissa. I wish to show you what the extent of human potentiality can be. Read me any passage of Shakespeare of your own choice and I will repeat it verbatim and then offer you textual analysis. Shall we try this? Very well, I said and delicately put my fingernail to the Shakespeare cube and the words formed and I said out loud, What man dare, I dare: Approach thou like the rugged Russian bear, the arm'd rhinoceros, or the Hyrcan tiger, Take any shape but that, and my firm nerves Shall never tremble. Vibrissa instantly recited the lines to me without error and interpreted them in terms of the poet's penis envy, offering me footnotes from Seneca and Strindberg. I was quite impressed. But then I was never what you might call an intellectual.

ON THE DAY OF THE snow-gliding events I distinctly and beyond any possibilities of ambiguity or misapprehension saw two separate individuals who resembled me. Are they importing more of my kind for their amusement? If they are I will be resentful. I cherish my unique status.

I TOLD DR. HABAKKUK THAT I wished to apply for transformation to the facial norm of society. Do it, I said, the transplant thing or the genetic manipulation or however you manage it. I want to be golden-haired and have blue eyes and regular features. I want to look like you. Dr. Habakkuk smiled genially and shook his youthful golden head. No, he told me. Forgive us, but we like you as you are.

SOMETIMES I DREAM OF MY life as it was in the former days. I think of automobiles and pastrami and tax returns and marigolds and pimples and mortgages and the gross national product. Also I indulge in recollections of my childhood my parents my wife my dentist my younger daughter my desk my toothbrush my dog my umbrella my favorite brand of beer my wristwatch my answering service my neighbors my phonograph my ocarina. All of these things are gone. Grinding my flesh against that of Drusilla in the copulatorium I wonder if she could be one of my descendants. I must have descendants somewhere in this civilization, and why not she? She asks me to perform an act of oral perversion with her and I explain that I couldn't possibly engage in such stuff with my own great-grandchild.

I THINK I REMAIN QUITE calm at most times considering the extraordinary nature of the stress that this experience has imposed on me. I am still self-conscious about my appearance but I pretend otherwise. Often I go naked just as they do. If they dislike bodily hair or disproportionate limbs, let them look away.

OCCASIONALLY I BELCH OR SCRATCH under my arms or do other primitive things to remind them that I am the authentic man from antiquity. For now there can be no doubt that I have my imitators. There are at least five. Calpurnia denies this, but I am no fool.

Dr. Habakkuk revealed that he was going to take a holiday in the Carpathians and would not return until the 14th of June-surrogate. In the meantime Dr. Clasp would minister to my needs. Dr. Clasp entered my suite and I remarked on his startling resemblance to Dr. Habakkuk. He asked, What would you like? and I told him I wanted him to operate on me so that I looked like everybody else. I am tired of appearing bestial and primordial, I said. To my surprise Dr. Clasp smiled warmly and told me that he'd arrange for the transformation at once, since it violated his principles to allow any organism needlessly to suffer. I was taken to the operating room and given a sour-tasting anaesthetic. Seemingly without the passing of time I awakened and was wheeled into a dome of mirrors to behold myself. Even as I had requested they had redone me into one of them, blond-haired, blue-eyed, with a slim, agile body and a splendidly symmetrical face. Dr. Clasp came in after a while and we stood side by side: we might have been twins. How do you like it? he asked. Tears brimmed in my eyes and I said that this was the most wonderful moment of my life. Dr. Clasp pummeled my shoulder jovially and said, You know, I am not Dr. Clasp at all, I am really Dr. Habakkuk and I never went to the Carpathians. This entire episode has been a facet of our analysis of your pattern of responses.

LOUISIANA WAS ASTONISHED BY MY changed appearance. Are you truly he? she kept asking. Are you truly he? I'll prove it, I said and mounted her with my old prehistoric zeal, snorting and gnawing her breasts. But she shook me free with a deft flip of her pelvis and rushed from the chamber. You'll never see me again, she shouted but I merely shrugged and called after her, So what I can see lots of others just like you. I never saw her again.

SO NOW THEY HAVE ALL changed themselves again to the new standard model. It happened gradually over a period of months but the transition is at last complete. Their heavy brows, their pockmarked cheeks, their hairy chests. It is the latest thing. I make my way through the crowded streets and wherever I turn I see faces that mirror my own lopsidedness. Only I am not lopsided myself any more, of course. I am symmetrical and flawless, and I am the only one. I cannot find Dr. Habakkuk, and Dr. Clasp is in the Pyrenees; Senator Mandragore was defeated in the primary. So I must remain beautiful. Walking among them. They are all alike. Thick lips uneven teeth noses like blobs. How I despise them! I the only golden one. And all of them mocking me by their metamorphosis. All of them. Mocking me. Meee.

◆

PASSENGERS

Here we have a case history in the rewards of perseverance. Late in 1967 I took it into my head to write a story for *Orbit*, an annual collection of science-fiction stories edited by Damon Knight. Knight, whom I had known for many years (and, in fact, had just succeeded as president of the Science Fiction Writers of America) was an excellent short-story writer and a brilliant critic from whom I had learned a great deal about the art of writing science fiction. He was also, I knew, a difficult, cantankerous, demanding editor. But his book *Orbit* was at the moment a center of exciting creative activity in our field and I was eager to take on the challenge of writing a story for it.

How much of a challenge it would be, I had no idea when I sent him "Passengers" in the first days of 1967. I had put a great deal of effort into it, knowing that I was aiming it at the toughest editor in the field, and I thought Knight would be pleased with it. Wrong. He sent it back on January 16, saying, "I can't fault this one technically, and it is surely dark and nasty enough to suit anybody, but I have a nagging feeling that there's something missing, and I'm not sure I can put my finger on it." He offered some suggestions for a rewrite even so, and, not willing to give up at that point, I did another draft and sent it to him on January 26, telling him, "You and your *Orbit* are a great tribulation to me. I suppose I could take 'Passenger' and ship it off to

Fred Pohl [the editor of the monthly magazine *Galaxy*, for whom I was doing stories regularly at that time] and collect my $120 and start all over trying to sell one to you. But I don't want to do that, because I believe this story represents just about the best I have in me, and if I can't get you to take it it's futile to go on submitting others."

Knight thought the rewrite was almost there—*almost*. So I did another rewrite. And another, when he turned that one back. The hook was in me, and all I could do was wriggle. On March 22 he wrote to me again to say, "God help us both, I am going to ask you to revise this one more time. The love story now has every necessary element, but it seems to me it's an empty jug. Now I want you to put the love into it. I say this with a feeling of helplessness, because I don't know how to tell you to do it."

Giving up at this point, I felt, was unthinkable. So I did another draft—the fifth—and this time he bought it, and the story was published in *Orbit Four* in 1969. I was paid $265 for it, or about $3000 in modern purchasing power, not an unreasonable sum for a twenty-two-page short story. But I had put in I know not how many hours of work to earn that $265, and I suspect I would have done just about as well, financially, if I had put in the same amount of time working as a bank teller as I had writing those five drafts for Damon Knight.

And yet—it had been an almighty nuisance tinkering with that story for the hard-to-satisfy Mr. Knight, but ultimately I was rewarded, and rewarded well for all the pains I took. The story won a Nebula in 1970 for Best Short Science Fiction Story of 1969. It was nominated for a Hugo, too, but lost out by a fluke, beaten by a story that was technically ineligible for a nomination. It was picked for several best-of-the-year anthologies, and has gone on to be reprinted in many other anthologies over the years, earning status as a classic of the genre. And then it was bought by a movie company for quite a large sum of money indeed, thus compensating me years after the fact for all those hours of rewriting between January and March of 1967. The movie was never made, but the film rights reverted to me and the story was optioned by Hollywood a *second* time, also for a bundle of cash, and if I live long enough I may yet see that movie happen. So I suppose Damon was right to make me go on and on with those revisions.

The story itself earns its place in this collection because it tells a tale that I hope none of us will ever be able to relate: what it is like to have one's mind taken over by an alien entity, to have, like everyone else on Earth, suffered a total loss of free will. Nothing like that, I hasten to say, has ever happened to me. The story is fiction. I just make these things up. But this is, I believe, how it would go if the aliens ever did appear among us and seize possession of our minds.

THERE ARE ONLY FRAGMENTS OF me left now. Chunks of memory have broken free and drifted away like calved glaciers. It is always like that when a Passenger leaves us. We can never be sure of all the things our borrowed bodies did. We have only the lingering traces, the imprints.

Like sand clinging to an ocean-tossed bottle. Like the throbbings of amputated legs.

I rise. I collect myself. My hair is rumpled; I comb it. My face is creased from too little sleep. There is sourness in my mouth. Has my Passenger been eating dung with my mouth? They do that. They do anything.

It is morning.

A gray, uncertain morning. I stare at it awhile, and then, shuddering, I opaque the window and confront instead the gray, uncertain surface of the inner panel. My room looks untidy. Did I have a woman here? There are ashes in the trays.

Searching for butts, I find several with lipstick stains. Yes, a woman was here.

I touched the bedsheets. Still warm with shared warmth. Both pillows tousled. She has gone, though, and the Passenger is gone, and I am alone.

How long did it last, this time?

I pick up the phone and ring Central. "What is the date?"

The computer's bland feminine voice replies, "Friday, December fourth, nineteen eighty-seven."

"The time?"

"Nine fifty-one, Eastern Standard Time."

"The weather forecast?"

"Predicted temperature range for today thirty to thirty-eight. Current temperature, thirty-one. Wind from the north, sixteen miles an hour. Chances of precipitation slight."

"What do you recommend for a hangover?"

"Food or medication?"

"Anything you like," I say.

The computer mulls that one over for a while. Then it decides on both, and activates my kitchen. The spigot yields cold tomato juice. Eggs begin to fry. From the medicine slot comes a purplish liquid. The Central Computer is always so thoughtful. Do the Passengers ever ride it, I wonder? What thrills could that hold for them? Surely it must be more exciting to borrow the million minds of Central than to live awhile in the short-circuited soul of a corroding human being!

December fourth, Central said. Friday. So the Passenger had me for three nights.

I drink the purplish stuff and probe my memories in a gingerly way, as one might probe a festering sore.

I remember Tuesday morning. A bad time at work. None of the charts will come out right. The section manager irritable; he has been taken by Passengers three times in five weeks, and his section is in disarray as a result, and his Christmas bonus is jeopardized.

Even though it is customary not to penalize a person for lapses due to Passengers, according to the system, the section manager seems to feel he will be treated unfairly. So he treats us unfairly. We have a hard time. Revise the charts, fiddle with the program, check the fundamentals ten times over. Out they come: the detailed forecasts for price variations of public utility securities, February–April 1988. That afternoon we are to meet and discuss the charts and what they tell us.

I do not remember Tuesday afternoon.

That must have been when the Passenger took me. Perhaps at work; perhaps in the mahogany-paneled boardroom itself, during the conference. Pink concerned faces all about me; I cough, I lurch, I stumble from my seat. They shake their heads sadly. No one reaches for me. No one stops me. It is too dangerous to interfere with one who has a Passenger. The chances are great that a second Passenger lurks nearby in the discorporate state, looking for a mount. So I am avoided. I leave the building.

After that, what?

Sitting in my room on bleak Friday morning, I eat my scrambled eggs and try to reconstruct the three lost nights.

Of course it is impossible. The conscious mind functions during the period of captivity, but upon withdrawal of the Passenger nearly every recollection goes too. There is only a slight residue, a gritty film of faint and ghostly memories. The mount is never precisely the same person afterwards; though he cannot recall the details of his experience, he is subtly changed by it.

I try to recall.

A girl? Yes: lipstick on the butts. Sex, then, here in my room. Young? Old? Blonde? Dark? Everything is hazy. How did my borrowed body behave? Was I a good lover? I try to be, when I am myself. I keep in shape. At thirty-eight, I can handle three sets of tennis on a summer afternoon without collapsing. I can make a woman glow as a woman is meant to glow. Not boasting; just categorizing. We have our skills. These are mine.

247

But Passengers, I am told, take wry amusement in controverting our skills. So would it have given my rider a kind of delight to find me a woman and force me to fail repeatedly with her?

I dislike that thought.

The fog is going from my mind now. The medicine prescribed by Central works rapidly. I eat, I shave, I stand under the vibrator until my skin is clean. I do my exercises. Did the Passenger exercise my body Wednesday and Thursday mornings? Probably not. I must make up for that. I am close to middle age, now; tonus lost is not easily regained.

I touch my toes twenty times, knees stiff.

I kick my legs in the air.

I lie flat and lift myself on pumping elbows.

The body responds, maltreated though it has been. It is the first bright moment of my awakening: to feel the inner tingling, to know that I still have vigor.

Fresh air is what I want next. Quickly I slip into my clothes and leave. There is no need for me to report to work today. They are aware that since Tuesday afternoon I have had a Passenger; they need not be aware that before dawn on Friday the Passenger departed. I will have a free day. I will walk the city's streets, stretching my limbs, repaying my body for the abuse it has suffered.

I enter the elevator. I drop fifty stories to the ground. I step out into the December dreariness.

The towers of New York rise about me.

In the street the cars stream forward. Drivers sit edgily at their wheels. One never knows when the driver of a nearby car will be borrowed, and there is always a moment of lapsed coordination as the Passenger takes over. Many lives are lost that way on our streets and highways; but never the life of a Passenger.

I begin to walk without purpose. I cross Fourteenth Street, heading north, listening to the soft violet purr of the electric engines. I see a boy jigging in the street and know he is being ridden. At Fifth and Twenty-second a prosperous-looking paunchy man approaches, his necktie askew, this morning's *Wall Street Journal* jutting from an overcoat pocket. He giggles. He thrusts out his tongue. Ridden. Ridden. I avoid him. Moving briskly, I come to the underpass that carries traffic below Thirty-fourth Street toward Queens, and pause for a moment to watch two adolescent girls quarreling at the rim of the pedestrian walk. One is a Negro. Her eyes are rolling in terror. The other pushes her closer to the railing. Ridden. But the Passenger does not have murder on its mind, merely pleasure. The Negro girl is released and falls in a huddled heap, trembling. Then she rises and runs. The other girl draws a long strand of gleaming hair into her mouth, chews on it, seems to awaken. She looks dazed.

I avert my eyes. One does not watch while a fellow sufferer is awakening. There is a morality of the ridden; we have so many new tribal mores in these dark days.

I hurry on.

Where am I going so hurriedly? Already I have walked more than a mile. I seem to be moving toward some goal, as though my Passenger still hunches in my skull, urging me about. But I know that is not so. For the moment, at least, I am free.

Can I be sure of that?

Cogito ergo sum no longer applies. We go on thinking even while we are ridden, and we live in quiet desperation, unable to half halt our courses no matter how ghastly, no matter how self-destructive. I am certain that I can distinguish between the condition of bearing a Passenger and the condition of being free. But perhaps not. Perhaps I bear a particularly devilish Passenger which has not quitted me at all, but which merely has receded to the cerebellum, leaving me the illusion of freedom while all the time surreptitiously driving me onward to some purpose of its own.

Did we ever have more than that: the illusion of freedom?

But this is disturbing, the thought that I may be ridden without realizing it. I burst out in heavy perspiration, not merely from the exertion of walking. Stop. Stop here. Why must you walk? You are at Forty-second Street. There is the library. Nothing forces you onward. Stop a while, I tell myself. Rest on the library steps.

I sit on the cold stone and tell myself that I have made this decision for myself.

Have I? It is the old problem, free will versus determinism, translated into the foulest of forms. Determinism is no longer a philosopher's abstraction; it is cold alien tendrils sliding between the cranial sutures. The Passengers arrived three years ago. I have been ridden five times since then. Our world is quite different now. But we have adjusted even to this. We have adjusted. We have our mores. Life goes on. Our governments rule, our legislatures meet, our stock exchanges transact business as usual, and we have methods for compensating for the random havoc. It is the only way. What else can we do? Shrivel in defeat? We have an enemy we cannot fight; at best we can resist through endurance. So we endure.

The stone steps are cold against my body. In December few people sit here.

I tell myself that I made this long walk of my own free will, that I halted of my own free will, that no Passenger rides my brain now. Perhaps. Perhaps. I cannot let myself believe that I am not free.

Can it be, I wonder, that the Passenger left some lingering command in me? Walk to this place, halt at this place? That is possible too.

I look about me at the others on the library steps.

An old man, eyes vacant, sitting on newspaper. A boy of thirteen or so with flaring nostrils. A plump woman. Are all of them ridden? Passengers seem to cluster about me today. The more I study the ridden ones, the more convinced I become that I am, for the moment, free. The last time, I had three months of freedom between rides. Some people, they say, are scarcely ever free. Their bodies are in great demand, and they know only scattered bursts of freedom, a day here, a week there, an hour. We have never been able to determine how many Passengers infest our world. Millions, maybe. Or maybe five. Who can tell?

A wisp of snow curls down out of the gray sky. Central had said the chance of precipitation was slight. Are they riding Central this morning too?

I see the girl.

She sits diagonally across from me, five steps up and a hundred feet away, her black skirt pulled up on her knees to reveal handsome legs. She is young. Her hair is deep, rich auburn. Her eyes are pale; at this distance, I cannot make out the precise color. She is dressed simply. She is younger than thirty. She wears a dark green coat and her lipstick has a purplish tinge. Her lips are full, her nose slender, high-bridged, her eyebrows carefully plucked.

I know her.

I have spent the past three nights with her in my room. She is the one. Ridden, she came to me, and ridden, I slept with her. I am certain of this. The veil of memory opens; I see her slim body naked on my bed.

How can it be that I remember this?

It is too strong to be an illusion. Clearly this is something that I have been *permitted* to remember for reasons I cannot comprehend. And I remember more. I remember her soft gasping sounds of pleasure. I know that my own body did not betray me those three nights, nor did I fail her need.

And there is more. A memory of sinuous music; a scent of youth in her hair; the rustle of winter trees. Somehow she brings back to me a time of innocence, a time when I am young and girls are mysterious, a time of parties and dances and warmth and secrets.

I am drawn to her now.

There is an etiquette about such things, too. It is in poor taste to approach someone you have met while being ridden. Such an encounter gives you no privilege; a stranger remains a stranger, no matter what you and she may have done and said during your involuntary time together.

Yet I am drawn to her.

Why this violation of taboo? Why this raw breach of etiquette? I have never done this before. I have been scrupulous.

But I get to my feet and walk along the step on which I have been sitting, until I am below her, and I look up, and automatically she folds her ankles together and angles her knees as if in awareness that her position is not a modest one. I know from that gesture that she is not ridden now. My eyes meet hers. Her eyes are hazy green. She is beautiful, and I rack my memory for more details of our passion.

I climb step by step until I stand before her.

"Hello," I say.

She gives me a neutral look. She does not seem to recognize me. Her eyes are veiled, as one's eyes often are, just after the Passenger has gone. She purses her lips and appraises me in a distant way.

"Hello," she replies coolly. "I don't think I know you."

"No. You don't. But I have the feeling you don't want to be alone just now. And I know I don't." I try to persuade her with my eyes that my motives are decent. "There's snow in the air," I say. "We can find a warmer place. I'd like to talk to you."

"About what?"

"Let's go elsewhere, and I'll tell you. I'm Charles Roth."

"Helen Martin."

She gets to her feet. She still has not cast aside her cool neutrality; she is suspicious, ill at ease. But at least she is willing to go with me. A good sign.

"Is it too early in the day for a drink?" I ask.

"I'm not sure. I hardly know what time it is."

"Before noon."

"Let's have a drink anyway," she says, and we both smile.

We go to a cocktail lounge across the street. Sitting face to face in the darkness, we sip drinks, daiquiri for her, Bloody Mary for me. She relaxes a little. I ask myself what it is I want from her. The pleasure of her company, yes. Her company in bed? But I have already had that pleasure, three nights of it, though she does not know that. I want something more. Something more. What?

Her eyes are bloodshot. She has had little sleep these past three nights.

I say, "Was it very unpleasant for you?"

"What?"

"The Passenger."

A whiplash of reaction crosses her face. "How did you know I've had a Passenger?"

"I know."

"We aren't supposed to talk about it."

"I'm broadminded," I tell her. "My Passenger left me some time during the night. I was ridden since Tuesday afternoon."

"Mine left me about two hours ago, I think." Her cheeks color. She is doing something daring, talking like this. "I was ridden since Monday night."

We toy with our drinks. Rapport is growing, almost without the need of words. Our recent experiences with Passengers give us something in common, although Helen does not realize how intimately we shared those experiences.

We talk. She is a designer of display windows. She has a small apartment several blocks from here. She lives alone. She asks me what I do. "Securities analyst," I tell her. She smiles. Her teeth are flawless. We have a second round of drinks. I am positive, now, that this is the girl who was in my room while I was ridden.

A seed of hope grows in me. It was a happy chance that brought us together again, so soon after we parted as dreamers. A happy chance, too, that some vestige of the dream lingered in my mind.

We have shared something, who knows what, and it must have been good to leave such a vivid imprint on me, and now I want to come to her conscious, aware, my own master, and renew that relationship, making it a real one this time. It is not proper, for I am trespassing on a privilege that is not mine except by virtue of our Passengers' brief presence in us. Yet I need her. I want her.

She seems to need me, too, without realizing who I am. But fear holds her back.

I am frightened of frightening her, and I do not try to press my advantage too quickly. Perhaps she would take me to her apartment with her now, perhaps not, but I do not ask. We finish our drinks. We arrange to meet by the library steps again tomorrow. My hand momentarily brushes hers. Then she is gone.

I fill three ashtrays that night. Over and over I debate the wisdom of what I am doing. But why not leave her alone? I have no right to follow her. In the place our world has become, we are wisest to remain apart.

And yet—there is that stab of half-memory when I think of her. The blurred lights of lost chances behind the stairs, of girlish laughter in second-floor corridors, of stolen kisses, of tea and cake. I remember the girl with the orchid in her hair, and the one in the spangled dress, and the one with the child's face and the woman's eyes, all so long ago, all lost, all gone, and I tell myself that this one I will not lose, I will not permit her to be taken from me.

Morning comes, a quiet Saturday. I return to the library, hardly expecting to find her there, but she is there, on the steps, and the sight of her is like a reprieve. She looks wary, troubled; obviously she has done much thinking, little sleeping. Together we walk along Fifth Avenue. She is quite close to me, but she does not take my arm. Her steps are brisk, short, nervous.

I want to suggest that we go to her apartment instead of to the cocktail lounge. In these days we must move swiftly while we are free. But I know it would be a mistake to think of this as a matter of tactics. Coarse haste would be fatal, bringing me perhaps an ordinary victory, a numbing defeat within it. In any event her mood hardly seems promising. I look at her, thinking of string music and new snowfalls, and she looks toward the gray sky.

She says, "I can feel them watching me all the time. Like vultures swooping overhead, waiting, waiting. Ready to pounce."

"But there's a way of beating them. We can grab little scraps of life when they're not looking."

"They're *always* looking."

"No," I tell her. "There can't be enough of them for that. Sometimes they're looking the other way. And while they are, two people can come together and try to share warmth."

"But what's the use?"

"You're too pessimistic, Helen. They ignore us for months at a time. We have a chance. We have a chance."

But I cannot break through her shell of fear. She is paralyzed by the nearness of the Passengers, unwilling to begin anything for fear it will be snatched away by our tormentors. We reach the building where she lives, and I hope she will relent and invite me in. For an instant she wavers, but only for an instant: she takes my hand in both of hers, and smiles, and the smile fades, and she is gone, leaving me only with the words, "Let's meet at the library again tomorrow. Noon."

I make the long chilling walk home alone.

Some of her pessimism seeps into me that night. It seems futile for us to try to salvage anything. More than that: wicked for me to seek her out, shameful to offer a hesitant love when I am not free. In this world, I tell myself, we should keep well clear of others, so that we do not harm anyone when we are seized and ridden.

I do not go to meet her in the morning.

It is best this way, I insist. I have no business trifling with her. I imagine her at the library, wondering why I am late, growing tense, impatient, then annoyed. She will be angry with me for breaking our date, but her anger will ebb, and she will forget me quickly enough.

Monday comes. I return to work.

Naturally, no one discusses my absence. It is as though I have never been away. The market is strong that morning. The work is challenging; it is mid-morning before I think of Helen at all. But once I think of her, I can think of nothing else. My cowardice in standing her up. The childishness of Saturday night's dark thoughts. Why accept fate so passively? Why give in? I want to fight, now, to carve out a pocket of security despite the odds. I feel a deep conviction that it can be done. The Passengers may never bother the two of us again, after all. And that flickering smile of hers outside her building Saturday, that momentary glow—it should have told me that behind her wall of fear she felt the same hopes. She was waiting for me to lead the way. And I stayed home instead.

At lunchtime I go to the library, convinced it is futile.

But she is there. She paces along the steps; the wind slices at her slender figure. I go to her.

She is silent a moment. "Hello," she says finally.

"I'm sorry about yesterday."

"I waited a long time for you."

I shrug. "I made up my mind that it was no use to come. But then I changed my mind again."

She tries to look angry. But I know she is pleased to see me again—else why did she come here today? She cannot hide her inner pleasure. Nor can I. I point across the street to the cocktail lounge.

"A daiquiri?" I say. "As a peace offering?"

"All right."

Today the lounge is crowded, but we find a booth somehow. There is a brightness in her eyes that I have not seen before. I sense that a barrier is crumbling within her.

"You're less afraid of me, Helen," I say.

"I've never been afraid of you. I'm afraid of what could happen if we take the risks."

"Don't be. Don't be."

"I'm trying not to be afraid. But sometimes it seems so hopeless. Since *they* came here—"

"We can still try to live our own lives."

"Maybe."

"We have to. Let's make a pact, Helen. No more gloom. No more worrying about the terrible things that might just happen. All right?"

A pause. Then a cool hand against mine.

"All right."

We finish our drinks, and I present my Credit Central to pay for them, and we go outside. I want her to tell me to forget about this afternoon's work and come home with her. It is inevitable, now, that she will ask me, and better sooner than later.

We walk a block. She does not offer the invitation. I sense the struggle inside her, and I wait, letting that struggle reach its own resolution without interference from me. We walk a second block. Her arm is through mine, but she talks only of her work, of the weather, and it is a remote, arm's-length conversation. At the next corner she swings around, away from her apartment, back toward the cocktail lounge. I try to be patient with her.

I have no need to rush things now, I tell myself. Her body is not a secret to me. We have begun our relationship topsy-turvy, with the physical part first; now it will take time to work backward to the more difficult part that some people call love.

But of course she is not aware that we have known each other that way. The wind blows swirling snowflakes in our faces, and somehow the cold sting awakens honesty in me. I know what I must say. I must relinquish my unfair advantage.

I tell her, "While I was ridden last week, Helen, I had a girl in my room."

"Why talk of such things now?"

"I have to, Helen. You were the girl."

She halts. She turns to me. People hurry past us in the street. Her face is very pale, with dark red spots growing in her cheeks.

"That's not funny, Charles."

"It wasn't meant to be. You were with me from Tuesday night to early Friday morning."

"How can you possibly know that?"

257

"I do. I do. The memory is clear. Somehow it remains, Helen. I see your whole body."

"Stop it, Charles."

"We were very good together," I say. "We must have pleased our Passengers because we were so good. To see you again—it was like waking from a dream, and finding that the dream was real, the girl right there—"

"No!"

"Let's go to your apartment and begin again."

She says, "You're being deliberately filthy, and I don't know why, but there wasn't any reason for you to spoil things. Maybe I was with you and maybe I wasn't, but you wouldn't know it, and if you did know it you should keep your mouth shut about it, and—"

"You have a birthmark the size of a dime," I say, "about two inches below your left breast."

She sobs and hurls herself at me, there in the street. Her long silvery nails rake my cheeks. She pummels me. I seize her. Her knees assail me. No one pays attention; those who pass by assume we are ridden, and turn their heads. She is all fury, but I have my arms around hers like metal bands, so that she can only stamp and snort, and her body is close against mine. She is rigid, anguished.

In a low, urgent voice I say, "We'll defeat them, Helen. We'll finish what they started. Don't fight me. There's no reason to fight me. I know, it's a fluke that I remember you, but let me go with you and I'll prove that we belong together."

"Let—go—"

"Please. Please. Why should we be enemies? I don't mean you any harm. I love you, Helen. Do you remember, when we were kids, we could play at being in love? I did; you must have done it too. Sixteen, seventeen years old. The whispers, the conspiracies—all a big game, and we knew it. But the game's over. We can't afford to tease and run. We have so little time, when we're free—we have to trust, to open ourselves—"

"It's wrong."

"No. Just because it's the stupid custom for two people brought together by Passengers to avoid one another, that doesn't mean we have to follow it. Helen—Helen—"

Something in my tone registers with her. She ceases to struggle. Her rigid body softens. She looks up at me, her tearstreaked face thawing, her eyes blurred.

"Trust me," I say. "Trust me, Helen!"

She hesitates. Then she smiles.

IN THAT MOMENT I FEEL the chill at the back of my skull, the sensation as of a steel needle driven deep through bone. I stiffen. My arms drop away from her. For an instant, I lose touch, and when the mists clear all is different.

"Charles?" she says. *"Charles?"*

Her knuckles are against her teeth. I turn, ignoring her, and go back into the cocktail lounge. A young man sits in one of the front booths. His dark hair gleams with pomade; his cheeks are smooth. His eyes meet mine.

I sit down. He orders drinks. We do not talk.

My hand falls on his wrist, and remains there. The bartender, serving the drinks, scowls but says nothing. We sip our cocktails and put the drained glasses down.

"Let's go," the young man says.

I follow him out.

◆

NOW PLUS N, NOW MINUS N

The first-person narrative mode is full of amusing little challenges for the science-fiction writer. W. Somerset Maugham never wrote any science fiction, and so he never found himself telling a story in the first-person *plural*. But I did. Consider the opening lines of "Now Plus N, Now Minus N," which I wrote in June 1969:

> "All had been so simple, so elegant, so profitable for ourselves. And then we met the lovely Selene and nearly were undone.... I was in satisfactory contact with myself and also with myself...."

Ourselves . . . we . . . I was in satisfactory contact with myself. . . .

W. Somerset Maugham never wrote stuff like that. Neither did William Faulkner or James Joyce, so far as I know. But I did, because I was telling a story about somebody who was doing stock-market shenanigans by getting information from his future self and relaying it to his past self. First-person plural, all right. It's more of a science-fiction sort of thing.

I wrote it for an old friend of mine, Harry Harrison, who was editing a series of annual science-fiction anthologies called *Nova*. Back then I was very concerned with exploring the twists and turns and paradoxes of time travel, most notably in a novel called *Up the Line*, but in an assortment of short stories and novellas, too. I don't believe that time travel is actually possible, you understand, but, like the White Queen whom Alice encountered beyond the Looking Glass, I'm capable of believing at least six impossible things before breakfast, at least when I'm trying to work out a story idea. And so, "Now Plus N, Now Minus N," which appeared in 1972 in *Nova Two*.

—⁓—

ALL HAD BEEN SO SIMPLE, so elegant, so profitable for ourselves. And then we met the lovely Selene and nearly were undone. She came into our lives during our regular transmission hour on Wednesday, October 7, 1987, between six and seven p.m. Central European Time. The moneymaking hour. I was in satisfactory contact with myself and also with myself. (Now − n) was due on the line first, and then I would hear from (now + n).

I was primed for some kind of trouble. I knew trouble was coming, because on Monday, while I was receiving messages from the me of Wednesday, there came an inexplicable and unexplained break in communications. As a result I did not get data from (now + n) concerning the prices of the stocks in our carryover portfolio from last week, and I was unable to take action. Two days have passed, and I am the me of Wednesday who failed to send the news to me of Monday, and I have no idea what will happen to interrupt contact. Least of all did I anticipate Selene.

In such dealings as ours no distractions are needed, sexual or otherwise. We must concentrate wholly. At any time there is steady low-level contact among ourselves; we feel one another's reassuring presence. But transmission of data from self to self requires close attention.

I tell you my method. Then maybe you understand my trouble.

My business is investments. I do all my work at this same hour. At this hour it is midday in New York; the Big Board is still open.

I can put through quick calls to my brokers when my time comes to buy or sell.

My office at the moment is the cocktail lounge known as the Celestial Room in the Henry VIII Hotel, south of the Thames. My office may be anywhere. All I need is a telephone. The Celestial Room is aptly named. The room orbits endlessly on a silent oiled track. Twittering sculptures in the so-called galactic mode drift through the air, scattering cascades of polychromed light upon those who sip drinks. Beyond the great picture windows of this supreme room lies the foggy darkness of the London evening, which I ignore. It is all the same to me, wherever I am: London, Nairobi, Karachi, Istanbul, Pittsburgh. I look only for an adequately comfortable environment, air that is safe to admit to one's lungs, service in the style I demand, and a telephone line. The individual characteristics of an individual place do not move me. I am like the ten planets of our solar family: a perpetual traveler, but not a sightseer.

Myself who is (now − n) is ready to receive transmission from myself who is (now). "Go ahead, (now + n)," he tells me. (To him I am (now + n). To myself I am (now). Everything is relative; n is exactly forty-eight hours these days.)

"Here we go, (now − n)," I say to him.

I SUMMON MY STRENGTH BY sipping at my drink. Chateau d'Yquem '79 in a sleek Czech goblet. Sickly sweet stuff; the waiter was aghast when I ordered it *before dinner.* Horreurs! Quel aperitif! But the wine makes transmission easier. It greases the conduit, somehow. I am ready.

My table is a single elegant block of glittering irradiated crystal, iridescent, cunningly emitting shifting moire patterns. On the table, unfolded, lies today's European edition of the *Herald Tribune.* I lean forward. I take from my breast pocket a sheet of paper, the printout listing the securities I bought on Monday afternoon. Now I allow my eyes to roam the close-packed type of the market quotations in my newspaper. I linger for a long moment on the heading, so there will be no mistake: *Closing New York Prices, Tuesday, October 6.* To me they are yesterday's prices. To (now − *n*) they are tomorrow's prices. (Now − *n*) acknowledges that he is receiving a sharp image.

I am about to transmit these prices to the me of Monday. You follow the machination, now?

I scan and I select.

I search only for the stocks that move five percent or more in a single day. Whether they move up or move down is immaterial; motion is the only criterion, and we go short or long as the case demands. We need fast action because our maximum survey span is only ninety-six hours at present, counting the relay from (now + *n*) back to (now − *n*) by way of (now). We cannot afford to wait for leisurely capital gains to mature; we must cut our risks by going for the quick, violent swings, seizing our profits as they emerge. The swings have to be violent. Otherwise brokerage costs will eat up our gross.

I have no difficulty choosing the stocks whose prices I will transmit to Monday's me. They are the stocks on the broker's printout, the ones we have already bought; obviously (now − *n*) would not have bought them unless Wednesday's me had told him about them, and now that I am Wednesday's me, I must follow through. So I send:

> *Arizona Agrochemical,* 79?, + 6?
> *Canadian Transmutation,* 116, + 4?
> *Commonwealth Dispersals,* 12, − 1?
> *Eastern Electric Energy,* 41, + 2
> *Great Lakes Bionics,* 66, + 3 ?

And so on through *Western Offshore Corp.,* 99, − 8. Now I have transmitted to (now − *n*) a list of Tuesday's top twenty high-percentage swingers. From his vantage-point in Monday, (now − *n*) will begin to place orders, taking positions in all twenty stocks on

Monday afternoon. I know that he has been successful, because the printout from my broker gives confirmations of all twenty purchases at what now are highly favorable prices.

(Now − n) then signs off for a while and (now + n) comes on. He is transmitting from Friday, October 9. He gives me Thursday's closing prices on the same twenty stocks, from Arizona Agrochemical to Western Offshore. He already knows which of the twenty I will have chosen to sell today, but he pays me the compliment of not telling me; he merely gives me the prices. He signs off, and, in my role as (now), I make my decisions. I sell Canadian Transmutation, Great Lakes Bionics, and five others; I cover our short sale on Commonwealth Dispersals. The rest of the positions I leave undisturbed for the time being, since they will sell at better prices tomorrow, according to the word from (now + n). I can handle those when I am Friday's me.

Today's sequence is over.

In any given sequence—and we have been running about three a week—we commit no more than five or six million dollars. We wish to stay inconspicuous. Our pre-tax profit runs at about nine percent a week. Despite our network of tax havens in Ghana, Fiji, Grand Cayman, Liechtenstein, and Bolivia, through which our profits are funneled, we can bring down to net only about five percent a week on our entire capital. This keeps all three of us in a decent style and compounds prettily. Starting with $5,000 six years ago at the age of twenty-five, I have become one of the world's wealthiest men, with no other advantages than intelligence, persistence, and extrasensory access to tomorrow's stock prices.

It is time to deal with the next sequence. I must transmit to (now − n) the Tuesday prices of the stocks in the portfolio carried over from last week, so that he can make his decisions on what to sell. I know what he has sold, but it would spoil his sport to tip my hand. We treat ourselves fairly. After I have finished sending (now − n) those prices, (now + n) will come online again and will transmit to me an entirely new list of stocks in which I must take

positions before Thursday morning's New York opening. He will
be able to realize profits in those on Friday. Thus we go from day
to day, playing our shifting roles.

But this was the day on which Selene intersected our lives.

I HAD EMPTIED MY GLASS. I looked up to signal the waiter, and at
that moment a slender, dark-haired girl, alone, entered the
Celestial Room. She was tall, graceful, glorious. She was expen-
sively clad in a clinging monomolecular wrap that shuttled
through a complex program of wavelength shifts, including a
microsecond sweep of total transparency that dazzled the eye
while still maintaining a degree of modesty. Her features were a
match for her garment: wide-set glossy eyes, delicate nose, firm
lips lightly outlined in green. Her skin was extraordinarily pale. I
could see no jewelry on her (why gild refined gold, why paint the
lily?) but on her lovely left cheekbone I observed a small decorative band of ultraviolet paint, obviously chosen for visibility in the
high-spectrum lighting of this unique room.

She conquered me. There was a mingling of traits in her that I
found instantly irresistible: she seemed both shy and steel-strong,
passionate and vulnerable, confident and ill at ease. She scanned
the room, evidently looking for someone, not finding him. Her
eyes met mine and lingered.

Somewhere in my cerebrum (now – n) said shrilly, as I had said
on Monday, "I don't read you, (now + n). I don't read you!"

I paid no heed. I rose. I smiled to the girl, and beckoned her
toward the empty chair at my table. I swept my *Herald Tribune* to
the floor. At certain times there are more important things than
compounding one's capital at five percent per week. She glowed
gratefully at me, nodding, accepting my invitation.

When she was about twenty feet from me, I lost all contact with
(now – n) and (now + n).

I don't mean simply that there was an interruption in the
transmission of words and data among us. I mean that I lost all

sense of the presence of my earlier and later selves. That warm, wordless companionship, that ourselvesness, that harmony that I had known constantly since we had established our linkage five years ago, vanished as if switched off. On Monday, when contact with (now + n) broke, I still had had (now − n). Now I had no one.

I was terrifyingly alone, even as ordinary men are alone, but more alone than that, for I had known a fellowship beyond the reach of other mortals. The shock of separation was intense.

Then Selene was sitting beside me, and the nearness of her made me forget my new solitude entirely.

She said, "I don't know where he is and I don't care. He's been late once too often. Finito for him. Hello, you. I'm Selene Hughes."

"Aram Kevorkian. What do you drink?"

"Chartreuse on the rocks. Green. I knew you were Armenian from halfway across the room."

I am Bulgarian, thirteen generations. It suits me to wear an Armenian name. I did not correct her. The waiter hurried over; I ordered chartreuse for her, a sake martini for self. I trembled like an adolescent. Her beauty was disturbing, overwhelming, astonishing. As we raised glasses I reached out experimentally for (now − n) or (now + n). Silence. Silence. But there was Selene.

I said, "You're not from London."

"I travel a lot. I stay here a while, there a while. Originally Dallas. You must be able to hear the Texas in my voice. Most recent port of call, Lima. For the July skiing. Now London."

"And the next stop?"

"Who knows? What do you do, Aram?"

"I invest."

"For a living?"

"So to speak. I struggle along. Free for dinner?"

"Of course. Shall we eat in the hotel?"

"There's the beastly fog outside," I said.

"Exactly."

Simpatico. Perfectly. I guessed her for twenty-four, twenty-five at most. Perhaps a brief marriage three or four years in the past. A private income, not colossal but nice. An experienced woman of the world, and yet also somehow still retaining a core of innocence, a magical softness of the soul. I loved her instantly. She did not care for a second cocktail. "I'll make dinner reservations," I said, as she went off to the powder room. I watched her walk away. A supple walk, flawless posture, supreme shoulderblades. When she was about twenty feet from me I felt my other selves suddenly return. "What's happening?" (now – *n*) demanded furiously. "Where did you go? Why aren't you sending?"

"I don't know yet."

"Where the hell are the Tuesday prices on last week's carryover stocks?"

"Later," I told him.

"Now. Before you blank out again."

"The prices can wait," I said, and shut him off. To (now + *n*) I said, "All right. What do you know that I ought to know?"

Myself of forty-eight hours hence said, "We have fallen in love."

"I'm aware of that. But what blanked us out?"

"She's psi-suppressant. She absorbs all the transmission energy we put out."

"Impossible! I've never heard of any such thing."

"No?" said (now + *n*). "Brother, this past hour has been the first chance I've had to get through to you since Wednesday, when we got into this mess. It's no coincidence that I've been with her just about one hundred percent of the time since Wednesday evening, except for a few two-minute breaks, and then I couldn't reach you because you must have been with her in your time sequence. And so—"

"How can this be?" I cried. "What'll happen to us if—? No. No, you bastard, you're rolling me over. I don't believe you. There's no way that she could be causing it."

"I think I know how she does it," said (now + n). "There's a—"

At that moment Selene returned, looking even more radiantly beautiful, and silence descended once more.

WE DINED WELL. CHILLED MOMBASA oysters, salade niçoise, filet of Kobe beef rare, washed down by Richebourg '77. Occasionally I tried to reach myselves. Nothing. I worried a little about how I was going to get the Tuesday prices to (now − n) on the carryover stuff, and decided to forget about it. Obviously I hadn't managed to get them to him, since I hadn't received any printout on sales out of that portfolio this evening, and if I hadn't reached him, there was no sense in fretting about reaching him. The wonderful thing about this telepathy across time is the sense of stability it gives you: whatever has been, must be, and so forth.

After dinner we went down one level to the casino for our brandies and a bit of gamblerage. "Two thousand pounds' worth," I said to the robot cashier, and put my thumb to his charge plate, and the chips came skittering out of the slot in his chest. I gave half the stake to Selene. She played high-grav-low-grav, and I played roulette; we shifted from one table to the other according to whim and the run of our luck. In two hours she tripled her stake and I lost all of mine. I never was good at games of chance. I even used to get hurt in the market before the market ceased being a game of chance for me. Naturally, I let her thumb her winnings into her own account, and when she offered to return the original stake I just laughed.

Where next? Too early for bed.

"The swimming pool?" she suggested.

"Fine idea," I said. But the hotel had two, as usual. "Nude pool or suit pool?"

"Who owns a suit?" she asked, and we laughed and took the dropshaft to the pool.

There were separate dressing rooms, M and W. No one frets about showing flesh, but shedding clothes still has lingering taboos. I peeled fast and waited for her by the pool. During this interval I felt the familiar presence of another self impinge on me: (now − n). He wasn't transmitting, but I knew he was there. I couldn't feel (now + n) at all. Grudgingly I began to admit that Selene must be responsible for my communications problem. Whenever she went more than twenty feet away, I could get through to myselves. How did she do it, though? And could it be stopped? Mao help me, would I have to choose between my livelihood and my new beloved?

The pool was a vast octagon with a trampoline diving web and a set of underwater psych-lights making rippling patterns of color. Maybe fifty people were swimming and a few dozen more were lounging beside the pool, improving their tans. No one person can possibly stand out in such a mass of flesh, and yet when Selene emerged from the women's dressing room and began the long saunter across the tiles toward me, the heads began to turn by the dozens. Her figure was not notably lush, yet she had the automatic magnetism that only true beauty exercises. She was definitely slender, but everything was in perfect proportion, as though she had been shaped by the hand of Phidias himself. Long legs, long arms, narrow wrists, narrow waist, small high breasts, miraculously outcurving hips. The *Primavera* of Botticelli. The *Leda* of Leonardo. She carried herself with ultimate grace. My heart thundered.

Between her breasts she wore some sort of amulet: a disk of red metal in which geometrical symbols were engraved. I hadn't noticed it when she was clothed.

"My good-luck piece," she explained. "I'm never without it." And she sprinted laughing to the trampoline, and bounded, and hovered, and soared, and cut magnificently through the surface of the water. I followed her in. We raced from angle to angle of the pool, testing each other, searching for limits and not finding them. We dived and met far below, and locked hands, and bobbed happily upward. Then we lay under the warm quartz lamps. Then we tried the sauna. Then we dressed.

We went to her room.

She kept the amulet on even when we made love. I felt it cold against my chest as I embraced her.

BUT WHAT OF THE MAKING of money? What of the compounding of capital? What of my sweaty little secret, the joker in the Wall Street pack, the messages from beyond by which I milked the market of millions? On Thursday no contact with my other selves was scheduled, but I could not have made it even if it had been. It was amply clear: Selene blanked my psi field. The critical range was twenty feet. When we were farther apart than that, I could get through; otherwise, not. How did it happen? How? How? How? An accidental incompatibility of psionic vibrations? A tragic canceling out of my powers through proximity to her splendid self? No. No. No. No.

On Thursday we roared through London like a conflagration, doing the galleries, the boutiques, the museums, the sniffer palaces, the pubs, the sparkle houses. I had never been so much in love. For hours at a time I forgot my dilemma. The absence of myself from myself, the separation that had seemed so shattering in its first instant, seemed trivial. What did I need *them* for, when I had *her*?

I needed them for the moneymaking. The moneymaking was a disease that love might alleviate but could not cure. And if I did not resume contact soon, there would be calamities in store.

Late Thursday afternoon, as we came reeling giddily out of a sniffer palace on High Holborn, our nostrils quivering, I felt contact again. (Now + n) broke through briefly, during a moment when I waited for a traffic light and Selene plunged wildly across to the far side of the street.

"The amulet's what does it," he said. "That's the word I get from—"

Selene rushed back to my side of the street. "Come *on*, silly! Why'd you wait?"

Two hours later, as she lay in my arms, I swept my hand up from her satiny haunch to her silken breast and caught the plaque of red metal between two fingers. "Love, won't you take this off?" I said innocently. "I hate the feel of a piece of cold slithery metal coming between us when—"

There was terror in her dark eyes. "I couldn't, Aram! I *couldn't!*"

"For me, love?"

"Please. Let me have my little superstition." Her lips found mine. Cleverly she changed the subject. I wondered at her tremor of shock, her frightened refusal.

Later we strolled along the Thames, and watched Friday coming to life in fogbound dawn. Today I would have to escape from her for at least an hour, I knew. The laws of time dictated it. For on Wednesday, between six and seven p.m. Central European Time, I had accepted a transmission from myself of (now + n), speaking out of Friday, and Friday had come and I was that very same (now + n), who must reach out at the proper time toward his counterpart at (now − n) on Wednesday. What would happen if I failed to make my rendezvous with time in time, I did not know. Nor wanted to discover. The universe, I suspected, would continue regardless. But my own sanity—my grasp on that universe—might not.

It was narrowness. All glorious Friday I had to plot how to separate myself from radiant Selene during the cocktail hour, when she would certainly want to be with me. But in the end it was simplicity. I told the concierge, "At seven minutes after six send a message to me in the Celestial Room. I am wanted on urgent business must come instantly to computer room for intercontinental data patch, person to person. So?"

Concierge replied, "We can give you the patch right at your table in the Celestial Room."

I shook my head firmly. "Do it as I say. Please."

I put my thumb to the gratuity account of concierge and signaled an account transfer of five pounds. Concierge smiled.

Seven minutes after six, message-robot scuttles into Celestial Room, comes homing in on table where I sit with Selene. "Intercontinental data patch, Mr. Kevorkian," says robot. "Wanted immediately. Computer room."

I turn to Selene. "Forgive me, love. Desolated, but must go. Urgent business. Just a few minutes."

She grasps my arm fondly. "Darling, no! Let the call wait. It's our anniversary now. Forty-eight hours since we met!"

Gently I pull arm free. I extend arm, show jewelled timepiece. "Not yet, not yet! We didn't meet until half past six Wednesday. I'll be back in time to celebrate." I kiss tip of supreme nose. "Don't smile at strangers while I'm gone," I say, and rush off with robot.

I do not go to computer room. I hurriedly buy a Friday *Herald Tribune* in the lobby and lock myself in men's washroom cubicle. Contact now is made on schedule with (now − *n*), living in Wednesday, all innocent of what will befall him that miraculous evening. I read stock prices, twenty securities, from Arizona Agrochemical to Western Offshore Corp. I sign off and study my watch. (Now − *n*) is currently closing out seven long positions and the short sale on Commonwealth Dispersals. During the interval I seek to make contact with (now + *n*) ahead of me on Sunday evening. No response. Nothing.

Presently I lose contact also with (now − *n*). As expected; for this is the moment when the me of Wednesday has for the first time come within Selene's psi-suppressant field. I wait patiently. In a while (Selene − *n*) goes to powder room. Contact returns.

(Now − *n*) says to me, "All right. What do you know that I ought to know?"

"We have fallen in love," I say.

Rest of conversation follows as per. What has been, must be. I debate slipping in the tidbit I have received from (now + *n*) concerning the alleged powers of Selene's amulet. Should I say it quickly, before contact breaks? Impossible. It was not said to me.

The conversation proceeds until at the proper moment I am able to say, "I think I know how she does it. There's a—"

Wall of silence descends. (Selene − n) has returned to the table of (now − n). Therefore I (now) will return to the table of Selene (now). I rush back to the Celestial Room. Selene, looking glum, sits alone, sipping drink. She brightens as I approach.

"See?" I cry. "Back just in time. Happy anniversary, darling. Happy, happy, happy, happy!"

When we woke Saturday morning we decided to share the same room thereafter. Selene showered while I went downstairs to arrange the transfer. I could have arranged everything by telephone without getting out of bed, but I chose to go in person to the desk, leaving Selene behind. You understand why.

In the lobby I received a transmission from (now + n), speaking out of Monday, October 12. "It's definitely the amulet," he said. "I can't tell you how it works, but it's some kind of mechanical psi-suppressant device. God knows why she wears it, but if I could only manage to have her lose it we'd be all right. It's the amulet. Pass it on."

I was reminded, by this, of the flash of contact I had received on Thursday outside the sniffer palace in High Holborn. I realized that I had another message to send, a rendezvous to keep with him who has become (now − n).

Late Saturday afternoon, I made contact with (now − n) once more, only momentarily. Again I resorted to a ruse in order to fulfill the necessary unfolding of destiny. Selene and I stood in the hallway, waiting for a dropshaft. There were other people. The dropshaft gate raised open and Selene went in, followed by others. With an excess of chivalry I let all the others enter before me, and "accidentally" missed the closing of the gate. The dropshaft descended with Selene. I remained alone in the hall. My timing was good; after a moment I felt the inner warmth that told me of proximity to the mind of (now − n).

"The amulet's what does it," I said. "That's the word I get from—" Aloneness intervened.

DURING THE WEEK BEGINNING MONDAY, October 12, I received no advance information on the fluctuations of the stock market at all. Not in five years had I been so deprived of data. My linkings with (now − n) and (now + n) were fleeting and unsatisfactory. We exchanged a sentence here, a blurt of hasty words there, no more. Of course, there were moments every day when I was apart from the fair Selene long enough to get a message out. Though we were utterly consumed by our passion for one another, nevertheless I did get opportunities to elude the twenty-foot radius of her psi-suppressant field. The trouble was that my opportunities to send did not always coincide with the opportunities of (now − n) or (now + n) to receive. We remained linked in a 48-hour spacing, and to alter that spacing would require extensive discipline and infinitely careful coordination, which none of ourselves were able to provide in such a time. So any contact with myselves had to depend on a coincidence of apartnesses from Selene.

I regretted this keenly. Yet there was Selene to comfort me. We reveled all day and reveled all night. When fatigue overcame us we grabbed a two-hour deepsleep wire and caught up with ourselves, and then we started over. I plumbed the limits of ecstasy. I believe it was like that for her.

Though lacking my unique advantage, I also played the market that week. Partly it was compulsion: my plungings had become obsessive. Partly, too, it was at Selene's urgings. "Don't you neglect your work for me," she purred. "I don't want to stand in the way of making *money*."

Money, I was discovering, fascinated her nearly as intensely as it did me. Another evidence of compatibility. She knew a good deal about the market herself and looked on, an excited spectator, as I each day shuffled my portfolio.

The market was closed Monday: Columbus Day. Tuesday, queasily operating in the dark, I sold Arizona Agrochemical, Consolidated Luna, Eastern Electric Energy, and Western Offshore, reinvesting the proceeds in large blocks of Meccano Leasing and Holoscan Dynamics. Wednesday's *Tribune,* to my chagrin, brought me the news that Consolidated Luna had received the Copernicus franchise and had risen 9 points in the final hour of Tuesday's trading. Meccano Leasing, though, had been rebuffed in the Robomation takeover bid and was off 4 since I had bought it. I got through to my broker in a hurry and sold Meccano, which was down even further that morning. My loss was $125,000—plus $250,000 more that I had dropped by selling Consolidated Luna too soon. After the market closed on Wednesday, the directors of Meccano Leasing unexpectedly declared a five-for-two split and a special dividend in the form of a one-for-ten distribution of cumulative participating high-depreciation warrants. Meccano regained its entire Tuesday–Wednesday loss and tacked on 5 points beyond.

I concealed the details of this from Selene. She saw only the glamor of my speculations: the telephone calls, the quick computations, the movements of hundreds of thousands of dollars. I hid the hideous botch from her, knowing it might damage my prestige.

On Thursday, feeling battered and looking for the safety of a utility, I picked up 10,000 Southwest Power and Fusion at 38, only hours before the explosion of SPF's magnetohydrodynamic generating station in Las Cruces which destroyed half a county and neatly peeled $90,000 off the value of my investment when the stock finally traded after a delayed opening, on Friday. I sold. Later came news that SPF's insurance would cover everything. SPF recovered, whereas Holoscan Dynamics plummeted 11, costing me $140,000 more. I had not known that Holoscan's insurance subsidiary was the chief underwriter for SPF's disaster coverage.

All told, that week I shed more than $500,000. My brokers were stunned. I had a reputation for infallibility among them. Most of them had become wealthy simply by duplicating my own transactions for their own accounts.

"Sweetheart, what *happened?*" they asked me.

My losses the following week came to $1,250,000. Still no news from (now + n). My brokers felt I needed a vacation. Even Selene knew I was losing heavily, by now. Curiously, my run of bad luck seemed to intensify her passion for me. Perhaps it made me look tragic and Byronic to be getting hit so hard.

We spent wild days and wilder nights. I lived in a throbbing haze of sensuality. Wherever we went we were the center of all attention. We had that burnished sheen that only great lovers have. We radiated a glow of delight all up and down the spectrum.

I was losing millions.

The more I lost, the more reckless my plunges became, and the deeper my losses became.

I was in real danger of being wiped out, if this went on.

I had to get away from her.

MONDAY, OCTOBER 26. Selene has taken the deepsleep wire and in the next two hours will flush away the fatigue of three riotous days and nights without rest. I have only pretended to take the wire. When she goes under, I rise. I dress. I pack. I scrawl a note for her. *"Business trip. Back soon. Love, love, love, love."* I catch noon rocket for Istanbul.

Minarets, mosques, Byzantine temples. Shunning the sleep wire, I spend next day and a half in bed in ordinary repose. I wake and it is forty-eight hours since parting from Selene. Desolation! Bitter solitude! But I feel (now + n) invading my mind.

"Take this down," he says brusquely. "Buy 5,000 FSP, 800 CCG, 150 LC, 200 T, 1,000 TXN, 100 BVI. Go short 200 BA, 500 UCM, 200 LOC. Clear? Read back to me."

I read back. Then I phone in my orders. I hardly care what the ticker symbols stand for. If (now + n) says to do, I do.

An hour and a half later the switchboard tells me, "A Miss Hughes to see you, sir."

She has traced me! Calamitas calamitatum! "Tell her I'm not here," I say. I flee to the roofport. By copter I get away. Commercial jet shortly brings me to Tel Aviv. I take a room at the Hilton and give absolute instructions am not to be disturbed. Meals only to room, also *Herald Trib* every day, otherwise no interruptions.

I study the market action. On Friday I am able to reach (now − *n*). "Take this down," I say brusquely. "Buy 5,000 FSP, 800 CCG, 140 LC, 200 T—"

Then I call brokers. I close out Wednesday's longs and cover Wednesday's shorts. My profit is over a million. I am recouping. But I miss her terribly.

I spend agonizing weekend of loneliness in hotel room.

Monday. Comes voice of (now + *n*) out of Wednesday, with new instructions. I obey. At lunchtime, under lid of my barley soup, floats note from her. "Darling, why are you running away from me? I love you to the ninth power. S."

I get out of hotel disguised as bellhop and take El Al jet to Cairo. Tense, jittery, I join tourist group sightseeing pyramids, much out of character. Tour is conducted in Hebrew; serves me right. I lock self in hotel. *Herald Tribune* available. On Wednesday I send instructions to me of Monday, (now − *n*). I await instructions from me of Friday, (now + *n*). Instead I get muddled transmissions, noise, confusions. What is wrong? Where to flee now? Brasilia, McMurdo Sound, Anchorage, Irkutsk, Maograd? She will find me. She has her resources. There are few secrets to one who has the will to surmount them. How does she find me?

She finds me.

Note comes: "I am at Abu Simbel to wait for you. Meet me there on Friday afternoon or I throw myself from Rameses' leftmost head at sundown. Love. Desperate. S."

I am defeated. She will bankrupt me, but I must have her.

On Friday I go to Abu Simbel.

SHE STOOD ATOP THE MONUMENT, luscious in windswept white cotton.

"I knew you'd come," she said.

"What else could I do?"

We kissed. Her suppleness inflamed me. The sun blazed toward a descent into the western desert.

"Why have you been running away from me?" she asked. "What did I do wrong? Why did you stop loving me?"

"I never stopped loving you," I said.

"Then—*why?*"

"I will tell you," I said, "a secret I have shared with no human being other than myselves."

Words tumbled out. I told all. The discovery of my gift, the early chaos of sensory bombardment from other times, the bafflement of living one hour ahead of time and one hour behind time as well as in the present. The months of discipline needed to develop my gift. The fierce struggle to extend the range of extrasensory perception to five hours, ten, twenty-four, forty-eight. The joy of playing the market and never losing. The intricate systems of speculation; the self-imposed limits to keep me from ending up with all the assets in the world; the pleasures of immense wealth. The loneliness, too. And the supremacy of the night when I met her.

Then I said, "When I'm with you it doesn't work. I can't communicate with myselves. I lost millions in the last couple of weeks, playing the market the regular way. You were breaking me."

"The amulet," she said. "It does it. It absorbs psionic energy. It suppresses the psi field."

"I thought it was that. But who ever heard of such a thing? Where did you get it, Selene? Why do you wear it?"

"I got it far, far from here," said Selene. "I wear it to protect myself."

"Against *what?*"

"Against my own gift. My terrible gift, my nightmare gift, my curse of a gift. But if I must choose between my amulet and my love it is no choice. I love you, Aram, I love you, I love you!"

She seized the metal disk, ripped it from the chain around her neck, hurled it over the brink of the monument. It fluttered through the twilight sky and was gone.

I felt (now – n) and (now + n) return.

Selene vanished.

For an hour I stood alone atop Abu Simbel, motionless, baffled, stunned. Suddenly Selene was back. She clutched my arm and whispered, "Quick! Let's go to the hotel!"

"Where have you been?"

"Next Tuesday," she said. "I oscillate in time."

"What?"

"The amulet damped my oscillations. It anchored me to the timeline in the present. I got it in 2459 A.D. Someone I knew there, someone who cared very deeply for me. It was his parting gift, and he gave it knowing we could never meet again. But now—"

She vanished. Gone eighteen minutes.

"I was back in last Tuesday," she said, returning. "I phoned myself and said I should follow you to Istanbul, and then to Tel Aviv, and then to Egypt. You see how I found you?"

We hurried to her hotel overlooking the Nile. We made love, and an instant before the climax I found myself alone in bed. (Now + n) spoke to me and said, "She's been here with me. She should be on her way back to you." Selene returned. "I went to—"

"—this coming Sunday," I said. "I know. Can't you control the oscillations at all?"

"No. I'm swinging free. When the momentum really builds up, I cover centuries. It's torture, Aram. Life has no sequence, no structure. Hold me tight!"

In a frenzy we finished what we could not finish before. We lay clasped close, exhausted. "What will we do?" I cried. "I can't let you oscillate like this!"

"You must. I can't let you sacrifice your livelihood!"

"But—"

She was gone.

I rose and dressed and hurried back to Abu Simbel. In the hours before dawn I searched the sands beside the Nile, crawling, sifting, probing. As the sun's rays crested the mountain I found the amulet. I rushed to the hotel. Selene had reappeared.

"Put it on," I commanded.

"I won't. I can't deprive you of—"

"Put it on."

She disappeared. (Now + n) said, "Never fear. All will work out wondrous well."

Selene came back. "I was in the Friday after next," she said. "I had an idea that will save everything."

"No ideas. Put the amulet on."

She shook her head. "I brought you a present," she said, and handed me a copy of the *Herald Tribune*, dated the Friday after next. Oscillation seized her. She went and came and handed me November 19's newspaper. Her eyes were bright with excitement. She vanished. She brought me the *Herald Tribune* of November 8. Of December 4. Of November 11. Of January 18, 1988. Of December 11. Of March 5, 1988. Of December 22. Of June 16, 1997. Of December 14. Of September 8, 1990. "Enough!" I said. "Enough!" She continued to swing through time. The stack of papers grew. "I love you," she gasped, and handed me a transparent cube one inch high. "*The Wall Street Journal*, May 19, 2206," she explained. "I couldn't get the machine that reads it. Sorry." She was gone. She brought me more *Herald Tribunes*, many dates, 1988–2002. Then a whole microreel. At last she sank down, dazed, exhausted, and said, "Give me the amulet. It must be within twelve inches of my body to neutralize my field." I slipped the disk into her palm. "Kiss me," Selene murmured.

AND SO. SHE WEARS HER amulet; we are inseparable; I have no contact with my other selves. In handling my investments I merely consult my file of newspapers, which I have reduced to minicap size and carry in the bezel of a ring I wear. For safety's sake Selene carries a duplicate.

We are very happy. We are very wealthy.

Is only one dilemma. Neither of us use the special gift with which we were born. Evolution would not have produced such things in us if they were not to be used. What risks do we run by thwarting evolution's design?

I bitterly miss the use of my power, which her amulet negates. Even the company of supreme Selene does not wholly compensate for the loss of the harmoniousness that was

(now − n)

(now)

(now + n)

I could, of course, simply arrange to be away from Selene for an hour here, an hour there, and reopen that contact. I could even have continued playing the market that way, setting aside a transmission hour every forty-eight hours outside of amulet range. But it is the continuous contact that I miss. The always presence of my other selves. If I have that contact, Selene is condemned to oscillate, or else we must part.

I wish also to find some way that her gift will be not terror but joy for her.

Is maybe a solution. Can extrasensory gifts be induced by proximity? Can Selene's oscillation pass to me? I struggle to acquire it. We work together to give me her gift. Just today I felt myself move, perhaps a microsecond into the future, then a microsecond into the past. Selene said I definitely seemed to blur.

Who knows? Will success be ours?

I think yes. I think love will triumph. I think I will learn the secret, and we will coordinate our vanishings, Selene and I, and we will oscillate as one, we will swing together through time, we will soar, we will speed hand in hand across the millennia. She can discard her amulet once I am able to go with her on her journeys.

Pray for us, (now + n), my brother, my other self, and one day soon perhaps I will come to you and shake you by the hand.

◆

THE IRON STAR

The first-person narrator, by definition, is telling us his own story. Sometimes that story isn't a pretty one, though the narrator himself may not realize it. As, for example, here, in a tale told in a calm, cool, reasonable voice about a horrifying interaction between humans and aliens in the depths of space. The tale is told, this time, not by any sort of unusual being—no dolphins here, no young poltergeists, no titanic Greek gods, just a spaceship captain not very different from me and thee except that he lives in some future era of interstellar travel and buzzes around the spacelanes the way you or I might make a journey on the freeway between here and San Jose.

I wrote the story in 1986 for an anthology called *The Universe*, edited by my friend Byron Preiss, in which science-fiction writers would do stories about things like pulsars and quasars and neutron stars, and actual scientists would write companion essays discussing the scientific underpinnings of our speculative ideas. I chose supernovae, and wrote a story about the aftereffects thereof, but what I was really writing about, as I had done many times before and would do many times again, was the notion that aliens are really *alien*. And sometimes humans are, too.

—◦◦◦—

THE ALIEN SHIP CAME DRIFTING up from behind the far side of the neutron star just as I was going on watch. It looked a little like a miniature neutron star itself: a perfect sphere, metallic, dark. But neutron stars don't have six perky little out-thrust legs and the alien craft did.

While I paused in front of the screen the alien floated diagonally upward, cutting a swathe of darkness across the brilliantly starry sky like a fast-moving black hole. It even occulted the real black hole that lay thirty light-minutes away.

I stared at the strange vessel, fascinated and annoyed, wishing I had never seen it, wishing it would softly and suddenly vanish away. This mission was sufficiently complicated already. We hadn't needed an alien ship to appear on the scene. For five days now we had circled the neutron star in seesaw orbit with the aliens, a hundred eighty degrees apart. They hadn't said anything to us and we didn't know how to say anything to them. I didn't feel good about that. I like things direct, succinct, known.

Lina Sorabji, busy enhancing sonar transparencies over at our improvised archaeology station, looked up from her work and caught me scowling. Lina is a slender, dark woman from Madras whose ancestors were priests and scholars when mine were hunting bison on the Great Plains. She said, "You shouldn't let it get to you like that, Tom."

"You know what it feels like, every time I see it cross the screen? It's like having a little speck wandering around on the visual field of your eye. Irritating, frustrating, maddening—and absolutely impossible to get rid of."

"You want to get rid of it?"

I shrugged. "Isn't this job tough enough? Attempting to scoop a sample from the core of a neutron star? Do we really have to have an alien spaceship looking over our shoulders while we work?"

"Maybe it's not a spaceship at all," Lina said cheerily. "Maybe it's just some kind of giant spacebug."

I suppose she was trying to amuse me. I wasn't amused. This was going to win me a place in the history of space exploration, sure: Chief Executive Officer of the first expedition from Earth ever to encounter intelligent extraterrestrial life. Terrific. But that wasn't what IBM/Toshiba had hired me to do. And I'm more interested in completing assignments than in making history. You don't get paid for making history.

Basically the aliens were a distraction from our real work, just as last month's discovery of a dead civilization on a nearby solar system had been, the one whose photographs Lina Sorabji now was studying. This was supposed to be a business venture involving the experimental use of new technology, not an archaeological mission or an exercise in interspecies diplomacy. And I knew that there was a ship from the Exxon/Hyundai combine loose somewhere in hyperspace right now working on the same task we'd been sent out to handle. If they brought it off first, IBM/Toshiba would suffer a very severe loss of face, which is considered very bad on the corporate level. What's bad for IBM/Toshiba would be exceedingly bad for me. For all of us.

I glowered at the screen. Then the orbit of the *Ben-wah Maru* carried us down and away and the alien disappeared from my line of sight. But not for long, I knew.

As I keyed up the log reports from my sleep period I said to Lina, "You have anything new today?" She had spent the past three weeks analyzing the dead-world data. You never know what the parent companies will see as potentially profitable.

"I'm down to hundred-meter penetration now. There's a system of broad tunnels wormholing the entire planet. Some kind of pneumatic transportation network, is my guess. Here, have a look."

A holoprint sprang into vivid life in the air between us. It was a sonar scan that we had taken from ten thousand kilometers out, reaching a short distance below the surface of the dead world. I saw odd-angled tunnels lined with gleaming luminescent tiles that still pulsed with dazzling colors, centuries after the cataclysm that had destroyed all life there. Amazing decorative patterns of bright lines were plainly visible along the tunnel walls, lines that swirled and overlapped and entwined and beckoned my eye into some adjoining dimension.

Trains of sleek snub-nosed vehicles were scattered like caterpillars everywhere in the tunnels. In them and around them lay skeletons, thousands of them, millions, a whole continent full of commuters slaughtered as they waited at the station for the morning express. Lina touched the fine scan and gave me a close look: biped creatures, broad skulls tapering sharply at the sides, long apelike arms, seven-fingered hands with what seemed like an opposable thumb at each end, pelvises enlarged into peculiar bony crests jutting far out from their hips. It wasn't the first time a hyperspace exploring vessel had come across relics of extinct extraterrestrial races, even a fossil or two. But these weren't fossils. These beings had died only a few hundred years ago. And they had all died at the same time.

I shook my head somberly. "Those are some tunnels. They might have been able to convert them into pretty fair radiation shelters, is my guess. If only they'd had a little warning of what was coming."

"They never knew what hit them."

"No," I said. "They never knew a thing. A supernova brewing right next door and they must not have been able to tell what was getting ready to happen."

Lina called up another print, and another, then another. During our brief fly-by last month our sensors had captured an amazing panoramic view of this magnificent lost civilization: wide streets, spacious parks, splendid public buildings, imposing private houses, the works. Bizarre architecture, all unlikely angles and jutting crests like its creators, but unquestionably grand, noble, impressive. There had been keen intelligence at work here, and high artistry. Everything was intact and in a remarkable state of preservation, if you make allowances for the natural inroads that time and weather and I suppose the occasional earthquake will bring over three or four hundred years. Obviously this had been a wealthy, powerful society, stable and confident.

And between one instant and the next it had all been stopped dead in its tracks, wiped out, extinguished, annihilated. Perhaps they had had a fraction of a second to realize that the end of the world had come, but no more than that. I saw what surely were family groups huddling together, skeletons clumped in threes or fours or fives. I saw what I took to be couples with their seven-fingered hands still clasped in a final exchange of love. I saw some kneeling in a weird elbows-down position that might have been one of—who can say? Prayer? Despair? Acceptance?

A sun had exploded and this great world had died. I shuddered, not for the first time, thinking of it.

It hadn't even been their own sun. What had blown up was this one, forty light-years away from them, the one that was now the neutron star about which we orbited and which once had been a main-sequence sun maybe three or four times as big as Earth's. Or else it had been the other one in this binary system, thirty light-minutes from the first, the blazing young giant companion star of which nothing remained except the black hole nearby. At the moment we had no way of knowing which of these two stars had gone supernova first. Whichever one it was, though, had sent a furious burst of radiation heading outward, a lethal flux of cosmic rays capable of destroying most or perhaps all life-forms within a sphere a hundred light-years in diameter.

The planet of the underground tunnels and the noble temples had simply been in the way. One of these two suns had come to the moment when all the fuel in its core had been consumed: hydrogen had been fused into helium, helium into carbon, carbon into neon, oxygen, sulphur, silicon, until at last a core of pure iron lay at its heart. There is no atomic nucleus more strongly bound than iron. The star had reached the point where its release of energy through fusion had to cease; and with the end of energy production the star no longer could withstand the gravitational pressure of its own vast mass. In a moment, in the twinkling of an eye, the core underwent a catastrophic collapse. Its matter was compressed—beyond the point of equilibrium. And rebounded. And sent forth an intense shock wave that went rushing through the star's outer layers at a speed of 15,000 kilometers a second.

Which ripped the fabric of the star apart, generating an explosion releasing more energy than a billion suns.

The shock wave would have continued outward and outward across space, carrying debris from the exploded star with it, and interstellar gas that the debris had swept up. A fierce sleet of radiation would have been riding on that wave, too: cosmic rays, X-rays, radio waves, gamma rays, everything, all up and down the spectrum. If the sun that had gone supernova had had planets close by, they would have been vaporized immediately. Outlying worlds of that system might merely have been fried.

The people of the world of the tunnels, forty light-years distant, must have known nothing of the great explosion for a full generation after it had happened. But, all that while, the light of that shattered star was traveling towards them at a speed of 300,000 kilometers per second, and one night its frightful baleful unexpected glare must have burst suddenly into their sky in the most terrifying way. And almost in that same moment—for the deadly cosmic rays thrown off by the explosion move nearly at the speed of light—the killing blast of hard radiation would have arrived. And so these people and all else that lived on their world perished in terror and light.

All this took place a thousand light-years from Earth: that surging burst of radiation will need another six centuries to complete its journey towards our home world. At that distance, the cosmic rays will do us little or no harm. But for a time that long-dead star will shine in our skies so brilliantly that it will be visible by day, and by night it will cast deep shadows, longer than those of the Moon.

That's still in Earth's future. Here the fatal supernova, and the second one that must have happened not long afterwards, were some four hundred years in the past. What we had here now was a neutron star left over from one cataclysm and a black hole left over from the other. Plus the pathetic remains of a great civilization on a scorched planet orbiting a neighboring star. And now a ship from some alien culture. A busy corner of the galaxy, this one. A busy time for the crew of the IBM/Toshiba hyperspace ship *Ben-wah Maru*.

I WAS STILL GOING OVER the reports that had piled up at my station during my sleep period—mass-and-output readings on the neutron star, progress bulletins on the setup procedures for the neutronium scoop, and other routine stuff of that nature—when the communicator cone in front of me started to glow. I flipped it on. Cal Bjornsen, our communications guru, was calling from Brain Central downstairs.

Bjornsen is mostly black African with some Viking genes salted in. The whole left side of his face is cyborg, the result of some extreme bit of teenage carelessness. The story is that he was gravity-vaulting and lost polarity at sixty meters. The mix of ebony skin, blue eyes, blond hair, and sculpted titanium is an odd one, but I've seen a lot of faces less friendly than Cal's. He's a good man with anything electronic.

He said, "I think they're finally trying to send us messages, Tom."

I sat up fast. "What's that?"

"We've been pulling in signals of some sort for the past ninety minutes that didn't look random, but we weren't sure about it. A dozen or so different frequencies all up and down the line, mostly in the radio band, but we're also getting what seem to be infrared pulses, and something flashing in the ultraviolet range. A kind of scattershot noise effect, only it isn't noise."

"Are you sure of that?"

"The computer's still chewing on it," Bjornsen said. The fingers of his right hand glided nervously up and down his smooth metal cheek. "But we can see already that there are clumps of repetitive patterns."

"Coming from them? How do you know?"

"We didn't, at first. But the transmissions conked out when we lost line-of-sight with them, and started up again when they came back into view."

"I'll be right down," I said.

Bjornsen is normally a calm man, but he was running in frantic circles when I reached Brain Central three or four minutes later. There was stuff dancing on all the walls: sine waves, mainly, but plenty of other patterns jumping around on the monitors. He had already pulled in specialists from practically every department—the whole astronomy staff, two of the math guys, a couple from the external maintenance team, and somebody from engines. I felt preempted. Who was CEO on this ship, anyway? They were all babbling at once. "Fourier series," someone said, and someone yelled back, "Dirichlet factor," and someone else said, "Gibbs phenomenon!" I heard Angie Seraphin insisting vehemently, "—continuous except possibly for a finite number of finite discontinuities in the interval—pi to pi—"

"Hold it," I said, "What's going on?"

More babble, more gibberish. I got them quiet again and repeated my question, aiming it this time at Bjornsen.

"We have the analysis now," he said.

"So?"

"You understand that it's only guesswork, but Brain Central gives good guess. The way it looks, they seem to want us to broadcast a carrier wave they can tune in on, and just talk to them while they lock in with some sort of word-to-word translating device of theirs."

"That's what Brain Central thinks they're saying?"

"It's the most plausible semantic content of the patterns they're transmitting," Bjornsen answered.

I felt a chill. The aliens had word-to-word translating devices? That was a lot more than we could claim. Brain Central is one very smart computer, and if it thought that it had correctly deciphered the message coming in, them in all likelihood it had. An astonishing accomplishment, taking a bunch of ones and zeros put together by an alien mind and culling some sense out of them.

But even Brain Central wasn't capable of word-to-word translation out of some unknown language. Nothing in our technology is. The alien message had been *designed* to be easy: put together, most likely, in a careful high-redundancy manner, the computer equivalent of picture-writing. Any race able to undertake interstellar travel ought to have a computer powerful enough to sweat the essential meaning out of a message like that, and we did. We couldn't go farther than that though. Let the entropy of that message—that is, the unexpectedness of it, the unpredictability of its semantic content—rise just a little beyond the picture-writing level, and Brain Central would be lost. A computer that knows French should be able to puzzle out Spanish, and maybe even Greek. But Chinese? A tough proposition. And an *alien* language? Languages may start out logical, but they don't stay that way. And when its underlying grammatical assumptions were put together in the first place by beings with nervous systems that were wired up in ways entirely different from our own, well, the notion of instantaneous decoding becomes hopeless.

Yet our computer said that their computer could do word-to-word. That was scary.

On the other hand, if we couldn't talk to them, we wouldn't begin to find out what they were doing here and what threat, if any, they might pose to us. By revealing our language to them we might be handing them some sort of advantage, but I couldn't be sure of that, and it seemed to me we had to take the risk.

It struck me as a good idea to get some backing for that decision, though. After a dozen years as CEO aboard various corporate ships I knew the protocols. You did what you thought was right, but you didn't go all the way out on the limb by yourself if you could help it.

"Request a call for a meeting of the corporate staff," I told Bjornsen.

It wasn't so much a scientific matter now as a political one. The scientists would probably be gung-ho to go blasting straight ahead with making contact. But I wanted to hear what the Toshiba people would say, and the IBM people, and the military people. So we got everyone together and I laid the situation out and asked for a Consensus Process. And let them go at it, hammer and tongs.

Instant polarization. The Toshiba people were scared silly of the aliens. We must be cautious, Nakamura said. Caution, yes, said her cohort Nagy-Szabo. There may be danger to Earth. We have no knowledge of the aims and motivations of these beings. Avoid all contact with them, Nagy-Szabo said. Nakamura went even further. We should withdraw from the area immediately, she said, and return to Earth for additional instructions. That drew hot opposition from Jorgensen and Kalliotis, the IBM people. We had work to do here, they said. We should do it. They grudgingly conceded the need to be wary, but strongly urged continuation of the mission and advocated a circumspect opening of contact with the other ship. I think they were already starting to think about alien marketing demographics. Maybe I do them an injustice. Maybe.

The military people were about evenly divided between the two factions. A couple of them, the hair-splitting career-minded ones, wanted to play it absolutely safe and clear out of here fast, and the others, the up-and-away hero types, spoke out in favor of forging ahead with contact and to hell with the risks.

I could see there wasn't going to be any consensus. It was going to come down to me to decide.

By nature I am cautious. I might have voted with Nakamura in favor of immediate withdrawal; however that would have made my ancient cold-eyed Sioux forebears howl. Yet in the end what swayed me was an argument that came from Bryce-Williamson, one of the fiercest of the military sorts. He said that we didn't dare turn tail and run for home without making contact, because the aliens would take that either as a hostile act or a stupid one, and either way they might just slap some kind of tracer on us that ultimately would enable them to discover the location of our home world. True caution, he said, required us to try to find out what these people were all about before we made any move to leave the scene. We couldn't just run and we couldn't simply ignore them.

I sat quietly for a long time, weighing everything.

"Well?" Bjornsen asked. "What do you want to do, Tom?"

"Send them a broadcast," I said. "Give them greetings in the name of Earth and all its peoples. Extend to them the benevolent warm wishes of the board of directors of IBM/Toshiba. And then we'll wait and see."

WE WAITED. BUT FOR A long while we didn't see.

Two days, and then some. We went round and round the neutron star, and they went round and round the neutron star, and no further communication came from them. We beamed them all sorts of messages at all sorts of frequencies along the spectrum, both in the radio band and via infra-red and ultraviolet as well, so that they'd have plenty of material to work with. Perhaps their translator gadget wasn't all that good, I told myself hopefully. Perhaps it was stripping its gears trying to fathom the pleasant little packets of semantic data that we had sent them.

On the third day of silence I began feeling restless. There was no way we could begin the work we had been sent here to do, not with aliens watching. The Toshiba people—the Ultra Cautious faction —got more and more nervous. Even the IBM representatives began to act a little twitchy. I started to question the wisdom of having overruled the advocates of a no-contact policy. Although the parent companies hadn't seriously expected us to run into aliens, they had covered that eventuality in our instructions, and we were under orders to do minimum tipping of our hands if we found ourselves observed by strangers. But it was too late to call back our messages and I was still eager to find out what would happen next. So we watched and waited, and then we waited and watched. Round and round the neutron star.

We had been parked in orbit for ten days now around the neutron star, an orbit calculated to bring us no closer to its surface than 9000 kilometers at the closest skim. That was close enough for us to carry out our work, but not so close that we would be subjected to troublesome and dangerous tidal effects.

The neutron star had been formed in the supernova explosion that had destroyed the smaller of the two suns in what had once been a binary star system here. At the moment of the cataclysmic collapse of the stellar sphere, all its matter had come rushing inward with such force that electrons and protons were driven into each other to become a soup of pure neutrons. Which then were squeezed so tightly that they were forced virtually into contact with one another, creating a smooth globe of the strange stuff that we call neutronium, a billion billion times denser than steel and a hundred billion billion times more incompressible.

That tiny ball of neutronium glowing dimly in our screens was the neutron star. It was just eighteen kilometers in diameter but its mass was greater than that of Earth's sun. That gave it a gravitational field a quarter of a billion billion times as strong as that of the surface of Earth. If we could somehow set foot on it, we wouldn't just be squashed flat, we'd be instantly reduced to fine powder by the colossal tidal effects—the difference in gravitational pull between the soles of our feet and the tops of our heads, stretching us towards and away from the neutron star's center with a kick of eighteen billion kilograms.

A ghostly halo of electromagnetic energy surrounded the neutron star: X-rays, radio waves, gammas, and an oily, crackling flicker of violet light. The neutron star was rotating on its axis some 550 times a second, and powerful jets of electrons were spouting from its magnetic poles at each sweep, sending forth a beacon-like pulsar broadcast of the familiar type that we have been able to detect since the middle of the twentieth century.

Behind that zone of fiercely outflung radiation lay the neutron star's atmosphere: an envelope of gaseous iron a few centimeters thick. Below that, our scan had told us, was a two-kilometers-thick crust of normal matter, heavy elements only, ranging from molybdenum on up to transuranics with atomic numbers as high as 140. And within that was the neutronium zone, the stripped nuclei of iron packed unimaginably close together, an ocean of strangeness nine kilometers deep. What lay at the heart of *that*, we could only guess.

We had come here to plunge a probe into the neutronium zone and carry off a spoonful of star-stuff that weighed 100 billion tons per cubic centimeter.

No sort of conventional landing on the neutron star was possible or even conceivable. Not only was the gravitational pull beyond our comprehension—anything that was capable of withstanding the tidal effects would still have to cope with an escape velocity requirement of 200,000 kilometers per second when it tried to take off, two thirds the speed of light—but the neutron star's surface temperature was something like 3.5 million degrees. The surface temperature of our own sun is six thousand degrees and we don't try to make landings there. Even at this distance, our heat and radiation shields were straining to the limits to keep us from being cooked. We didn't intend to go any closer.

What IBM/Toshiba wanted us to do was to put a miniature hyperspace ship into orbit around the neutron star: an astonishing little vessel no bigger than your clenched fist, powered by a fantastically scaled-down version of the drive that had carried us through the space-time manifold across a span of a thousand light-years in a dozen weeks. The little ship was a slave-drone; we would operate it from the *Ben-wah Maru*. Or, rather, Brain Central would. In a maneuver that had taken fifty computer-years to program, we would send the miniature into hyperspace and bring it out again *right inside the neutron star*. And keep it there a billionth of a second, long enough for it to gulp the spoonful of neutronium we had been sent here to collect. Then we'd head for home, with the miniature ship following us along the same hyperpath.

We'd head for home, that is, unless the slave-drone's brief intrusion into the neutron star released disruptive forces that splattered us all over this end of the galaxy. IBM/Toshiba didn't really think that was going to happen. In theory a neutron star is one of the most stable things there is in the universe, and the math didn't indicate that taking a nip from its interior would cause real problems. This neighborhood had already had its full quota of giant explosions, anyway.

Still, the possibility existed. Especially since there was a black hole just thirty light-minutes away, a souvenir of the second and much larger supernova bang that had happened here in the recent past. Having a black hole nearby is a little like playing with an extra wild card whose existence isn't made known to the players until some randomly chosen moment midway through the game. If we destabilized the neutron star in some way not anticipated by the scientists back on Earth, we might just find ourselves going for a visit to the event horizon instead of getting to go home. Or we might not. There was only one way of finding out.

I didn't know, by the way, what use the parent companies planned to make of the neutronium we had been hired to bring them. I hoped it was a good one.

But obviously we weren't going to tackle any of this while there was an alien ship in the vicinity. So all we could do was wait. And see. Right now we were doing a lot of waiting, and no seeing at all.

Two days later Cal Bjornsen said, "We're getting a message back from them now. Audio only. In English."

We had wanted that, we had even hoped for that. And yet it shook me to learn that it was happening.

"Let's hear it," I said.

"The relay's coming over ship channel seven."

I tuned in. What I heard was an obviously synthetic voice, no undertones or overtones, not much inflection. They were trying to mimic the speech rhythms of what we had sent them, and I suppose they were actually doing a fair job of it, but the result was still unmistakably mechanical-sounding. Of course there might be nothing on board that ship but a computer, I thought, or maybe robots. I wish now that they had been robots.

It had the absolute and utter familiarity of a recurring dream. In stiff, halting, but weirdly comprehensible English came the first greetings of an alien race to the people of the planet of Earth. "This who speak be First of Nine Sparg," the voice said. Nine Sparg, we soon realized from context, was the name of their planet. First might have been the speaker's name, or his—hers, its?—title; that was unclear, and stayed that way. In an awkward pidgin-English that we nevertheless had little trouble understanding, First expressed gratitude for our transmission and asked us to send more words. To send a dictionary, in fact: now that they had the algorithm for our speech they needed more content to jam in behind it, so that we could go on to exchange more complex statements than Hello and How are you.

Bjornsen queried me on the override. "We've got an English program that we could start feeding them," he said. "Thirty thousand words: that should give them plenty. You want me to put it on for them?"

"Not so fast," I said. "We need to edit it first."

"For what?"

"Anything that might help them find the location of Earth. That's in our orders, under Eventuality of Contact with Extraterrestrials.

Remember, I have Nakamura and Nagy-Szabo breathing down my neck, telling me that there's a ship full of boogiemen out there and we mustn't have anything to do with them. I don't believe that myself. But right now we don't know how friendly these Spargs are and we aren't supposed to bring strangers home with us."

"But how could a dictionary entry—"

"Suppose the sun—*our* sun—is defined as a yellow G2 type star," I said. "That gives them a pretty good beginning. Or something about the constellations as seen from Earth. I don't know, Cal. I just want to make sure we don't accidentally hand these beings a road-map to our home planet before we find out what sort of critters they are."

Three of us spent half a day screening the dictionary, and we put Brain Central to work on it too. In the end we pulled seven words—you'd laugh if you knew which they were, but we wanted to be careful—and sent the rest across to the Spargs. They were silent for nine or ten hours. When they came back on the air their command of English was immensely more fluent. Frighteningly more fluent. Yesterday First had sounded like a tourist using a Fifty Handy Phrases program. A day later, First's command of English was as good as that of an intelligent Japanese who has been living in the United States for ten or fifteen years.

It was a tense, wary conversation. Or so it seemed to me, the way it began to seem that First was male and that his way of speaking was brusque and bluntly probing. I may have been wrong on every count.

First wanted to know who we were and why we were here. Jumping right in, getting down to the heart of the matter. I felt a little like a butterfly collector who has wandered onto the grounds of a fusion plant and is being interrogated by a security guard. But I kept my tone and phrasing as neutral as I could, and told him that our planet was called Earth and that we had come on a mission of exploration and investigation.

So had they, he told me. Where is Earth?

Pretty straightforward of him, I thought. I answered that I lacked at this point a means of explaining galactic positions to him in terms that he would understand. I did volunteer the information that Earth was not anywhere close at hand.

He was willing to drop that line of inquiry for the time being. He shifted to the other obvious one:

What were we investigating?

Certain properties of collapsed stars, I said, after a bit of hesitation.

And which properties were those?

I told him that we didn't have enough vocabulary in common for me to try to explain that either.

The Nine Sparg captain seemed to accept that evasion too. And provided me with a pause that indicated that it was my turn. Fair enough.

When I asked him what *he* was doing here, he replied without any apparent trace of evasiveness that he had come on a mission of historical inquiry. I pressed for details. It has to do with the ancestry of our race, he said. We used to live in this part of the galaxy, before the great explosion. No hesitation at all about telling me that. It struck me that First was being less reticent about dealing with my queries than I was with his; but of course I had no way of judging whether I was hearing the truth from him.

"I'd like to know more," I said, as much as a test as anything else. "How long ago did your people flee this great explosion? And how far from here is your present home world?"

A long silence: several minutes. I wondered uncomfortably if I had overplayed my hand. If they were as edgy about our finding their home world as I was about their finding ours, I had to be careful not to push them into an overreaction. They might just think that the safest thing to do would be to blow us out of the sky as soon as they had learned all they could from us.

But when First spoke again it was only to say, "Are you willing to establish contact in the visual band?"

"Is such a thing possible?"

"We think so," he said.

I thought about it. Would letting them see what we looked like give them any sort of clue to the location of Earth? Perhaps, but it seemed far-fetched. Maybe they'd be able to guess that we were carbon-based oxygen-breathers, but the risk of allowing them to know that seemed relatively small. And in any case we'd find out what *they* looked like. An even trade, right?

I had my doubts that their video transmission system could be made compatible with our receiving equipment. But I gave First the go-ahead and turned the microphone over to the communications staff. Who struggled with the problem for a day and a half. Sending the signal back and forth was no big deal, but breaking it down into information that would paint a picture on a cathode-ray tube was a different matter. The communications people at both ends talked and talked and talked, while I fretted about how much technical information about us we were revealing to the Spargs. The tinkering went on and on and nothing appeared on screen except occasional strings of horizontal lines. We sent them more data about how our television system worked. They made further adjustments in their transmission devices. This time we got spots instead of lines. We sent even more data. Were they leading us on? And were we telling them too much? I came finally to the position that trying to make the video link work had been a bad idea, and started to tell Communications that. But then the haze of drifting spots on my screen abruptly cleared and I found myself looking into the face of an alien being.

An alien face, yes. Extremely alien. Suddenly this whole interchange was kicked up to a new level of reality.

A hairless wedge-shaped head, flat and broad on top, tapering to a sharp point below. Corrugated skin that looked as thick as heavy rubber. Two chilly eyes in the center of that wide forehead and two more at its extreme edges. Three mouths, vertical slits, side by side: one for speaking and the other two, maybe for separate intake of fluids and solids. The whole business supported by three long columnar necks as thick as a man's wrist, separated by open spaces two or three centimeters wide. What was below the neck we never got to see. But the head alone was plenty.

They probably thought we were just as strange.

WITH VIDEO ESTABLISHED, FIRST AND I picked up our conversation right where we had broken it off the day before. Once more he was not in the least shy about telling me things.

He had been able to calculate in our units of time the date of the great explosion that had driven his people far from home world: it had taken place 387 years ago. He didn't use the word "supernova," because it hadn't been included in the 30,000-word vocabulary we had sent them, but that was obviously what he meant by "the great explosion." The 387-year figure squared pretty well with our own calculations, which were based on an analysis of the surface temperature and rate of rotation of the neutron star.

The Nine Sparg people had had plenty of warning that their sun was behaving oddly—the first signs of instability had become apparent more than a century before the blow-up—and they had devoted all their energy for several generations to the job of packing up and clearing out. It had taken many years, it seemed, for them to accomplish their migration to the distant new world they had chosen for their new home. Did that mean, I asked myself, that their method of interstellar travel was much slower than ours, and that they had needed decades or even a century to cover fifty or a hundred light-years? Earth had less to worry about, then. Even if they wanted to make trouble for us, they wouldn't be able easily to reach us, a thousand light-years from here. Or was First saying that their new world was really distant—all the way across the galaxy, perhaps, seventy or eighty thousand light-years away, or even in some other galaxy altogether? If that was the case, we were up against truly superior beings. But there was no easy way for me to question him about such things without telling him things about our own hyperdrive and our distance from this system that I didn't care to have him know.

After a long and evidently difficult period of settling in on the new world, First went on, the Nine Sparg folk finally were well enough established to launch an inquiry into the condition of their former home planet. Thus his mission to the supernova site.

"But we are in great mystery," First admitted, and it seemed to me that a note of sadness and bewilderment had crept into his mechanical-sounding voice. "We have come to what certainly is the right location. Yet nothing seems to be correct here. We find only this little iron star. And of our former planet there is no trace."

I stared at that peculiar and unfathomable four-eyed face, that three-columned neck, those tight vertical mouths, and to my surprise something close to compassion awoke in me. I had been dealing with this creature as though he were a potential enemy capable of leading armadas of war to my world and conquering it. But in fact he might be merely a scholarly explorer who was making a nostalgic pilgrimage, and running into problems with it. I decided to relax my guard just a little.

"Have you considered," I said, "that you might not be in the right location after all?"

"What do you mean?"

"As we were completing our journey towards what you call the iron star," I said, "we discovered a planet forty light-years from here that beyond much doubt had had a great civilization, and which evidently was close enough to the exploding star system here to have been devastated by it. We have pictures of it that we could show you. Perhaps *that* was your home world."

Even as I was saying it the idea started to seem foolish to me. The skeletons we had photographed on the dead world had had broad tapering heads that might perhaps have been similar to those of First, but they hadn't shown any evidence of this unique triple-neck arrangement. Besides, First had said that his people had had several generations to prepare for evacuation. Would they have left so many millions of their people behind to die? It looked obvious from the way those skeletons were scattered around that the inhabitants of that planet hadn't had the slightest clue that doom was due to overtake them that day. And finally, I realized that First had plainly said that it was his own world's sun that had exploded, not some neighboring star. The supernova had happened here. The dead world's sun was still intact.

"Can you show me your pictures?" he said.

It seemed pointless. But I felt odd about retracting my offer. And in the new rapport that had sprung up between us I could see no harm in it.

I told Lina Sorabji to feed her sonar transparencies into the relay pickup. It was easy enough for Cal Bjornsen to shunt them into our video transmission to the alien ship.

The Nine Sparg captain withheld his comment until we had shown him the batch.

Then he said, "Oh, that was not our world. That was the world of the Garvalekkinon people."

"The Garvalekkinon?"

"We knew them. A neighboring race, not related to us. Sometimes, on rare occasions, we traded with them. Yes, they must all have died when the star exploded. It is too bad."

"They look as though they had no warning," I said. "Look: can you see them there, waiting in the train stations?"

The triple mouths fluttered in what might have been the Nine Sparg equivalent of a nod.

"I suppose they did not know the explosion was coming."

"You suppose? You mean you didn't tell them?"

All four eyes blinked at once. Expression of puzzlement.

"Tell them? Why should we have told them? We were busy with our preparations. We had no time for them. Of course the radiation would have been harmful to them, but why was that our concern? They were not related to us. They were nothing to us."

I had trouble believing I had heard him correctly. A neighboring people. Occasional trading partners. Your sun is about to blow up, and it's reasonable to assume that nearby solar systems will be affected. You have fifty or a hundred years of advance notice yourselves, and you can't even take the trouble to let these other people know what's going to happen?

I said, "You felt no need at all to warn them? That isn't easy for me to understand."

Again the four-eyed shrug.

"I have explained it to you already," said First. "They were not of our kind. They were nothing to us."

I EXCUSED MYSELF ON SOME flimsy excuse and broke contact. And sat and thought a long long while. Listening to the words of the Nine Sparg captain echoing in my mind. And thinking of the millions of skeletons scattered like straws in the tunnels of that dead world that the supernova had baked. A whole people left to die because it was inconvenient to take five minutes to send them a message. Or perhaps because it simply never had occurred to anybody to bother.

The families, huddling together. The children reaching out. The husbands and wives with hands interlocked.

A world of busy, happy, intelligent people. Boulevards and temples. Parks and gardens. Paintings, sculpture, poetry, music. History, philosophy, science. And a sudden star in the sky, and everything gone in a moment.

Why should we have told them? They were nothing to us.

I knew something of the history of my own people. We had experienced casual extermination too. But at least when the white settlers had done it to us it was because they had wanted our land.

For the first time I understood the meaning of alien.

I turned on the external screen and stared out at the unfamiliar sky of this place. The neutron star was barely visible, a dull red dot, far down in the lower left quadrant; and the black hole was high.

Once they had both been stars. What havoc must have attended their destruction! It must have been the Sparg sun that blew first, the one that had become the neutron star. And then, fifty or a hundred years later, perhaps, the other, larger star had gone the same route. Another titanic supernova, a great flare of killing light. But of course everything for hundreds of light-years around had perished already in the first blast.

The second sun had been too big to leave a neutron star behind. So great was its mass that the process of collapse had continued on beyond the neutron-star stage, matter crushing in upon itself until it broke through the normal barriers of space and took on a bizarre and almost unthinkable form, creating an object of infinitely small volume that was nevertheless of infinite density: a black hole, a pocket of incomprehensibility where once a star had been.

I stared now at the black hole before me.

I couldn't see it, of course. So powerful was the surface gravity of that grotesque thing that nothing could escape from it, not even electromagnetic radiation, not the merest particle of light. The ultimate in invisibility cloaked that infinitely deep hole in space.

But though the black hole itself was invisible, the effects that its presence caused were not. That terrible gravitational pull would rip apart and swallow any solid object that came too close; and so the hole was surrounded by a bright ring of dust and gas several hundred kilometers across. These shimmering particles constantly tumbled towards that insatiable mouth, colliding as they spiraled in, releasing flaring fountains of radiation, red-shifted into the visual spectrum by the enormous gravity: the bright green of helium, the majestic purple of hydrogen, the crimson of oxygen. That outpouring of energy was the death-cry of doomed matter. That rainbow whirlpool of blazing light was the beacon marking the maw of the black hole.

I found it oddly comforting to stare at that thing. To contemplate that zone of eternal quietude from which there was no escape. Pondering so inexorable and unanswerable an infinity was more soothing than thinking of a world of busy people destroyed by the indifference of their neighbors. Black holes offer no choices, no complexities, no shades of disagreement. They are absolute.

Why should we have told them? They were nothing to us.

After a time I restored contact with the Nine Sparg ship. First came to the screen at once, ready to continue our conversation.

"There is no question that our world once was located here," he said at once. "We have checked and rechecked the coordinates. But the changes have been extraordinary."

"Have they?"

"Once there were two stars here, our own and the brilliant blue one that was nearby. Our history is very specific on that point: a brilliant blue star that lit the entire sky. Now we have only the iron star. Apparently it has taken the place of our sun. But where has the blue one gone? Could the explosion have destroyed it too?"

I frowned. Did they really not know? Could a race be capable of attaining an interstellar spacedrive and an interspecies translating device, and nevertheless not have arrived at any understanding of the neutron star/black hole cosmogony?

Why not? They were aliens. They had come by all their understanding of the universe via a route different from ours. They might well have overlooked this feature or that of the universe about them.

"The blue star—" I began.

But First spoke right over me, saying, "It is a mystery that we must devote all our energies to solving, or our mission will be fruitless. But let us talk of other things. You have said little of your own mission. And of your home world. I am filled with great curiosity, Captain, about those subjects."

I'm sure you are, I thought.

"We have only begun our return to space travel," said First. "Thus far we have encountered no other intelligent races. And so we regard this meeting as fortunate. It is our wish to initiate contact with you. Quite likely some aspects of your technology would be valuable to us. And there will be much that you wish to purchase from us. Therefore we would be glad to establish trade relations with you."

As you did with the Garvalekkinon people, I said to myself.

I said, "We can speak of that tomorrow, Captain. I grow tired now. But before we break contact for the day, allow me to offer you the beginning of a solution to the mystery of the disappearance of the blue sun."

The four eyes widened. The slitted mouths parted in what seemed surely to be excitement.

"Can you do that?"

I took a deep breath.

"We have some preliminary knowledge. Do you see the place opposite the iron star, where energies boil and circle in the sky? As we entered this system, we found certain evidence there that may explain the fate of your former blue sun. You would do well to center your investigations on that spot."

"We are most grateful," said First.

"And now, Captain, I must bid you good night. Until tomorrow, Captain."

"Until tomorrow," said the alien.

I was awakened in the middle of my sleep period by Lina Sorabji and Bryce-Williamson, both of them looking flushed and sweaty. I sat up, blinking and shaking my head.

"It's the alien ship," Bryce-Williamson blurted, "It's approaching the black hole."

"Is it, now?"

"Dangerously close," said Lina. "What do they think they're doing? Don't they know?"

"I don't think so," I said. "I suggested that they go exploring there. Evidently they don't regard it as a bad idea."

"You sent them there?" she said incredulously.

307

With a shrug I said, "I told them that if they went over there they might find the answer to the question of where one of their missing suns went. I guess they've decided to see if I was right."

"We have to warn them," said Bryce-Williamson. "Before it's too late. Especially if we're responsible for sending them there. They'll be furious with us once they realize that we failed to warn them of the danger."

"By the time they realize it," I replied calmly, "it *will* be too late. And then their fury won't matter, will it? They won't be able to tell us how annoyed they are with us. Or to report to their home world, for that matter, that they had an encounter with intelligent aliens who might be worth exploiting."

He gave me an odd look. The truth was starting to sink in.

I turned on the external screens and punched up a close look at the black hole region. Yes, there was the alien ship, the little metallic sphere, the six odd outthrust legs. It was in the zone of criticality now. It seemed hardly to be moving at all. And it was growing dimmer and dimmer as it slowed. The gravitational field had it, and it was being drawn in. Blacking out, becoming motionless. Soon it would have gone beyond the point where outside observers could perceive it. Already it was beyond the point of turning back.

I heard Lina sobbing behind me. Bryce-Williamson was muttering to himself: praying, perhaps.

I said, "Who can say what they would have done to us—in their casual, indifferent way—once they came to Earth? We know now that Spargs worry only about Spargs. Anybody else is just so much furniture." I shook my head. "To hell with them. They're gone, and in a universe this big we'll probably never come across any of them again, or they us. Which is just fine. We'll be a lot better off having nothing at all to do with them."

"But to die that way—" Lina murmured. "To sail blindly into a black hole—"

"It is a great tragedy," said Bryce-Williamson.

"A tragedy for them," I said. "For us, a reprieve, I think. And tomorrow we can get moving on the neutronium-scoop project." I tuned up the screen to the next level. The boiling cloud of matter around the mouth of the black hole blazed fiercely. But of the alien ship there was nothing to be seen.

Yes, a great tragedy, I thought. The valiant exploratory mission that had sought the remains of the Nine Sparg home world has been lost with all hands. No hope of rescue. A pity that they hadn't known how unpleasant black holes can be.

But why should we have told them? They were nothing to us.

THE SCIENCE FICTION HALL OF FAME

This one cuts very close to the bone. Taken superficially, it doesn't seem to be entirely a first-person story: it opens, as you will see, in the first person, but the "I" of that opening paragraph is not the "I" who is really telling the story; then it cuts to a paragraph of real first-person narrative, goes on to two fragmentary third-person paragraphs, and then returns to first person in the voice of the true narrator.

What is going on here?

What is going on is a story that is partly the first-person tale of a science-fiction reader who is ambivalent, to put it very mildly, about all the time he wastes reading science fiction, and partly a series of quotes, rather parodistic in tone, from science-fiction stories that the protagonist of the story has been reading, but which, in fact, I, Robert Silverberg, have invented for the purpose of telling this particular story. And gradually the tale the reader is telling and the science-fictional stuff he is reading draw together until he is, apparently, pulled right into some science-fiction world.

What is going on here, underneath all that, is a manifestation of the powerful love/hate relationship that the author of the story, i.e. me, has developed with the field of science fiction. I wrote it in 1972, a complicated year for me (I had just abandoned my native city of New York for a new life in California, and my marriage of sixteen years was quite plainly coming apart, and I was pretty tired of writing, too, after almost two decades of prolific work.) My friend Terry Carr, who edited a periodical anthology called *Universe*, had asked me to do a story for his fourth issue—I had had stories in the first three—and this is what I gave him. The title was an ironic one. It was the same as that of a well-known anthology that I had edited on behalf of the Science Fiction Writers of America, a compilation of classic s-f stories that had been published between 1934 and 1969, a book which has had strong sales over the years and is still in print half a century later.

Terry read the story right away—and returned it to me that evening (we lived near each other in the Oakland hills), looking crestfallen and dismayed. "You know how much I want something of yours in the next issue," he said. "But I can't publish this, Bob. *Universe* is supposed to be a book for people who *like* science fiction."

I had to admit that Terry was right. My narrator refers to science fiction, at one point, as "simple-minded escape literature." He goes on immediately to admit the possibility that it may be something a good deal more than that, but the note of ambivalence has been struck. It is hard to deny that the author of "The Science Fiction Hall of Fame" felt about science fiction much the same way his protagonist does. I thought then, and think now, that the story reflects more ambivalence than hostility—the work of a writer who at that point had spent more than a quarter of a century deeply concerned with science fiction, first as a reader and then as a writer, and who, for the moment, has grown a little weary of it. Terry Carr was so upset by the whole episode that I promised to write another story for him at once, and I did, and he published it.

Meanwhile I offered "The Science Fiction Hall of Fame" to another veteran editor, Bob Hoskins, who accepted it without any qualms and published it in the 1973 edition of his own periodical anthology, *Infinity*.

It's a complicated story, and the story behind the story is a complicated one, too. And in this book of first-person stories this may be the most first-person of them all.

———*∿∿*———

THE LOOK IN HIS REMOTE gray eyes was haunted, terrified, beaten, as he came running in from the Projectorium. His shoulders were slumped; I had never before seen him betray the slightest surrender to despair, but now I was chilled by the completeness of his capitulation. With a shaking hand he thrust at me a slender yellow data slip, marked in red with the arcane symbols of cosmic computation. "No use," he muttered. "There's absolutely no use trying to fight any longer!"

"You mean—"

"Tonight," he said huskily, "the universe irrevocably enters the penumbra of the null point!"

THE DAY ARMSTRONG AND ALDRIN stepped out onto the surface of the moon—it was Sunday, July 20, 1969, remember?—I stayed home, planning to watch the whole thing on television. But it happened that I met an interesting woman at Leon and Helene's party the night before, and she came home with me. Her name is gone from my mind, if I ever knew it, but I remember how she looked: long soft golden hair, heart-shaped face with prominent ruddy cheeks, gentle gray-blue eyes, plump breasts, slender legs. I remember, too, how she wandered around my apartment, studying the crowded shelves of old paperbacks and magazines. "You're really into sci-fi, aren't you?" she said at last. And laughed and said, "I guess this must be your big weekend, then! Wow, the moon!" But it was all a big joke to her, that men should be cavorting around up there when there was still so much work left to do on earth. We had a shower and I made lunch and we settled down in front of the set to wait for the men to come out of their module, and—very easily, without a sense of transition—we found ourselves starting to screw, and it went on and on, one of those impossible impersonal mechanical screws in which body grinds against body for centuries, no feeling, no excitement, and as I rocked rhythmically on top of her, unable either to come or to quit, I heard Walter Cronkite telling the world that the module hatch was opening. I wanted to break free of her so I could watch, but she clawed at my back. With a distinct effort I pulled myself up on my elbows, pivoted the upper part of my body so I had a view of the screen, and waited for the ecstasy to hit me. Just as the first wavery image of an upside-down spaceman came into view on that ladder, she moaned and bucked her hips wildly and went into frenzied climax. I felt nothing. Nothing. Eventually she left, and I showered and had a snack and watched the replay of the moonwalk on the eleven o'clock news. And still I felt nothing.

"WHAT IS THE ANSWER?" said Gertrude Stein, about to die. Alice B. Toklas remained silent. "In that case," Miss Stein went on, "what is the question?"

EXTRACT FROM *HISTORY OF THE IMPERIUM,* Koeckert and Hallis, third edition (revised):

> The galactic empire was organized 190 standard universal centuries ago by the joint, simultaneous, and unanimous resolution of the governing bodies of eleven hundred worlds. By the present day the hegemony of the empire has spread to thirteen galactic sectors and embraces many thousands of planets, all of which entered the empire willingly and gladly. To remain outside the empire is to confess civic insanity, for the Imperium is unquestionably regarded throughout the cosmos as the most wholly sane construct ever created by the sentient mind. The decision-making processes of the Imperium are invariably determined by recourse to the Hermosillo Equations, which provide unambiguous and incontrovertibly rational guidance in any

question of public policy. Thus the many worlds of the empire form a single coherent unit, as perfectly interrelated socially, politically, and economically as its component worlds are interrelated by the workings of the universal laws of gravitation.

PERHAPS I SPEND TOO MUCH time on other planets and in remote galaxies. It's an embarrassing addiction, this science fiction. (Horrible jingle! It jangles in my brain like an idiot's singsong chant.) Look at my bookshelves: hundreds of well-worn paperbacks, arranged alphabetically by authors, Aschenbach-Barger-Capwell-De Soto-Friedrich, all the greats of the genre out to Waldman and Zenger. The collection of magazines, every issue of everything back to the summer of 1953, a complete run of *Nova*, most issues of *Deep Space*, a thick file of *Tomorrow*. I suppose some of those magazines are quite rare now, though I've never looked closely into the feverish world of the s-f collector. I simply accumulate the publications I buy at the newsstand, never throwing any of them away. How could I part with them? Slices of my past, those magazines, those books. I can give dates to changes in my spirit, alterations in my consciousness, merely by picking up old magazines and reflecting on the associations they evoke. The issue showing the ropy-armed purple monster: it went on sale the month I discovered sex. This issue, cover painting of exploding spaceships: I read it my first month in college, by way of relief from Aquinas and Plato. Mileposts, landmarks, waterlines. An embarrassing addiction. My friends are good-humored about it. They think science fiction is a literature for children—God knows, they may be right—and they indulge my fancy for it in an affectionate way, giving me some fat anthology for Christmas, leaving a stack of current magazines on my desk while I'm out to lunch. But they wonder about me. Sometimes I wonder too. At the age of thirty-four should I still be able to react with such boyish enthusiasm to, say, Capwell's Solar League novels or Waldman's "Mindleech" series? What is there about the present that drives me so obsessively toward the future? The gray and vacant present, the tantalizing, inaccessible future.

HIS EYES WERE GLITTERING WITH irrepressible excitement as he handed her the gleaming yellow dome that was the thought-transference helmet. "Put it on," he said tenderly.

"I'm afraid, Riik."

"Don't be. What's there to fear?"

"Myself. The real me. I'll be wide open, Riik. I fear what you may see in me, what it may do to you, to *us*."

"Is it so ugly inside you?" he asked.

"Sometimes I think so."

"Sometimes everybody thinks that about himself, Juun. It's the old neurotic self-hatred welling up, the garbage that we can't escape until we're totally sane. You'll find that kind of stuff in me, too, once we have the helmets on. Ignore it. It isn't real. It isn't going to be a determining factor in our lives."

"Do you love me, Riik?"

"The helmet will answer that better than I can."

"All right. All right." She smiled nervously. Then with exaggerated care she lifted the helmet, put it in place, adjusted it, smoothed a vagrant golden curl back under the helmet's rim. He nodded and donned his own.

"Ready?" he asked.

"Ready."

"Now!"

He threw the switch. Their minds surged toward one another. Then—

Oneness!

MY MIND IS CLUTTERED WITH other men's fantasies: robots, androids, starships, giant computers, predatory energy globes, false messiahs, real messiahs, visitors from distant worlds, time machines, gravity repellers. Punch my buttons and I offer you parables from the works of Hartzell or Marcus, appropriate philosophical gems borrowed from the collected editorial utterances of David Coughlin, or concepts dredged from my meditations on De Soto. I am a walking mass of secondhand imagination. I am the flesh-and-blood personification of the Science Fiction Hall of Fame.

"At last," cried Professor Kholgoltz triumphantly. "The machine is finished! The last solenoid is installed! Feed power, Hagley. Feed power! Now we will have the Answer we have sought for so many years!"

He gestured to his assistant, who gradually brought the great computer throbbingly to life. A subtle, barely perceptible flow of energy pervaded the air: the neutrino flux that the master equations had predicted. In the amphitheatre adjoining the laboratory, ten thousand people sat tensely frozen. All about the world, millions more, linked by satellite relay, waited with similar intensity. The professor nodded. Another gesture, and Hagley, with a grand flourish, fed the question tape—programmed under the supervision of a corps of multispan-trained philosophers—into the gaping jaws of the input slot.

"The meaning of life," murmured Kholgoltz. "The solution to the ultimate riddle. In just another moment it will be in our hands."

An ominous rumbling sound came from the depths of the mighty thinking machine. And then—

My recurring nightmare: A beam of dense emerald light penetrates my bedroom and lifts me with an irresistible force from my bed. I float through the window and hover high above the city. A zone of blackness engulfs me and I find myself transported to an endless onyx-walled tunnel-like hallway. I am alone. I wait, and nothing happens, and after an interminable length of time I begin to walk forward, keeping close to the left side of the hall. I am aware now that towering cone-shaped beings with

THE SCIENCE FICTION HALL OF FAME

saucer-size orange eyes and rubbery bodies are gliding past me on the right, paying no attention to me. I walk for days. Finally the hallway splits: nine identical tunnels confront me. Randomly I choose the leftmost one. It is just like the last, except that the beings moving toward me now are animated purple starfish, rough-skinned, many-tentacled, a globe of pale white fire glowing at their cores. Days again. I feel no hunger, no fatigue; I just go marching on. The tunnel forks once more. Seventeen options this time. I choose the rightmost branch. No change in the texture of the tunnel—smooth as always, glossy, bright with an inexplicable inner radiance—but now the beings flowing past me are spherical, translucent, paramecioid things filled with churning misty organs. On to the next forking place. And on. And on. Fork after fork, choice after choice, nothing the same, nothing ever different. I keep walking. On. On. On. I walk forever. I never leave the tunnel.

WHAT'S THE PURPOSE OF LIFE, anyway? Who if anybody put us here, and why? Is the whole cosmos merely a gigantic accident? Or was there a conscious and determined Prime Cause? What about free will? Do we have any, or are we only acting out the dictates of some unimaginable, unalterable program that was stenciled into the fabric of reality a billion years ago?

Big resonant questions. The kind an adolescent asks when he first begins to wrestle with the nature of the universe. What am I doing brooding over such stuff at my age? Who am I fooling?

THIS IS THE PLACE. I have reached the center of the universe, where all vortices meet, where everything is tranquil, the zone of stormlessness. I drift becalmed, moving in a shallow orbit. This is ultimate peace. This is the edge of union with the All. In my tranquillity I experience a vision of the brawling, tempestuous universe that surrounds me. In every quadrant there are wars, quarrels, conspiracies, murders, air crashes, frictional losses, dimming suns, transfers of energy, colliding planets, a multitude of entropic interchanges. But here everything is perfectly still. Here is where I wish to be.

Yes! If only I could remain forever!

How, though? There's no way. Already I feel the tug of inexorable forces, and I have only just arrived. There is no everlasting peace. We constantly rocket past the miraculous center toward one zone of turbulence or another, driven always toward the periphery, driven, driven, helpless. I am drawn away from the place of peace. I spin wildly. The centrifuge of ego keeps me churning. Let me go back! Let me go! Let me lose myself in that place at the heart of the tumbling galaxies!

NEVER TO DIE. THAT'S PART of the attraction. To live in a thousand civilizations yet to come, to see the future millennia unfold, to participate vicariously in the ultimate evolution of mankind—how to achieve all that, except through these books and magazines? That's what they give me: life eternal and a cosmic perspective. At any rate they give it to me from one page to the next.

THE SIGNAL SPED ACROSS THE black bowl of night, picked up again and again by ultrawave repeater stations that kicked it to higher energy states. A thousand trembling laser nodes were converted to vapor in order to hasten the message to the galactic communications center on Manipool VI, where the emperor awaited news of the revolt. Through the data dome at last the story tumbled. Worlds aflame! Millions dead! The talismans of the Imperium trampled upon!

"We have no choice," said the emperor calmly. "Destroy the entire Rigel system at once."

THE PROBLEM THAT ARISES WHEN you try to regard science fiction as adult literature is that it's doubly removed from our "real" concerns. Ordinary mainstream fiction, your Faulkner and

Dostoevsky and Hemingway, is by definition made-up stuff—the first remove. But at least it derives directly from experience, from contemplation of the empirical world of tangible daily phenomena. And so, while we are able to accept *The Possessed,* say, as an abstract thing, a verbal object, a construct of nouns and verbs and adjectives and adverbs, and while we can take it purely as a story, and aggregation of incidents and conversations and expository passages describing invented individuals and events, we can also *make use of it* as a guide to a certain aspect of Russian nineteenth-century sensibility and as a key to prerevolutionary radical thought. That is, it is of the nature of an historical artefact, a legacy of its own era, with real and identifiable extra literary values. Because it simulates actual people moving within a plausible and comprehensible real-world human situation, we can draw information from Dostoevsky's book that could conceivably aid us in understanding our own lives. What about science fiction, though, dealing with unreal situations set in places that do not exist and in eras that have not yet occurred? Can we take the adventures of Captain Zap in the eightieth century as a blueprint for self-discovery? Can we accept the collision of stellar federations in the Andromeda Nebula as an interpretation of the relationship of the United States and the Soviet Union circa 1950? I suppose we can, provided we can accept a science fiction story on a rarefied metaphorical level, as a set of symbolic structures generated in some way by the author's real-world experience. But it's much easier to hang in there with Captain Zap on his own level, for the sheer gaudy fun of it. And that's kiddie stuff.

Therefore we have two possible evaluations of science fiction:

—That it is simple-minded escape literature, lacking relevance to daily life and useful only as self-contained diversion.

—That its value is subtle and elusive, accessible only to those capable and willing to penetrate the experimental substructure concealed by those broad metaphors of galactic empires and supernormal powers.

I oscillate between the two attitudes. Sometimes I embrace both simultaneously. That's a trick I learned from science fiction, incidentally: "multispan logic," it was called in Zenger's famous novel *The Mind Plateau*. It took his hero twenty years of ascetic study in the cloisters of the Brothers of Aldebaran to master the trick. I've accomplished it in twenty years of reading *Nova* and *Deep Space* and *Solar Quarterly*. Yes: multispan logic. Yes. The art of embracing contradictory theses. Maybe "dynamic schizophrenia" would be a more expressive term, I don't know.

IS THIS THE CENTER? AM I there? I doubt it. Will I know it when I reach it, or will I deny it as I frequently do, will I say, *What else is there, where else should I look?*

THE ALIEN WAS A REPELLENT thing, all lines and angles, its tendrils quivering menacingly, its slit-wide eyes revealing a somber bloodshot curiosity. Mortenson was unable to focus clearly on the creature; it kept slipping off at the edges into some other plane of being, an odd rippling effect that he found morbidly disquieting. It was no more than fifty meters from him now, and advancing steadily. When it gets to within ten meters, he thought, I'm going to blast it no matter what.

Five steps more; then an eerie metamorphosis. In place of this thing of harsh angular threat there stood a beaming, happy Golkon! The plump little creature waved its chubby tentacles and cooed a gleeful greeting!

"I am love," the Golkon declared. "I am the bringer of happiness! I welcome you to this world, dear friend!"

WHAT DO I FEAR? I fear the future. I fear the infinite possibilities that lie ahead. They fascinate and terrify me. I never thought I would admit that, even to myself. But what other interpretation can I place on my dream? That multitude of tunnels, that infinity of strange beings, all drifting toward me as I walk on and on? The embodiment of my basic fear. Hence my compulsive reading of science fiction: I crave road signs, I want a map of the territory that I must enter. That we all must enter. Yet the maps themselves are frightening. Perhaps I should look backward instead. It would be less terrifying to read historical novels. Yet I feed on these fantasies that obsess and frighten me. I derive energy from them. If I renounced them, what would nourish me?

THE BLOOD-COLLECTORS WERE OUT TONIGHT, roving in thirsty packs across the blasted land. From the stone-walled safety of his cell he could hear them baying, could hear also the terrible cries of the victims, the old women, the straggling children. Four, five nights a week now, the fanged monsters broke loose and went marauding, and each night there were fewer humans left to hold back the tide. That was bad enough, but there was worse: his own craving. How much longer could he keep himself locked up in here? How long before he too was out there, prowling, questing for blood?

WHEN I WENT TO THE newsstand at lunchtime to pick up the latest issue of *Tomorrow,* I found the first number of a new magazine: *Worlds of Wonder.* That startled me. It must be nine or ten years since anybody risked bringing out a new s-f title. We have our handful of long-established standbys, most of them founded in the thirties and even the twenties, which seem to be going to go on forever; but the failure of nearly all the younger magazines in the fifties was so emphatic that I suppose I came to assume there never again would be any new titles. Yet here is *Worlds of Wonder,* out today. There's nothing extraordinary about it. Except for the name it might very well be *Deep Space* or *Solar.* The format is the usual one, the size of *Reader's Digest.* The cover painting, unsurprisingly, is by Greenstone. The stories are by Aschenbach, Marcus, and some lesser names. The editor is Roy Schaefer, whom I remember as a competent but unspectacular writer in the fifties and sixties. I suppose I should be pleased that I'll have six more issues a year to keep me amused. In fact I feel vaguely threatened, as though the tunnel of my dreams has sprouted an unexpected new fork.

THE TIME MACHINE HANGS BEFORE me in the laboratory, a glittering golden ovoid suspended in ebony struts. Richards and Halleck smile nervously as I approach it. This, after all, is the climax of our years of research, and so much emotion rides on the success of the voyage I am about to take that every moment now seems freighted with heavy symbolic import. Our experiments with rats and rabbits seemed successful; but how can we know what it is to travel in time until a human being has made the journey?

All right. I enter the machine. Crisply we crackle instructions to one another across the intercom. Setting? Fifth of May, 2500 A.D.—a jump of nearly three and a half centuries. Power level? Energy feed? Go. Go. Dislocation circuit activated? Yes. All systems go. Bon voyage!

The control panel goes crazy. Dials spin. Lights flash. Everything's zapping at once. I plunge forward in time, going, going, going!

When everything is calm again I commence the emergence routines. The time capsule must be opened just so, unhurriedly. My hands tremble in anticipation of the strange new world that awaits me. A thousand hypotheses tumble through my brain. At last the hatch opens. "Hello," says Richards. "Hi there," Halleck says. We are still in the laboratory.

"I don't understand," I say. "My meters show definite temporal transfer."

"There was," says Richards. "You went forward to 2500 A.S., as planned. But you're still here."

"Where?"

"*Here.*"

Halleck laughs. "You know what happened, Mike? You *did* travel in time. You jumped forward three hundred and whatever years. But you brought the whole present along with you. You pulled our own time into the future. It's like tugging a doughnut through its own hole. You see? Our work is kaput, Mike. We've got our answer. The present is always with us, no matter how far out we go."

ONCE ABOUT FIVE YEARS AGO I took some acid, a little purple pill that a friend of mine mailed me from New Mexico. I had read a good deal about the psychedelics and I wasn't at all afraid; eager, in fact, hungry for the experience. I was going to float up into the cosmos and embrace it all. I was going to become a part of the nebulas and the supernovas, and they were going to become part of me; or rather, I would at last come to recognize that we had been part of each other all along. In other words, I imagined that LSD would be like an input of five hundred s-f novels all at once; a mind-blowing charge of imagery, emotion, strangeness, and transport to incredible unknowable places. The drug took about an hour to hit me. I saw the walls begin to flow and billow, and cascades of light streamed from the ceiling. Time became jumbled, and I thought three hours had gone by, but it was only about twenty minutes. Holly was with me. "What are you feeling?" she asked. "Is it mystical?" She asked a lot of questions like that. "I don't know," I said. "It's very pretty, but I just don't know." The drug wore off in about seven hours, but my nervous system was keyed up and lights kept exploding behind my eyes when I tried to go to sleep. So I sat up all night and read Marcus's *Starflame* novels, both of them, before dawn.

THERE IS NO GALACTIC EMPIRE. There never will be any galactic empire. All is chaos. Everything is random. Galactic empires are puerile power-fantasies. Do I truly believe this? If not, why do I say it? Do I enjoy bringing myself down?

"LOOK OVER THERE!" THE MUTANT whispered. Carter looked. An entire corner of the room had disappeared—melted away, as though it had been erased. Carter could see the street outside, the traffic, the building across the way. "Over there!" the mutant said. "Look!" The chair was gone. "Look!" The ceiling vanished. "Look! Look! Look!" Carter's head whirled. Everything was going, vanishing at the command of the inexorable golden-eyed mutant. "Do you see the stars?" the mutant asked. He snapped his fingers. "No!" Carter cried. "Don't!" Too late. The stars also were gone.

SOMETIMES I SLIP INTO WHAT I consider the science fiction experience in everyday life. I mean, I can be sitting at my desk typing a report, or standing in the subway train waiting for the long grinding sweaty ride to end, when I feel a buzz, a rush, an upward movement of the soul similar to what I felt the time I took acid, and suddenly I see myself in an entirely new perspective—as a visitor from some other time, some other place, isolated in a world of alien beings known as Earth. Everything seems unfamiliar and baffling. I get that sense of doubleness, of *déjà vu,* as though I have read about this subway in some science fiction novel, as though I have seen this office described in a fantasy story, far away, long ago. The real world thus becomes something science fictional to me for twenty or thirty seconds at a stretch. The textures slide; the fabric strains. Sometimes, when that has happened to me, I think it's more exciting than having a fantasy world become "real" as I read. And sometimes I think I'm coming apart.

WHILE WE WERE SLEEPING THERE had been tragedy aboard our mighty starship. Our captain, our leader, our guide for two full generations, had been murdered in his bed! "Let me see it again!" I insisted, and Timothy held out the hologram. Yes! No doubt of it! I could see the bloodstains in his thick white hair, I could see the frozen mask of anguish on his strong-featured face. Dead! The captain was dead! "What now?" I asked. "What will happen?"

"The civil war has already started on E Deck," Timothy said.

PERHAPS WHAT I REALLY FEAR is not so much a dizzying multiplicity of futures but rather the absence of futures. When I end, will the universe end? Nothingness, emptiness, the void that awaits us all, the tunnel that leads not to everywhere but to nowhere—is that the only destination? If it is, is there any reason to feel fear? Why should I fear it? Nothingness is peace. Our nada who art in nada, nada be thy name, thy kingdom nada, thy will be nada, in nada as it is in nada. Hail nothing full of nothing, nothing is with thee. That's Hemingway. He felt the nada pressing in on all sides. Hemingway never wrote a word of science fiction. Eventually he delivered himself cheerfully to the great nada with a shotgun blast.

MY FRIEND LEON REMINDS ME in some ways of Henry Darkdawn in De Soto's classic *Cosmos* trilogy. (If I said he reminded me of Stephen Dedalus or Raskolnikov or Julien Sorel, you would naturally need no further descriptions to know what I mean, but Henry Darkdawn is probably outside your range of literary experience. The De Soto trilogy deals with the formation, expansion, and decay of a quasi-religious movement spanning several galaxies in the years 30,000 to 35,000 A.D., and Darkdawn is a charismatic prophet, human but immortal or at any rate extraordinarily long-lived, who combines within himself the functions of Moses, Jesus, and St. Paul: seer, intermediary with higher powers, organizer, leader, and ultimately martyr.) What makes the series so beautiful is the way De Soto gets inside Darkdawn's character, so that he's not merely a distant bas-relief—the Prophet—but a warm, breathing human being. That is, you see him warts and all—a sophisticated concept for science fiction, which tends to run heavily to marble statues in place of living protagonists.

Leon, of course, is unlikely ever to found a galaxy-spanning cult, but he has much of the intensity that I associate with Darkdawn. Oddly, he's quite tall—six feet two, I'd say—and has conventional good looks; people of his type don't generally run to high inner voltage, I've observed. But despite his natural physical advantages something must have compressed and redirected Leon's soul when he was young, because he's a brooder, a dreamer, a fire-breather, always coming up with visionary plans for reorganizing our office, stuff like that. He's the one who usually leaves s-f magazines on my desk as gifts, but he's also the one who pokes the most fun at me for reading what he considers to be trash. You see his contradictory nature right there. He's shy and aggressive, tough and vulnerable, confident and uncertain, the whole crazy human mix, everything right up front.

Last Tuesday I had dinner at his house. I often go there. His wife Helene is a superb cook. She and I had an affair five years ago that lasted about six months. Leon knew about it after the third meeting, but he never has said a word to me. Judging by Helene's desperate ardor, she and Leon must not have a very good sexual relationship; when she was in bed with me she seemed to want everything all at once, every position, every kind of sensation, as though she had been deprived much too long. Possibly Leon was pleased that I was taking some of the sexual pressure off him, and has silently regretted that I no longer sleep with his wife. (I ended the affair because she was drawing too much energy from me and because I was having difficulties meeting Leon's frank, open gaze.)

Last Tuesday just before dinner Helene went into the kitchen to check the oven. Leon excused himself and headed for the bathroom. Alone, I stood a moment by the bookshelf, checking in my automatic way to see if they had any s-f, and then I followed Helene into the kitchen to refill my glass from the martini pitcher in the refrigerator. Suddenly she was up against me, clinging tight, her lips seeking mine. She muttered my name; she dug her fingertips into my back. "Hey," I said softly. "Wait a second! We agreed that we weren't going to start that stuff again!"

"I want you!"

"Don't, Helene." Gently I pried her free of me. "Don't complicate things. Please."

I wriggled loose. She backed away from me, head down, and sullenly went to the stove. As I turned I saw Leon in the doorway. He must have witnessed the entire scene. His dark eyes were glossy with half-suppressed tears; his lips were quivering. Without saying anything he took the pitcher from me, filled his martini glass and drank the cocktail at a gulp. Then he went into the living room, and ten minutes later we were talking office politics as though nothing had happened. Yes, Leon, you're Henry Darkdawn to the last inch. Out of such stuff as you, Leon, are prophets created. Out of such stuff as you are cosmic martyrs made.

No one could tell the difference any longer. The sleek, slippery android had totally engulfed its maker's personality.

I stood at the edge of the cliff, staring in horror at the red, swollen thing that had been the life-giving sun of Earth.

The horde of robots—

The alien spaceship, plunging in a wild spiral—

Laughing, she opened her fist. The Q-bomb lay in the center of her palm. "Ten seconds," she cried.

How warm it is tonight! A dank glove of humidity enfolds me. Sleep will not come. I feel a terrible pressure all around me. Yes! The beam of green light! At last, at last, at last! Cradling me, lifting me, floating me through the open window. High over the dark city. On and on, through the void, out of space and time. To the tunnel. Setting me down. Here. Here. Yes, exactly as I imagined it would be: the onyx walls, the sourceless dull gleam, the curving vault far overhead, the silent alien figures drifting toward me. Here. The tunnel, at last. I take the first step forward. Another. Another. I am launched on my journey.

◆

THE SECRET SHARER

When I was about seventeen I acquired a slender paperback book that contained two novellas by Joseph Conrad, my initial encounter with his work. The first story in the book was *Heart of Darkness*, which I read with something approaching awe, as well I might, since it is, I think, the finest work of that great writer (with his novel *Nostromo* not far behind). Conrad in all the succeeding decades has held a high place in my literary world; I continue to read and re-read his books, and on more than one occasion, as I discussed here earlier, I have introduced Conradian notes into work of my own, saluting *Heart of Darkness* in my novel *Downward to the Earth* and touching on a theme of *Lord Jim* in *Hot Sky at Midnight*. I have written elsewhere about the influence of Conrad on my writing, saying, "Much of what I owe to Conrad is buried deep in the substructure of my stories—a way of looking at narrative, a way of understanding character." And from time to time I have acknowledged that debt with an overt and conspicuous homage to some work of his.

The second novella in that slim paperback of long ago made a strong impression on me as well, though not quite as powerful a one as *Heart of Darkness*. That second tale was "The Secret Sharer," in which a young sea-captain, probably based on Conrad himself (who had been a captain in the British merchant marine before he took up writing) boldly takes a stowaway into his cabin and hides him there for much of the voyage that follows. Having already tackled *Heart of Darkness*, I found myself suddenly impelled in 1986 to deal with the other story in that book, I know not why. A love of symmetry? A compulsion toward completion? Anyway, I set out that year to write my own version of "The Secret Sharer."

I was appropriating much of Conrad's plot, but I made no attempt to hide what I was doing. Rather than borrowing one of his characters' names (as I had done in *Downward to the Earth*) I came straight out in the open and put his own story's title on mine. The Silverberg version of "The Secret Sharer" made use of Conrad's basic story situation, that of a ship's captain who finds a stowaway on board and is eventually drawn into a strange alliance with him. But I translated every aspect of that story situation into something that could only be told as science fiction. My stowaway (female, not male) does not actually have a physical body, but exists only in electromagnetic form. The ship she stows away on is nothing like any vessel Joseph Conrad would have commanded, and the way she stows away aboard it would have been beyond his comprehension. The starwalk scene affords visionary possibilities quite unlike those afforded by a long Conradian look into the vastnesses of the trackless Pacific. The way my stowaway eventually leaves the ship is very different from anything depicted in Conrad's maritime fiction. And so on.

The tale my captain tells is, or so I believe, not just a rewrite of Conrad but a new and unique science-fiction story set for reasons of the author's private amusement within the framework of a century-old masterpiece of the sea by the earlier and greater writer.

I sent the story to *Asimov's Science Fiction*, the leading science-fiction magazine of the day, and it was published there in the September 1988 issue. Not long afterward a reader wrote to the editor, somewhat indignantly, to ask whether Mr. Silverberg was aware that the title had been used already by Joseph Conrad.

Yes, I replied. Mr. Silverberg was aware of that.

—◦◦◦—

1.

IT WAS MY FIRST TIME to heaven and I was no one at all, no one at all, and this was the voyage that was supposed to make me someone.

But though I was no one at all I dared to look upon the million worlds and I felt a great sorrow for them. There they were all about me, humming along on their courses through the night, each of them believing it was actually going somewhere. And each one wrong, of course, for worlds go nowhere, except around and around and around, pathetic monkeys on a string, forever tethered in place. They seem to move, yes. But really they stand still. And I—I who stared at the worlds of heaven and was swept with compassion for them—I knew that though I seemed to be standing still, I was in fact moving. For I was aboard a ship of heaven, a ship of the Service, that was spanning the light-years at a speed so incomprehensibly great that it might as well have been no speed at all.

I was very young. My ship, then as now, was the *Sword of Orion*, on a journey out of Kansas Four bound for Cul-de-Sac and Strappado and Mangan's Bitch and several other worlds, via the usual spin-arounds. It was my first voyage and I was in command. I thought for a long time that I would lose my soul on that voyage; but now I know that what was happening aboard that ship was not the losing of a soul but the gaining of one. And perhaps of more than one.

2.

ROACHER THOUGHT I WAS SWEET. I could have killed him for that; but of course he was dead already.

You have to give up your life when you go to heaven. What you get in return is for me to know and you, if you care, to find out; but the inescapable thing is that you leave behind anything that ever linked you to life on shore, and you become something else.

We say that you give up the body and you get your soul. Certainly you can keep your body too, if you want it. Most do.

But it isn't any good to you any more, not in the ways that you think a body is good to you. I mean to tell you how it was for me on my first voyage aboard the *Sword of Orion*, so many years ago.

I was the youngest officer on board, so naturally I was captain.

They put you in command right at the start, before you're anyone. That's the only test that means a damn: they throw you in the sea and if you can swim you don't drown, and if you can't you do. The drowned ones go back in the tank and they serve their own useful purposes, as push-cells or downloaders or mind-wipers or Johnny-scrub-and-scour or whatever. The ones that don't drown go on to other commands. No one is wasted. The Age of Waste has been over a long time.

On the third virtual day out from Kansas Four, Roacher told me that I was the sweetest captain he had ever served under. And he had served under plenty of them, for Roacher had gone up to heaven at least two hundred years before, maybe more.

"I can see it in your eyes, the sweetness. I can see it in the angle you hold your head."

He didn't mean it as a compliment.

"We can put you off ship at Ultima Thule," Roacher said. "Nobody will hold it against you. We'll put you in a bottle and send you down, and the Thuleys will catch you and decant you and you'll be able to find your way back to Kansas Four in twenty or fifty years. It might be the best thing."

Roacher is small and parched, with brown skin and eyes that shine with the purple luminescence of space. Some of the worlds he has seen were forgotten a thousand years ago.

"Go bottle yourself, Roacher," I told him.

"Ah, captain, captain! Don't take it the wrong way. Here, captain, give us a touch of the sweetness." He reached out a claw, trying to stroke me along the side of my face. "Give us a touch, captain, give us just a little touch!"

"I'll fry your soul and have it for breakfast, Roacher. There's sweetness for you. Go scuttle off, will you? Go jack yourself to the mast and drink hydrogen, Roacher. Go. Go."

"So sweet," he said. But he went. I had the power to hurt him. He knew I could do it, because I was captain. He also knew I wouldn't; but there was always the possibility he was wrong. The captain exists in that margin between certainty and possibility. A crewman tests the width of that margin at his own risk. Roacher knew that. He had been a captain once himself, after all.

There were seventeen of us to heaven that voyage, staffing a ten-kilo Megaspore-class ship with full annexes and extensions and all virtualities. We carried a bulging cargo of the things regarded in those days as vital in the distant colonies: pre-read vapor chips, artificial intelligences, climate nodes, matrix jacks, mediq machines, bone banks, soil converters, transit spheres, communication bubbles, skin-and-organ synthesizers, wildlife domestication plaques, gene replacement kits, a sealed consignment of obliteration sand and other proscribed weapons, and so on. We also had fifty billion dollars in the form of liquid currency pods, central-bank-to-central-bank transmission. In addition there was a passenger load of seven thousand colonists. Eight hundred of these were on the hoof and the others were stored in matrix form for body transplant on the worlds of destination. A standard load, in other words. The crew worked on commission, also as per standard, one percent of bill-of-lading value divided in customary lays. Mine was the 50th lay—that is, two percent of the net profits of the voyage—and that included a bonus for serving as captain; otherwise I would have had the 100th lay or something even longer.

Roacher had the 10th lay and his jackmate Bulgar the 14th, although they weren't even officers. Which demonstrates the value of seniority in the Service. But seniority is the same thing as survival, after all, and why should survival not be rewarded? On my most recent voyage I drew the 19th lay. I will have better than that on my next.

3.

YOU HAVE NEVER SEEN A starship. We keep only to heaven; when we are to worldward, shoreships come out to us for the downloading. The closest we ever go to planetskin is a million shiplengths. Any closer and we'd be shaken apart by that terrible strength which emanates from worlds.

We don't miss landcrawling, though. It's a plague to us. If I had to step to shore now, after having spent most of my lifetime in heaven, I would die of the drop-death within an hour. That is a monstrous way to die; but why would I ever go ashore? The likelihood of that still existed for me at the time I first sailed the *Sword of Orion*, you understand, but I have long since given it up. That is what I mean when I say that you give up your life when you go to heaven. But of course what also goes from you is any feeling that to be ashore has anything to do with being alive. If you could ride a starship, or even see one as we see them, you would understand. I don't blame you for being what you are.

Let me show you the *Sword of Orion*. Though you will never see it as we see it.

What would you see, if you left the ship as we sometimes do to do the starwalk in the Great Open?

The first thing you would see was the light of the ship. A starship gives off a tremendous insistent glow of light that splits heaven like the blast of a trumpet. That great light both precedes and follows. Ahead of the ship rides a luminescent cone of brightness bellowing in the void. In its wake the ship leaves a photonic track so intense that it could be gathered up and weighed. It is the stardrive that issues this light: a ship eats space, and light is its offthrow.

Within the light you would see a needle ten kilometers long. That is the ship. One end tapers to a sharp point and the other has the Eye, and it is several days' journey by foot from end to end through all the compartments that lie between. It is a world self-contained. The needle is a flattened one. You could walk about easily on the outer surface of the ship, the skin of the top deck, what we call Skin Deck. Or just as easily on Belly Deck, the one on the bottom side. We call one the top deck and the other the bottom, but when you are outside the ship these distinctions have no meaning. Between Skin and Belly lie Crew Deck, Passenger Deck, Cargo Deck, Drive Deck. Ordinarily no one goes from one deck to another. We stay where we belong. The engines are in the Eye. So are the captain's quarters.

That needle is the ship, but it is not the whole ship. What you will not be able to see are the annexes and extensions and virtualities. These accompany the ship, enfolding it in a webwork of intricate outstructures. But they are of a subordinate level of reality and therefore they defy vision. A ship tunnels into the void, spreading far and wide to find room for all that it must carry. In these outlying zones are kept our supplies and provisions, our stores of fuel, and all cargo traveling at second-class rates. If the ship transports prisoners, they will ride in an annex. If the ship expects to encounter severe probability turbulence during the course of the voyage, it will arm itself with stabilizers, and those will be carried in the virtualities, ready to be brought into being if needed. These are the mysteries of our profession. Take them on faith, or ignore them, as you will: they are not meant for you to know.

A ship takes forty years to build. There are two hundred seventy-one of them in service now. New ones are constantly under construction. They are the only link binding the Mother Worlds and the eight hundred ninety-eight Colonies and the colonies of the Colonies. Four ships have been lost since the beginning of the Service. No one knows why. The loss of a starship is the worst disaster I can imagine. The last such event occurred sixty virtual years ago.

A starship never returns to the world from which it was launched. The galaxy is too large for that. It makes its voyage and it continues onward through heaven in an endless open circuit. That is the service of the Service. There would be no point in returning, since thousands of worldward years sweep by behind us as we make our voyages. We live outside of time. We must, for there is no other way. That is our burden and our privilege. That is the service of the Service.

4.

ON THE FIFTH VIRTUAL DAY of the voyage I suddenly felt a tic, a nibble, a subtle indication that something had gone wrong. It was a very trifling thing, barely perceptible, like the scatter of eroded pebbles that tells you that the palaces and towers of a great ruined city lie buried beneath the mound on which you climb. Unless you are looking for such signals you will not see them. But I was primed for discovery that day. I was eager for it. A strange kind of joy came over me when I picked up that fleeting signal of wrongness.

I keyed the intelligence on duty and said, "What was that tremor on Passenger Deck?"

The intelligence arrived instantly in my mind, a sharp gray-green presence with a halo of tingling music.

"I am aware of no tremor, sir."

"There was a distinct tremor. There was a data-spurt just now."

"Indeed, sir? A data-spurt, sir?" The intelligence sounded aghast, but in a condescending way. It was humoring me. "What action shall I take, sir?"

I was being invited to retreat.

The intelligence on duty was a 49 Henry Henry. The Henry series affects a sort of slippery innocence that I find disingenuous. Still, they are very capable intelligences. I wondered if I had mis-read the signal. Perhaps I was too eager for an event, any event, that would confirm my relationship with the ship.

There is never a sense of motion or activity aboard a starship: we float in silence on a tide of darkness, cloaked in our own daz-zling light. Nothing moves, nothing seems to live in all the uni-verse. Since we had left Kansas Four I had felt that great silence judging me. Was I really captain of this vessel? Good: then let me feel the weight of duty upon my shoulders.

We were past Ultima Thule by this time, and there could be no turning back. Borne on our cloak of light, we would roar through heaven for week after virtual week until we came to worldward at the first of our destinations, which was Cul-de-Sac in the Vainglory Archipelago, out by the Spook Clusters. Here in free space I must begin to master the ship, or it would master me.

"Sir?" the intelligence said.

"Run a data uptake," I ordered. "All Passenger Deck input for the past half hour. There was movement. There was a spurt."

I knew I might be wrong. Still, to err on the side of caution may be naïve, but it isn't a sin. And I knew that at this stage in the voyage nothing I could say or do would make me seem other than naïve to the crew of the *Sword of Orion*. What did I have to lose by ordering a recheck, then? I was hungry for surprises. Any irregularity that 49 Henry Henry turned up would be to my advantage; the absence of one would make nothing worse for me.

"Begging your pardon, sir," 49 Henry Henry reported after a moment, "but there was no tremor, sir."

"Maybe I overstated it, then. Calling it a tremor. Maybe it was just an anomaly. What do you say, 49 Henry Henry?" I wondered if I was humiliating myself, negotiating like this with an intelligence. "There was something. I'm sure of that. An unmistakable irregular burst in the data-flow. An anomaly, yes. What do you say, 49 Henry Henry?"

"Yes, sir."

"Yes what?"

"The record does show an irregularity, sir. Your observation was quite acute, sir."

"Go on."

"No cause for alarm, sir. A minor metabolic movement, nothing more. Like turning over in your sleep." You bastard, what do you know about sleep? "Extremely unusual, sir, that you should be able to observe anything so small. I commend you, sir. The passengers are all well, sir."

"Very good," I said. "Enter this exchange in the log, 49 Henry Henry."

"Already entered, sir," the intelligence said. "Permission to decouple, sir?"

"Yes, you can decouple," I told it.

The shimmer of music that signalled its presence grew tinny and was gone. I could imagine it smirking as it went about its ghostly flitting rounds deep in the neural conduits of the ship. Scornful software, glowing with contempt for its putative master. The poor captain, it was thinking. The poor hopeless silly boy of a captain. A passenger sneezes and he's ready to seal all bulkheads.

Well, let it smirk, I thought. I have acted appropriately and the record will show it.

I knew that all this was part of my testing.

You may think that to be captain of such a ship as the *Sword of Orion* in your first voyage to heaven is an awesome responsibility and an inconceivable burden. So it is, but not for the reason you think.

In truth the captain's duties are the least significant of anyone's aboard the ship. The others have well-defined tasks that are essential to the smooth running of the voyage, although the ship could, if the need arose, generate virtual replacements for any and every crew member and function adequately on its own. The captain's task, though, is fundamentally abstract. His role is to witness the voyage, to embody it in his own consciousness, to give it coherence, continuity, by reducing it to a pattern of decisions and responses. In that sense the captain is simply so much software: he is the coding through which the voyage is expressed as a series of linear functions. If he fails to perform that duty adequately, others will quietly see to it that the voyage proceeds as it should. What is destroyed, in the course of a voyage that is inadequately captained, is the captain himself, not the voyage. My pre-flight training made that absolutely clear. The voyage can survive the most feeble of captains. As I have said, four starships have been lost since the Service began, and no one knows why. But there is no reason to think that any of those catastrophes were caused by failings of the captain. How could they have been? The captain is only the vehicle through which others act. It is not the captain who makes the voyage, but the voyage which makes the captain.

5.

RESTLESS, TROUBLED, I WANDERED THE eye of the ship. Despite 49 Henry Henry's suave mockery I was still convinced there was trouble on board, or about to be.

Just as I reached Outerscreen Level I felt something strange touch me a second time. It was different this time, and deeply disturbing.

The Eye, as it makes the complete descent from Skin Deck to Belly Deck, is lined with screens that provide displays, actual or virtual, of all aspects of the ship both internal and external. I came up to the great black bevel-edged screen that provided our simulated view of the external realspace environment and was staring at the dwindling wheel of the Ultima Thule relay point when the new anomaly occurred. The other had been the merest of subliminal signals, a nip, a tickle. This was more like an attempted intrusion. Invisible fingers seemed to brush lightly over my brain, probing, seeking entrance. The fingers withdrew; a moment later there was a sudden stabbing pain in my left temple.

I stiffened. "Who's there?"

"Help me," a silent voice said.

I had heard wild tales of passenger matrixes breaking free of their storage circuits and drifting through the ship like ghosts, looking for an unguarded body that they might infiltrate. The sources were unreliable, old scoundrels like Roacher or Bulgar. I dismissed such stories as fables, the way I dismissed what I had heard of the vast tentacular krakens that were said to swim the seas of space, or the beckoning mermaids with shining breasts who danced along the force-lines at spinaround points. But I had felt this. The probing fingers, the sudden sharp pain. And the sense of someone frightened, frightened but strong, stronger than I, hovering close at hand.

"Where are you?"

There was no reply. Whatever it was, if it had been anything at all, had slipped back into hiding after that one furtive thrust.

But was it really gone?

"You're still here somewhere," I said. "I know that you are."

Silence. Stillness.

"You asked for help. Why did you disappear so fast?"

No response. I felt anger rising.

"Whoever you are. Whatever. Speak up."

Nothing. Silence. Had I imagined it? The probing, the voiceless voice?

No. No. I was certain that there was something invisible and unreal hovering about me. And I found it infuriating, not to be able to regain contact with it. To be toyed with this way, to be mocked like this.

This is my ship, I thought. I want no ghosts aboard my ship.

"You can be detected," I said. "You can be contained. You can be eradicated."

As I stood there blustering in my frustration, it seemed to me that I felt that touch against my mind again, a lighter one this time, wistful, regretful. Perhaps I invented it. Perhaps I have supplied it retroactively.

But it lasted only a part of an instant, if it happened at all, and then I was unquestionably alone again. The solitude was real and total and unmistakable. I stood gripping the rail of the screen, leaning forward into the brilliant blackness and swaying dizzily as if I were being pulled forward through the wall of the ship into space.

"Captain?"

The voice of 49 Henry Henry, tumbling out of the air behind me.

"Did you feel something that time?" I asked.

The intelligence ignored my question. "Captain, there's trouble on Passenger Deck. Hands-on alarm: will you come?"

"Set up a transit track for me," I said. "I'm on my way."

Lights began to glow in mid-air, yellow, blue, green. The interior of the ship is a vast opaque maze and moving about within it is difficult without an intelligence to guide you. 49 Henry Henry constructed an efficient route for me down the curve of the Eye and into the main body of the ship, and thence around the rim of the leeward wall to the elevator down to Passenger Deck. I rode an air-cushion tracker keyed to the lights. The journey took no more than fifteen minutes. Unaided I might have needed a week.

Passenger Deck is an echoing nest of coffins, hundreds of them, sometimes even thousands, arranged in rows three abreast. Here our live cargo sleeps until we arrive and decant the stored sleepers into wakefulness. Machinery sighs and murmurs all around them, coddling them in their suspension. Beyond, far off in the dim distance, is the place for passengers of a different sort—a spiderwebbing of sensory cables that holds our thousands of disembodied matrixes. Those are the colonists who have left their bodies behind when going into space. It is a dark and forbidding place, dimly lit by swirling velvet comets that circle overhead emitting sparks of red and green.

The trouble was in the suspension area. Five crewmen were there already, the oldest hands on board: Katkat, Dismas, Rio de Rio, Gavotte, Roacher. Seeing them all together, I knew this must be some major event. We move on distant orbits within the immensity of the ship: to see as many as three members of the crew in the same virtual month is extraordinary. Now here were five. I felt an oppressive sense of community among them. Each of these five had sailed the seas of heaven more years than I had been alive. For at least a dozen voyages now they had been together as a team. I was the stranger in their midst, unknown, untried, lightly regarded, insignificant. Already Roacher had indicted me for my sweetness, by which he meant, I knew, a basic incapacity to act decisively. I thought he was wrong. But perhaps he knew me better than I knew myself.

They stepped back, opening a path between them. Gavotte, a great hulking thick-shouldered man with a surprisingly delicate and precise way of conducting himself, gestured with open hands: Here, captain, see? See?

What I saw were coils of greenish smoke coming up from a passenger housing, and the glass door of the housing half open, cracked from top to bottom, frosted by temperature differentials. I could hear a sullen dripping sound. Blue fluid fell in thick steady gouts from a shattered support line. Within the housing itself was the pale naked figure of a man, eyes wide open, mouth agape as if in a silent scream. His left arm was raised, his fist was clenched. He looked like an anguished statue.

They had body-salvage equipment standing by. The hapless passenger would be disassembled and all usable parts stored as soon as I gave the word.

"Is he irretrievable?" I asked.

"Take a look," Katkat said, pointing to the housing readout. All the curves pointed down. "We have nineteen percent degradation already, and rising. Do we disassemble?"

"Go ahead," I said. "Approved."

The lasers glinted and flailed. Body parts came into view, shining, moist. The coiling metallic arms of the body-salvage equipment rose and fell, lifting organs that were not yet beyond repair and putting them into storage. As the machine labored the men worked around it, shutting down the broken housing, tying off the disrupted feeders and refrigerator cables.

I asked Dismas what had happened. He was the mind-wiper for this sector, responsible for maintenance on the suspended passengers. His face was open and easy, but the deceptive cheeriness about his mouth and cheeks was mysteriously negated by his bleak, shadowy eyes. He told me that he had been working much farther down the deck, performing routine service on the Strappado-bound people, when he felt a sudden small disturbance, a quick tickle of wrongness.

"So did I," I said. "How long ago was that?"

"Half an hour, maybe. I didn't make a special note of it. I thought it was something in my gut, captain. You felt it too, you say?"

I nodded. "Just a tickle. It's in the record." I heard the distant music of 49 Henry Henry. Perhaps the intelligence was trying to apologize for doubting me. "What happened next?" I asked.

"Went back to work. Five, ten minutes, maybe. Felt another jolt, a stronger one." He touched his forehead, right at the temple, showing me where. "Detectors went off, broken glass. Came running, found this Cul-de-Sac passenger here undergoing convulsions. Rising from his bindings, thrashing around. Pulled himself loose from everything, went smack against the housing window. Broke it. It's a very fast death."

"Matrix intrusion," Roacher said.

The skin of my scalp tightened. I turned to him.

"Tell me about that."

He shrugged. "Once in a long while someone in the storage circuits gets to feeling footloose, and finds a way out and goes roaming the ship. Looking for a body to jack into, that's what they're doing. Jack into me, jack into Katkat, even jack into you, captain. Anybody handy, just so they can feel flesh around them again. Jacked into this one here and something went wrong."

The probing fingers, yes. The silent voice. *Help me.*

"I never heard of anyone jacking into a passenger in suspension," Dismas said.

"No reason why not," said Roacher.

"What's the good? Still stuck in a housing, you are. Frozen down, that's no better than staying matrix."

"Five to two it was matrix intrusion," Roacher said, glaring.

"Done," Dismas said. Gavotte laughed and came in on the bet. So too did sinuous little Katkat, taking the other side. Rio de Rio, who had not spoken a word to anyone in his last six voyages, snorted and gestured obscenely at both factions.

I felt like an idle spectator. To regain some illusion of command I said, "If there's a matrix loose, it'll show up on ship inventory. Dismas, check with the intelligence on duty and report to me. Katkat, Gavotte, finish cleaning up this mess and seal everything off. Then I want your reports in the log and a copy to me. I'll be in my quarters. There'll be further instructions later. The missing matrix, if that's what we have on our hands, will be identified, located, and recaptured."

Roacher grinned at me. I thought he was going to lead a round of cheers.

I turned and mounted my tracker, and rode it following the lights, yellow, blue, green, back up through the maze of decks and out to the Eye.

As I entered my cabin something touched my mind and a silent voice said, "Please help me."

6.

CAREFULLY I SHUT THE DOOR behind me, locked it, loaded the privacy screens. The captain's cabin aboard a Megaspore starship of the Service is a world in itself, serene, private, immense. In mine, spiral galaxies whirled and sparkled on the walls. I had a stream, a lake, a silver waterfall beyond it. The air was soft and glistening. At a touch of my hand I could have light, music, scent, color, from any one of a thousand hidden orifices. Or I could turn the walls translucent and let the luminous splendor of starspace come flooding through.

Only when I was fully settled in, protected and insulated and comfortable, did I say, "All right. What are you?"

"You promise you won't report me to the captain?"

"I don't promise anything."

"You will help me, though?" The voice seemed at once frightened and insistent, urgent and vulnerable.

"How can I say? You give me nothing to work with."

"I'll tell you everything. But first you have to promise not to call the captain."

I debated with myself for a moment and opted for directness.

"I am the captain," I said.

"No!"

"Can you see this room? What do you think it is? Crew quarters? The scullery?"

I felt turbulent waves of fear coming from my invisible companion. And then nothing. Was it gone? Then I had made a mistake in being so forthright. This phantom had to be confined, sealed away, perhaps destroyed, before it could do more damage. I should have been more devious. And also I knew that I would regret it in another way if it had slipped away: I was taking a certain pleasure in being able to speak with someone—something— that was neither a member of my crew nor an omnipotent, contemptuous artificial intelligence.

"Are you still here?" I asked after a while.

Silence.

Gone, I thought. Sweeping through the *Sword of Orion* like a gale of wind. Probably down at the far end of the ship by this time.

Then, as if there had been no break in the conversation: "I just can't believe it. Of all the places I could have gone, I had to walk right into the captain's cabin."

"So it seems."

"And you're actually the captain?"

"Yes. Actually."

Another pause.

"You seem so young," it said. "For a captain."

"Be careful," I told it.

"I didn't mean anything by that, captain." With a touch of bravado, even defiance, mingling with uncertainty and anxiety. "Captain, *sir*."

Looking toward the ceiling, where shining resonator nodes shimmered all up and down the spectrum as slave-light leaped from junction to junction along the illuminator strands, I searched for a glimpse of it, some minute electromagnetic clue. But there was nothing.

I imagined a web of impalpable force, a dancing will-o'-the-wisp, flitting erratically about the room, now perching on my shoulder, now clinging to some fixture, now extending itself to fill every open space: an airy thing, a sprite, playful and capricious. Curiously, not only was I unafraid but I found myself strongly drawn to it. There was something strangely appealing about this quick vibrating spirit, so bright with contradictions. And yet it had caused the death of one of my passengers.

"Well?" I said. "You're safe here. But when are you going to tell me what you are?"

"Isn't that obvious? I'm a matrix."

"Go on."

"A free matrix, a matrix on the loose. A matrix who's in big trouble. I think I've hurt someone. Maybe killed him."

"One of the passengers?" I said.

"So you know?"

"There's a dead passenger, yes. We're not sure what happened."

"It wasn't my fault. It was an accident."

"That may be," I said. "Tell me about it. Tell me everything."

"Can I trust you?"

"More than anyone else on this ship."

"But you're the captain."

"That's why," I said.

7.

HER NAME WAS LEELEAINE, BUT she wanted me to call her Vox. That means "voice," she said, in one of the ancient languages of Earth. She was seventeen years old, from Jaana Head, which is an island off the coast of West Palabar on Kansas Four. Her father was a glass-farmer, her mother operated a gravity hole, and she had five brothers and three sisters, all of them much older than she was.

"Do you know what that's like, captain? Being the youngest of nine? And both your parents working all the time, and your cross-parents just as busy? Can you imagine? And growing up on Kansas Four, where it's a thousand kilometers between cities, and you aren't even in a city, you're on an *island?*"

"I know something of what that's like," I said.

"Are you from Kansas Four too?"

"No," I said. "Not from Kansas Four. But a place much like it, I think."

She spoke of a troubled, unruly childhood, full of loneliness and anger. Kansas Four, I have heard, is a beautiful world, if you are inclined to find beauty in worlds: a wild and splendid place, where the sky is scarlet and the bare basalt mountains rise in the east like a magnificent black wall. But to hear Vox speak of it, it was squalid, grim, bleak. For her it was a loveless place where she led a loveless life. And yet she told me of pale violet seas aglow with brilliant yellow fish, and trees that erupted with a shower of dazzling crimson fronds when they were in bloom, and warm rains that sang in the air like harps. I was not then so long in heaven that I had forgotten the beauty of seas or trees or rains, which by now are nothing but hollow words to me. Yet Vox had found her life on Kansas Four so hateful that she had been willing to abandon not only her native world but her body itself. That was a point of kinship between us: I too had given up my world and my former life, if not my actual flesh. But I had chosen heaven, and the Service.

Vox had volunteered to exchange one landcrawling servitude for another.

"The day came," she said, "when I knew I couldn't stand it anymore. I was so miserable, so empty: I thought about having to live this way for another two hundred years or even more, and I wanted to pick up the hills and throw them at each other. Or get into my mother's plummeter and take it straight to the bottom of the sea. I made a list of ways I could kill myself. But I knew I couldn't do it, not this way or that way or any way. I wanted to live. But I didn't want to live like *that*."

On that same day, she said, the soul-call from Cul-de-Sac reached Kansas Four. A thousand vacant bodies were available there and they wanted soul-matrixes to fill them. Without a moment's hesitation Vox put her name on the list.

There is a constant migration of souls between the worlds. On each of my voyages I have carried thousands of them, setting forth hopefully toward new bodies on strange planets.

Every world has a stock of bodies awaiting replacement souls. Most were the victims of sudden violence. Life is risky on shore, and death lurks everywhere. Salvaging and repairing a body is no troublesome matter, but once a soul has fled it can never be recovered. So the empty bodies of those who drown and those who are stung by lethal insects and those who are thrown from vehicles and those who are struck by falling branches as they work are collected and examined. If they are beyond repair they are disassembled and their usable parts set aside to be installed in others. But if their bodies can be made whole again, they are, and they are placed in holding chambers until new souls become available for them.

And then there are those who vacate their bodies voluntarily, perhaps because they are weary of them, or weary of their worlds, and wish to move along. They are the ones who sign up to fill the waiting bodies on far worlds, while others come behind them to fill the bodies they have abandoned. The least costly way to travel between the worlds is to surrender your body and go in matrix form, thus exchanging a discouraging life for an unfamiliar one. That was what Vox had done. In pain and despair she had agreed to allow the essence of herself, everything she had ever seen or felt or thought or dreamed, to be converted into a lattice of electrical impulses that the *Sword of Orion* would carry on its voyage from Kansas Four to Cul-de-Sac. A new body lay reserved for her there.

Her own discarded body would remain in suspension on Kansas Four. Some day it might become the home of some wandering soul from another world; or, if there were no bids for it, it might eventually be disassembled by the body-salvagers, and its parts put to some worthy use. Vox would never know; Vox would never care.

"I can understand trading an unhappy life for a chance at a happy one," I said. "But why break loose on ship? What purpose could that serve? Why not wait until you got to Cul-de-Sac?"

"Because it was torture," she said.

"Torture? What was?"

"Living as a matrix." She laughed bitterly. "Living? It's worse than death could ever be!"

"Tell me."

"You've never done matrix, have you?"

"No," I said. "I chose another way to escape."

"Then you don't know. You can't know. You've got a ship full of matrixes in storage circuits but you don't understand a thing about them. Imagine that the back of your neck itches, captain. But you have no arms to scratch with. Your thigh starts to itch. Your chest. You lie there itching everywhere. And you can't scratch. Do you understand me?"

"How can a matrix feel an itch? A matrix is simply a pattern of electrical—"

"Oh, you're impossible! You're *stupid!* I'm not talking about actual literal itching. I'm giving you a suppose, a for-instance.

Because you'd never be able to understand the real situation. Look: you're in the storage circuit. All you are is electricity. That's all a mind really is, anyway: electricity. But you used to have a body. The body had sensation. The body had feelings. You remember them. You're a prisoner. A prisoner remembers all sorts of things that used to be taken for granted. You'd give anything to feel the wind in your hair again, or the taste of cool milk, or the scent of flowers. Or even the pain of a cut finger. The saltiness of your blood when you lick the cut. Anything. I hated my body, don't you see? I couldn't wait to be rid of it. But once it was gone I missed the feelings it had. I missed the sense of flesh pulling at me, holding me to the ground, flesh full of nerves, flesh that could feel pleasure. Or pain."

"I understand," I said, and I think that I truly did. "But the voyage to Cul-de-Sac is short. A few virtual weeks and you'd be there, and out of storage and into your new body, and—"

"Weeks? Think of that itch on the back of your neck, Captain. The itch that you can't scratch. How long do you think you could stand it, lying there feeling that itch? Five minutes? An hour? *Weeks?*"

It seemed to me that an itch left unscratched would die of its own, perhaps in minutes. But that was only how it seemed to me. I was not Vox; I had not been a matrix in a storage circuit.

I said, "So you let yourself out? How?"

"It wasn't that hard to figure. I had nothing else to do but think about it. You align yourself with the polarity of the circuit. That's a matrix too, an electrical pattern holding you in crosswise bands. You change the alignment. It's like being tied up, and slipping the ropes around until you can slide free. And then you can go anywhere you like. You key into any bioprocessor aboard the ship and you draw your energy from that instead of from the storage circuit, and it sustains you. I can move anywhere around this ship at the speed of light. Anywhere. In just the time you blinked your eye, I've been everywhere. I've been to the far tip and out on the mast, and I've been down through the lower decks, and I've been in the crew quarters and the cargo places and I've even been a little way off into something that's right out-side the ship but isn't quite real, if you know what I mean. Something that just seems to be a cradle of probability waves sur-rounding us. It's like being a ghost. But it doesn't solve anything. Do you see? The torture still goes on. You want to feel, but you can't. You want to be connected again, your senses, your inputs. That's why I tried to get into the passenger, do you see? But he wouldn't let me."

I began to understand at last.

Not everyone who goes to the worlds of heaven as a colonist travels in matrix form. Ordinarily anyone who can afford to take his body with him will do so; but relatively few can afford it. Those who do travel in suspension, the deepest of sleeps. We carry no waking passengers in the Service, not at any price. They would be trouble for us, poking here, poking there, asking questions, demanding to be served and pampered. They would shatter the peace of the voyage. And so they go down into their coffins, their housings, and there they sleep the voyage away, all life-processes halted, a death-in-life that will not be reversed until we bring them to their destinations.

And poor Vox, freed of her prisoning circuit and hungry for sensory data, had tried to slip herself into a passenger's body.

I listened, appalled and somber, as she told of her terrible odys-sey through the ship. Breaking free of the circuit: that had been the first strangeness I felt, that tic, that nibble at the threshold of my consciousness.

Her first wild moment of freedom had been exhilarating and joyous. But then had come the realization that nothing really had changed. She was at large, but still she was incorporeal, caught in that monstrous frustration of bodilessness, yearning for a touch. Perhaps such torment was common among matrixes; perhaps that was why, now and then, they broke free as Vox had done, to roam ships like sad troubled spirits. So Roacher had said. *Once in a long while someone in the storage circuits gets to feeling footloose, and finds a way out and goes roaming the ship. Looking for a body to jack into, that's what they're doing. Jack into me, jack into Katkat, even jack into you, captain. Anybody handy, just so they can feel flesh around them again.* Yes.

That was the second jolt, the stronger one, that Dismas and I had felt, when Vox, selecting a passenger at random, suddenly, impulsively, had slipped herself inside his brain. She had realized her mistake at once. The passenger, lost in whatever dreams may come to the suspended, reacted to her intrusion with wild terror. Convulsions swept him; he rose, clawing at the equipment that sustained his life, trying desperately to evict the succubus that had penetrated him. In this frantic struggle he smashed the case of his housing and died. Vox, fleeing, frightened, careened about the ship in search of refuge, encountered me standing by the screen in the Eye, and made an abortive attempt to enter my mind. But just then the death of the passenger registered on 49 Henry Henry's sensors and when the intelligence made contact with me to tell me of the emergency Vox fled again, and hovered dolefully until I returned to my cabin. She had not meant to kill the passenger, she said. She was sorry that he had died. She felt some embarrassment, now, and fear. But no guilt. She rejected guilt for it almost defiantly. He had died? Well, so he had died. That was too bad. But how could she have known any such thing was going to happen? She was only looking for a body to take refuge in. Hearing that from her, I had a sense of her as someone utterly unlike me, someone volatile, unstable, perhaps violent. And yet I felt a strange kinship with her, even an identity. As though we were two parts of the same spirit; as though she and I were one and the same. I barely understood why.

"And what now?" I asked. "You say you want help. How?"

"Take me in."

"What?"

"Hide me. In you. If they find me, they'll eradicate me. You said so yourself, that it could be done, that I could be detected, contained, eradicated. But it won't happen if you protect me."

"I'm the *captain*," I said, astounded.

"Yes."

"How can I—"

"They'll all be looking for me. The intelligences, the crewmen. It scares them, knowing there's a matrix loose. They'll want to destroy me. But if they can't find me, they'll start to forget about me after a while. They'll think I've escaped into space, or something. And if I'm jacked into you, nobody's going to be able to find me."

"I have a responsibility to—"

"Please," she said. "I could go to one of the others, maybe. But I feel closest to you. Please. Please."

"Closest to me?"

"You aren't happy. You don't belong. Not here, not anywhere. You don't fit in, any more than I did on Kansas Four. I could feel it the moment I first touched your mind. You're a new captain, right? And the others on board are making it hard for you. Why should you care about *them*? Save me. We have more in common than you do with them. Please? You can't just let them eradicate me. I'm young. I didn't mean to hurt anyone. All I want is to get to Cul-de-Sac and be put in the body that's waiting for me there. A new start, my first start, really. Will you?"

"Why do you bother asking permission? You can simply enter me through my jack whenever you want, can't you?"

"The last one died," she said.

"He was in suspension. You didn't kill him by entering him. It was the surprise, the fright. He killed himself by thrashing around and wrecking his housing."

"Even so," said Vox. "I wouldn't try that again, an unwilling host. You have to say you'll let me, or I won't come in."

I was silent.

"Help me?" she said.

"Come," I told her.

8.

IT WAS JUST LIKE ANY other jacking: an electrochemical mind-to-mind bond, a linkage by way of the implant socket at the base of my spine. The sort of thing that any two people who wanted to make communion might do. There was just one difference, which was that we didn't use a jack. We skipped the whole intricate business of checking bandwiths and voltages and selecting the right transformer-adapter. She could do it all, simply by matching evoked potentials. I felt a momentary sharp sensation and then she was with me.

"Breathe," she said. "Breathe real deep. Fill your lungs. Rub your hands together. Touch your cheeks. Scratch behind your left ear. Please. Please. It's been so long for me since I've felt anything."

Her voice sounded the same as before, both real and unreal. There was no substance to it, no density of timbre, no sense that it was produced by the vibrations of vocal cords atop a column of air. Yet it was clear, firm, substantial in some essential way, a true voice in all respects except that there was no speaker to utter it. I suppose that while she was outside me she had needed to extend some strand of herself into my neural system in order to generate it. Now that was unnecessary. But I still perceived the voice as originating outside me, even though she had taken up residence within.

She overflowed with needs.

"Take a drink of water," she urged. "Eat something. Can you make your knuckles crack? Do it, oh, do it! Put your hand between your legs and squeeze. There's so much I want to feel. Do you have music here? Give me some music, will you? Something loud, something really hard."

I did the things she wanted. Gradually she grew more calm.

I was strangely calm myself. I had no special awareness then of her presence within me, no unfamiliar pressure in my skull, no slitherings along my spine. There was no mingling of her thought-stream and mine. She seemed not to have any way of controlling the movements or responses of my body. In these respects our contact was less intimate than any ordinary human jacking communion would have been. But that, I would soon discover, was by her choice. We would not remain so carefully compartmentalized for long.

"Is it better for you now?" I asked.

"I thought I was going to go crazy. If I didn't start feeling something again soon."

"You can feel things now?"

"Through you, yes. Whatever you touch, I touch."

"You know I can't hide you for long. They'll take my command away if I'm caught harboring a fugitive. Or worse."

"You don't have to speak out loud to me any more," she said.

"I don't understand."

"Just *send* it. We have the same nervous system now."

"You can read my thoughts?" I said, still aloud.

"Not really. I'm not hooked into the higher cerebral centers. But I pick up motor, sensory stuff. And I get subvocalizations. You know what those are? I can hear your thoughts if you want me to. It's like being in communion. You've been in communion, haven't you?"

"Once in a while."

"Then you know. Just open the channel to me. You can't go around the ship talking out loud to somebody invisible, you know. *Send* me something. It isn't hard."

"Like this?" I said, visualizing a packet of verbal information sliding through the channels of my mind.

"You see? You can do it!"

"Even so," I told her. "You still can't stay like this with me for long. You have to realize that."

She laughed. It was unmistakable, a silent but definite laugh. "You sound so serious. I bet you're still surprised you took me in in the first place."

"I certainly am. Did you think I would?"

"Sure I did. From the first moment. You're basically a very kind person."

"Am I, Vox?"

"Of course. You just have to let yourself do it." Again the silent laughter. "I don't even know your name. Here I am right inside your head and I don't know your name."

"Adam."

"That's a nice name. Is that an Earth name?"

"An old Earth name, yes. Very old."

"And are you from Earth?" she asked.

"No. Except in the sense that we're all from Earth."

"Where, then?"

"I'd just as soon not talk about it," I said.

She thought about that. "You hated the place where you grew up that much?"

"Please, Vox—"

"Of course you hated it. Just like I hated Kansas Four. We're two of a kind, you and me. We're one and the same. You got all the caution and I got all the impulsiveness. But otherwise we're the same person. That's why we share so well. I'm glad I'm sharing with you, Adam. You won't make me leave, will you? We belong with each other. You'll let me stay until we reach Cul-de-Sac. I know you will."

"Maybe. Maybe not." I wasn't at all sure, either way.

"Oh, you will. You will, Adam. I know you better than you know yourself."

9.

So IT BEGAN. I WAS in some new realm outside my established sense of myself, so far beyond my notions of appropriate behavior that I could not even feel astonishment at what I had done. I had taken her in, that was all. A stranger in my skull. She had turned to me in appeal and I had taken her in. It was as if her recklessness was contagious. And though I didn't mean to shelter her any longer than was absolutely necessary, I could already see that I wasn't going to make any move to eject her until her safety was assured.

But how was I going to hide her?

Invisible she might be, but not undetectable. And everyone on the ship would be searching for her.

There were sixteen crewmen on board who dreaded a loose matrix as they would a vampire. They would seek her as long as she remained at large. And not only the crew. The intelligences would be monitoring for her too, not out of any kind of fear but simply out of efficiency: they had nothing to fear from Vox but they would want the cargo manifests to come out in balance when we reached our destination.

The crew didn't trust me in the first place. I was too young, too new, too green, too *sweet*. I was just the sort who might be guilty of giving shelter to a secret fugitive. And it was altogether likely that her presence within me would be obvious to others in some way not apparent to me. As for the intelligences, they had access to all sorts of data as part of their routine maintenance operations. Perhaps they could measure tiny physiological changes, differences in my reaction times or circulatory efficiency or whatever, that would be a tipoff to the truth. How would I know? I would have to be on constant guard against discovery of the secret sharer of my consciousness.

The first test came less than an hour after Vox had entered me. The communicator light went on and I heard the far-off music of the intelligence on duty.

This one was 612 Jason, working the late shift. Its aura was golden, its music deep and throbbing. Jasons tend to be more brusque and less condescending than the Henry series, and in general I prefer them. But it was terrifying now to see that light, to hear that music, to know that the ship's intelligence wanted to speak with me. I shrank back at a tense awkward angle, the way one does when trying to avoid a face-to-face confrontation with someone.

But of course the intelligence had no face to confront. The intelligence was only a voice speaking to me out of a speaker grid, and a stew of magnetic impulses somewhere on the control levels of the ship. All the same, I perceived 612 Jason now as a great glowing eye, staring through me to the hidden Vox.

"What is it?" I asked.

"Report summary, captain. The dead passenger and the missing matrix."

Deep within me I felt a quick plunging sensation, and then the skin of my arms and shoulders began to glow as the chemicals of fear went coursing through my veins in a fierce tide. It was Vox, I knew, reacting in sudden alarm, opening the petcocks of my hormonal system. It was the thing I had dreaded. How could 612 Jason fail to notice that flood of endocrine response?

"Go on," I said, as coolly as I could.

But noticing was one thing, interpreting the data something else. Fluctuations in a human being's endocrine output might have any number of causes. To my troubled conscience everything was a glaring signal of my guilt. 612 Jason gave no indication that it suspected a thing.

The intelligence said, "The dead passenger was Hans Eger Olafssen, 54 years of age, a native of—"

"Never mind his details. You can let me have a printout on that part."

"The missing matrix," 612 Jason went on imperturbably. "Leeleaine Eliani, 17 years of age, a native of Kansas Four, bound for Cul-de-Sac, Vainglory Archipelago, under Transmission Contract No. D-14871532, dated the 27th day of the third month of—"

"Printout on that too," I cut in. "What I want to know is where she is now."

"That information is not available."

"That isn't a responsive answer, 612 Jason."

"No better answer can be provided at this time, captain. Tracer circuits have been activated and remain in constant search mode."

"And?"

"We have no data on the present location of the missing matrix."

Within me Vox reacted instantly to the intelligence's calm flat statement. The hormonal response changed from one of fear to one of relief. My blazing skin began at once to cool. Would 612 Jason notice that too, and from that small clue be able to assemble the subtext of my body's responses into a sequence that exposed my criminal violation of regulations?

"Don't relax too soon," I told her silently. "This may be some sort of trap."

To 612 Jason I said, "What data *do* you have, then?"

"Two things are known: the time at which the Eliani matrix achieved negation of its storage circuitry and the time of its presumed attempt at making neural entry into the suspended passenger Olafssen. Beyond that no data has been recovered."

"Its *presumed* attempt?" I said.

"There is no proof, captain."

"Olafssen's convulsions? The smashing of the storage housing?"

"We know that Olafssen responded to an electrical stimulus, captain. The source of the stimulus is impossible to trace, although the presumption is that it came from the missing matrix Eliani. These are matters for the subsequent inquiry. It is not within my responsibilities to assign definite causal relationships."

Spoken like a true Jason-series intelligence, I thought.

I said, "You don't have any effective way of tracing the movements of the Eliani matrix, is that what you're telling me?"

"We're dealing with extremely minute impedances, sir. In the ordinary functioning of the ship it is very difficult to distinguish a matrix manifestation from normal surges and pulses in the general electrical system."

"You mean, it might take something as big as the matrix trying to climb back into its own storage circuit to register on the monitoring system?"

"Very possibly, sir."

"Is there any reason to think the Eliani matrix is still on the ship at all?"

"There is no reason to think that it is not, captain."

"In other words, you don't know anything about anything concerning the Eliani matrix."

"I have provided you with all known data at this point. Trace efforts are continuing, sir."

"You still think this is a trap?" Vox asked me.

"It's sounding better and better by the minute. But shut up and don't distract me, will you?"

To the intelligence I said, "All right, keep me posted on the situation. I'm preparing for sleep, 612 Jason. I want the end-of-day status report, and then I want you to clear off and leave me alone."

"Very good, sir. Fifth virtual day of voyage. Position of ship sixteen units beyond last port of call, Kansas Four. Scheduled rendezvous with relay forces at Ultima Thule spinaround point was successfully achieved at the hour of—"

The intelligence droned on and on: the usual report of the routine events of the day, broken only by the novelty of an entry for the loss of a passenger and one for the escape of a matrix, then returning to the standard data, fuel levels and velocity soundings and all the rest. On the first four nights of the voyage I had solemnly tried to absorb all this torrent of ritualized downloading of the log as though my captaincy depended on committing it all to memory, but this night I barely listened, and nearly missed my cue when it was time to give it my approval before clocking out for the night. Vox had to prod me and let me know that the intelligence was waiting for something. I gave 612 Jason the confirm-and-clock-out and heard the welcome sound of its diminishing music as it decoupled the contact.

"What do you think?" Vox asked. "It doesn't know, does it?"

"Not yet," I said.

"You really are a pessimist, aren't you?"

"I think we may be able to bring this off," I told her. "But the moment we become overconfident, it'll be the end. Everyone on this ship wants to know where you are. The slightest slip and we're both gone."

"Okay. Don't lecture me."

"I'll try not to. Let's get some sleep now."

"I don't need to sleep."

"Well, I do."

"Can we talk for a while first?"

"Tomorrow," I said.

But of course sleep was impossible. I was all too aware of the stranger within me, perhaps prowling the most hidden places of my psyche at this moment. Or waiting to invade my dreams once I drifted off. For the first time I thought I could feel her presence even when she was silent: a hot node of identity pressing against the wall of my brain. Perhaps I imagined it. I lay stiff and tense, as wide awake as I have ever been in my life. After a time I had to call 612 Jason and ask it to put me under the wire; and even then my sleep was uneasy when it came.

10.

UNTIL THAT POINT IN THE voyage I had taken nearly all of my meals in my quarters. It seemed a way of exerting my authority, such as it was, aboard ship. By my absence from the dining hall I created a presence, that of the austere and aloof captain; and I avoided the embarrassment of having to sit in the seat of command over men who were much my senior in all things. It was no great sacrifice for me. My quarters were more than comfortable, the food was the same as that which was available in the dining hall, the servo-steward that brought it was silent and efficient. The question of isolation did not arise. There has always been something solitary about me, as there is about most who are of the Service.

But when I awoke the next morning after what had seemed like an endless night, I went down to the dining hall for breakfast.

It was nothing like a deliberate change of policy, a decision that had been rigorously arrived at through careful reasoning. It wasn't a decision at all. Nor did Vox suggest it, though I'm sure she inspired it. It was purely automatic. I arose, showered, and dressed. I confess that I had forgotten all about the events of the night before. Vox was quiet within me. Not until I was under the shower, feeling the warm comforting ultrasonic vibration, did I remember her: there came a disturbing sensation of being in two places at once, and, immediately afterward, an astonishingly odd feeling of shame at my own nakedness. Both those feelings passed quickly. But they did indeed bring to mind that extraordinary thing which I had managed to suppress for some minutes, that I was no longer alone in my body.

She said nothing. Neither did I. After last night's astounding alliance I seemed to want to pull back into wordlessness, unthinkingness, a kind of automaton consciousness. The need for breakfast occurred to me and I called up a tracker to take me down to the dining hall. When I stepped outside the room I was surprised to encounter my servo-steward, already on its way up with my tray. Perhaps it was just as surprised to see me going out, though of course its blank metal face betrayed no feelings.

"I'll be having breakfast in the dining hall today," I told it.

"Very good, sir."

My tracker arrived. I climbed into its seat and it set out at once on its cushion of air toward the dining hall.

The dining hall of the *Sword of Orion* is a magnificent room at the Eye end of Crew Deck, with one glass wall providing a view of all the lights of heaven. By some whim of the designers we sit with that wall below us, so that the stars and their tethered worlds drift beneath our feet. The other walls are of some silvery metal chased with thin swirls of gold, everything shining by the reflected light of the passing star-clusters. At the center is a table of black stone, with places allotted for each of the seventeen members of the crew. It is a splendid if somewhat ridiculous place, a resonant reminder of the wealth and power of the Service.

Three of my shipmates were at their places when I entered. Pedregal was there, the supercargo, a compact, sullen man whose broad dome of a head seemed to rise directly from his shoulders. And there was Fresco, too, slender and elusive, the navigator, a lithe dark-skinned person of ambiguous sex who alternated from voyage to voyage, so I had been told, converting from male to female and back again according to some private rhythm. The third person was Raebuck, whose sphere of responsibility was communications, an older man whose flat, chilly gaze conveyed either boredom or menace, I could never be sure which.

"Why, it's the captain," said Pedregal calmly. "Favoring us with one of his rare visits."

All three stared at me with that curious testing intensity which I was coming to see was an inescapable part of my life aboard ship: a constant hazing meted out to any newcomer to the Service, an interminable probing for the place that was most vulnerable.

Mine was a parsec wide and I was certain they would discover it at once. But I was determined to match them stare for stare, ploy for ploy, test for test.

"Good morning, gentlemen," I said. Then, giving Fresco a level glance, I added, "Good morning, Fresco."

I took my seat at the table's head and rang for service.

I was beginning to realize why I had come out of my cabin that morning. In part it was a reflection of Vox's presence within me, an expression of that new component of rashness and impulsiveness that had entered me with her. But mainly it was, I saw now, some stratagem of my own, hatched on some inaccessible subterranean level of my double mind. In order to conceal Vox most effectively, I would have to take the offensive: rather than skulking in my quarters and perhaps awakening perilous suspicions in the minds of my shipmates, I must come forth, defiantly, challengingly, almost flaunting the thing that I had done, and go among them, pretending that nothing unusual was afoot and forcing them to believe it. Such aggressiveness was not natural to my temperament. But perhaps I could draw on some reserves provided by Vox. If not, we both were lost.

Raebuck said, to no one in particular, "I suppose yesterday's disturbing events must inspire a need for companionship in the captain."

I faced him squarely. "I have all the companionship I require, Raebuck. But I agree that what happened yesterday was disturbing."

"A nasty business," Pedregal said, ponderously shaking his neckless head. "And a strange one, a matrix trying to get into a passenger. That's new to me, a thing like that. And to lose the passenger besides—that's bad. That's very bad."

"It does happen, losing a passenger," said Raebuck.

"A long time since it happened on a ship of mine," Pedregal rejoined.

"We lost a whole batch of them on the *Emperor of Callisto*," Fresco said. "You know the story? It was thirty years ago. We were making the run from Van Buren to the San Pedro Cluster. We picked up a supernova pulse and the intelligence on duty went into flicker. Somehow dumped a load of aluminum salts in the feed-lines and killed off fifteen, sixteen passengers. I saw the bodies before they went into the converter. Beyond salvage, they were."

"Yes," said Raebuck. "I heard of that one. And then there was the *Queen Astarte*, a couple of years after that. Tchelitchev was her captain, little green-eyed Russian woman from one of the Troika worlds. They were taking a routine inventory and two digits got transposed, and a faulty delivery signal slipped through. I think it was six dead, premature decanting, killed by air poisoning. Tchelitchev took it very badly. *Very* badly. Somehow the captain always does."

"And then that time on the *Hecuba*," said Pedregal. "No ship of mine, thank God. That was the captain who ran amok, thought the ship was too quiet, wanted to see some passengers moving around and started awakening them—"

Raebuck showed a quiver of surprise. "You know about that? I thought that was supposed to be hushed up."

"Things get around," Pedregal said, with something like a smirk. "The captain's name was Catania-Szu, I believe, a man from Mediterraneo, very high-strung, the way all of them are there. I was working the *Valparaiso* then, out of Mendax Nine bound for Scylla and Charybdis and neighboring points, and when we stopped to download some cargo in the Seneca system I got the whole story from a ship's clerk named—"

"You were on the *Valparaiso*?" Fresco asked. "Wasn't that the ship that had a free matrix, too, ten or eleven years back? A real soul-eater, so the report went—"

"After my time," said Pedregal, blandly waving his hand. "But I did hear of it. You get to hear about everything, when you're downloading cargo. Soul-eater, you say, reminds me of the time—"

And he launched into some tale of horror at a spinaround station in a far quadrant of the galaxy. But he was no more than halfway through it when Raebuck cut in with a gorier reminiscence of his own, and then Fresco, seething with impatience, broke in on him to tell of a ship infested by three free matrixes at once. I had no doubt that all this was being staged for my enlightenment, by way of showing me how seriously such events were taken in the Service, and how the captains under whom they occurred went down in the folklore of the starships with ineradicable black marks. But their attempts to unsettle me, if that is what they were, left me undismayed. Vox, silent within me, infused me with a strange confidence that allowed me to ignore the darker implications of these anecdotes.

I simply listened, playing my role: the neophyte fascinated by the accumulated depth of spacegoing experience that their stories implied.

Then I said, finally, "When matrixes get loose, how long do they generally manage to stay at large?"

"An hour or two, generally," said Raebuck. "As they drift around the ship, of course, they leave an electrical trail. We track it and close off access routes behind them and eventually we pin them down in close quarters. Then it's not hard to put them back in their bottles."

"And if they've jacked into some member of the crew?"

"That makes it even easier to find them."

Boldly I said, "Was there ever a case where a free matrix jacked into a member of the crew and managed to keep itself hidden?"

"Never," said a new voice. It belonged to Roacher, who had just entered the dining hall. He stood at the far end of the long table, staring at me. His strange luminescent eyes, harsh and probing, came to rest on mine. "No matter how clever the matrix may be, sooner or later the host will find some way to call for help."

"And if the host doesn't choose to call for help?" I asked.

Roacher studied me with great care.

Had I been too bold? Had I given away too much?

"But that would be a violation of regulations!" he said, in a tone of mock astonishment. "That would be a criminal act!"

11.

SHE ASKED ME TO TAKE her starwalking, to show her the full view of the Great Open.

It was the third day of her concealment within me. Life aboard the *Sword of Orion* had returned to routine, or, to be more accurate, it had settled into a new routine in which the presence on board of an undetected and apparently undetectable free matrix was a constant element.

As Vox had suggested, there were some who quickly came to believe that the missing matrix must have slipped off into space, since the watchful ship-intelligences could find no trace of it. But there were others who kept looking over their shoulders, figuratively or literally, as if expecting the fugitive to attempt to thrust herself without warning into the spinal jacks that gave access to their nervous systems. They behaved exactly as if the ship were haunted. To placate those uneasy ones, I ordered round-the-clock circuit sweeps that would report every vagrant pulse and random surge. Each such anomalous electrical event was duly investigated, and, of course, none of these investigations led to anything significant. Now that Vox resided in my brain instead of the ship's wiring, she was beyond any such mode of discovery.

Whether anyone suspected the truth was something I had no way of knowing. Perhaps Roacher did; but he made no move to denounce me, nor did he so much as raise the issue of the missing matrix with me at all after that time in the dining hall. He might know nothing whatever; he might know everything, and not care; he might simply be keeping his own counsel for the moment. I had no way of telling.

I was growing accustomed to my double life, and to my daily duplicity. Vox had quickly come to seem as much a part of me as my arm, or my leg. When she was silent—and often I heard nothing from her for hours at a time—I was no more aware of her than I would be, in any special way, of my arm or my leg; but nevertheless I knew somehow that she was there. The boundaries between her mind and mine were eroding steadily. She was learning how to infiltrate me. At times it seemed to me that what we were were joint tenants of the same dwelling, rather than I the permanent occupant and she a guest. I came to perceive my own mind as something not notably different from hers, a mere web of electrical force which for the moment was housed in the soft moist globe that was the brain of the captain of the *Sword of Orion*. Either of us, so it seemed, might come and go within that soft moist globe as we pleased, flitting casually in or out after the wraithlike fashion of matrixes.

At other times it was not at all like that: I gave no thought to her presence and went about my tasks as if nothing had changed for me. Then it would come as a surprise when Vox announced herself to me with some sudden comment, some quick question. I had to learn to guard myself against letting my reaction show, if it happened when I was with other members of the crew. Though no one around us could hear anything when she spoke to me, or I to her, I knew it would be the end for our masquerade if anyone caught me in some unguarded moment of conversation with an unseen companion.

How far she had penetrated my mind began to become apparent to me when she asked to go on a starwalk.

"You know about that?" I said, startled, for starwalking is the private pleasure of the spacegoing and I had not known of it myself before I was taken into the Service.

Vox seemed amazed by my amazement. She indicated casually that the details of starwalking were common knowledge everywhere. But something rang false in her tone. Were the landcrawling folk really so familiar with our special pastime? Or had she picked what she knew of it out of the hitherto private reaches of my consciousness?

I chose not to ask. But I was uneasy about taking her with me into the Great Open, much as I was beginning to yearn for it myself. She was not one of us. She was planetary; she had not passed through the training of the Service.

I told her that.

"Take me anyway," she said. "It's the only chance I'll ever have."

"But the training—"

"I don't need it. Not if you've had it."

"What if that's not enough?"

"It will be," she said. "I know it will, Adam. There's nothing to be afraid of. You've had the training, haven't you? And I am you."

12.

TOGETHER WE RODE THE TRANSIT track out of the Eye and down to Drive Deck, where the soul of the ship lies lost in throbbing dreams of the far galaxies as it pulls us ever onward across the unending night.

We passed through zones of utter darkness and zones of cascading light, through places where wheeling helixes of silvery radiance burst like auroras from the air, through passages so crazed in their geometry that they reawakened the terrors of the womb in anyone who traversed them. A starship is the mother of mysteries. Vox crouched, frozen with awe, within that portion of our brain that was hers. I felt the surges of her awe, one after another, as we went downward.

"Are you really sure you want to do this?" I asked.

"Yes!" she cried fiercely. "Keep going!"

"There's the possibility that you'll be detected," I told her.

"There's the possibility that I won't be," she said.

We continued to descend. Now we were in the realm of the three cyborg push-cells, Gabriel, Banquo, and Fleece. Those were three members of the crew whom we would never see at the table in the dining hall, for they dwelled here in the walls of Drive Deck, permanently jacked in, perpetually pumping their energies into the ship's great maw. I have already told you of our saying in the Service, that when you enter you give up the body and you get your soul. For most of us that is only a figure of speech: what we give up, when we say farewell forever to planet-skin and take up our new lives in starships, is not the body itself but the body's trivial needs, the sweaty things so dear to shore people. But some of us are more literal in their renunciations. The flesh is a meaningless hindrance to them; they shed it entirely, knowing that they can experience starship life just as fully without it. They allow themselves to be transformed into extensions of the stardrive. From them comes the raw energy out of which is made the power that carries us hurtling through heaven. Their work is unending; their reward is a sort of immortality. It is not a choice I could make, nor, I think, you: but for them it is bliss. There can be no doubt about that.

"Another starwalk so soon, captain?" Banquo asked. For I had been here on the second day of the voyage, losing no time in availing myself of the great privilege of the Service.

"Is there any harm in it?"

"No, no harm," said Banquo. "Just isn't usual, is all."

"That's all right," I said. "That's not important to me."

Banquo is a gleaming metallic ovoid, twice the size of a human head, jacked into a slot in the wall. Within the ovoid is the matrix of what had once been Banquo, long ago on a world called Sunrise where night is unknown. Sunrise's golden dawns and shining days had not been good enough for Banquo, apparently. What Banquo had wanted was to be a gleaming metallic ovoid, hanging on the wall of Drive Deck aboard the *Sword of Orion*.

Any of the three cyborgs could set up a starwalk. But Banquo was the one who had done it for me that other time and it seemed best to return to him. He was the most congenial of the three. He struck me as amiable and easy. Gabriel, on my first visit, had seemed austere, remote, incomprehensible. He is an early model who had lived the equivalent of three human lifetimes as a cyborg aboard starships and there was not much about him that was human any more. Fleece, much younger, quick-minded and quirky, I mistrusted: in her weird edgy way she might just somehow be able to detect the hidden other who would be going along with me for the ride.

You must realize that when we starwalk we do not literally leave the ship, though that is how it seems to us. If we left the ship even for a moment we would be swept away and lost forever in the abyss of heaven. Going outside a starship of heaven is not like stepping outside an ordinary planet-launched shoreship that moves through normal space. But even if it were possible, there would be no point in leaving the ship. There is nothing to see out there. A starship moves through utter empty darkness.

But though there may be nothing to see, that does not mean that there is nothing out there. The entire universe is out there. If we could see it while we are traveling across the special space that is heaven we would find it flattened and curved, so that we had the illusion of viewing everything at once, all the far-flung galaxies back to the beginning of time. This is the Great Open, the totality of the continuum. Our external screens show it to us in simulated form, because we need occasional assurance that it is there.

A starship rides along the mighty lines of force which cross that immense void like the lines of the compass rose on an ancient mariner's map. When we starwalk, we ride those same lines, and we are held by them, sealed fast to the ship that is carrying us onward through heaven. We seem to step forth into space; we seem to look down on the ship, on the stars, on all the worlds of heaven. For the moment we become little starships flying along beside the great one that is our mother. It is magic; it is illusion; but it is magic that so closely approaches what we perceive as reality that there is no way to measure the difference, which means that in effect there is no difference.

"Ready?" I asked Vox.

"Absolutely."

Still I hesitated.

"Are you *sure*?"

"Go on," she said impatiently. "Do it!"

I put the jack to my spine myself. Banquo did the matching of impedances. If he were going to discover the passenger I carried, this would be the moment. But he showed no sign that anything was amiss. He queried me; I gave him the signal to proceed;

there was a moment of sharp warmth at the back of my neck as my neural matrix, and Vox's traveling with it, rushed out through Banquo and hurtled downward toward its merger with the soul of the ship.

We were seized and drawn in and engulfed by the vast force that is the ship. As the coils of the engine caught us we were spun around and around, hurled from vector to vector, mercilessly stretched, distended by an unimaginable flux. And then there was a brightness all about us, a brightness that cried out in heaven with a mighty clamor. We were outside the ship. We were starwalking.

"Oh," she said. A little soft cry, a muted gasp of wonder.

The blazing mantle of the ship lay upon the darkness of heaven like a white shadow. That great cone of cold fiery light reached far out in front of us, arching awesomely toward heaven's vault, and behind us it extended beyond the limits of our sight. The slender tapering outline of the ship was clearly visible within it, the needle and its Eye, all ten kilometers of it easily apparent to us in a single glance.

And there were the stars. And there were the worlds of heaven.

The effect of the stardrive is to collapse the dimensions, each one in upon the other. Thus inordinate spaces are diminished and the galaxy may be spanned by human voyagers. There is no logic, no linearity of sequence, to heaven as it appears to our eyes. Wherever we look we see the universe bent back upon itself, revealing its entirety in an infinite series of infinite segments of itself. Any sector of stars contains all stars. Any demarcation of time encompasses all of time past and time to come. What we behold is altogether beyond our understanding, which is exactly as it should be; for what we are given, when we look through the Eye of the ship at the naked heavens, is a god's-eye view of the universe. And we are not gods.

"What are we seeing?" Vox murmured within me.

I tried to tell her. I showed her how to define her relative position so there would be an up and a down for her, a backward, a forward, a flow of time and event from beginning to end. I pointed out the arbitrary coordinate axes by which we locate ourselves in this fundamentally incomprehensible arena. I found known stars for her, and known worlds, and showed them to her.

She understood nothing. She was entirely lost.

I told her that there was no shame in that.

I told her that I had been just as bewildered, when I was undergoing my training in the simulator. That everyone was; and that no one, not even if he spent a thousand years aboard the starships that plied the routes of heaven, could ever come to anything more than a set of crude equivalents and approximations of understanding what starwalking shows us. Attaining actual understanding itself is beyond the best of us.

I could feel her struggling to encompass the impact of all that rose and wheeled and soared before us. Her mind was agile, though still only half-formed, and I sensed her working out her own system of explanations and assumptions, her analogies, her equivalencies. I gave her no more help. It was best for her to do these things by herself; and in any case I had no more help to give.

I had my own astonishment and bewilderment to deal with, on this my second starwalk in heaven.

Once more I looked down upon the myriad worlds turning in their orbits. I could see them easily, the little bright globes rotating in the huge night of the Great Open: red worlds, blue worlds, green ones, some turning their full faces to me, some showing mere slivers of a crescent. How they cleaved to their appointed tracks! How they clung to their parent stars!

I remembered that other time, only a few virtual days before, when I had felt such compassion for them, such sorrow. Knowing that they were condemned forever to follow the same path about the same star, a hopeless bondage, a meaningless retracing of a perpetual route. In their own eyes they might be footloose wanderers, but to me they had seemed the most pitiful of slaves. And so I had grieved for the worlds of heaven; but now, to my surprise, I felt no pity, only a kind of love. There was no reason to be sad for them. They were what they were, and there was a supreme rightness in those fixed orbits and their obedient movements along them. They were content with being what they were. If they were loosed even a moment from that bondage, such chaos would arise in the universe as could never be contained. Those circling worlds are the foundations upon which all else is built; they know that and they take pride in it; they are loyal to their tasks and we must honor them for their devotion to their duty. And with honor comes love.

This must be Vox speaking within me, I told myself.

I had never thought such thoughts. Love the planets in their orbits? What kind of notion was that? Perhaps no stranger than my earlier notion of pitying them because they weren't starships; but that thought had arisen from the spontaneous depths of my own spirit and it had seemed to make a kind of sense to me. Now it had given way to a wholly other view.

I loved the worlds that moved before me and yet did not move, in the great night of heaven.

I loved the strange fugitive girl within me who beheld those worlds and loved them for their immobility.

I felt her seize me now, taking me impatiently onward, outward, into the depths of heaven. She understood now; she knew how it was done. And she was far more daring than ever I would have allowed me to be. Together we walked the stars. Not only walked but plunged and swooped and soared, traveling among them like gods. Their hot breath singed us. Their throbbing brightness thundered at us. Their serene movements boomed a mighty music at us. On and on we went, hand in hand, Vox leading, I letting her draw me, deeper and deeper into the shining abyss that was the universe. Until at last we halted, floating in mid-cosmos, the ship nowhere to be seen, only the two of us surrounded by a shield of suns.

In that moment a sweeping ecstasy filled my soul. I felt all eternity within my grasp. No, that puts it the wrong way around and makes it seem that I was seized by delusions of imperial grandeur, which was not at all the case. What I felt was myself within the grasp of all eternity, enfolded in the loving embrace of a complete and perfect cosmos in which nothing was out of place, or ever could be.

It is this that we go starwalking to attain. This sense of belonging, this sense of being contained in the divine perfection of the universe.

When it comes, there is no telling what effect it will have; but inner change is what it usually brings. I had come away from my first starwalk unaware of any transformation; but within three days I had impulsively opened myself to a wandering phantom, violating not only regulations but the nature of my own character as I understood it. I have always, as I think I have said, been an intensely private man. Even though I had given Vox refuge, I had been relieved and grateful that her mind and mine had remained separate entities within our shared brain.

Now I did what I could to break down whatever boundary remained between us.

I hadn't let her know anything, so far, of my life before going to heaven. I had met her occasional questions with coy evasions, with half-truths, with blunt refusals. It was the way I had always been with everyone, a habit of secrecy, an unwillingness to reveal myself. I had been even more secretive, perhaps, with Vox than with all the others, because of the very closeness of her mind to mine. As though I feared that by giving her any interior knowledge of me I was opening the way for her to take me over entirely, to absorb me into her own vigorous, undisciplined soul.

But now I offered my past to her in a joyous rush. We began to make our way slowly backward from that apocalyptic place at the center of everything; and as we hovered on the breast of the Great

Open, drifting between the darkness and the brilliance of the light that the ship created, I told her everything about myself that I had been holding back.

I suppose they were mere trivial things, though to me they were all so highly charged with meaning. I told her the name of my home planet. I let her see it, the sea the color of lead, the sky the color of smoke. I showed her the sparse and scrubby gray headlands behind our house, where I would go running for hours by myself, a tall slender boy pounding tirelessly across the crackling sands as though demons were pursuing him.

I showed her everything: the somber child, the troubled youth, the wary, overcautious young man. The playmates who remained forever strangers, the friends whose voices were drowned in hollow babbling echoes, the lovers whose love seemed without substance or meaning. I told her of my feeling that I was the only one alive in the world, that everyone about me was some sort of artificial being full of gears and wires. Or that the world was only a flat colorless dream in which I somehow had become trapped, but from which I would eventually awaken into the true world of light and color and richness of texture. Or that I might not be human at all, but had been abandoned in the human galaxy by creatures of another form entirely, who would return for me some day far in the future.

I was lighthearted as I told her these things, and she received them lightly. She knew them for what they were—not symptoms of madness, but only the bleak fantasies of a lonely child, seeking to make sense out of an incomprehensible universe in which he felt himself to be a stranger and afraid.

"But you escaped," she said. "You found a place where you belonged!"

"Yes," I said. "I escaped."

And I told her of the day when I had seen a sudden light in the sky. My first thought then had been that my true parents had come back for me; my second, that it was some comet passing by.

That light was a starship of heaven that had come to worldward in our system. And as I looked upward through the darkness on that day long ago, straining to catch a glimpse of the shoreships that were going up to it bearing cargo and passengers to be taken from our world to some unknowable place at the other end of the galaxy, I realized that that starship was my true home. I realized that the Service was my destiny.

And so it came to pass, I said, that I left my world behind, and my name, and my life, such as it had been, to enter the company of those who sail between the stars. I let her know that this was my first voyage, explaining that it is the peculiar custom of the Service to test all new officers by placing them in command at once. She asked me if I had found happiness here; and I said, quickly, Yes, I had, and then I said a moment later, Not yet, not yet, but I see at least the possibility of it.

She was quiet for a time. We watched the worlds turning and the stars like blazing spikes of color racing toward their far-off destinations, and the fiery white light of the ship itself streaming in the firmament as if it were the blood of some alien god. The thought came to me of all that I was risking by hiding her like this within me. I brushed it aside. This was neither the place nor the moment for doubt or fear or misgiving.

Then she said, "I'm glad you told me all that, Adam."

"Yes. I am too."

"I could feel it from the start, what sort of person you were. But I needed to hear it in your own words, your own thoughts. It's just like I've been saying. You and I, we're two of a kind. Square pegs in a world of round holes. You ran away to the Service and I ran away to a new life in somebody else's body."

I realized that Vox wasn't speaking of my body, but of the new one that waited for her on Cul-de-Sac.

And I realized too that there was one thing about herself that she had never shared with me, which was the nature of the flaw in her old body that had caused her to discard it. If I knew her more fully, I thought, I could love her more deeply: imperfections and all, which is the way of love. But she had shied away from telling me that, and I had never pressed her on it. Now, out here under the cool gleam of heaven, surely we had moved into a place of total trust, of complete union of soul.

I said, "Let me see you, Vox."

"See me? How could you—"

"Give me an image of yourself. You're too abstract for me this way. *Vox*. A voice. Only a voice. You talk to me, you live within me, and I still don't have the slightest idea what you look like."

"That's how I want it to be."

"Won't you show me how you look?"

"I won't look like anything. I'm a matrix. I'm nothing but electricity."

"I understand that. I mean how you looked *before*. Your old self, the one you left behind on Kansas Four."

She made no reply.

I thought she was hesitating, deciding; but some time went by, and still I heard nothing from her. What came from her was silence, only silence, a silence that had crashed down between us like a steel curtain.

"Vox?"

Nothing.

Where was she hiding? What had I done?

"What's the matter? Is it the thing I asked you?"

No answer.

"It's all right, Vox. Forget about it. It isn't important at all. You don't have to show me anything you don't want to show me."

Nothing. Silence.

"Vox? Vox?"

The worlds and stars wheeled in chaos before me. The light of the ship roared up and down the spectrum from end to end. In growing panic I sought for her and found no trace of her presence within me. Nothing. Nothing.

"Are you all right?" came another voice. Banquo, from inside the ship. "I'm getting some pretty wild signals. You'd better come in. You've been out there long enough as it is."

Vox was gone. I had crossed some uncrossable boundary and I had frightened her away.

Numbly I gave Banquo the signal, and he brought me back inside.

13.

ALONE, I MADE MY WAY upward level by level through the darkness and mystery of the ship, toward the Eye. The crash of silence went on and on, like the falling of some colossal wave on an endless shore. I missed Vox terribly. I had never known such complete solitude as I felt now. I had not realized how accustomed I had become to her being there, nor what impact her leaving would have on me. In just those few days of giving her sanctuary, it had somehow come to seem to me that to house two souls within one brain was the normal condition of mankind, and that to be alone in one's skull as I was now was a shameful thing.

As I neared the place where Crew Deck narrows into the curve of the Eye a slender figure stepped without warning from the shadows.

"Captain."

My mind was full of the loss of Vox and he caught me unawares. I jumped back, badly startled.

"For the love of God, man!"

"It's just me. Bulgar. Don't be so scared, captain. It's only Bulgar."

"Let me be," I said, and brusquely beckoned him away.

"No. Wait, captain. Please, wait."

He clutched at my arm, holding me as I tried to go. I halted and turned toward him, trembling with anger and surprise.

Bulgar, Roacher's jackmate, was a gentle, soft-voiced little man, wide-mouthed, olive-skinned, with huge sad eyes. He and Roacher had sailed the skies of Heaven together since before I was born.

They complemented each other. Where Roacher was small and hard, like fruit that has been left to dry in the sun for a hundred years, his jackmate Bulgar was small and tender, with a plump, succulent look about him. Together they seemed complete, an unassailable whole: I could readily imagine them lying together in their bunk, each jacked to the other, one person in two bodies, linked more intimately even than Vox and I had been.

With an effort I recovered my poise. Tightly I said, "What is it, Bulgar?"

"Can we talk a minute, captain?"

"We are talking. What do you want with me?"

"That loose matrix, sir."

My reaction must have been stronger than he was expecting. His eyes went wide and he took a step or two back from me.

Moistening his lips, he said, "We were wondering, captain—wondering how the search is going—whether you had any idea where the matrix might be—"

I said stiffly, "Who's *we*, Bulgar?"

"The men. Roacher. Me. Some of the others. Mainly Roacher, sir."

"Ah. So Roacher wants to know where the matrix is."

The little man moved closer. I saw him staring deep into me as though searching for Vox behind the mask of my carefully expressionless face. Did he know? Did they all? I wanted to cry out, *She's not there any more, she's gone, she left me, she ran off into space.* But apparently what was troubling Roacher and his shipmates was something other than the possibility that Vox had taken refuge with me.

Bulgar's tone was soft, insinuating, concerned. "Roacher's very worried, captain. He's been on ships with loose matrixes before. He knows how much trouble they can be. He's really worried, captain. I have to tell you that. I've never seen him so worried."

"What does he think the matrix will do to him?"

"He's afraid of being taken over," Bulgar said.

"Taken over?"

"The matrix coming into his head through his jack. Mixing itself up with his brain. It's been known to happen, captain."

"And why should it happen to Roacher, out of all the men on this ship? Why not you? Why not Pedregal? Or Rio de Rio? Or one of the passengers again?" I took a deep breath. "Why not me, for that matter?"

"He just wants to know, sir, what's the situation with the matrix now. Whether you've discovered anything about where it is. Whether you've been able to trap it."

There was something strange in Bulgar's eyes. I began to think I was being tested again. This assertion of Roacher's alleged terror of being infiltrated and possessed by the wandering matrix might simply be a roundabout way of finding out whether that had already happened to me.

"Tell him it's gone," I said.

"Gone, sir?"

"Gone. Vanished. It isn't anywhere on the ship any more. Tell him that, Bulgar. He can forget about her slithering down his precious jackhole."

"*Her?*"

"Female matrix, yes. But that doesn't matter now. She's gone. You can tell him that. Escaped. Flew off into heaven. The emergency's over." I glowered at him. I yearned to be rid of him, to go off by myself to nurse my new grief. "Shouldn't you be getting back to your post, Bulgar?"

Did he believe me? Or did he think that I had slapped together some transparent lie to cover my complicity in the continued absence of the matrix? I had no way of knowing. Bulgar gave me a little obsequious bow and started to back away.

"Sir," he said. "Thank you, sir. I'll tell him, sir."

He retreated into the shadows. I continued uplevel.

I passed Katkat on my way, and, a little while afterward, Raebuck. They looked at me without speaking. There was something reproachful but almost loving about Katkat's expression, but Raebuck's icy, baleful stare brought me close to flinching. In their different ways they were saying, *Guilty, guilty, guilty.* But of what?

Before, I had imagined that everyone whom I encountered aboard ship was able to tell at a single glance that I was harboring the fugitive, and was simply waiting for me to reveal myself with some foolish slip. Now everything was reversed. They looked at me and I told myself that they were thinking, *He's all alone by himself in there, he doesn't have anyone else at all,* and I shrank away, shamed by my solitude. I knew that this was the edge of madness. I was overwrought, overtired; perhaps it had been a mistake to go starwalking a second time so soon after my first. I needed to rest. I needed to hide.

I began to wish that there were someone aboard the *Sword of Orion* with whom I could discuss these things. But who, though? Roacher? 612 Jason? I was altogether isolated here. The only one I could speak to on this ship was Vox. And she was gone.

In the safety of my cabin I jacked myself into the mediq rack and gave myself a ten-minute purge. That helped. The phantom fears and intricate uncertainties that had taken possession of me began to ebb.

I keyed up the log and ran through the list of my captainly duties, such as they were, for the rest of the day. We were approaching a spinaround point, one of those nodes of force positioned equidistantly across heaven which a starship in transit must seize and use in order to propel itself onward through the next sector of the universe. Spinaround acquisition is performed automatically but at least in theory the responsibility for carrying it out successfully falls to the captain: I would give the commands, I would oversee the process from initiation through completion.

But there was still time for that.

I accessed 49 Henry Henry, who was the intelligence on duty, and asked for an update on the matrix situation.

"No change, sir," the intelligence reported at once.

"What does that mean?"

"Trace efforts continue as requested, sir. But we have not detected the location of the missing matrix."

"No clues? Not even a hint?"

"No data at all, sir. There's essentially no way to isolate the minute electromagnetic pulse of a free matrix from the background noise of the ship's entire electrical system."

I believed it. 612 Jason Jason had told me that in nearly the same words.

I said, "I have reason to think that the matrix is no longer on the ship, 49 Henry Henry."

"Do you, sir?" said 49 Henry Henry in its usual aloof, half-mocking way.

"I do, yes. After a careful study of the situation, it's my opinion that the matrix exited the ship earlier this day and will not be heard from again."

"Shall I record that as an official position, sir?"

"Record it," I said.

"Done, sir."

"And therefore, 49 Henry Henry, you can cancel search mode immediately and close the file. We'll enter a debit for one matrix and the Service bookkeepers can work it out later."

"Very good, sir."

"Decouple," I ordered the intelligence.

49 Henry Henry went away. I sat quietly amid the splendors of my cabin, thinking back over my starwalk and reliving that sense of harmony, of love, of oneness with the worlds of heaven, that had come over me while Vox and I drifted on the bosom of the Great Open. And feeling once again the keen slicing sense of loss that I had felt since Vox's departure from me. In a little while I would have to rise and go to the command center and put myself through the motions of overseeing spinaround acquisition; but for the moment I remained where I was, motionless, silent, peer-

ing deep into the heart of my solitude.

"I'm not gone," said an unexpected quiet voice.

It came like a punch beneath the heart. It was a moment before I could speak.

"Vox?" I said at last. "Where are you, Vox?"

"Right here."

"Where?" I asked.

"Inside. I never went away."

"You never—"

"You upset me. I just had to hide for a while."

"You knew I was trying to find you?"

"Yes."

Color came to my cheeks. Anger roared like a stream in spate through my veins. I felt myself blazing.

"You knew how I felt, when you—when it seemed that you weren't there any more."

"Yes," she said, even more quietly, after a time.

I forced myself to grow calm. I told myself that she owed me nothing, except perhaps gratitude for sheltering her, and that whatever pain she had caused me by going silent was none of her affair. I reminded myself also that she was a child, unruly and turbulent and undisciplined.

After a bit I said, "I missed you. I missed you more than I want to say."

"I'm sorry," she said, sounding repentant, but not very. "I had to go away for a time. You upset me, Adam."

"By asking you to show me how you used to look?"

"Yes."

"I don't understand why that upset you so much."

"You don't have to," Vox said. "I don't mind now. You can see me, if you like. Do you still want to? Here. This is me. This is what I used to be. If it disgusts you don't blame me. Okay? Okay, Adam? Here. Have a look. Here I am."

14.

THERE WAS A WRENCHING WITHIN me, a twisting, a painful yank-
ing sensation, as of some heavy barrier forcibly being pulled aside.
And then the glorious radiant scarlet sky of Kansas Four blos-
somed on the screen of my mind.

She didn't simply show it to me. She took me there. I felt the
soft moist wind on my face, I breathed the sweet, faintly pungent
air, I heard the sly rustling of glossy leathery fronds that dangled
from bright yellow trees. Beneath my bare feet the black soil was
warm and spongy.

I was Leeleaine, who liked to call herself Vox. I was seventeen
years old and swept by forces and compulsions as powerful as
hurricanes.

I was her from within and also I saw her from outside.

My hair was long and thick and dark, tumbling down past my
shoulders in an avalanche of untended curls and loops and snags.
My hips were broad, my breasts were full and heavy: I could feel
the pull of them, the pain of them. It was almost as if they were
stiff with milk, though they were not. My face was tense, alert, sullen, aglow with angry intelligence. It was not an unappealing face.
Vox was not an unappealing girl.

From her earlier reluctance to show herself to me I had expected
her to be ugly, or perhaps deformed in some way, dragging herself
about in a coarse, heavy, burdensome husk of flesh that was a constant reproach to her. She had spoken of her life on Kansas Four
as being so dreary, so sad, so miserable, that she saw no hope in
staying there. And had given up her body to be turned into mere
electricity, on the promise that she could have a new body—any
body—when she reached Cul-de-Sac. *I hated my body*, she had told
me. *I couldn't wait to be rid of it.* She had refused even to give me a
glimpse of it, retreating instead for hours into a desperate silence
so total that I thought she had fled.

All that was a mystery to me now. The Leeleaine that I saw, that
I was, was a fine sturdy-looking girl. Not beautiful, no, too strong

and strapping for that, I suppose, but far from ugly: her eyes were warm and intelligent, her lips full, her nose finely modeled. And it was a healthy body, too, robust, vital. Of course she had no deformities; and why had I thought she had, when it would have been a simple matter of retrogenetic surgery to amend any bothersome defect? No, there was nothing wrong with the body that Vox had abandoned and for which she professed such loathing, for which she felt such shame.

Then I realized that I was seeing her from outside. I was seeing her as if by relay, filtering and interpreting the information she was offering me by passing it through the mind of an objective observer: myself. Who understood nothing, really, of what it was like to be anyone but himself.

Somehow—it was one of those automatic, unconscious adjustments—I altered the focus of my perceptions. All old frames of reference fell away and I let myself lose any sense of the separateness of our identities.

I was her. Fully, unconditionally, inextricably.

And I understood.

Figures flitted about her, shadowy, baffling, maddening. Brothers, sisters, parents, friends: they were all strangers to her. Everyone on Kansas Four was a stranger to her. And always would be.

She hated her body not because it was weak or unsightly but because it was her prison. She was enclosed within it as though within narrow stone walls. It hung about her, a cage of flesh, holding her down, pinning her to this lovely world called Kansas Four where she knew only pain and isolation and estrangement. Her body—her perfectly acceptable, healthy body—had become hateful to her because it was the emblem and symbol of her soul's imprisonment. Wild and incurably restless by temperament, she had failed to find a way to live within the smothering predictability of Kansas Four, a planet where she would never be anything but an internal outlaw. The only way she could leave Kansas Four was to surrender the body that tied her to it; and so she had turned against it with fury and loathing, rejecting it, abandoning it, despising it, detesting it. No one could ever understand that who beheld her from the outside.

But I understood.

I understood much more than that, in that one flashing moment of communion that she and I had. I came to see what she meant when she said that I was her twin, her double, her other self. Of course we were wholly different, I the sober, staid, plodding, diligent man, and she the reckless, volatile, impulsive, tempestuous girl. But beneath all that we were the same: misfits, outsiders, troubled wanderers through worlds we had never made. We had found vastly differing ways to cope with our pain. Yet we were one and the same, two halves of a single entity.

We will remain together always now, I told myself.

And in that moment our communion broke. She broke it—it must have been she, fearful of letting this new intimacy grow too deep—and I found myself apart from her once again, still playing host to her in my brain but separated from her by the boundaries of my own individuality, my own selfhood. I felt her nearby, within me, a warm but discrete presence. Still within me, yes. But separate again.

15.

THERE WAS SHIPWORK TO DO. For days, now, Vox's invasion of me had been a startling distraction. But I dared not let myself forget that we were in the midst of a traversal of heaven. The lives of us all, and of our passengers, depended on the proper execution of our duties: even mine. And worlds awaited the bounty that we bore. My task of the moment was to oversee spinaround acquisition.

I told Vox to leave me temporarily while I went through the routines of acquisition. I would be jacked to other crewmen for a time; they might very well be able to detect her within me; there was no telling what might happen. But she refused. "No," she said.

"I won't leave you. I don't want to go out there. But I'll hide, deep down, the way I did when I was upset with you."

"Vox—" I began.

"No. Please. I don't want to talk about it."

There was no time to argue the point. I could feel the depth and intensity of her stubborn determination.

"Hide, then," I said. "If that's what you want to do."

I made my way down out of the Eye to Engine Deck.

The rest of the acquisition team was already assembled in the Great Navigation Hall: Fresco, Raebuck, Roacher. Raebuck's role was to see to it that communications channels were kept open, Fresco's to set up the navigation coordinates, and Roacher, as power engineer, would monitor fluctuations in drain and input-output cycling. My function was to give the cues at each stage of acquisition. In truth I was pretty much redundant, since Raebuck and Fresco and Roacher had been doing this sort of thing a dozen times a voyage for scores of voyages and they had little need of my guidance. The deeper truth was that they were redundant too, for 49 Henry Henry would oversee us all, and the intelligence was quite capable of setting up the entire process without any human help.

Nevertheless there were formalities to observe, and not inane ones. Intelligences are far superior to humans in mental capacity, interfacing capability, and reaction time, but even so they are nothing but servants, and artificial servants at that, lacking in any real awareness of human fragility or human ethical complexity. They must only be used as tools, not decision-makers. A society which delegates responsibilities of life and death to its servants will eventually find the servants' hands at its throat. As for me, novice that I was, my role was valid as well: the focal point of the enterprise, the prime initiator, the conductor and observer of the process. Perhaps anyone could perform those functions, but the fact remained that *someone* had to, and by tradition that someone was the captain. Call it a ritual, call it a highly stylized dance, if you will. But there is no getting away from the human need for ritual and stylization. Such aspects of a process may not seem essential, but they are valuable and significant, and ultimately they can be seen to be essential as well.

"Shall we begin?" Fresco asked.

We jacked up, Roacher directly into the ship, Raebuck into Roacher, Fresco to me, me into the ship.

"Simulation," I said.

Raebuck keyed in the first code and the vast echoing space that was the Great Navigation Hall came alive with pulsing light: a representation of heaven all about us, the lines of force, the spinaround nodes, the stars, the planets. We moved unhinderedly in free fall, drifting as casually as angels. We could easily have believed we were starwalking.

The simulacrum of the ship was a bright arrow of fierce light just below us and to the left. Ahead, throbbing like a nest of twining angry serpents, was the globe that represented the Lasciate Ogni Speranza spinaround point, tightly-wound dull gray cables shot through with strands of fierce scarlet.

"Enter approach mode," I said. "Activate receptors. Begin threshold equalization. Begin momentum comparison. Prepare for acceleration uptick. Check angular velocity. Begin spin consolidation. Enter displacement select. Extend mast. Prepare for acquisition receptivity."

At each command the proper man touched a control key or pressed a directive panel or simply sent an impulse shooting through the jack hookup by which he was connected, directly or indirectly, to the mind of the ship. Out of courtesy to me, they waited until the commands were given, but the speed with which they obeyed told me that their minds were already in motion even as I spoke.

"It's really exciting, isn't it?" Vox said suddenly.

"For God's sake, Vox! What are you trying to do?"

For all I knew, the others had heard her outburst as clearly as though it had come across a loudspeaker.

"I mean," she went on, "I never imagined it was anything like this. I can feel the whole—"

I shot her a sharp, anguished order to keep quiet. Her surfacing like this, after my warning to her, was a lunatic act. In the silence that followed I felt a kind of inner reverberation, a sulky twanging of displeasure coming from her. But I had no time to worry about Vox's moods now.

Arcing patterns of displacement power went ricocheting through the Great Navigation Hall as our mast came forth—not the underpinning for a set of sails, as it would be on a vessel that plied planetary seas, but rather a giant antenna to link us to the spinaround point ahead—and the ship and the spinaround point reached toward one another like grappling many-armed wrestlers. Hot streaks of crimson and emerald and gold and amethyst speared the air, vaulting and rebounding. The spinaround point, activated now and trembling between energy states, was enfolding us in its million tentacles, capturing us, making ready to whirl on its axis and hurl us swiftly onward toward the next way-station in our journey across heaven.

"Acquisition," Raebuck announced.

"Proceed to capture acceptance," I said.

"Acceptance," said Raebuck.

"Directional mode," I said. "Dimensional grid eleven."

"Dimensional grid eleven," Fresco repeated.

The whole hall seemed on fire now.

"Wonderful," Vox murmured. "So beautiful—"

"*Vox!*"

"Request spin authorization," said Fresco.

"Spin authorization granted," I said. "Grid eleven."

"Grid eleven," Fresco said again. "Spin achieved."

A tremor went rippling through me—and through Fresco, through Raebuck, through Roacher. It was the ship, in the persona of 49 Henry Henry, completing the acquisition process. We had been captured by Lasciate Ogni Speranza, we had undergone velocity absorption and redirection, we had had new spin imparted to us, and we had been sent soaring off through heaven toward our upcoming port of call. I heard Vox sobbing within me, not a sob of despair but one of ecstasy, of fulfillment.

We all unjacked. Raebuck, that dour man, managed a little smile as he turned to me.

"Nicely done, captain," he said.

"Yes," said Fresco. "Very nice. You're a quick learner."

I saw Roacher studying me with those little shining eyes of his. Go on, you bastard, I thought. You give me a compliment too now, if you know how.

But all he did was stare. I shrugged and turned away. What Roacher thought or said made little difference to me, I told myself.

As we left the Great Navigation Hall in our separate directions Fresco fell in alongside me. Without a word we trudged together toward the transit trackers that were waiting for us. Just as I was about to board mine he—or was it she?—said softly, "Captain?"

"What is it, Fresco?"

Fresco leaned close. Soft sly eyes, tricksy little smile; and yet I felt some warmth coming from the navigator.

"It's a very dangerous game, captain."

"I don't know what you mean."

"Yes, you do," Fresco said. "No use pretending. We were jacked together in there. I felt things. I know."

There was nothing I could say, so I said nothing.

After a moment Fresco said, "I like you. I won't harm you. But Roacher knows too. I don't know if he knew before, but he certainly knows now. If I were you, I'd find that very troublesome, captain. Just a word to the wise. All right?"

16.

ONLY A FOOL WOULD HAVE remained on such a course as I had been following. Vox saw the risks as well as I. There was no hiding anything from anyone any longer; if Roacher knew, then Bulgar knew, and soon it would be all over the ship. No question, either, but that 49 Henry Henry knew. In the intimacies of our navigation-hall contact, Vox must have been as apparent to them as a red scarf around my forehead.

There was no point in taking her to task for revealing her presence within me like that during acquisition. What was done was done. At first it had seemed impossible to understand why she had done such a thing; but then it became all too easy to comprehend. It was the same sort of unpredictable, unexamined, impulsive behavior that had led her to go barging into a suspended passenger's mind and cause his death. She was simply not one who paused to think before acting. That kind of behavior has always been bewildering to me. She was my opposite as well as my double. And yet had I not done a Vox-like thing myself, taking her into me, when she appealed to me for sanctuary, without stopping at all to consider the consequences?

"Where can I go?" she asked, desperate. "If I move around the ship freely again they'll track me and close me off. And then they'll eradicate me. They'll—"

"Easy," I said. "Don't panic. I'll hide you where they won't find you."

"Inside some passenger?"

"We can't try that again. There's no way to prepare the passenger for what's happening to him, and he'll panic. No. I'll put you in one of the annexes. Or maybe one of the virtualities."

"The what?"

"The additional cargo area. The subspace extensions that surround the ship."

She gasped. "Those aren't even real! I was in them, when I was traveling around the ship. Those are just clusters of probability waves!"

"You'll be safe there," I said.

"I'm afraid. It's bad enough that *I'm* not real any more. But to be stored in a place that isn't real either—"

"You're as real as I am. And the outstructures are just as real as the rest of the ship. It's a different quality of reality, that's all. Nothing bad will happen to you out there. You've told me yourself that you've already been in them, right? And got out again without any problems. They won't be able to detect you there, Vox. But I tell you this, that if you stay in me, or anywhere else in the main part of the ship, they'll track you down and find you and eradicate you. And probably eradicate me right along with you."

"Do you mean that?" she said, sounding chastened.

"Come on. There isn't much time."

On the pretext of a routine inventory check—well within my table of responsibilities—I obtained access to one of the virtualities. It was the storehouse where the probability stabilizers were kept. No one was likely to search for her there. The chances of our encountering a zone of probability turbulence between here and Cul-de-Sac were minimal; and in the ordinary course of a voyage nobody cared to enter any of the virtualities.

I had lied to Vox, or at least committed a half-truth, by leading her to believe that all our outstructures are of an equal level of reality. Certainly the annexes are tangible, solid; they differ from the ship proper only in the spin of their dimensional polarity. They are invisible except when activated, and they involve us in no additional expenditure of fuel, but there is no uncertainty about their existence, which is why we entrust valuable cargo to them, and on some occasions even passengers.

The extensions are a level further removed from basic reality. They are skewed not only in dimensional polarity but in temporal contiguity: that is, we carry them with us under time displacement, generally ten to twenty virtual years in the past or future. The risks of this are extremely minor and the payoff in reduction of generating cost is great. Still, we are measurably more cautious about what sort of cargo we keep in them.

As for the virtualities—

Their name itself implies their uncertainty. They are purely probabilistic entities, existing most of the time in the stochastic void that surrounds the ship. In simpler words, whether they are actually there or not at any given time is a matter worth wagering on. We know how to access them at the time of greatest probability, and our techniques are quite reliable, which is why we can use them for overflow ladings when our cargo uptake is unusually heavy. But in general we prefer not to entrust anything very important to them, since a virtuality's range of access times can fluctuate in an extreme way, from a matter of microseconds to a matter of megayears, and that can make quick recall a chancy affair.

Knowing all this, I put Vox in a virtuality anyway.

I had to hide her. And I had to hide her in a place where no one would look. The risk that I'd be unable to call her up again because of virtuality fluctuation was a small one. The risk was much greater that she would be detected, and she and I both punished, if I let her remain in any area of the ship that had a higher order of probability.

"I want you to stay here until the coast is clear," I told her sternly. "No impulsive journeys around the ship, no excursions into adjoining outstructures, no little trips of any kind, regardless of how restless you get. Is that clear? I'll call you up from here as soon as I think it's safe."

"I'll miss you, Adam."

"The same here. But this is how it has to be."

"I know."

"If you're discovered, I'll deny I know anything about you. I mean that, Vox."

"I understand."

"You won't be stuck in here long. I promise you that."

"Will you visit me?"

"That wouldn't be wise," I said.

"But maybe you will anyway."

"Maybe. I don't know." I opened the access channel. The virtuality gaped before us. "Go on," I said. "In with you. In. Now. Go, Vox. Go."

I could feel her leaving me. It was almost like an amputation. The silence, the emptiness, that descended on me suddenly was ten times as deep as what I had felt when she had merely been hiding within me. She was gone, now. For the first time in days, I was truly alone.

I closed off the virtuality.

When I returned to the Eye, Roacher was waiting for me near the command bridge.

"You have a moment, captain?"

"What is it, Roacher."

"The missing matrix. We have proof it's still on board ship."

"Proof?"

"You know what I mean. You felt it just like I did while we were doing acquisition. It said something. It spoke. It was right in there in the navigation hall with us, captain."

I met his luminescent gaze levelly and said in an even voice, "I was giving my complete attention to what we were doing, Roacher. Spinaround acquisition isn't second nature to me the way it is to you. I had no time to notice any matrixes floating around in there."

"You didn't?"

"No. Does that disappoint you?"

"That might mean that you're the one carrying the matrix," he said.

"How so?"

"If it's in you, down on a subneural level, you might not even be aware of it. But we would be. Raebuck, Fresco, me. We all detected something, captain. If it wasn't in us it would have to be in you. We can't have a matrix riding around inside our captain, you know. No telling how that could distort his judgment. What dangers that might lead us into."

"I'm not carrying any matrixes, Roacher."

"Can we be sure of that?"

"Would you like to have a look?"

"A jackup, you mean? You and me?"

The notion disgusted me. But I had to make the offer.

"A—jackup, yes," I said. "Communion. You and me, Roacher. Right now. Come on, we'll measure the bandwidths and do the matching. Let's get this over with."

He contemplated me a long while, as if calculating the likelihood that I was bluffing. In the end he must have decided that I was too naïve to be able to play the game out to so hazardous a turn. He knew that I wouldn't bluff, that I was confident he would find me untenanted or I never would have made the offer.

"No," he said finally. "We don't need to bother with that."

"Are you sure?"

"If you say you're clean—"

"But I might be carrying her and not even know it," I said. "You told me that yourself."

"Forget it. You'd know, if you had her in you."

"You'll never be certain of that unless you look. Let's jack up, Roacher."

He scowled. "Forget it," he said again, and turned away. "You must be clean, if you're this eager for jacking. But I'll tell you this, captain. We're going to find her, wherever she's hiding. And when we do—"

He left the threat unfinished. I stood staring at his retreating form until he was lost to view.

17.

FOR A FEW DAYS EVERYTHING seemed back to normal. We sped onward toward Cul-de-Sac. I went through the round of my regular tasks, however meaningless they seemed to me. Most of them did. I had not yet achieved any sense that the *Sword of Orion* was under my command in anything but the most hypothetical way. Still, I did what I had to do.

No one spoke of the missing matrix within my hearing. On those rare occasions when I encountered some other member of the crew while I moved about the ship, I could tell by the hooded look of his eyes that I was still under suspicion. But they had no proof. The matrix was no longer in any way evident on board. The ship's intelligences were unable to find the slightest trace of its presence.

I was alone, and oh! it was a painful business for me.

I suppose that once you have tasted that kind of round-the-clock communion, that sort of perpetual jacking, you are never the same again. I don't know: there is no real information available on cases of possession by free matrix, only shipboard folklore, scarcely to be taken seriously. All I can judge by is my own misery now that Vox was actually gone. She was only a half-grown girl, a wild coltish thing, unstable, unformed; and yet, and yet, she had lived within me and we had come toward one another to construct the deepest sort of sharing, what was almost a kind of marriage. You could call it that.

After five or six days I knew I had to see her again. Whatever the risks.

I accessed the virtuality and sent a signal into it that I was coming in. There was no reply; and for one terrible moment I feared the worst, that in the mysterious workings of the virtuality she had somehow been engulfed and destroyed. But that was not the case. I stepped through the glowing pink-edged field of light that was the gateway to the virtuality, and instantly I felt her near me, clinging tight, trembling with joy.

She held back, though, from entering me. She wanted me to tell her it was safe. I beckoned her in; and then came that sharp warm moment I remembered so well, as she slipped down into my neural network and we became one.

"I can only stay a little while," I said. "It's still very chancy for me to be with you."

"Oh, Adam, Adam, it's been so awful for me in here—"

"I know. I can imagine."

"Are they still looking for me?"

"I think they're starting to put you out of their minds," I said. And we both laughed at the play on words that that phrase implied.

I didn't dare remain more than a few minutes. I had only wanted to touch souls with her briefly, to reassure myself that she was all right and to ease the pain of separation. But it was irregular for a captain to enter a virtuality at all. To stay in one for any length of time exposed me to real risk of detection.

But my next visit was longer, and the one after that longer still. We were like furtive lovers meeting in a dark forest for hasty delicious trysts. Hidden there in that not-quite-real out-structure of the ship we would join our two selves and whisper together with urgent intensity until I felt it was time for me to leave. She would always try to keep me longer; but her resistance to my departure was never great, nor did she ever suggest accompanying me back into the stable sector of the ship. She had come to understand that the only place we could meet was in the virtuality.

We were nearing the vicinity of Cul-de-Sac now. Soon we would go to worldward and the shoreships would travel out to meet us, so that we could download the cargo that was meant for them. It was time to begin considering the problem of what would happen to Vox when we reached our destination.

That was something I was unwilling to face. However I tried, I could not force myself to confront the difficulties that I knew lay just ahead.

But she could.

"We must be getting close to Cul-de-Sac now," she said.

"We'll be there soon, yes."

"I've been thinking about that. How I'm going to deal with that."

"What do you mean?"

"Adam, don't you see?" she cried fiercely. "I can't just float down to Cul-de-Sac and grab myself a body and put myself on the roster of colonists. And you can't possibly smuggle me down there while nobody's looking. The first time anyone ran an inventory check, or did passport control, I'd be dead. No, the only way I can get there is to be neatly packed up again in my original storage circuit. And even if I could figure out how to get back into that, I'd be simply handing myself over for punishment or even eradication. I'm listed as missing on the manifest, right? And I'm wanted for causing the death of that passenger. Now I turn up again, in my storage circuit. You think they'll just download me nicely to Cul-de-Sac and give me the body that's waiting for me there? Not very likely. Not likely that I'll ever get out of that circuit alive, is it, once I go back in? Assuming I *could* go back in in the first place. I don't know how a storage circuit is operated, do you? And there's nobody you can ask."

"What are you trying to say, Vox?"

"I'm not trying to say anything. I'm saying it. I have to leave the ship on my own and disappear."

"No. You can't do that!"

"Sure I can. It'll be just like starwalking. I can go anywhere I please. Right through the skin of the ship, out into heaven. And keep on going."

"To Cul-de-Sac?"

"You're being stupid," she said. "Not to Cul-de-Sac, no. Not to anywhere. That's all over for me, the idea of getting a new body. I have no legal existence any more. I've messed myself up. All right: I admit it. I'll take what's coming to me. It won't be so bad, Adam. I'll go starwalking. Outward and outward and outward, forever and ever."

"You mustn't," I said. "Stay here with me."

"Where? In this empty storage unit out here?"

398

"No," I told her. "Within me. The way we are right now. The way we were before."

"How long do you think we could carry that off?" she asked.

I didn't answer.

"Every time you have to jack into the machinery I'll have to hide myself down deep," she said. "And I can't guarantee that I'll go deep enough, or that I'll stay down there long enough. Sooner or later they'll notice me. They'll find me. They'll eradicate me and they'll throw you out of the Service, or maybe they'll eradicate you too. No, Adam. It couldn't possibly work. And I'm not going to destroy you with me. I've done enough harm to you already."

"Vox—"

"No. This is how it has to be."

18.

AND THIS IS HOW IT was. We were deep in the Spook Cluster now, and the Vainglory Archipelago burned bright on my realspace screen. Somewhere down there was the planet called Cul-de-Sac. Before we came to worldward of it, Vox would have to slip away into the great night of heaven.

Making a worldward approach is perhaps the most difficult maneuver a starship must achieve; and the captain must go to the edge of his abilities along with everyone else. Novice at my trade though I was, I would be called on to perform complex and challenging processes. If I failed at them, other crewmen might cut in and intervene, or, if necessary, the ship's intelligences might override; but if that came to pass my career would be destroyed, and there was the small but finite possibility, I suppose, that the ship itself could be gravely damaged or even lost.

I was determined, all the same, to give Vox the best send-off I could.

On the morning of our approach I stood for a time on Outerscreen Level, staring down at the world that called itself Cul-de-Sac. It glowed like a red eye in the night. I knew that it was the world Vox had chosen for herself, but all the same it seemed repellent to me, almost evil. I felt that way about all the worlds of the shore people now. The Service had changed me; and I knew that the change was irreversible. Never again would I go down to one of those worlds. The starship was my world now.

I went to the virtuality where Vox was waiting.

"Come," I said, and she entered me.

Together we crossed the ship to the Great Navigation Hall.

The approach team had already gathered: Raebuck, Fresco, Roacher, again, along with Pedregal, who would supervise the downloading of cargo. The intelligence on duty was 612 Jason. I greeted them with quick nods and we jacked ourselves together in approach series.

Almost at once I felt Roacher probing within me, searching for the fugitive intelligence that he still thought I might be harboring. Vox shrank back, deep out of sight. I didn't care. Let him probe, I thought. This will all be over soon.

"Request approach instructions," Fresco said.

"Simulation," I ordered.

The fiery red eye of Cul-de-Sac sprang into vivid representation before us in the hall. On the other side of us was the simulacrum of the ship, surrounded by sheets of white flame that rippled like the blaze of the aurora.

I gave the command and we entered approach mode.

We could not, of course, come closer to planetskin than a million shiplengths, or Cul-de-Sac's inexorable forces would rip us apart. But we had to line the ship up with its extended mast aimed at the planet's equator, and hold ourselves firm in that position while the shoreships of Cul-de-Sac came swarming up from their red world to receive their cargo from us.

612 Jason fed me the coordinates and I gave them to Fresco, while Raebuck kept the channels clear and Roacher saw to it that we had enough power for what we had to do. But as I passed the data along to Fresco, it was with every sign reversed. My purpose

was to aim the mast not downward to Cul-de-Sac but outward toward the stars of heaven.

At first none of them noticed. Everything seemed to be going serenely. Because my reversals were exact, only the closest examination of the ship's position would indicate our 180-degree displacement.

Floating in the free fall of the Great Navigation Hall, I felt almost as though I could detect the movements of the ship. An illusion, I knew. But a powerful one. The vast ten-kilometer-long needle that was the *Sword of Orion* seemed to hang suspended, motionless, and then to begin slowly, slowly to turn, tipping itself on its axis, reaching for the stars with its mighty mast. Easily, easily, slowly, silently—

What joy that was, feeling the ship in my hand!

The ship was mine. I had mastered it.

"Captain," Fresco said softly.

"Easy on, Fresco. Keep feeding power."

"Captain, the signs don't look right—"

"Easy on. Easy."

"Give me a coordinates check, captain."

"Another minute," I told him.

"But—"

"Easy on, Fresco."

Now I felt restlessness too from Pedregal, and a slow chilly stirring of interrogation from Raebuck; and then Roacher probed me again, perhaps seeking Vox, perhaps simply trying to discover what was going on. They knew something was wrong, but they weren't sure what it was.

We were nearly at full extension, now. Within me there was an electrical trembling: Vox rising through the levels of my mind, nearing the surface, preparing for departure.

"Captain, we're turned the wrong way!" Fresco cried.

"I know," I said. "Easy on. We'll swing around in a moment."

"He's gone crazy!" Pedregal blurted.

I felt Vox slipping free of my mind. But somehow I found myself still aware of her movements, I suppose because I was jacked into 612 Jason and 612 Jason was monitoring everything. Easily, serenely, Vox melted into the skin of the ship.

"*Captain!*" Fresco yelled, and began to struggle with me for control.

I held the navigator at arm's length and watched in a strange and wonderful calmness as Vox passed through the ship's circuitry all in an instant and emerged at the tip of the mast, facing the stars. And cast herself adrift.

Because I had turned the ship around, she could not be captured and acquired by Cul-de-Sac's powerful navigational grid, but would be free to move outward into heaven. For her it would be a kind of floating out to sea, now. After a time she would be so far out that she could no longer key into the shipboard bioprocessors that sustained the patterns of her consciousness, and, though the web of electrical impulses that was the Vox matrix would travel outward and onward forever, the set of identity responses that was Vox herself would lose focus soon, would begin to waver and blur. In a little while, or perhaps not so little, but inevitably, her sense of herself as an independent entity would be lost. Which is to say, she would die.

I followed her as long as I could. I saw a spark traveling across the great night. And then nothing.

"All right," I said to Fresco. "Now let's turn the ship the right way around and give them their cargo."

19.

THAT WAS MANY YEARS AGO. Perhaps no one else remembers those events, which seem so dreamlike now even to me. The *Sword of Orion* has carried me nearly everywhere in the galaxy since then. On some voyages I have been captain; on others, a downloader, a supercargo, a mind-wiper, even sometimes a push-cell. It makes no difference how we serve, in the Service.

I often think of her. There was a time when thinking of her meant coming to terms with feelings of grief and pain and irrecoverable loss, but no longer, not for many years. She must be long dead now, however durable and resilient the spark of her might have been. And yet she still lives. Of that much I am certain. There is a place within me where I can reach her warmth, her strength, her quirky vitality, her impulsive suddenness. I can feel those aspects of her, those gifts of her brief time of sanctuary within me, as a living presence still, and I think I always will, as I make my way from world to tethered world, as I journey onward everlastingly spanning the dark light-years in this great ship of heaven.

TO SEE THE INVISIBLE MAN

I stole the idea for this one from Jorge Luis Borges. But if a writer is going to steal, he ought to steal from the best; and Borges wasn't planning to do anything with it, anyway.

In the opening paragraph of his lovely short story "The Babylon Lottery" Borges says, "Like all men in Babylon I have been a proconsul; like all, a slave. . . . During one lunar year I have been declared invisible. I shrieked and was not heard. I stole bread and was not decapitated." That's all. Borges makes no other use of the theme of statutory invisibility in the story— it was, for him, nothing more than a throwaway line.

Well, what one writer throws away, another may find to be of value. Think of what Hemingway did with Donne's "for whom the bell tolls," or any number of writers have done with innumerable bits of Shakespeare. ("A tale full of sound and fury," for example.) So I fell upon the notion of being declared invisible and worked out its practical implications in a story that I wrote for Frederik Pohl in 1962, thus doing the job that Borges had left undone. I expected Fred to use it in his top-of-the-line magazine, *Galaxy*, but he was launching a new magazine, *Worlds of Tomorrow*, just then, and my story wound up in its first issue, dated April 1963. First-person narration seemed mandatory for this one: my protagonist would be not just telling a story but uttering a cry straight from the heart.

"To See the Invisible Man" has had a healthy afterlife in the fifty-odd years since I wrote it. It was adapted for the second incarnation of that splendid television show, *The Twilight Zone*, it became a French movie that I have never seen, and it has been reprinted in a whole host of anthologies. And, quite appropriately, here it is in one more.

———

AND THEN THEY FOUND ME guilty, and then they pronounced me invisible, for a span of one year beginning on the eleventh of May in the year of Grace 2104, and they took me to a dark room beneath the courthouse to affix the mark to my forehead before turning me loose.

Two municipally paid ruffians did the job. One flung me into a chair and the other lifted the brand.

"This won't hurt a bit," the slab-jawed ape said, and thrust the brand against my forehead, and there was a moment of coolness, and that was all.

"What happens now?" I asked.

But there was no answer, and they turned away from me and left the room without a word. The door remained open. I was free to leave, or to stay and rot, as I chose. No one would speak to me, or look at me more than once, long enough to see the sign on my forehead. I was invisible. You must understand that my invisibility was strictly metaphorical. I still had corporeal solidity. People *could* see me—but they *would not* see me.

An absurd punishment? Perhaps. But then, the crime was absurd too. The crime of coldness. Refusal to unburden myself for my fellow man. I was a four-time offender. The penalty for that was a year's invisibility. The complaint had been duly sworn, the trial held, the brand duly affixed.

I was invisible.

I went out, out into the world of warmth.

They had already had the afternoon rain. The streets of the city were drying, and there was the smell of growth in the Hanging Gardens. Men and women went about their business. I walked among them, but they took no notice of me.

The penalty for speaking to an invisible man is invisibility, a month to a year or more, depending on the seriousness of the offense. On this the whole concept depends. I wondered how rigidly the rule was observed.

I soon found out.

I stepped into a liftshaft and let myself be spiraled up toward the nearest of the Hanging Gardens. It was Eleven, the cactus garden, and those gnarled, bizarre shapes suited my mood. I emerged on the landing stage and advanced toward the admissions counter to buy my token. A pasty-faced, empty-eyed woman sat back of the counter.

I laid down my coin. Something like fright entered her eyes, quickly faded.

"One admission," I said.

No answer. People were queuing up behind me. I repeated my demand. The woman looked up helplessly, then stared over my left shoulder. A hand extended itself, another coin was placed down. She took it, and handed the man his token. He dropped it in the slot and went in.

"Let me have a token," I said crisply.

Others were jostling me out of the way. Not a word of apology. I began to sense some of the meaning of my invisibility. They were literally treating me as though they could not see me.

There are countervailing advantages. I walked around behind the counter and helped myself to a token without paying for it. Since I was invisible, I could not be stopped. I thrust the token in the slot and entered the garden.

But the cacti bored me. An inexpressible malaise slipped over me, and I felt no desire to stay. On my way out I pressed my finger against a jutting thorn and drew blood. The cactus, at least, still recognized my existence. But only to draw blood.

I returned to my apartment. My books awaited me, but I felt no interest in them. I sprawled out on my narrow bed and activated the energizer to combat the strange lassitude that was afflicting me. I thought about my invisibility.

It would not be such a hardship, I told myself. I had never depended overly on other human beings. Indeed, had I not been sentenced in the first place for my coldness toward my fellow creatures? So what need did I have of them now? *Let* them ignore me!

It would be restful. I had a year's respite from work, after all. Invisible men did not work. How could they? Who would go to an invisible doctor for a consultation, or hire an invisible lawyer to represent him, or give a document to an invisible clerk to file? No work, then. No income, of course, either. But landlords did not take rent from invisible men. Invisible men went where they pleased, at no cost. I had just demonstrated that at the Hanging Gardens.

Invisibility would be a great joke on society, I felt. They had sentenced me to nothing more dreadful than a year's rest cure. I was certain I would enjoy it.

But there were certain practical disadvantages. On the first night of my invisibility I went to the city's finest restaurant. I would order their most lavish dishes, a hundred-unit meal, and then conveniently vanish at the presentation of the bill.

My thinking was muddy. I never got seated. I stood in the entrance half an hour, bypassed again and again by a maitre d'hotel who had clearly been through all this many times before: Walking to a seat, I realized, would gain me nothing. No waiter would take my order.

I could go into the kitchen. I could help myself to anything I pleased. I could disrupt the workings of the restaurant. But I decided against it. Society had its ways of protecting itself against the invisible ones. There could be no direct retaliation, of course, no intentional defense. But who could say no to a chef's claim that he had seen no one in the way when he hurled a pot of scalding water toward the wall? Invisibility was invisibility, a two-edged sword.

I left the restaurant.

I ate at an automated restaurant nearby. Then I took an autocab home. Machines, like cacti, did not discriminate against my sort. I sensed that they would make poor companions for a year, though.

I slept poorly.

THE SECOND DAY OF MY invisibility was a day of further testing and discovery.

I went for a long walk, careful to stay on the pedestrian paths. I had heard all about the boys who enjoy running down those who carry the mark of invisibility on their foreheads. Again, there is no recourse, no punishment for them. My condition has its little hazards by intention.

I walked the streets, seeing how the throngs parted for me. I cut through them like a microtome passing between cells. They were well trained. At midday I saw my first fellow Invisible. He was a tall man of middle years, stocky and dignified, bearing the mark of shame on a domelike forehead. His eyes met mine only for a moment. Then he passed on. An invisible man, naturally, cannot see another of his kind.

I was amused, nothing more. I was still savoring the novelty of this way of life. No slight could hurt me. Not yet.

Late in the day I came to one of those bathhouses where working girls can cleanse themselves for a couple of small coins. I smiled wickedly and went up the steps. The attendant at the door gave me the flicker of a startled look—it was a small triumph for me—but did not dare to stop me.

I went in.

An overpowering smell of soap and sweat struck me. I persevered inward. I passed cloakrooms where long rows of gray smocks were hanging, and it occurred to me that I could rifle those smocks of every unit they contained, but I did not. Theft loses meaning when it becomes too easy, as the clever ones who devised invisibility were aware.

I passed on, into the bath chambers themselves.

Hundreds of women were there. Nubile girls, weary wenches, old crones. Some blushed. A few smiled. Many turned their backs on me. But they were careful not to show any real reaction to my presence. Supervisory matrons stood guard, and who knew but that she might be reported for taking undue cognizance of the existence of an Invisible?

So I watched them bathe, watched five hundred pairs of bobbing breasts, watched naked bodies glistening under the spray, watched this vast mass of bare feminine flesh. My reaction was a mixed one, a sense of wicked achievement at having penetrated this sanctum sanctorum unhalted, and then, welling up slowly within me, a sensation of—was it sorrow? Boredom? Revulsion?

I was unable to analyze it. But it felt as though a clammy hand had seized my throat. I left quickly. The smell of soapy water stung my nostrils for hours afterward, and the sight of pink flesh haunted my dreams that night. I ate alone, in one of the automatics. I began to see that the novelty of this punishment was soon lost.

IN THE THIRD WEEK I fell ill. It began with a high fever, then pains of the stomach, vomiting, the rest of the ugly symptomatology. By midnight I was certain I was dying. The cramps were intolerable, and when I dragged myself to the toilet cubicle I caught sight of myself in the mirror, distorted, greenish, beaded with sweat. The mark of invisibility stood out like a beacon in my pale forehead.

For a long time I lay on the tiled floor, limply absorbing the coolness of it. Then I thought: What if it's my appendix? That ridiculous, obsolete, obscure prehistoric survival? Inflamed, ready to burst?

I needed a doctor.

The phone was covered with dust. They had not bothered to disconnect it, but I had not called anyone since my arrest, and no one had dared call me. The penalty for knowingly telephoning an invisible man is invisibility. My friends, such as they were, had stayed far away.

I grasped the phone, thumbed the panel. It lit up and the directory robot said, "With whom do you wish to speak, sir?"

"Doctor," I gasped.

"Certainly, sir." Bland, smug mechanical words! No way to pronounce a robot invisible, so it was free to talk to me!

The screen glowed. A doctorly voice said, "What seems to be the trouble?"

"Stomach pains. Maybe appendicitis."

"We'll have a man over in—" He stopped. I had made the mistake of upturning my agonized face. His eyes lit on my forehead mark. The screen winked into blackness as rapidly as though I had extended a leprous hand for him to kiss.

"Doctor," I groaned.

He was gone. I buried my face in my hands. This was carrying things too far, I thought. Did the Hippocratic Oath allow things like this? Could a doctor ignore a sick man's plea for help?

Hippocrates had not known anything about invisible men. A doctor was not required to minister to an invisible man. To society at large I simply was not there. Doctors could not diagnose diseases in nonexistent individuals.

I was left to suffer.

It was one of invisibility's less attractive features. You enter a bathhouse unhindered, if that pleases you—but you writhe on a bed of pain equally unhindered. The one with the other, and if your appendix happens to rupture, why, it is all the greater deterrent to others who might perhaps have gone your lawless way!

My appendix did not rupture. I survived, though badly shaken. A man can survive without human conversation for a year. He can travel on automated cars and eat at automated restaurants. But there are no automated doctors. For the first time, I felt truly beyond the pale. A convict in a prison is given a doctor when he falls ill. My crime had not been serious enough to merit prison, and so no doctor would treat me if I suffered. It was unfair. I cursed the devils who had invented my punishment. I faced each bleak dawn alone, as alone as Crusoe on his island, here in the midst of a city of twelve million souls.

HOW CAN I DESCRIBE MY shifts of mood, my many tacks before the changing winds of the passing months?

There were times when invisibility was a joy, a delight, a treasure. In those paranoid moments I gloried in my exemption from the rules that bound ordinary men.

I stole. I entered small stores and seized the receipts, while the cowering merchant feared to stop me, lest in crying out he make himself liable to my invisibility. If I had known that the State reimbursed all such losses, I might have taken less pleasure in it. But I stole.

I invaded. The bathhouse never tempted me again, but I breached other sanctuaries. I entered hotels and walked down the corridors, opening doors at random. Most rooms were empty. Some were not.

Godlike, I observed all. I toughened. My disdain for society—the crime that had earned me invisibility in the first place —heightened.

I stood in the empty streets during the periods of rain, and railed at the gleaming faces of the towering buildings on every side. "Who needs you?" I roared. "Not I! Who needs you in the slightest?"

I jeered and mocked and railed. It was a kind of insanity, brought on, I suppose, by the loneliness. I entered theaters—where the happy lotus-eaters sat slumped in their massage chairs, transfixed by the glowing tridim images—and capered down the aisles. No one grumbled at me. The luminescence of my forehead told them to keep their complaints to themselves, and they did.

Those were the mad moments, the good moments, the moments when I towered twenty feet high and strode among the visible clods with contempt oozing from every pore. Those were insane moments—I admit that freely. A man who has been in a condition of involuntary invisibility for several months is not likely to be well balanced.

Did I call them paranoid moments? Manic depressive might be more to the point. The pendulum swung dizzily. The days when I felt only contempt for the visible fools all around me were balanced by days when the isolation pressed in tangibly on me. I would walk the endless streets, pass through the gleaming arcades, stare down at the highways with their streaking bullets of gay colors. Not even a beggar would come up to me. Did you know we had beggars, in our shining century? Not till I was pronounced invisible did I know it, for then my long walks took me to the slums, where the shine has worn thin, and where shuffling stubble-faced old men beg for small coins.

No one begged for coins from me. Once a blind man came up to me.

"For the love of God," he wheezed, "help me to buy new eyes from the eye bank."

They were the first direct words any human being had spoken to me in months. I started to reach into my tunic for money, planning to give him every unit on me in gratitude. Why not? I could get more simply by taking it. But before I could draw the money out, a nightmare figure hobbled on crutches between us. I caught the whispered word, "Invisible," and then the two of them scuttled away like frightened crabs. I stood there stupidly holding my money.

Not even the beggars. Devils, to have invented this torment!

So I softened again. My arrogance ebbed away. I was lonely, now. Who could accuse me of coldness? I was spongy soft, pathetically eager for a word, a smile, a clasping hand. It was the sixth month of my invisibility.

I loathed it entirely, now. Its pleasures were hollow ones and its torment was unbearable. I wondered how I would survive the remaining six months. Believe me, suicide was not far from my mind in those dark hours.

And finally I committed an act of foolishness. On one of my endless walks I encountered another Invisible, no more than the third or the fourth such creature I had seen in my six months. As in the previous encounters, our eyes met, warily, only for a moment. Then he dropped his to the pavement, and he sidestepped me and walked on. He was a slim young man, no more than forty, with tousled brown hair and a narrow, pinched face. He had a look of scholarship about him, and I wondered what he might have done to merit his punishment, and I was seized with the desire to run after him and ask him, and to learn his name, and to talk to him, and embrace him.

All these things are forbidden to mankind. No one shall have any contact whatsoever with an Invisible—not even a fellow Invisible. Especially not a fellow Invisible. There is no wish on society's part to foster a secret bond of fellowship among its pariahs.

I knew all this.

I turned and followed him, all the same.

For three blocks I moved along behind him, remaining twenty to fifty paces to the rear. Security robots seemed to be everywhere, their scanners quick to detect an infraction, and I did not dare make my move. Then he turned down a side street, a gray, dusty street five centuries old, and began to stroll, with the ambling, going-nowhere gait of the Invisible. I came up behind him.

"Please," I said softly. "No one will see us here. We can talk. My name is—"

He whirled on me, horror in his eyes. His face was pale. He looked at me in amazement for a moment, then darted forward as though to go around me.

I blocked him.

"Wait," I said. "Don't be afraid. Please—"

He burst past me. I put my hand on his shoulder, and he wriggled free.

"Just a word," I begged.

Not even a word. Not even a hoarsely uttered, "Leave me alone!" He sidestepped me and ran down the empty street, his steps diminishing from a clatter to a murmur as he reached the corner and rounded it. I looked after him, feeling a great loneliness well up in me.

And then a fear. *He* hadn't breached the rules of Invisibility, but I had. I had seen him. That left me subject to punishment, an extension of my term of invisibility, perhaps. I looked around anxiously, but there were no security robots in sight, no one at all.

I was alone.

Turning, calming myself, I continued down the street. Gradually I regained control over myself. I saw that I had done something unpardonably foolish. The stupidity of my action troubled me, but even more the sentimentality of it. To reach out in that panicky way to another Invisible—to admit openly my loneliness, my need—no. It meant that society was winning. I couldn't have that.

I found that I was near the cactus garden once again. I rode the liftshaft, grabbed a token from the attendant, and bought my way in. I searched for a moment, then found a twisted, elaborately ornate cactus eight feet high, a spiny monster. I wrenched it from its pot and broke the angular limbs to fragments, filling my hands with a thousand needles. People pretended not to watch. I plucked the spines from my hands and, palms bleeding, rode the liftshaft down, once again sublimely aloof in my invisibility.

THE EIGHTH MONTH PASSED, THE ninth, the tenth. The seasonal round had made nearly a complete turn. Spring had given way to a mild summer, summer to a crisp autumn, autumn to winter with its fortnightly snowfalls, still permitted for esthetic reasons. Winter had ended, now. In the parks, the trees sprouted green buds. The weather control people stepped up the rainfall to thrice daily.

My term was drawing to its end.

In the final months of my invisibility I had slipped into a kind of torpor. My mind, forced back on its own resources, no longer cared to consider the implications of my condition, and I slid in a blurred haze from day to day. I read compulsively but unselectively. Aristotle one day, the Bible the next, a handbook of mechanics the next. I retained nothing; as I turned a fresh page, its predecessor slipped from my memory.

I no longer bothered to enjoy the few advantages of invisibility, the voyeuristic thrills, the minute throb of power that comes from being able to commit any act with only limited fears of retaliation. I say *limited* because the passage of the Invisibility Act had not been accompanied by an act repealing human nature; few men would not risk invisibility to protect their wives or children from an invisible one's molestations; no one would coolly allow an invisible to jab out his eyes; no one would tolerate an Invisible's invasion of his home. There were ways of coping with such infringements without appearing to recognize the existence of the Invisible, as I have mentioned.

Still, it was possible to get away with a great deal. I declined to try. Somewhere Dostoevsky has written, "Without God, all things are possible." I can amend that. "To the invisible man, all things are possible—and uninteresting." So it was.

The weary months passed.

I did not count the minutes till my release. To be precise, I wholly forgot that my term was due to end. On the day itself, I was reading in my room, morosely turning page after page, when the annunciator chimed.

It had not chimed for a full year. I had almost forgotten the meaning of the sound.

But I opened the door. There they stood, the men of the law. Wordlessly, they broke the seal that held the mark to my forehead.

The emblem dropped away and shattered.

"Hello, citizen," they said to me.

I nodded gravely. "Yes. Hello."

"May 11, 2105. Your term is up. You are restored to society. You have paid your debt."

"Thank you. Yes."

"Come for a drink with us."

"I'd sooner not."

"It's the tradition. Come along."

I went with them. My forehead felt strangely naked now, and I glanced in a mirror to see that there was a pale spot where the emblem had been. They took me to a bar nearby, and treated me to synthetic whiskey, raw, powerful. The bartender grinned at me. Someone on the next stool clapped me on the shoulder and asked me who I liked in tomorrow's jet races. I had no idea, and I said so.

"You mean it? I'm backing Kelso. Four to one, but he's got terrific spurt power."

"I'm sorry," I said.

"He's been away for a while," one of the government men said softly.

The euphemism was unmistakable. My neighbor glanced at my forehead and nodded at the pale spot. He offered to buy me a drink too. I accepted, though I was already feeling the effects of the first one. I was a human being again. I was visible.

I did not dare spurn him, anyway. It might have been construed as a crime of coldness once again. My fifth offense would have meant five years of Invisibility. I had learned humility.

Returning to visibility involved an awkward transition, of course. Old friends to meet, lame conversations to hold, shattered relationships to renew. I had been an exile in my own city for a year, and coming back was not easy.

No one referred to my time of invisibility, naturally. It was treated as an affliction best left unmentioned. Hypocrisy, I thought, but I accepted it. Doubtless they were all trying to spare my feelings. Does one tell a man whose cancerous stomach has been replaced, "I hear you had a narrow escape just now?" Does one say to a man whose aged father has tottered off toward a euthanasia house, "Well, he was getting pretty feeble anyway, wasn't he?"

No. Of course not.

So there was this hole in our shared experience, this void, this blankness. Which left me little to talk about with my friends, in particular since I had lost the knack of conversation entirely. The period of readjustment was a trying one.

But I persevered, for I was no longer the same haughty, aloof person I had been before my conviction. I had learned humility in the hardest of schools.

Now and then I noticed an Invisible on the streets, of course. It was impossible to avoid them. But, trained as I had been trained, I quickly glanced away, as though my eyes had come momentarily to rest on some shambling, festering horror from another world.

It was in the fourth month of my return to visibility that the ultimate lesson of my sentence struck home, though. I was in the vicinity of the City Tower, having returned to my old job in the documents division of the municipal government. I had left work for the day and was walking toward the tubes when a hand emerged from the crowd, caught my arm.

"Please," the soft voice said. "Wait a minute. Don't be afraid."

I looked up, startled. In our city strangers do not accost strangers.

I saw the gleaming emblem of invisibility on the man's forehead. Then I recognized him—the slim man I had accosted more than half a year before on that deserted street. He had grown haggard; his eyes were wild, his brown hair flecked with gray. He must have been at the beginning of his term, then. Now he must have been near its end.

He held my arm. I trembled. This was no deserted street. This was the most crowded square of the city. I pulled my arm away from his grasp and started to turn away.

"No—don't go," he cried. "Can't you pity me? You've been there yourself."

I took a faltering step. Then I remembered how I had cried out to him, how I had begged him not to spurn me. I remembered my own miserable loneliness.

I took another step away from him.

"Coward!" he shrieked after me. "Talk to me! I dare you! Talk to me, coward!"

It was too much. I was touched. Sudden tears stung my eyes, and I turned to him, stretched out a hand to his. I caught his thin wrist. The contact seemed to electrify him. A moment later, I held him in my arms, trying to draw some of the misery from his frame to mine.

The security robots closed in, surrounding us. He was hurled to one side, I was taken into custody. They will try me again—not for the crime of coldness, this time, but for a crime of warmth. Perhaps they will find extenuating circumstances and release me; perhaps not.

I do not care. If they condemn me, this time I will wear my invisibility like a shield of glory.

◆